SPINWARD FRINGE BROADCAST 11

REVENGE

RANDOLPH LALONDE

BOOKS BY RANDOLPH LALONDE

THE CHAOS CORE SERIES

Trapped

Cool Pursuit

Savage Stars

THE SPINWARD FRINGE SERIES

Spinward Fringe Broadcast 0: Origins

Spinward Fringe Broadcast 1 and 2: Resurrection and Awakening

Spinward Fringe Broadcast 3: Triton

Spinward Fringe Broadcast 4: Frontline

Spinward Fringe Broadcast 5: Fracture

Spinward Fringe Broadcast 6: Fragments

Spinward Fringe Broadcast 6.5: The Expendable Few

Spinward Fringe Broadcast 7: Framework

Spinward Fringe Broadcast 8: Renegades

Spinward Fringe Broadcast 9: Warpath

Spinward Fringe Broadcast 10: Freeground

Spinward Fringe Broadcast 10.5: Carnie's Tale

Spinward Fringe Broadcast 11: Revenge

Spinward Fringe Broadcast 12: Invasion

Spinward Fringe Broadcast 13: Warriors

Spinward Fringe Broadcast 14: Rebel

Spinward Fringe Broadcast 15: Pursuit

FANTASY

Brightwill

Highshield

NEM: Awakening

HORROR

Dark Arts

For more information please visit:

www.RandolphLalonde.com

Revision 4

Thank you for supporting the author by purchasing this book. Every honest reader counts.

EBook ISBN: 978-1-988175-12-6

Print ISBN: 978-1-988175-15-7

SPECIAL THANKS

I owe a lot to everyone who worked on this book, read the rough version of Alice's story on Patreon and offered their input and to you, the reader. It isn't abnormal for a novel to take between one to two years to surface, but in the Indie EBook world expectations are high. This book became two novels: Spinward Fringe Broadcast 10.5: Carnie's Tale and Spinward Fringe Broadcast 11: Revenge because readers saw material that was cut from the series and wanted to see that story.

In the last two years, constructive reader input has been helpful in bringing more of the Spinward Fringe story into the world. With that in mind, I have to emphasize how important it is to read the rest of the series including Broadcast 10.5: Carnie's Tale before reading this book.

I would also like to thank everyone who has hosted, organized or assisted with events centred around Spinward Fringe. There have been events in the UK, USA and Australia as far as I know. I'm always amazed and humbled at how this series can bring people together.

Thank you for your support and your efforts.

PREAMBLE

Alice Valent

After completing a significant step in her Haven Fleet training, Alice Valent is moving on to the next phase. All the while she wonders where her father and the crew of the Revenge are, and why they aren't expected to arrive with the rest of the fleet coming from the Iron Head Nebula.

Jacob Valent

The agility and reflexes Jacob had before the framework system was removed are returning as he works with his crew to rescue a multitude of crewmembers. The battle to defend Freeground Alpha was fought by the entire Freeground Fleet from a distance, but the Revenge tipped the balance as it closed the distance and gave Samurai Squadron time to damage the capabilities of the largest Order of Eden ship any of them had ever seen, the Glorious.

It was the right choice, but the results leave no room or time for pride as he joins the crew of the Revenge in rescuing their fellow crew mates from wherever they may be stranded or trapped in damaged sections of their ship. Days of working shoulder-to-shoulder with them, leading his own rescue squad and working longer hours than anyone else has earned their respect and admiration.

Rescue and repair has been his only focus for nearly two weeks. All the while he has taken comfort in the knowledge that Ayan Anderson and Alice Valent are both safely home in the Rega Gain System, which has been renamed the Haven System in his absence.

This is the last day of his rescue mission. Not because he is too exhausted to continue, but because they've finally reached the last life sign. Trapped behind more rubble and warped metal than anyone else, their lead Medical Technician, Ensign Zac Levine has been in and out of stasis as he waits for crews to clear their way to him.

The Triton & Admiral Terry Ozark (Oz) McPatrick

After suffering massive damage, the Triton and crew travels alongside Freeground Fleet and Freeground Alpha as they continue their journey away from the Iron Head Nebula in a long-distance wormhole. The Nafalli Fleet that has allied with them sent repair crews to Freeground Alpha in order to repair and improve its wormhole generator and have made great progress, cannibalizing whatever they can from Freeground Fleet ships, the station itself and some of their own vessels to restore and improve the essential travel technology. By all estimates, the large gathering of allies is a long way from Order of Eden territory, and will arrive in the Rega Gain system, now renamed the Haven System, in days, not weeks.

All the while, Admiral McPatrick (Oz) wonders what happened to his friend, Jacob Valent, and his ship, the Revenge.

As they escaped the Revenge had to take a separate wormhole provided by one of their allies, and the heavily damaged ship hasn't been seen on scanners since, indicating that their escape route has taken them well off course.

The Revenge

The damage to the nose of the ship and the port side have destroyed a quarter of the ship, an entire hangar, thousands of tons of supplies, equipment, many crew quarters and the medical bay. Engineering Chief Finn directs repairs on their primary power systems and main hull support structure. The First Officer, Stephanie Vega has been directing ship operations from the bridge.

Gunnery Chief Frost has been assigned the daunting task of directing robots and repair teams as they work frantically to restore functionality to thrusters and weapons. To the surprise of everyone aboard, the gruff Chief's people have been able to restore all but one of the ship's main thrusters, and two of their heavy railgun turrets are ready for action, making the Revenge a formidable threat despite its overall condition.

The crew collectively hope it will be enough, since the Revenge and the Hoarta will be emerging behind Order of Eden enemy lines.

ONE

Desire Versus Duty

WHILE ALICE DELIVERED the torso of her new android friend, Theodore, to the home of an android technician who owed her a favour, every part of her uniform changed. Her heavy jacket, which was one of her favourite things - a waist length, thick garment that had hidden sections that could generate a shield and expand into a heavy suit of armour - had turned black and gained thick red pinstripe running down the sides. The same pattern was repeated on her uniform vacsuit and heavy combat boots, where the rest of her heavy armour hid.

A check on her comm unit strapped to her left wrist revealed nothing. Her civilian file was still there, connected to Crewcast as usual so she could contact friends and anyone else in Haven Shore, but her military file was blocked completely. It had to have something to do with the Triton returning with Freeground Alpha and over a million Nafalli in tow. It probably had something to do with her father being reported missing in action along with the Revenge and the Hoarta, the Nafalli battle cruiser that helped them escape.

It was late, or early depending on how you looked at it. Oh four oh three in the morning. Thanks to the shield around Haven Shore, the whole island chain was embraced by a false night. It was part of an effort to get the island and all its inhabitants on a controlled, earth like twenty-four-hour schedule. Morale and sleep health were already on the rise after one week of the experiment, but Alice hadn't been exposed to it long enough to decide whether or not she liked it. Most of her time off after training was spent with the shades drawn, in front of holographic and audio data as she wrote the largest report of her life on Noah Lucas, the pilot known as Carnie, and his experiences on Iora. At the end she gladly helped him by tracking down his companion and friend, Theo, who was left in a state of disrepair thanks to a long line at the automation repair facilities in Haven Shore. Carnie was lost along with her father, so he wouldn't know about her helping hand until he returned, if he returned.

Considering the clearance level required to see the report, and who wrote it, Haven Fleet Command may have to ensure that he would never know she helped him. It may become a secret Theo had to keep as well, and he would, keeping secrets was something he was good at, something he was made for. There were important details in her report that could result in the execution of several missions and sealing the file would ensure low ranking members of the military or civilians couldn't discern what those missions might be. She tried not to think about never being able to take a little credit for helping Carnie, she'd come to admire him during the time she spent reviewing his lengthy narrated log. His voice had become familiar to her, even comforting.

Theo would be taken care of. That was the most important thing to her with regards to tying up Carnie's loose ends. Alice could turn all of her attention to making sure that her father, the Revenge, and everyone aboard were found and brought home.

The weeks old Haven Shore transit car took her from the edge of the jungle swiftly. "There's a lot happening in the fleet," Iruuk said. "Updates coming from the Triton every few seconds. More from the Nafalli Hub."

The comfortable seating in the transit car seemed like overkill for such a short distance, but she was happy it was there. It felt like she'd been awake for days. In the last few hours she'd tried getting in touch with everyone she knew above her Cadet rank, and no one was replying. The Triton had returned, her father was reported missing and she had no idea what to do. Iruuk's uniform changed to black with a gold pinstripe down his sides. "Well, someone picked you for their bridge crew, congratulations, Second Lieutenant," Alice said. The half slash on his shoulder told her his rank, and the hollow section in the middle told her it was probationary, she expected he was wanted for a higher rank, but he had to earn his way to it somehow.

He looked at himself, then his comm unit, wide eyed, excited. His nose twitched, he blinked at the message on his communicator, then very quietly said; "I'm on the Advance, due to complete final shipyard testing later today."

"Congratulations, Fur-Face," Alice said. The transit car slowed down at the base of the Everin Building. The rounded segments of the structure hung above them. A third of the units she could see had their lights on, which was unusual for the night cycle. There was a crowd of people waiting to get onto the transit car. Alice and Iruuk made their way off through the throng, many of whom looked like they were just waking up. "Looks like it's a busy morning."

"I'm not supposed to report for another six hours," Iruuk said. "What do I do until then?"

Alice turned to him once they were clear of the crowd. "Go home, get your kit together and then get some sleep. I don't need you to come with me to see my mother."

"But we don't even know where you've been assigned, or what's going on with your father, or the Revenge."

"I'll find out, don't worry. I'll send you a message as soon as I know. You have a new assignment to rest up for."

"I don't know if I could sleep, I'm too excited," Iruuk said. "Serving on the bridge of a ship already, and in the sciences section, it's my first pick for specialization."

"You're going to do great. Just knock yourself out for a few hours, show up on time, do your job and it'll turn out fine. Better than fine."

"I forgot about that, being able to get my own medication. I'm still used to my mother doing it."

Sometimes Alice forgot how young he was. His new rank, and the fact that he already had an assignment while her situation was unclear told her that they wouldn't be serving on the same ship, perhaps not in the same solar system, and she knew she'd miss him. "You'll be fine, Iruuk. Next time I meet you, you'll probably be giving me orders, or advice at least."

Iruuk laughed, a high-pitched yip, before taking her into an embrace that made the world disappear. "Thank you, Alice," he said as he stepped back. "You're my first real human friend, my best friend. I hope we end up on the same ship."

"We'll send messages if we don't," Alice said. "Now go get some sleep." She turned away, towards the Everin Building.

"Bye Alice, good luck!" he called after her.

She didn't turn around but pressed on into the foyer of the Everin Building. "I'm going to miss you so much, Fur-Face," she said under her breath. His new crew mates would love him, he would work with them beautifully because he enjoyed collaboration and knew how to follow orders. His keen mind would do the rest, he was so much more intelligent than she was. Sciences was where he belonged, and he'd thrive there.

In the middle of the foyer of the Everin Building was a giant planter with a broad column in the middle. Around the column small fruit and berry plants flourished. Some of them were flowering instead of producing food, filling in the gaps with red, yellow and blue splashes of colour. The central column was part of the aquarium system that had been woven throughout the building.

Colourful perch, sunfish and other fresh water life swam around, paying the people passing by no mind. The innermost wall of the foyer was a much larger tank, filling the space with a dimly lit exhibition of some of the larger species that were in the system, including a grey-blue Serza Shark that glided through the water with purpose. With its jagged, pointed nose it looked threatening even though it was less than a metre long. Alice leaned against the transparent metal wall of the aquarium and tapped the tank lightly as the elevator was on its way. In an instant it turned towards her, rolled its eyes up so only the whites were visible and charged her with its toothy maw open. Alice jumped back and laughed at herself for a moment as the shark turned away and swam on. "Now that's a predator."

The lift door opened and she was face to face with the woman she'd come to see. Ayan was in her black and silver Admiral's uniform, looking at a holographic projection that only she could see. Everyone around her only saw a scant haze of light coming from the command and control unit on her left wrist. She stepped out of the elevator and noticed Alice, looking her up and down and nodding. "I see your orders are about to go through."

"They're classified above my level," Alice said. "I don't know anything, only that I'm out of the Apex Program, and am to await orders."

"You won't be disappointed in where you end up if you keep your mind open," Ayan said. She turned to her entourage. "Go on ahead, I'll catch up."

The Major and two Lieutenants accompanying her moved on, leaving Ayan and Alice alone. "Is there an expedition coming together to go after the Revenge?" Alice asked quietly. "Am I part of it? Is that why I'm blacked out?"

"You're not blacked out," Ayan said, alarmed. "You remember the trainees who you saw in briefings, the ones who had their hoods up so you never saw their faces? They were blacked out until training completed, you were never blacked out."

"Who were they?"

"They were all officers from other military organizations, fallen ones. Aucharians, Nodins, and more than a dozen others. Even a few old Vindyne commanders who saw their entire sector fall apart. They volunteered for full memory scans so their loyalty could be verified, it's a secret program that will fill out the Haven Fleet's middle ranks while we keep filling Apex and other Officer training programs. They took classes with you and attended briefings while they got their qualifications, cloaked most of the time."

"Okay, that's creepy, but I get it. I always wondered why there were so many empty seats around. So, I'm not blacked out, I'm just in the dark."

"The uniform you're wearing is only assigned to Special Operations. The Admiralty has decided that you have nothing left to prove in or outside of the classroom. When you're fully activated, you'll learn more, and expect to be involved in classified missions, if not right away, soon enough."

"So, who won the bidding war for me?"

"Lieutenant Commander Robert Terran for Captain Frederick Coran. They were both blacked out officers for a while, qualifying early for a command. Captain Coran is a great commander and has already assumed command of the Eagle, a hybrid Regent Galactic and Haven Shore carrier. The refit isn't complete, they won't be ready for a week. I don't know what your assignment is going to be while the ship is unavailable."

Alice noticed that they were within a scrambling field, something Ayan must have turned on while they were talking. No one would be able to understand or record what they were saying unless they were within half a metre of them. "What's the mission?"

"You're staying close," Ayan said. "I couldn't play a part in the decision, but I support their thinking."

"So there is going to be an expedition to find the Revenge, and I'm not going to be part of it."

"I'm sorry, Alice," Ayan said. "You're capable of being a great asset to a rescue, but everyone knows your head won't be clear. You could be a danger to yourself, maybe worse. No captain who we were assigning to the expedition was allowed to bid on you."

"So, you did play a part in deciding to keep me here," Alice said.

"No, I abstained. There's nothing I'd rather do than get aboard the Clever Dream with you and go after the Revenge, but I know that would be self-serving, and cooler heads will get the job done better. There is one thing I was able to do for you just minutes ago, by the way. The Clever Dream is yours again. Your new command will require a ship, so I made sure the Clever Dream was put at the top of the upgrade list and that you'd have full ownership and control by the end of the day. The upgrades will take longer than that, but I think you'll like what we do."

Hearing that helped. She didn't normally want Ayan the Admiral, her new biological mother to pull strings for her, but if it got the Clever Dream back, if she got to be with Lewis again, she couldn't see the harm. It wasn't enough. The thought of having to stay near the Haven solar system while a whole expedition went after her father and the crew of the Revenge made her want to scream on the spot. Her instincts told her to find a way to go after them, but her services were promised to a higher cause, and she knew there was a lot of work to do in and near the solar system. It was up to her to prove that all the time and effort the fleet spent on her wasn't wasted. Besides, she knew Ayan loved her father as well, and if she wasn't pulling every string she had to be a part of the expedition, if she had that kind of restraint, then Alice had to fall in line. "Thank you, Admiral," she said. "I'll go where I'm told, do my best on whatever assignment I'm given. Thank you for getting me the Clever Dream."

"I'm glad I could help a little. I know you'll put your ship to good use and having Lewis will help you come back in one piece," Ayan said. "You know I'm always on your side, right? I'll give you anything I can."

An update appeared on Alice's comm unit telling her that she was to report to the War Forge at twelve hundred hours. The directions would take her into the bowels of the massive station, to the end of one of the smaller manufacturing lines. "I know," Alice said, looking up at her mother. When the framework system that brought her to life the last time was removed, she made the subconscious choice to combine Ayan Anderson's DNA with her fathers to remake herself one last time. That only made Ayan her biological mother. It made sense, even though it wasn't entirely likely. Ayan had betrayed Jacob's heart, breaking their relationship off for months to have a fling with another man. It was something that Alice still didn't understand, but Ayan and her father were close again, doubtlessly getting back together.

Alice would never forget that Ayan turned away from her father, but that didn't stop her from liking the woman. Ayan was an accomplished thinker and survivor, two things Alice respected deeply, and she was generally kind. It never seemed forced either; Ayan seemed to have more patience and kindness as she became more successful, something Alice had never seen before. An example of that was right in front of Alice then, as Ayan regarded her with concern. "I know you'll work for my best interests," Alice said. "Just don't pull too many strings, I'd like to do a few things on my own."

"Don't worry, after getting you the Clever Dream and pushing it to the top of the refit list, I'm all out of string," Ayan said. "I'm in your corner anyway. Remember that, okay?"

"I will," Alice said, stepping into a hug. "Thanks, Mom."

"I'm proud of you," Ayan said as they stepped apart.

"I know, thank you," Alice said. "I'm going to force myself to get some sleep, I didn't get to bed last night."

"I have emergency meetings and inspections filling my schedule, but between you and me, I wish I could go back to bed," Ayan said with a wink. "The Triton is going into the War Forge's main manufacturing and refit line at eleven. I'll be meeting Oz then, I'm sure he'd love to see you. I can send a shuttle down to pick you up."

"That sounds good, I'll see you then." The two parted and Alice made her way back to her house, deep within the protected military housing complex in the Haven Jungle. She took her own advice and used a mild dose of medication to force herself to sleep.

TWO

The Last Man

FOR FOURTEEN DAYS everyone thought Ensign Zac Levine died in the blast that put a hole through the port side of The Revenge. Jake looked through that through-and-through wound more times than he could count as he worked with the rescue crews, interfacing with the bridge from where he was, digging for crewmembers in the rubble. Whatever weapon was used didn't just cut a hole through their ship, but once it burned through the hull it forced material away from it, widening that wound.

Three hundred and eighteen people were dead, and Jake thought they were finished with the rescue effort until that morning. Several meters away from where the medical bay once was, faint life signs were detected. A concentrated scan revealed that it was Ensign Zac Levine, that he was intact inside his sealed suit, and that he was in deep stasis.

Jake led the effort as the crew cut their way to him, and after nearly two hours he saw a fully intact hand clad in a white glove. "We'll get you out of there, Doc," Jake said, making a mistake that Zac would have corrected if he were conscious. He was a medical technician, not an actual doctor, but he was the most highly trained medical officer the Revenge had.

They got closer to getting him loose, and that meant that the cutting slowed down, or at least it always seemed that way. Jake worked with his team, helping them cut through a twisted support beam that, from its markings, was from several meters down a hallway that no longer existed.

Everyone was still sealed in their suits, the section they were in was open to space. If any of the rescue team leaned back, they could see through the top and bottom of the ship's hull. The walls of the standard wormhole they travelled through lensed the stars, turning and stretching the light passing through the threshold.

The support came loose, and the rescue team handed the debris back so it could be handled by the pair of crewmembers who were assigned to salvage whatever they could while they cut and pulled broken pieces of their ship away.

Jake examined the warped deck plates in front of him and compared it to the scans on his heads-up display. "These must have protected him from most of the concussive damage, but they're not doing anything now." He said as he concluded that it was safe to pull the metal plates away.

"Hey, guys," Zac said groggily. "How long was I under?"

"Longer than you expected, I bet," Jake said. The rescue team stripped enough loose debris away to reveal most of Zac.

He shared his cocoon of metal and plastic with one of his narrow-bodied assistant bots. The pipe-thin body had been bent slightly, and the head was on his chest, still attached. Zac's hand rested on it as though he was comforting a child.

"Can you move? It's safe, just start slow."

"Yeah," Zac replied, "one sec." He carefully handed the body and attached head of his robotic assistant to Jake, who passed it back to the next rescuer. "She's still intact, just in power-saving mode because she got detached from her base, so don't recycle her."

"No problem," Jake said, attaching a tether to Zac's chest then taking his hands. "Come on out."

"I've got a little stasis fog in the head, but I'll be good to join in on the rescue effort in a few minutes," he said as he was gently pulled from the debris.

"You're our last rescue," Jake said. "We thought you were dead."

"Your medical bay is gone, man," said one of the rescue workers behind Jake. "Sorry. But hey, Nurse Thingy survived," he said, holding up the stalk and head of Zac's robotic assistant.

"Careful, she might not have real feelings, but it took me a long time to program her," Zac said as he gingerly took the robot's remains from his rescuer. He looked through the hole in the upper hull, then the lower hull and shook his head. "We lost a lot of people. Is there anyone I can help?"

"The survivors are stable," Jake said. "But they could use someone with a better trained eye. You're lucky we found you. Rescue efforts ended yesterday, you could have been trapped in there until we got back to Tamber. The transmission systems in your suit were destroyed when you got buried in this mess."

"Thanks, Captain," Zac said.

"Thank Stephanie and her people when you get the chance. She had her people do a focused scan so we could figure out how to dig in and get you."

THREE

Swimming in The Dark

ALICE'S REST was cut short when an emergency signal was sent up her arm from the small communications band she wore around her wrist at night. It took effort for her to open her eyes, they felt like old, heavy hangar doors, and she sat up as soon as she read the message. There was a briefing for HF Eagle officers in twenty minutes, at ten o'clock local time. "Holy crap!" she shouted, leaping out of bed and nearly falling on her face as her active blanket was hesitant to let her go. The gift from her biological mother, Ayan, was incredible when you wanted to get to sleep - the thick temperature adjusting blanket embraced the user - but she was discovering that they were difficult to leave in the morning. "Roomie, pour me a breakfast Pep and start the shower. Hot, high pressure!" she told her house artificial intelligence as she popped a denta tab into her mouth and leapt into the hard spray of the shower, chewing and scrubbing. "Call an automated shuttle that's cleared to go to the War Forge and tell it that I'll be about three minutes."

"Right away, Alice. I've analyzed your sleep cycle and have determined that you did, indeed get enough rest to function adequately during the day. I have to say that your schedule is in conflict with the hours you kept during the last five days, however. Going forward, you may want to go to bed earlier so you can have a more active morning."

"Who asked you?" Alice asked before spitting the leftover foam from the denta tab and wiping her mouth. "Is the shuttle coming?"

"An automated shuttle will arrive in two minutes and thirty-three seconds."

"Bring up a map leading me from where I'll be docking with the War Forge to the briefing room. Holographic, large size," she ordered as she pulled her uniform from the cleaning closet and started putting the thin under suit on. "Auto, please." In response to her request, the fabric stretched over her and sealed up to the neck as she grabbed her jacket from the closet, kicked her boots out so she could step into them and closed it behind. As she pulled the heavy jacket on she memorized the route she'd have to take through the War Forge to get to her briefing, noting that the War Forge's manufacturing systems were more than half complete, and the rest of the massive station was already host to three fighter squadrons and thousands of new inhabitants. It had already eclipsed the Solar Forge in size five times over.

With her route firmly in mind, she checked herself in a full length mirrored wall in the bathroom and finished straightening her uniform, then quickly brushed her hair. "I need a cut. More like a bob, something easy to manage."

"That would look good on you, youthful and fun," Roomie replied.

"I was thinking practical and easy to maintain," Alice said as she emerged from the bathroom. "Make the bed," she ordered as she marched through the bedroom.

"Yes, Alice."

"There you are," Alice said as she snatched her frosty drink from the kitchen then rushed through the living room, through the broad sliding door and onto the landing pad. With a firm draw on the straw, the thick, green, mint flavoured morning drink made her tongue tingle. Pep was something Iruuk had on his favourites list, and she had it a few times during training, when she felt she was low on energy, but it was her first time having it since she moved down to Tamber.

Half the drink was gone by the time a small armoured shuttle set down. A smooth, uplifting rush of energy replaced the ragged sleepiness that threatened to slow her mind and body down. The shuttle ride to the War Forge was uneventful. Alice sat in the rear seat closest to the passenger door, finishing her drink and looking for anything that may tell her more about her assignment.

There was nothing new about her specifically, but she discovered that the HF Eagle, the ship she would be serving on, had thousands of refugees from the Sol System assigned to it. They arrived while she was in training in a small fleet of freighters and starliners. They were called the Red Alliance, a disbanded group of fighters from Mars and the many stations that orbited the planet. They joined Haven Fleet, were tested, trained and she didn't notice. It was another event that proved something that Alice suspected for weeks; that Haven Fleet was growing faster than any one person could track.

There was more information about the Sol System, but it

was still unverified, so it hadn't gone public yet. What she could see thanks to her clearance level told her that there was some kind of final attack on Earth. Her heart sank as she viewed a holographic image of the planet shrouded in dark clouds, dressed in oceans that were more brown than blue. It had been rendered unliveable again, and all the evidence pointed to radical groups that once worked to restore the precious world.

Earth was never a place she consciously wanted to visit, not seriously, but seeing that the green and blue jewel, the origin point of her species was in ruins once again was heart rending. Even she knew that it took centuries to restore the planet to a state of balance and good health, she couldn't imagine the people who did that undid all their own work. Alice hoped that Haven Fleet would fail to verify the image she saw, the longer it took for that news to reach the primary data networks, the better. Knowing that Earth was in such a terrible state again was horrific, it was as though there was less hope in the galaxy.

The shuttle docked with the War Forge and she turned the hologram off. Alice dropped the nearly empty cup of Pep into the recycler and rushed through the station at a march to the briefing room. After spending some time training there, the glossy black and grey walls, the clean dark blue and white floors were unremarkable to her, especially after what she just learned. It took effort to put it from her mind, she could look into it when she wasn't required to focus on an important briefing.

Alice didn't recognize anyone except for Yawen, who smiled at her when she noticed her in the filling briefing room. Her uniform was the same; black with a thick red pinstripe down the side and absent rank. The rest of the uniforms on the hundred or so people gathering represented every department in the fleet, and Alice noticed that friendly reunions were rare.

As Yawen made her way over to her, where she stood close to the front of the plain space, Alice observed that few people seemed to know each other at all. There were a few tentative introductions between crew members who had markings from the same ships, but other than that, it was a room of strangers. She touched the arm of a young woman without a rank or ship emblem on her uniform. "I'm wondering, are you one of the officers who attended the Apex Program in a blacked out uniform?"

The young woman's brown eyes looked her up and down quickly, and she smiled a little. "Alice Valent, it's an honour to finally have the opportunity to introduce myself. I was. I'm Bailey Wilson," she replied in a thick, stately British accent.

Alice shook the woman's hand; her grip was firm and sure. "That had to be something, taking classes like a shadow."

"They did it so we couldn't interfere with your class, the main test group. Most of us preferred it for other reasons, though. When I joined your fleet I was a healthy seventy-nine-year-old, and I thought that would limit my service." The woman didn't look a day over twenty, but her eyes had a surety that was uncommon in someone so young. "I suppose you have no way of knowing, but all of us were undergoing an aggressive rollback process. Everyone who signed up agreed to it, and there were times when I was relieved to be a shadow, following you trainees. There are some stages for someone who looked like I did - a bit leathery like an old dog who spent her best years in the desert - that aren't pretty. No regrets, things turned out as promised."

"I'd say; you're a knockout. I'm Yawen," she said from Alice's side. "So, you were shadowing us the whole time?"

"I was only there for two weeks while I qualified on your fleet's technology and regulations. Many of the blacked out officers were there for a little longer," Bailey replied. "We only joined you for classes and to observe exercises though, we had a separate dormitory and galley."

A whistle sounded over the intercom and five officers entered the room. "Attention!" shouted one marked as a Lieutenant Commander in a black and gold vacsuit. He was a bridge officer. "Captain on deck!"

A man with salt and pepper hair cut sensibly, of average height and a runner's build entered the room and stopped in the middle of the far wall. He looked at the group assembled in the briefing room who were standing stiffly at attention with a little smile. Alice was in the third row, Yawen at her side.

"Targen," he said to himself, nodding at someone in the front. "Paragon? There you are," he said as he spotted someone Alice couldn't see. She wanted to - Paragon was the first android to serve in Haven Fleet. He'd proven absolute loyalty, individuality and finished every qualifier test they could devise. "Alice?" he asked, searching from where he stood, leaning and standing on his toes. "Ah, there you are," he said as their eyes met for a moment. He flashed her a smile and settled into a stance. "At ease. I'm happy to see all the late comers have made it. The rest of you have been aboard the Eagle and have met many of the people you will command."

Everyone relaxed a little, standing at ease. The Captain seemed lighter hearted than she expected, so she shuffled just a little so she made sure she could see him between the shoulders of the people standing in front of her. He wasn't what she'd expected.

"I am the doomsayer who grins and shows the way to the next paradise so the cycle may begin anew," he said in a clear, relaxed speaking voice. "You will find everything you need to know about me in that statement. It is by a failed colonist named Onan Yeth. He led his people from ruin to what he thought they would fancy as their new home. His colonists mutinied after several disasters and were successful under new leadership. He is a reminder to me. It takes a special kind of genius and drive to deliver a people from oppression and strife to a place where they have a chance at freedom, at grace, but the person who takes them there may not be the right one to lead them once they arrive."

He cleared his throat and straightened the top of his black and gold uniform so the gold pinstripe was perfectly straight. "I am Captain Frederick Coran, master of the Eagle, and I admit to you that I hope we all find ourselves as successful and eventually as obsolete as Oman Yeth. There are three great wars under way right now. Up until three months ago there were four. The civil war between Earth and the Red Alliance has concluded. Thousands of warriors from that conflict are obsolete in the Sol system; soldiers without a war to fight. I am one of them. I came here to join the next worthy cause, the fight against the Order and for the preservation of freedom for humanity. The Earth I set foot on before leaving the Sol system as a victor was a smouldering ruin. Our enemy did that after claiming to be its ultimate protectors for centuries. Despite their religious teachings, and against everything they preached, they made sure it would take a thousand years to repair the damage they caused as they scarred their own world as a final insult before losing to us. We, the Red Alliance, only wanted to have access to the planet of humanity's origin, and more freedom for ourselves. We never imagined that winning a civil war would drive the religiously driven caretakers of Earth to make it unlivable again. That is the crucible I come from. The Sol system, where Mars is green and glorious, Earth smoulders, and every soul within its sun's light mourns." He shook his head.

"I've gotten off track," he said to himself quietly before going on. "I was lured to the Haven System like so many of you. Like a whisper in the dark that had come to tell me that there was a place where humans were building while presenting open arms to the other races of the galaxy. There is mourning here, but there is a drive to create a truly advanced, democratic place that on one hand has no interest in fighting. Civilians can flourish in peace without fear that their personal ambitions will send them to a prison of debt, where they can become their best selves without worrying about where their next meal will come from, whether or not their home will be there when they return, or that they will lose dear friends and loved ones. On the other side of Haven is the tenacious fighting spirit to protect that lifestyle and to expand responsibly so millions of survivors of all races can enjoy it, enrich it with their diversity and have time to find peaceful, common ground. We fight ferociously, but intelligently so we can bring this vision to the galaxy and become obsolete as warriors. I may never see the day, but I will fight for the morning when many of you retire because the fight has come to an end. I may never see the day, but I fight so many of you can eventually put your guns into lockers, point the nose of your ships and become explorers and ambassadors. I may never see the day, but I fight harder still so the civilians I defend can someday look to the sky and instead of seeing endless war and fear the possibility of impending invasion but a sky filled with inviting stars. I was born on Earth in a place called New Chicago, and even after my family left, we still looked to our greatest icon, the eagle flying free, when we dreamt of equality and safety. The carrier you will serve on, the Eagle, was named to celebrate her purpose; that is to defend Tamber and the Haven System, where the seeds of a free society have been planted.

Welcome to the dream, now let's defend it with all our wit and vigour."

The Captain didn't spare the officers gathered in the briefing room a glance but turned and left as applause followed him. One of his underlings, a tall, extremely thin Lieutenant Commander, spoke as though he was barking. "Most of you officers know where you're going now. Brief your people and get them prepared to perform their duties at their temporary posts. The rest of you, the late comers, are free to leave for now. Your temporary assignments will come through sometime in the next three hours, so stand ready and watch your comms for more information on where you will be posted once the Eagle is ready. Dismissed."

Yawen looked from her comm unit to Alice, the rank of Ensign marked on her shoulder. "The first part of my instructions just came through; You're my commander," she said. "Guess losing all those points put me down a rung or two."

"I'm sorry," Alice replied quietly as most of the officers made their way from the room.

"At least I know who I'm under," Yawen replied. "Still no rank showing on your uniform."

Alice checked her command and control unit and shook her head. "My military rank and post are still blocked. There must be something wrong, I'm putting in a request for clarification."

"But it's all part of the grand design. What am I doing in the meantime, boss?" Yawen asked with a smirk.

"Let's go meet a pair of Admirals," Alice said.

Yawen chucked for a moment, then stopped. "Wait, you're serious?"

"Absolutely."

FOUR

To Embrace A System

THE WORST STATE of captivity follows you wherever you go. It is invisible and relentless. A prison only the captive can see. He was once again known as The Beast, no longer the Overlord. Within his mind he was increasingly something else; simply Clark Patterson.

His Issyrian senses were useless aboard the Glorious. He was surrounded by crewmembers in fully sealed suits whenever he was allowed out of his chambers. The white and dark green halls revealed nothing about his location inside the gargantuan base ship. He was seen by the soldiers and gave commands as he was instructed.

There was no choice in his existence, someone well out of sight was using an implant to make him walk where he was supposed to be seen next, to do and say whatever they commanded, then to return to his rejuvenation pool when they were finished with him. Clark knew the control implant they put in his head was still there, but he couldn't feel it anymore.

Before it was like a strong presence in his mind, and to his physical senses it was like a loose tooth he tried to jostle free. He couldn't help but toy with it, try to tamper with it in hopes that it would fail. Then, one morning perhaps a week ago, he couldn't feel it anymore. It must have still been there, since he was still not in control, but there was no more annoyance, or any sensation that it was there.

That was a problem. Before he had something to fight, something to try to extract himself, but now he could only make shallow attempts to move on his own or hold the words he was being forced to say back and it never worked.

That afternoon his imprisoned gait took him to an office somewhere in the most armoured section of the ship. He passed through a set of heavy doors and found himself in a room filled with intelligence officers reviewing holograms and screens. "Welcome, Patterson," Dron said. "Follow me."

Clark Patterson nearly fell to the floor as his body was suddenly released to him. The urge to lunge at Dron and take his throat into his hands was irresistible. Clark tried, and found himself stuck still for the duration of the attempt.

"Your attempt to attack comes from ignorance and impatience," Dron said coolly. "I should be your enemy, but I am not."

The analysts around Clark glanced at him uneasily. Sometimes it was easy to forget that he looked like a monster. Part human, but also Issyrian, Edxian and framework, with hard, crimson plates grown atop his skin that shifted and scraped together as he moved. The wary looks of the people around him was a clear reminder. Dron had never shrunk away, and only ever averted his eyes as a gesture of respect, though that may have been faked.

No effort to attack Dron led to movement. He wasn't in full control after all.

"I have an office just here," Dron said. "I have some things to tell you."

He followed him into an office that was alive with light. Ship movements and solar systems drifted through the air holographically. With a gesture, Dron dismissed them. His dark green uniform was perfect - a jacket over a simple cloth textured suit with the rank of Overlord on his shoulder. The door closed behind Clark and he stood in front of it.

"You are here because I decided that taking vengeance on you wasn't practical. I would say that my desire for it decreases faster all the time. My brother was a misguided creature. Lister Hampon was ruled by his obsessions, the worst of which was the Victory Machine and the messages it sent him. The best, most useful was the creation of this Order of Eden. This imperfect system that was built atop an even more imperfect system."

"Your brother was Lister Hampon?" Clark asked.

Dron nodded. "I've decided it's time to reveal everything to a certain few. You played a part in his downfall, and even though he was a half mad psychopath, everyone would understand if I took revenge. I will take control instead. You were a poor overlord. You have good military habits, I'll admit, but you were a terrible delegator, an uninspiring leader, and your strategies are rudimentary at best. There's something else too. You are a beast of too many races. I'd never accuse you of being sentimental, because you barely remember what it was to be human. You and Eve have wasted your opportunities as leaders. Not to be too harsh, but you're more iconic freaks than anything else.

The order runs well despite you, not because of you. I'm amazed no one else has picked up your leash."

"How am I supposed to respond to that?" Clark asked. He could imagine crossing the room and tearing Dron to pieces, but not act on it. "Is there a point?"

"The point? I'm only telling you what you need to know so you understand what's about to happen to you. I have complete control over every creature with our framework technology installed. My people have a complete understanding of how your physiology works, and what improvements we can apply to a new generation of Order Knight volunteers. Your experimentation has led to some incredible advancements, but your usefulness has come to an end. There is one thing I need to know before moving forward though. What did you do with the three framework copies of Valent that were aboard the Overlord? Did you hide them? Activate them and set them free? Destroy them?"

Clark did his best to avoid thinking about the Valents he discovered in stasis. They were fully imprinted with Jonas Valent's memories. Too dangerous to keep. He thought about his predicament, being trapped in his own body, unable to act on his urge to put Dron back in his place.

"You destroyed them, didn't you?" Dron asked as he looked at his command and control unit. He brought up a life-sized image of Jonas Valent. "You destroyed all three?"

"Dammit," Clark muttered as the memory of recycling the framework skeletons and disposing of the flesh that was Valent two, three, and four. He was tempted to activate one, to see what he would do, but that seemed cruel. They were all test subjects, and each thought they were the real Jonas Valent.

"Destroyed them," Dron said. "Just as well. One Jacob Valent is enough. So, we're going to put you to sleep now and modify your memories so you believe you are The Beast, a fully devout member of the Order and my personal hand. You will recall that Freeground Fleet murdered your family and friends, and that you joined the Order to fight them and anyone who would oppose us. You will be grateful to me as your mentor and defend me with your life. When you wake up all this," he gestured towards the rough plates covering Clark, "will be just an experimental armour that will help you lead Order Knights. Your Issyrian senses will be gone. Your new memories will justify and detail how you surrendered the rank of Overlord and backed my elevation to that level. The Order will thank you for it. Goodbye, Beast. Goodbye Clark Patterson," Dron said, turning away.

"I'll remember something, and I'll turn against you."

"Not soon enough to make any kind of difference. You'll be seeing some action in your new life. I'm sure you'll earn a great deal of glory before dying for the cause."

Once again, Clark lost control of his body as he turned towards the door and walked through. His mind started to feel numb, thought slowing and becoming more difficult until the world faded completely.

FIVE

Reunions

"I'M happy to be part of your unit, no matter how I fit in," Yawen told Alice as they waited for the small secondary transit car to take them to the bay where the Clever Dream was being prepared to undergo a refit that would remake the ship entirely. "Honestly, I'm a 'boots on the ground' kind of soldier, commanding from the middle." Her thick Northern Irish accent was in full evidence. "You're more of a big picture commander, I've always seen it, always said it."

"I don't think they pushed me up too far. I'm putting a request in for information on my assignment and rank, this is ridiculous," Alice said, quickly navigating the menus on her command and control unit. The windowless transit car hummed and shifted along as she waited for a response from the system, and then her uniform changed. The slash markings of her rank appeared on her shoulders and cuffs.

"Lieutenant, Junior Grade," Yawen said, sighing and pushing her hand through her short blonde hair. "With the mark of Captain for the Clever Dream. Looks like they're setting you up with a lot of responsibility; better you than me."

Alice knew that her former roommate and friend was covering. Being put in your place hurt most of the time, and Yawen came straight out of a war where she was a hero against the Order of Eden, went into regimented training where she didn't shine as brightly as she expected, and ended up under someone who didn't have as rich a history. No matter how close they were as friends, it had to hurt. "You're a great field commander, I'll be taking orders from you soon enough."

"That's bollocks, and you know it. Anyone who talks to me for a minute, then you, will say you're the born officer. Are you sure you don't remember anything past the last year or two? Look in the mirror sometime, really look. There's something there, in your eyes, when you don't think anyone's paying attention, it's as though you've seen three or four lifetimes and at least two of 'em went sour on you. There's something in there, maybe not the memories, but you learned some lessons. How else would you have cruised through boot camp with the Rangers, taken up arms as though guns were a part of your arm, then pushed through Apex hard enough to make the whole fleet take notice."

"I don't know about the whole..."

"Who do you think everyone's talking about right now?" Yawen asked with a slightly rueful chuckle. "The new Valent. Not the father, not your probably-soon-to-be Valent mother the Admiral, she's as much as disappeared, but you. To the rest of the fleet you're the one everyone is expecting something from, something amazing."

"I hope not, I don't even know what I'll be doing," Alice replied.

"With your own ship and a special operations team?" Yawen said. "I don't want to know. Not until it's run-and-gun time. They're not going to hold you back long, though, so if you wanted excitement, I bet you'll get it, and it's a good thing you're taking me with you. You'll need someone who can save your ass."

"I signed up to serve, that's all," Alice said. The transit car stopped for a moment. They could hear another one pass by, and it resumed. "I'm glad you're on my team. Really glad. You probably will save me more times than I can count by the time you get promoted."

The doors opened, and they stepped out into an airlock leading to a moderately sized hangar. Alice could see Ayan and Terry Ozark McPatrick talking within. She emerged from the airlock with Yawen at her side and was shocked to see the Clever Dream. Some of the armour plating had been warped by heat damage, there were patched holes across the starboard side of several different sizes and one of the missile launchers was stuck open, half ruined.

"You're just in time, Alice," Ayan said. She didn't greet her jovially. It was as though she had adjusted her tone and demeanour for a wake, and looking past her mother, Alice could see that Oz was more morose than ever. He turned away for a moment, then joined the three women with a put-on smile. "It's good to meet you again, Alice," Oz said, offering a hand.

Alice took it and shook it once but used it to lead herself into his arms. He was more than a head taller than her, but when he returned her embrace, it was clear that he needed it much more than she did. "What's wrong?" she asked as she stepped away.

"Haus Geist was killed in the last engagement with the Order," Oz said quietly. "It was as though they knew exactly where to hit the Triton, where he was. We're hiding the ship from the fleet so they can't see the hole one of their ships punched through the hull to get him."

"How? Few people even knew about him," Alice asked, more in disbelief than out of inquisitiveness.

"He said he could feel a human with telepathic enhancement aboard the Glorious. His name was Dron. Then they hit us with the biggest weapon they had and let us go. We got away quickly, but they could have slagged half the fleet as we were leaving. If it wasn't for your father, the Revenge, and Samurai Squadron, we wouldn't have had a chance at all."

"I'm sorry, Oz," Alice said. She was keenly aware that Yawen was watching as quietly as she could, staying out of the circle that Ayan, Alice and Oz had formed.

"Geist wouldn't want us to mourn him. He even left an active program aboard the Triton that was derived from his knowledge and thought patterns, so only the people who were telepathically linked with him would notice his absence. To most of the crew, there's no difference."

"If there's anything I can do, I'll be there," Alice offered.

"Thank you, but I'll be fine," Oz said. He was putting up a brave face, but she knew he wasn't fine, and it would be a long time before he felt right again. She wished he could give him a clean start like she had only months before but kept the thought to herself. Sometimes pain was as much a teacher as any other sensation or experience. "For now, there's an artificial intelligence here that has been waiting for you. He's refused to contact you using Crewcast or other normal channels, he's afraid he'll be hacked into while he's vulnerable."

"I know the damage looks rough," Ayan said, gesturing

towards the sleek, Arcyn Starskipper Luxury Combat vessel. It didn't look nearly as sleek or stylish as it once did. "We were in contact with the Triton early on while they were on their way back from the Iron Head Nebula and consulted with Lewis, got his permission to do a full refit once they were back here. The other condition was that you agree to the work as well, but with his permission, the Triton flight and repair crews stopped working on getting him back in shape. Lewis knows what we're proposing for the refit. You know the technology, it's in what you studied during your time with the Apex program."

"Should I go aboard?" Alice asked, staring at the patched holes.

"He's expecting you," Oz said.

Alice started walking towards her ship, wishing she could remember more than impressions and brief mental images of it. The feeling that she'd spent a long time aboard, that it was more than just a ship was ever present. This was a friend, a companion comparable to most of the friendships she'd made. She turned around and looked to Yawen.

"I'll stay here, I can meet him later," she said.

Alice nodded and boarded using the forward ramp. It was just large enough for one person, with narrow stairs. Without thinking, she found the cockpit. "Hello, Lewis," Alice said.

"Is that really you, Alice?" Lewis asked, his voice clear and a little gruffer than she remembered. "You are quite different from your last incarnation. It seems you've gone from woman, to girl, now back to woman. If it weren't for the records Oz and Lieutenant Garrison showed me, I would doubt it was you at all. You are more Ayan and Jacob's daughter than the person I knew."

"I had a rebirth. It's really me, Lewis, I missed you." She thought for a moment, there was a memory, no, a number of memories and a sensation but if she tried to recall more than tiny fragments of events, they dissipated like wisps of smoke in a breeze. "I missed having you in my head?"

"That's right, you used to have a communications node installed," Lewis said, his tone lightening a little. "You remember?"

"A little, here and there. It's hard, like I'm learning a new language or something, but looking around..." she leaned towards the forward entrance. "I recognize the recycler and cleaning system near the entrance. I got those two mixed up a few times, didn't I?"

"I always asked if you were sure you wanted to recycle something when you used that compartment after you destroyed a jacket in there," Lewis replied.

"There was one time, I had to use a waste line to get away. The smell was..."

"More than I wanted aboard!" Lewis laughed. "It's you! It's you, after all! When they transferred Garrison and the report on you showed that you didn't remember much of your old self, well, I was near panic."

"I'd hate to see what happens when you panic," Alice said, slowly sitting in the pilot's seat. "This feels familiar, but a little off somehow."

"You were eleven centimetres taller when you used to sit there," Lewis said. "And narrower, especially in the hips."

"Watch it," Alice warned with a chuckle.

"Yes, Ma'am."

"You've been through some serious adventures yourself, haven't you?"

"I'm the only ship in the fleet with seven layer cloaking technology and a variable missile launcher system. If you ask me, I was under-utilized."

"It doesn't look like it from the outside," Alice said. "If you don't mind me saying."

"I took extensive damage, it only makes sense that most of it looks worse from the outside than it does within. I still kept every member of the crew safe and sound, but I have to admit there were moments when I wished I had a few more layers of armour."

"What do you think of me taking command? Running missions with you?"

"Only if I can help you with your memories. Oh, and get that full refit. The thought of having over eighty four percent of my mass replaced and being rebuilt in a new design would frighten me if I hadn't already seen the intended results. Regenerative systems, new sensors, a dimension drive or two, a micro-fusion array and uni-generator would be more than enough to make me happy, but the design they plan on putting it all in with me is like upgrading to an embarrassment of riches."

"So, you're excited, not even a little afraid?" Alice asked.

"Afraid? Well, they're not transferring me to another computer system. Why? Do you know something I don't? Should I be afraid?"

Alice suddenly felt as though she was undoing a lot of work someone else did to reassure him. "I know less than you do. I'll just miss you while you're on the line being rebuilt, transferring a bit of my nervousness, sorry."

"Oh, you don't have to worry, Alice. Like you, I will come out the other end looking better than ever. Perhaps not as well rounded or bouncy, but better."

"Good, so I'll sign off on the work and you'll wake up later feeling like a new ship." She patted the dash before getting to her feet. "Then we'll have work to do."

"Thank you, Alice. I'm looking forward to it."

SIX

The Special Operations Combat Unit

WHEN THE ALERT CAME, Alice was walking back to Oz and Ayan, struggling to find something to say to Admiral McPatrick. He was so sullen, he looked so tired, that his mourning seemed to have crossed the line between emotional damage to physical harm. She could not have imagined that someone that sturdy, that confident could look so weakened.

"I gave my approval," Alice said. "Lewis is excited about the upgrade, a little unsure about being temporarily deactivated, but he's looking forward to the change."

"Good, he's up next on line fourteen," Ayan said. "We'll do an extra round of tests to make sure he doesn't wake up to a bunch of bugs and bad bends."

That's when the invasion alert jostled her nerves and chimed on all their command and control units. At a glance she could see the whole fleet was on yellow alert. Her muster point was only three decks down, in an unused squad room. Yawen compared her instructions quickly and nodded. "We're activated."

"We have to get to the command centre," Ayan said. "Good luck, you two."

"Keep your heads on a swivel," Oz added.

"You too," Alice replied, unsure of what to say in the moment. She looked to Yawen, starting for the stairway. "We'll make better time under our own power."

"Good thinking," Yawen said.

By the time they descended three decks on the steps and arrived at the squad room, which was laid out and set up with comfortable seats that looked a lot like they belonged in the cockpit of a fighter, Yawen and Alice knew who they would be in command of. Most of their squad members were cadets who they were responsible for watching and assisting during their time in the Apex program. "It looks like they took the best from both of our squads and made one functional group," Yawen said.

"Not bad thinking. I'm surprised we get any credit, we didn't have much time to help them out while we were in the middle of the academic curriculum."

"Speak for yourself; I'm sure my squad were praying to get rid of me. I was in their business and pushing them to get higher scores every day."

"That explains why you weren't around for days at a time," Alice said.

They entered the room, Regan, a tall trainee who looked to her for help more than once during training flashed a smile at her as she and Yawen made their way between the middle aisle between the seats. "Officer on deck!" he shouted.

All twelve members of their squad snapped to attention. "At ease," Alice said. "Our commander is on route with our orders. We're here first, so we sit first. Take the front row."

As they settled in, two more squads of fourteen arrived, filling half the seats. One other team, led by Titus and an Ensign she didn't recognize, wore the Special Operations uniforms, but the other two squads were marked with the insignia and colours of regular security staff. Titus nodded at her with a little smile and spotted something over her shoulder. "Officer on deck!" he shouted.

Lieutenant Commander Robert Terran strode in, looking at something on his command and control unit. "At ease," he barked without looking up. Several pilots followed him, taking seats where they could find them. "Good muster time," he said as he looked up. "There's no time for long introductions or speeches, thank all the Gods and stars. The Eagle won't be ready for action for at least seven more days. That doesn't mean that her personnel get time off when trouble has crossed our borders. I was supposed to begin group assessment for the security teams and give our Special Operations people time to settle in, but this is Haven Fleet. Nothing happens when it's supposed to, and the order of operations is always changing. The primary elements of our fleet are occupied. They are still executing rescue and recovery operations on what's left of Freeground Alpha and assisting the Nafalli. Our defence is..." He looked over everyone's head to the rear entrance as the doors slipped open.

Most of the soldiers turned in their seats to see what drew the Lieutenant Commander's attention. A tall, dark haired Junior Lieutenant stood in the doorway with a smaller, stockier man of the same rank who held his jacket in his hand. His

Special Operations uniform was only closed half way up his torso and he was out of breath. "In or out, gentlemen!" the Lieutenant Commander barked.

"I'm sorry, Sir," started the taller one. He and the fellow with him filed in and sat down in a hurry, their squads flowing in behind them. "We were using one of the closed storage bays for a football game between delta and beta squads."

"No one asked, no one cares. Sit down and listen up," Lieutenant Commander Terran said rapidly and coolly. "Twenty eight minutes ago, three ships from the Cefa System arrived on the edge of the Haven System. That's the Rega Gain system, our home, for anyone who is as mentally behind as Lieutenants Foran and Steno were late. The lead ship arrived dead. All souls lost in transit thanks to hundreds of Order of Eden driller scramblers that were aboard. This is the first time we've seen them use small attack bots that affix to an outer hull, drill through and go after crew or critical systems. Early intelligence reveals that this may have been a ship carrying an outspoken group of rebels. There was an automated message telling us simply that the Cefa System has been overrun and thousands of refugees are coming. You can play it back later. The other two ships were filled with civilians and the few rescue ships we could scramble got to them in time. There were no attack bots aboard. While they were doing their jobs, more ships began arriving. The rescue teams we have are overwhelmed, and if the Order of Eden or any of their allies decide to push against our border, we will have plenty of fighters, some good heavy fire support, but no boarding teams, no multi-role support staff to back them up and take up important secondary objectives as they come up. Our Captain volunteered his crew, and I am in charge of the Special Operations Division, so that takes us to this moment. You have each been assigned to an extended combat shuttle. Your current objective is to perform rescues on ships as assigned. Keep your eyes on your scanners. Watch for suicide bombers, do not attempt to dock with a ship that scans as empty. We are aware that some of these ships are arriving with failed life support systems and those tombs will be dealt with last until we've saved everyone we can. If anything looks wrong, if you even hear someone mutter; 'For the Order,' you will retreat back to your shuttle and back off unless you are Special Operations. The Order will do anything to infiltrate and interfere with us, we are tasking Special Operations with handling the more complicated situations. No one else should attempt to resolve a situation that may have a combat element today. Remember your training. We're in for a long day."

"Lieutenant Commander, Sir," called the short, half-dressed Lieutenant from behind. "How many ships are we up to?"

"Did you make it through training without learning to read, Lieutenant?" Terran asked. He held his command unit up; the thick arm band flashed a screen of quickly flowing text. "You have more information than you need right here. If you don't know how to read it, then have one of your people show you. Let's get to work, dismissed!"

A pair of pilots approached Alice and Yawen, they were both short, stout people. "Ensign Tamera Lott, reporting for duty, Lieutenant," said one. "This is my navigator; Ensign Manda Lott." She said, gesturing to her twin.

"Your shuttle awaits, Ma'am. Prep's all done," Manda said. "Engineering's got us set up with one of their brilliant newbies, he's waiting for us."

Alice took a brief look at the people in her charge. Everyone had all their gear on them, so their armour was complete, and each wore their sidearm and were checked in with their general kit. "All right, let's not keep these refugees waiting. If anyone forgot anything, now's your last chance."

"I could eat," Regan said. "I missed lunch."

Yawen tossed him a meal bar and moved past him, shaking her head.

"Lead the way, Ensign," Alice said to Tamera.

SEVEN

Big News

THE BRIEFING ROOM, the hallways around it, and most of the equipment areas on the command deck were wide open. The walls, doors, and all non-essential small circuitry had been repurposed for repairs. Any metal that could be recycled into armour and wasn't structurally required was pulled and utilized. Nothing aboard the Revenge was wasted. Not even the Captain's quarters were saved from the cannibalization. Jake was down to a bed, a footlocker and one light. The table, his food and drink dispenser, shelves, cupboard, drawers, sound buffering material and even his hygiene system had been pulled. He still had his privacy and a comfortable bed, even though the size of his quarters was cut in half so they could use the extra plating.

The Revenge was also shorter. Building a new shield system for the burnt out forward section was impractical, so while they were in the wormhole, teams of volunteers cut armour from the vulnerable forward section so it could be used to patch major breeches. One of the hangars was abandoned and its interior was stripped as well, giving the crew more than enough hardened metal to armour the hull breached sections. The engineer in Jake was thrilled at the damage control efforts.

In the time they spent within the wormhole, all critical repairs were completed under the direction of Finn, Agameg, and Frost. Direction came from elsewhere as well, but to a lesser extent.

Jake focused on leading rescue teams though the ship for long shifts. Remmy was his number two for that entire endeavour, leading a secondary team through the damaged areas of the ship. At first following life signs, and when they could detect no more, he and Remmy led their teams into difficult to scan areas that could have bodies or survivors. Zac, their only medical technician was the last one. It was a good way to end the rescue effort.

He emerged telling him that he should have a conversation with his first officer, and if they weren't both so busy, he would have approached Commander Stephanie Vega right away, but other duties took him away from that. It was the middle of her duty shift and the beginning of his when he approached her flight command seat. It was launch prep day, she was coordinating the final work necessary to have all the support Samurai Squadron needed to operate. It was one of the biggest advantages the Revenge had: an experienced and ready squadron of heavy attack fighters.

"Captain," she said, turning her seat towards him. "The deck crews are doing final testing and scanning. We're ship shape and fully operational in two hangars."

"Good, I never had a doubt," he said. "Zac is settling into his new med bay. Most of the injured are treated."

"I saw that. He's fast, and most of his patients are returning to duty with smiles on their faces."

"I know." Jake hesitated for a moment before going on. "He told me you had something important to talk to me about."

Any levity Stephanie had drained away. "I'm sorry, Sir," she whispered. "I blocked a medical detail before boarding the Revenge. There was a high chance I was pregnant, and it turns out that it took. Sorry, Jake," she said in a low whisper.

"Don't apologize for being pregnant," he replied, keeping his voice low as well. If anyone in flight control heard from their stations all around them, they didn't make any indication.

"I'm not," Stephanie scoffed. "I'm sorry for lying about it. I couldn't pass this post up. I needed to be here in case you needed me, and I'm glad I came."

"We needed you, but there's good intent behind the regulation that we don't put an innocent life at risk."

"I know," Stephanie said. "It was unplanned, I haven't even told Frost yet."

"Unplanned? How? Contraception either works or it doesn't now," Jake knew he was overstepping the moment he said the words. Some commanders believed that everything the people under them did was their business, but he wasn't one of them. Everyone had some personal choice. It was the repercussions that generally remained the same. What Stephanie did with her body, and how she conducted her relationship with Frost wasn't his business as long as she could do her duty. "From someone who has known you for a long time, I'd just like to know what's going on."

"Haven Shore, Frost, and his bloody family," Stephanie hissed. "I went off prevention on purpose for one week. Maybe I went a little baby crazy after seeing how amazing and safe Haven Shore looked, and there were so many kids there. I hadn't seen kids just playing and growing up in a safe place for a while. Then Shamus starts talking about how he should check on his brother and his nephew core ward, and I felt him slipping away. I turned the prevention meds off." She leaned onto her console and rested her forehead on her arms. "It was one week, Jake. It wasn't even like I was trying to trap Shamus with a baby. It was more like I love him so much that, if he's going to go off for a while and leave me behind, then I want something from him."

Jake put a comforting hand on her shoulder. "Leave you behind? I'm sure he would have taken you with him if he went to check on family."

"He never mentioned me going with him once, and even if he did I would tell him that I was staying here because this is where I'm most needed. If he went anyway, I'd follow him. I've had time to think about it, but I'd make sure he didn't see it coming."

A few of her staff definitely heard her, some couldn't avoid seeing that something dramatic was going on. "I'd miss you, but I'd understand."

"Would you though? Your daughter, and well, your Ayan are both in the Haven System. You sent Ayan back for her own good, but I don't know if I could leave Shamus if I were in her place."

"It was for the good of the Fleet. She wouldn't have gone otherwise. I could see you doing the same thing," he said.

"Now what happens?" Stephanie said. "I've looked through the regulations, I know what could happen, what's supposed to happen, but a lot of it is up to you as my commanding officer."

"Step into my office," Jake said, nodding in the general direction of his quarters.

"You have the hot seat, Apanowicz," she said as she stood and strode out of the flight command deck. It was no larger than the bridge, and relatively untouched by the salvage operations. Jake's quarters were less than twenty steps away.

As soon as the door closed, Jake faced her and realized they were almost nose to nose. "One of us has to sit," he said, gesturing to the bed that was a little too big for the space. It was a suspended membrane bed that adjusted to the user, the same technology as the beds and bunks on the Triton used. Stephanie sat down. "Okay, so you're keeping the baby?"

"Yes. That's the only thing I know for sure," she replied.

"Congratulations. Are you going to continue serving in Fleet even if you have to do it from a land base?"

"I plan on serving my three years at least. I was hoping to go career long term," Stephanie said. "Oh, God, how didn't I think about the maternity suspension. I'm going to be out of the loop for one to five years."

"They call it 'maternity leave,' I'm pretty sure," Jake corrected quietly.

"Unless you report me for blocking critical medical information," she said.

"No, I'm going to report that I ordered you to block the information so you could be my first officer on this trip. If there's a reprimand, I'll take it. It'll be less severe for me than it would be for you."

"What? How?"

"I can tell them that I needed you too much, or that I wasn't sure if the pregnancy would take because it was so early, or I can just say; 'oh, but she was only a little bit pregnant,' and pretend I'm an idiot. I've got a little more latitude to play with because I'm your commanding officer. If you admit to blocking critical information they could say you were emotionally compromised and start watching for a trend."

"Which they wouldn't find," Stephanie said. "You know that, right?"

"How long have we been serving together?" he asked. "I know. I'll take the heat, either way, it'll be a slap on the wrist. It'll look like I went to bat for one of my crewmembers to a lot of the fleet."

"It would look like I was just serving myself, if I took the blame," Stephanie said. "All right, I'm convinced. You did it. Wait, not the pregnancy, you made me lie about it."

"I'll make sure that's clear," Jake said.

A light ping from the doorway announced that someone wanted in and Jake opened it. Shamus Frost leaned in. "I heard something was going on and I might want to know about it?"

"Who told you?" Stephanie asked. "It was Olden, wasn't it?"

"I won't be revealing my sources, lass."

"Come in," Jake said. "I should go."

"I'm pregnant," Stephanie blurted. "Oh, thank God, I said it. I was sure I would lose my nerve and you'd have to tell him."

"That would have been awkward," Jake said.

Frost was stunned, standing between Jake, the bed and Stephanie. There was just enough room to walk around the queen sized intelligent membrane mattress. He looked to Jake, who put his hands up. "I had no part in it," he said.

"Is it mine?" Frost asked Stephanie.

Stephanie lashed out with an open hand so quickly that Jake heard the slap before he realized what happened. "Of course it's yours, you idiot!"

Frost shook his head, then resumed staring at Stephanie,

open mouthed with her staring back with a stormy expression. "What? Say something!" she shouted after a long moment.

Frost lifted her off the bed and held her up, laughing joyfully. "I'm the luckiest man in the galaxy!" Her head grazed the ceiling, but by some miracle, Frost managed to spin around once with her up in his arms without bumping into anything or bashing into something.

"It's going to change things," she said, smiling down at him, holding his broad face in her hands.

"I love ya, you're having our baby, that's all that matters," he said, looking up at her.

"You have the room," Jake said as he finally exited. One glance back at the pair smiling at each other as he'd rarely - if ever - seen was enough to keep him smiling for the rest of the day.

EIGHT

Orders

THE DETAILS of Alice's new commission came through as Yawen and her troops finished their equipment and armour check aboard their combat shuttle. The ship didn't look like anything special. A long slug with extra passenger space and a broad main deck. There were three turrets and thick armour made from the new type of advanced plating that the War Forge was building most of the new ships with. The section they were settling into was behind the cabin, could convert from seats to bunks in minutes, and had lockers for all their gear.

Alice was settled into heavy armour that had interceptor thrusters and a shield package added before anyone else had a chance to finish checking theirs. She wanted to check the details of her orders and commission more than anything, but she knew she had to get herself set up for the mission of the moment first.

"I'll make sure the rest of our people are set up and ready.

They're not qualified on Interceptor Armour though, so we won't be able to set them up with more than emergency thrusters," Yawen said. "You look your file over."

Alice nodded and stood beside the door leading to the passenger and cargo area. The shuttle jostled slightly as it left the deck. She could see the hangar surrounding the ship disappear through the transparent sections of hull, revealing a field of distant stars. They were just outside the Haven Solar System, near the end of the hyper speed deceleration zone, where ships that travelled at speeds faster than light were supposed to slow to normal transit velocities. She couldn't see them, but she knew that there were two whole squadrons of fighters out there already along with a small fleet of rescue ships already meeting the incoming refugee crafts.

Alice settled into her armour, letting it stand for her and leaning her weight on the inside of its shell. It was a trick she learned during suit week - when she had armour with its own strength augmentation systems, she could trick it so it stayed still while she used it as support - and it was a great way to conserve energy. At her mental urging her command and control unit started using the systems inside her helmet as a display. "Read me my orders, please," she requested.

"Second Lieutenant Alice Valent, you have been assigned to the First Special Operations Combat Unit," announced a gentle male voice that reminded her of Theodore, the android she knew was being repaired back on Tamber. It wasn't the same, but something in its clear, formal manner reminded her of him. "Assume duty immediately under the direction of Lieutenant Commander Robert Terran as a solitary operative with support. Your support is determined by your commanding officer and will change depending on mission requirements. Upon its completion, the Light Corvette - Clever Dream - will be remitted to your solitary ownership and will be used as your primary mission transportation system. Until then you will be provided with the temporary means you require."

"Stop," Alice said. "Clarify the last passage; the Clever Dream will be my property, no matter what upgrades are made?"

"That is correct. Notes from three superior commanders are attached to that part of your orders. All of them specifically guarantee your sole ownership of the Clever Dream. Would you like me to read them?"

"No, I think I know what they'll say. Continue reading my orders, please."

"As a member of the Special Operations Combat Unit, or SOCU, you are given the right to assume command of any personnel of a lesser rank, or to requisition any equipment if justifiable. You may also dismiss any member of your team at any time, and they will be reassigned elsewhere. The privileges and responsibilities of your rank in the Haven Shore Fleet apply as normal."

Astonished, Alice turned away from the small squad who were checking each other's armour and gear in the cabin. There was nothing about the Special Operations that covered the kind of position she had been assigned in her training. Academically, she understood the need for units like SOCU, they could break off from a battle group or smaller assembly of forces to accomplish more focused tasks, perform scouting duties, and complete a broad variety of more delicate missions, but she never thought she would be assigned to such a team. The amount of responsibility that came with being an independent operative in the Special Operations Combat Unit was staggering. It meant Yawen and the troops under her were temporarily assigned to her, they could be called away at any minute, and Alice could be given a mission that she had to undertake alone or she could assemble a team of her own from a broad roster if she needed to. That idea was incredible, but at the same time, she wanted to have a more permanent team around her, so there could be a feeling of comradery amongst her core people. It only took her a moment to realize that she could have that as long as she could justify it. "What is the mission of SOCU?"

"The Special Operations Combat Unit's mission is to address threats to Haven Shore that fall outside normal parameters, require specialists that are not available in a timely manner, or must be handled in secret."

"What is my current mission?" Alice asked, already looking at it on her display.

"To address any exceptional threats as they appear in the Haven Solar system in Arrival Zone Twenty-Eight. You are under the command of Lieutenant Commander Robert Terran. Your combat shuttle and squad are to wait for further orders."

Alice thought for a moment, pondering the full meaning of 'exceptional threats' according to regulations and nodded to herself as she felt she had a full grasp of what that meant. She closed her eyes and cleared her mind of the excitement at finally knowing her place in the military. It was a special position, filled with privileges that most officers didn't have, and it would be challenging, but she could ponder that at another time. Thoughts of the Clever Dream, and of Theo had to be pressed away too. Finally, she sent her hopes out to her father, who she wanted to go after herself more than anything and did her best to clear her mind of worry.

There was no way she could know what she and the green troops under her would face next. They were finished doing their checks, and already settling into the seats in the embarkation compartment. Alice took a few deep, slow breaths as she looked through their records. There wasn't much to learn since she'd had Regan, Trang and Luu as cadets during Apex training. They were all great soldiers and had solid secondary interests that could help in different situations. Private Fritz Regan was her favourite amongst them, he made an impression on her during her training, and only required her direct help once as a cadet. Knowing how much responsibility she had been given, she'd never reveal that, but it was good to see him anyway.

At the conclusion of one more deep breath, she turned to face her team. They perked up and paid attention immediately. "Now that I've finally had the details of my command cleared up, I can tell you why we're here," she said in a tone that was much sharper than she intended. By the time she was finished, everyone was on their feet.

She retracted her helmet, baring her face to her team and took a moment to relax a little. "We're not going to help any of the ships that come in with minimal problems. If the refugees aboard are in fair condition and their ships are in good enough shape to make it to one of our screening centres, then we won't be ordered to help. The Special Operations Units are here to address exceptional threats. That means we will be called in to board ships that may have a hostage situation in progress, or may be contaminated by a virus, one that is not responding to hails but has armed passengers, or anything that Fleet doesn't want a regular rescue team to touch. Until we are called on, we wait here. It may be a while before we're needed, so stay focused. On another note, I'm glad to see some familiar faces." She let her smile slip and looked across the group of seven Privates, then to Yawen. "It's a new career for all of us, in a new fleet in a place where we haven't been for much more than a year at the longest. So, when I saw who I'd be working with today, I couldn't have been happier. I couldn't think of a finer group to hurry up and wait with. That is all."

Alice was half way through a sigh of relief at finishing her short update when an alarm whooped in the cabin and the lights flashed red. Everyone closed their helmets and began to get ready. Alice watched her information stream for an update to her orders while she watched her group check in with Yawen. "Sorry! Sorry!" announced the pilot through the intercom. "We saw an assignment for SOCU Alpha come up and forgot that Lieutenant Valent is Special Operations Combat Unit Gamma. Won't happen again! Sorry,"

"If Mump and Smoot do that again, I'll make sure they don't make the mistake a third time," Private Beck said as she disengaged her head protection and ran her hand over the blonde stubble on her head.

"Easy, Tulsa, I think everyone's on edge."

Alice left her helmet in place and started looking up Lieutenant Garrison, the pilot who helmed the Clever Dream. He was still in the service, still assigned to the Triton as a combat pilot but on leave. Without an instant's hesitation she began filling out a request to have him assigned to her unit as the primary pilot. He outranked her, so it was just that, a request, but she hoped he would take a position on the Clever Dream one more time.

NINE

The Lucky Ones

"HOW DID THIS HAPPEN?" Ensign Sharim asked from the edge of a gurney. Things were finally under control in the medical bay, or what had been repurposed to be the new medical bay.

Zac was about to breathe a sigh of relief when Ensign Sharim stormed in, furious that the stop shot didn't work, she was pregnant. "You were pregnant when you boarded this ship and started duty. I can only assume that the scanners aboard were overtaxed by so many people being aboard at once. They installed new computers, but that doesn't mean all the connections in the system were perfect. How your own health monitor didn't pick up the pregnancy is beyond me."

"I shut most of the monitoring technology off on my comm unit," she said. "I was sick and tired of Fleet tracking everything

I was doing, where I was going, what was or wasn't in my uterus."

"Fleet doesn't gather that information until they need it. Until they do, it all stays right there," Zac said, pointing to the command and control unit. "The only way it sends information out on its own is if you're in some kind of trouble, or if there's a change that has to be addressed. If you didn't disconnect that, it would have stopped you from serving aboard the Revenge completely because you are pregnant." He checked her records quickly and realized that she was a member of the Refit and Repair staff. "How are you part of a technical crew if you don't know how your own comm works?" he muttered to himself.

"What was that?" she asked.

He flagged her as a security risk, something she wouldn't see. If she was just paranoid, they'd clear her with a reprimand for disconnecting from the Fleet computer system. If there was something worse going on, then the Captain should know. "Nothing," he took a breath and faced her. "Okay, I can temporarily slow your pregnancy so you can make decisions when we get back home."

"Terminate it," she said.

"No. You have every right to make that decision on your own, but I'm only a medical technician, not a properly trained doctor. Go find one of those and then make your choice, have it aborted, but I have the luxury of not having that duty."

"It's just a drug cocktail," she retorted.

"If it's that simple, then use your comms auto medic to administer it. Oh, wait, you disconnected it!"

"Don't get angry with me," she warned.

"Too late. Get out. I'll have someone find you with a new comm unit in hand, I'll make sure the auto medic system is working, and then you can do what you want after you're reprimanded."

"After I'm reprimanded?" she looked truly shocked. "Fleet's going to reprimand me for having an abort..."

"No, they're going to reprimand you for tampering with a piece of equipment that's made to save your life and attend to a long list of medical issues," Zac said. "If you left it alone, you would have never had to come to me. Can't you see I'm trying to make a new medical bay out of a half-blasted cafeteria? Oh, and by the way; please tell someone in damage control that I could use a hand. Thank you, goodbye." He already felt guilty about how he treated the Ensign, but he didn't watch her leave.

Once he heard the door close he dropped into one of the only good chairs. "You were too rough with her," said his medical assistant. Its narrow, dented head shook slowly. "I'm sure it was no small matter to her, you could have been supportive."

"I'll record an apology once I calm down. Maybe it'll lessen the penalty she'll get for tampering with her equipment," Zac replied. He brought up a hologram he'd watched a hundred, perhaps a thousand times. His boy, Brian and his little girl Andi were four and six when it was taken. They piled on top of him, trying to pin him to the floor as he pretended that they almost had him. They giggled and pounced over and over, squealing when he picked one of them up or pretended to pin them for a moment.

"Okay, that's enough for now. Wash up for lunch," Gabriella, his wife said. He stopped the recording, not ready to see her even in holographic form again.

"Why do I keep getting lucky when everyone else gets killed?" he asked, remembering the moment he thought he'd be crushed to death when his medical bay was destroyed.

"As an adult male, you are more well suited to survive challenging situations..." his medical assistant began to answer.

"It was rhetorical," Zac said quietly. He rested his eyes for a long moment, breathing, relaxing the muscles in his neck and shoulders. "Somewhere on this ship, there are at least two people who are very happy that Stephanie Vega is pregnant. That's good. There are fifty three people who are properly medicated, no longer in pain, and back on duty or recovering comfortably."

"There are five crewmembers who have restored sight," his medical assistant added.

"I play this game alone, remember?" Zac told him. "Still, thanks for that, I forgot about them."

"Sir? Can we help?" asked a meek voice from the hallway.

He sat up and opened his eyes. They were crewmembers from different departments; engineering, launch deck hands, and personnel support. He took a breath and cleared his throat. It was time to put a brave face on again.

"Our duty shifts are over, so we thought we'd offer some time to, you know, tidy up," said one of the youngest crewmembers he'd seen. His hair was perfect, and he was part of the operations team.

"You're right, I could use a hand. Please, call me Zac," he told them. "Do they train you guys in good timing before you leave the academy?"

TEN

So Close

LUCIUS WHEELER ENJOYED the warm breeze as he sat on the third storey balcony of the Star Worshipper Inn. He was so close to a Haven Shore recruitment centre that he could see it in the distance. Landing fields had been flattened, antennae and emitters pointed high in the sky on top of a large observation tower.

No one in the system knew who he was, or why he was there. He sipped his cup of Lil Spice tea. It was tart but pleasant, good for the nerves. There was a way in, and he waited for his contact to arrive.

"Sir, there is a priority message for you," said a waitress in old fashioned black and white wear. Humans had taken up the simple work, since no one outside of the Haven Government trusted bots anymore. He liked it, except for the new custom of gratuities. She held a small, round holoprojector in her hand. "Would you like me to tell them to contact you directly?"

"No, I can take it, thank you," he said, handing her a platinum pip. He activated the unit, an Echo Corporation logo appeared for a second, telling him that someone was using a quantum communications network to make contact. The face of a fairly average looking man of smaller stature appeared, he was in an Order of Eden uniform. For a moment he thought it was Hampon, and he did seem a little familiar. "Privacy mode," he said, engaging a system that would ensure that only he could see or hear the hologram. "Do you realize where I am right now?"

"Of course, how do you think I found you?" the man said calmly. "Your contact is one of my spies."

"Do you realize how much trouble I went through to get this close?" Wheeler asked.

"You had your DNA altered, which took some doing since you're a framework, have worn a few different faces, paid your crew off with the last of your money and took a small ship, which you do not own, to Tamber. A deal with Patrizia Salustri and her people facilitated... something, what you wanted to accomplish with her is still unclear, but now you're awaiting the arrival of my operative so you can become a citizen of the Haven Government. To what end, well, I can't be sure, but I'd guess you want to cause some harm."

"How long have you been watching me?" Wheeler asked. "And how?"

"Your whole framework system is detectable if you know the serial number. You think the model you're in is somehow special. In truth, it's just different. It's not like the one the Valents were using. The serial numbers were removed from our system for reasons I may never know, along with a number of others. We've always known where you are, Lucius. Your contact is not coming. Whatever you arranged with Salustri will most likely go through, there's nothing we can do to stop that, but you are being recalled."

"I'm done with the Order of Eden, with Regent Galactic. I just want to get even, then get gone," Wheeler said. "I'll get close enough somehow."

"No, you won't," Dron said. "I'm curious; what was your plan, anyway?"

"I don't know, I thought I'd send Ayan a selection of pretty dresses, maybe a bouquet with a hornet in it. What do you think? They put a bounty on me, ruined my life in any sector where the British Alliance has a foothold. They've gotta die."

"But, how?"

"I was going to figure something out once I became a citizen. Until then, I can't get a good look at anything. What passes for Hart News these days doesn't go into detail about anything. Those so-called journalists won't even hop a fence to get better footage, so I have to go in."

"Not an unwise plan. Perhaps you can give us a few tips on how we can get more people over the fence when you join my fleet. It's time, Lucius."

"Not a chance," Wheeler said.

The man in the hologram smiled a little. "It's not your choice. Who do you think is ultimately in control of you now that the whole framework development vault has been opened? Now that the entire database has been decrypted? When you regain consciousness, you will be standing right in front of me. We'll talk then."

The hologram disappeared. Wheeler felt himself slowly stand. He knew he was going back to his small ship. There he would chart a course then execute it. He tried to fight for control, but his body would not respond. Then all sensation stopped, as though someone flipped an off switch in his head.

ELEVEN

The Team

BEING FURTHER DOWN than Alice would have liked on the list of Special Operations teams to be called on was wearing on her people. They waited, all geared up and ready, within the cabin of their armoured shuttle as it held position.

The only good thing about having the extra time was getting the opportunity for her to introduce herself to the new people on her team. They were all from Yawen's group of cadets, people her friend spent so much time with that it cost her several points in the Apex program. Yawen was always doing something with the cadets, so much so that Alice felt that she had neglected hers, even though she made herself available for questions, guidance and spent as many combat and physical training exercises with them as she could, which amounted to more than half the sessions they had. It seemed like a lot, but it was nothing compared to Yawen's level of attentiveness.

Oscar Holm, a thin, slightly short man with new strands of hair filling in a horseshoe shaped void on his head introduced himself first. He noticed that Alice glanced at his newly carpeted scalp right away and rubbed the new growth with a smile. "You like? I just started gene-meds for premature loss, couldn't afford it where I came from but Fleet's helping me out for free."

"It's going to look great," Alice said, glad that Holm set a casual tone to the introductions. Everyone was ready to go, they all had one eye on their status feeds, so there was no need for strict behaviour at the moment. "How long has it been coming in?"

"About two days. They waited until my file was set up for active duty before telling me I could get it done."

Not knowing exactly what to say, Alice fell back on her command training and mentioned what she remembered from his file. "You were an electrician on Xono Drift before you joined up? That had to be interesting."

"Yeah, I think I learned how to wire half the ships ever made there. Xono was half scrap, and half whatever ships they could weld in or hard dock. I pulled a lot of wire and ran even more with Jessen, here." He pointed at a dark haired woman at his side. Her gaze was cool and calm. Naja Jessen looked like she was observing everything around her, drinking it all in from moment to moment. "She's the one who I had to listen to over there. Lady has a nose for when you're about to cut through the wrong beam and make a whole pier crumple."

"I had two year's training in structural engineering before I started running guns for the Zulitch family. They turned on each other and I ended up stuck on the Xono Drift. This is a much better career move, thanks for having us on your team."

"I didn't get to choose this time," Alice said, prompting

several nervous glances and raised eyebrows. "But I don't think I'd have chosen differently if I had the choice."

"Yeah, you'll learn to love us," Holm said, pushing the conversation along and bumping into a taller, broad faced man who looked like he was straight out of a Viking epic. "This is Knud and the tall beauty behind him is Beck. They're both one hundred percent hunter - as in former bounty hunters - and were marooned on Iora for three weeks before they got their ship flying again and got to Haven Shore."

"The Southern Refugee Centre, but close enough," Beck said. "It's not really an interesting story."

"Iora was a mess," Alice said, accepting Knud's outstretched hand. It was huge, nearly twice as wide as her own. It seemed like Beck did the talking while Knud nodded politely.

"You've been? I thought it was actually pretty quiet until the Order showed up."

"I've had some experiences," Alice replied. "I have to ask; what are two bounty hunters doing at this level of the military?"

"We were gunners and runners for Victoria Bell, so we bagged a few bounties, sure, but she was the star. We were just support."

"Thank you for signing up, I'm glad you're on my team."

"It feels like this is where I'm needed," Knud said shyly.

"You're right, it is," Alice said.

It was impossible to ignore Yawen, standing proudly beside Alice as she was introduced to the four people who followed her into service from her cadet group. For the first time since the introductions began, Alice looked directly at her. After a moment her former roommate subtly tilted her head towards Regan and the rest of the cadets from Alice's group. "Right, I'm happy to introduce the service men and woman that I've been able to take from training," she said, moving to stand beside

Regan. "This is Private Fitz Regan, the resident joker and secret deep thinker of the group."

"A farm boy who went to university for starship engineering but got caught in this adventure of a war. Real Tamber original resident," he said with a nod. "You have signed on with two of the most kick-ass ladies I've ever seen, if you'll pardon my language, Lieutenant," he said, pointing to Alice and Yawen from above.

"No worries," Yawen replied.

"This is Sang Tran," Alice introduced. If Minh-Chu had a serious minded younger brother, she could easily see it being Sang. "He's our hacker, one of the white-hats who kept on trying to break into the Academy computers while he was in training."

"With permission," he added. "I found seven vulnerabilities, but if I tell you what they were, you'll have to take another oath of secrecy."

"I'm his not-so-serious side," Cara Luu said. "We were both born in the core worlds on the Stellar Mark, one of the ships that crash landed on Tamber in the early days of Haven Shore. I don't know if the Lieutenant remembers, but we met her when she was with the Rangers. She was one of the people who helped get us out of the wreck."

"I wish I did, I'm sorry," Alice said.

"It's all right, you've changed so much that I didn't realize you were the same person until a month ago. Anyway, I used to do repairs on the Stellar Mark, now I can get into any ship you like, kinda the best counter-part for my boyfriend here."

"I am not your boyfriend," Sang said without a hint of humour.

"You're lucky fraternization rules protect you," Luu said with a wink.

"What kind of ship was the Stellar Mark?" asked Holm.

"Part passenger transport, part bulk freighter. Most of the crew were third or fourth generation, just making our way around the galaxy getting paid to pick up and drop off. It was a huge ship, I grew up there and I don't think I saw..."

The alarm whooped loudly, and all of their command and control systems populated with new information on a ship that just came into the area. It was a small, hundred and fifty metre long passenger ship named the Gibson, it was the thirty ninth ship to arrive. It set off an antimatter alarm on every ship within seventy million kilometres.

"Scans are coming in, Ma'am. There's just shy of five hundred fifty litres of liquid antimatter on that ship and it is losing power," Beck said.

Alice saw that her team had been assigned to dealing with whatever was aboard the Gibson, but there were no orders yet. "Get set, we may have to go aboard."

There were a few groans, but Alice didn't get a chance to see who they came from before Yawen barked; "Get set! Whatever we're doing, we're going to have to do it with clear heads, and we'll have to get it done quickly!"

Everything that could fly started moving out of the blast radius as quickly as possible. From her training, Alice knew that someone with a much higher rank than hers was making a decision about their next move. Destroying the ship once everything was out of its destructive range was an option, it was the easiest option, but if there were refugees aboard or some other complication, her team could be sent in. They waited in silence, with no access to the scan data that the fleet must have had.

Lieutenant Commander Terran's voice was in Alice's ear then. "Lieutenant; the crew on that ship has reported that an Order of Eden Commander has taken control of the vessel and is holding a trigger that is wired into the reserve power. If he presses that trigger, it will cut off the reserve power that is maintaining the field around the antimatter, turning the ship into a bomb. We have identified this man as Commander Darius Pope, a significant figure in the nearest solar systems held by the Order of Eden and I want him in custody. Convince him that we are willing to trade anything feasible for him to turn to our side after taking control of the antimatter aboard that ship."

"How did he end up on a refugee ship?"

"The refugees tell us that they captured him on their way out of the system, but he got loose. We must take him into custody. The secondary objective is to save the refugees aboard. There are several government officials, so these are some of the most important people we'll see today, and Pope knows it."

Alice glanced at the tactical map in her helmet and almost shook her head. Their shuttle was the only ship not running from the Gibson. "I copy, Sir. I'll have him in custody immediately."

"Let me be clear, Lieutenant: you are clear to use whatever means necessary to get this done, good hunting," Terran said. "I'm making the channel to the Gibson available to you now, Pope has control of the cockpit and all systems."

Alice made sure that the channel was muted and turned to her team. Before addressing them, she signalled the shuttle cockpit crew to close and dock with the Gibson. "All right, I need Regan, Luu, Tran and Holm to go space walking. You have to covertly get through the hull of that ship and connect a backup power supply to the antimatter containment system as fast as you can. We need that under our control. The rest of you are with me. Yawen, you will take Jessen, Knud, and Beck and file in right behind me. You will be cloaked."

"Yes, Ma'am," Yawen replied along with the rest of her team. "What will you be doing? Helping us with the refugees?"

"Commander Pope, from the Order of Eden is aboard that ship, and he has a trigger set to deactivate the reserve power keeping the antimatter from exploding. I'm going to keep him calm long enough for our people to get another power source connected so his trigger doesn't work. That's the safest version of this plan, but there is another contingency. Team two, led by Yawen will move in on him and get the trigger out of his hand if you can create a real opportunity to do so safely. If I say; 'lock' in any context, you will back off. If I say; 'up' then get the trigger away from him as quickly as you can."

"Good thing we all have full scans on file," Tran muttered. Alice knew exactly what he meant, and it made her want to kick him. The theory was that if soldiers died on a mission, Haven Fleet would construct a new body for them, memories included, using a scan that their helmets could take intermittently. The scans were encrypted then sent to Haven Fleet Intelligence.

Some people believe that it gave soldiers permission to sacrifice themselves, that it made people more disposable. Tran seemed like one of those people. "If that helps you keep your head clear, then go on thinking it," Alice replied. There was a whole lecture she wanted to shout at him, but it wasn't the time. "Team one - Holm, Luu, Tran, Regan - get to the emergency hatch at the rear and start depressurizing. I want you to cloak and get out as soon as we dock."

While the shuttle closed in on the Gibson from a little over two million kilometres away, into the hottest area of the blast zone, Alice concentrated on calming down. Before long she found herself thinking about what the previous teams faced.

Alpha team was sent in when a refugee ship's hull couldn't be penetrated by scanners and there was no reply to hails. It turned out that it was a ghost ship, the life support systems failed and everyone aboard asphyxiated before arriving.

Beta team was sent after a ship that attempted to flee as soon as it arrived. It turned out that they weren't part of the influx of refugee ships at all, but were raiders and smugglers returning from a looting spree somewhere nearby. It was something the rescue teams didn't have to attend to, but any group of marines would have done a fine job, they didn't actually need Special Operations for that one. As Alice gave it some thought, she realized that the first call didn't require Special Operations either, but there could have been anything on that ship, so it wasn't a waste of a team.

They crossed the one million kilometre mark, Alice felt much calmer, and she decided it was time to open a dialog. With a glance at an icon inside her helmet, she started a playback of Commander Pope's first and only communication with Haven Fleet Command.

"I am Commander Pope of the Order of Eden. I have enough antimatter here to obliterate everything within a million kilometres, and I will detonate it if my demands are not met. I also have most of the ruling body of Bienla, one of the most important Commonwealths in the sector, and their children aboard. They are alive, which is something I cannot say for their security team. Send a representative immediately."

"Commander, we hear you and will be happy to begin discussions with you right away. My name is Major Larn, and..."

"A representative in person! An officer with your fleet will be on this deck within the hour or I will set course for the largest ship in the area and detonate my payload." The communication ended. Further attempts at communications with him failed.

Alice took a deep breath, steeled herself and opened the channel. "I'm Lieutenant Alice Valent. My ship is approaching from your port side. I would like permission to come aboard so we can discuss the particulars of your visit to our system."

"Lieutenant..." Pope replied as he crackled onto the channel. For a moment Alice didn't know if there was a problem with the connection or if he paused, then she heard him breathe into the pickup. "Wait, Lieutenant Valent?"

It was then that Alice realized why she was sent on that mission. "Of Haven Fleet, yes, Sir."

"Come aboard," he replied, sounding intrigued.

Alice watched the airlock of the Gibson draw closer as her combat shuttle decelerated. "We could begin this discussion right now, if you like," she offered.

"No, I want to conduct this in person. Especially knowing who you are," Pope replied.

TWELVE

A Good Rest

JAKE SAT in the command seat of the Revenge, looking through the data they collected from the distant mouth of the wormhole. They would come out in a difficult spot, but it presented an incredible opportunity.

The security door to his left opened and Agameg emerged. "How was your time off?" Jake asked.

"Five days of deep sleep is just what I needed, Captain," he replied. "I'm good for at least another month."

"I thought you were going to sleep in for a while there," Liara said from the communications station, pulling her brown hair free of a band. "It's good to see you."

"I did extend my rest for three hours," he replied. "Hit the snooze button as you'd say. I knew I would be on time for our emergence from wormhole transit though. How dangerous does the space look?"

He took a seat beside Captain Valent, and Jake made sure he could see the holographic displays of the star chart in front of him. "We've spotted one patrol, but they moved on hours ago. I think we'll get a chance to find a hiding spot for both ships while we figure a few things out. The Nafalli are low on food and water. We don't have enough to help much. Our fabrication systems are breaking down, and we could use some raw materials."

"I expected the fabrication heads would begin to break down," Agameg said. "How many are still operational?"

"Two, almost three. Only one of them is full sized," Jake said. "It's been that way for a couple days."

"We have to get the other eight main units back up and running if we expect to continue repairs."

"You're right," Jake said. "Our emergency course took us behind enemy lines. I want to be prepared if we have to fight. The good news is that our intelligence tells us that we're not going to be too far from a supply post. There are a lot of them along the frontline. Stephanie and I think a raid would work, especially if the Nafalli are up for it."

Agameg looked at the schematics for a standard Order of Eden Supply Outpost for a moment then shook his head. "This is not recent data on the outpost," he said.

"You're right, but it's what was here last time an Order ship had to report there, well, before we got the intelligence we're using. That data's about two weeks old."

"What is my role in this?" he asked.

"I need you to assume command while I lead my team. You'll have to make do without Liara and Finn. I'll need them down there with me."

"I'd feel more comfortable if someone else led the team."

"Stephanie isn't going to be leading any teams for a while unless it's from her command seat," Jake whispered.

"Because she's pregnant," Agameg said. "I understand. No need to put an innocent life at risk."

"You knew?"

"I could sense the change, you couldn't?" Agameg asked.

"Humans aren't that sensitive," Jake replied. "Next time, tell me about serious changes in physiology, all right?"

"Liara's ovulating right now," Agameg said.

"And welcome back Agameg," Ashley laughed.

"That's a bit personal, no?" Liara asked.

"Right, so if someone's pregnant or ill, you should make sure the medical technician knows," Jake said, trying not to smirk. "That way, if it's too personal for everyone to know, you're not in the wrong."

"Ah, I'll have to suggest that Fleet add that to the regulations."

"Hey, how'd you sleep?" Finn asked as he entered the bridge.

"Very well," Agameg replied. "How did the repairs go while I was resting?"

"Better than expected, the crew have fallen into a rhythm. We had to abandon the nose section though, so we're cannibalizing it for plating. That was a good suggestion, by the way."

"I was so tired the last couple days before going to sleep, I don't remember making it," he said. "Is there anything I can do right now?"

"Catch up on the logs while you manage things from the bridge," Finn said. "A lot has happened in the last five days, system wise. We have our old shields back up everywhere except the nose. Two of our main turrets are working, and the dampeners are set up so the whole ship won't shake when they fire. There's a lot more in the logs."

"I'll assume my place at the engineering station then," Agameg said, looking at the Captain.

"Thank you, Agameg," Jake said.

"I'm on my way back down there, then," Finn said "We missed you, glad you're back."

"Thank you," Agameg replied. "The greetings I receive after a rest from humans are always nice, it's as if you all think I was on a trip for the better part of a week."

"Well, we don't see you, Aggie," Ashley said. "So we're happy when you get back. I mean, we sleep for a few hours a night, so we're used to seeing each other pretty regularly."

"Oh, I don't object to the welcome," Agameg said. "I just find it odd every time."

Ashley turned back to her station. "We're coming out of the wormhole in nine minutes," she announced.

They were already ready for combat; final checks were being made across the ship according to Jake's status display. All departments were reporting ready. He hoped they didn't miss something, that there wasn't a surprise waiting for them past the end of the wormhole.

THIRTEEN

Negotiations

THE INNER AIRLOCK let Alice pass into the Gibson. Yawen was close behind, cloaked with her part of the team, but only she had time to slip through behind Alice before the rest were cut off. There was no way Commander Pope could know that he'd trapped Yawen's three soldiers in the airlock, there was no way the Gibson, an older transport vessel, could have scanners that would see through the cloaking systems.

"I wonder how many of you there actually are?" Pope said as he emerged from the narrow cockpit door, holding one hand behind his back. A simple needle pistol was in his other hand, it was no threat to Alice. "This ship is so old that I couldn't get a reading on the volume of air you displaced as the pressure equalized. I'm guessing there are at least three of you."

The left side of his face was red, with cuts on his cheekbone and his brow. The swelling confirmed that he must have gotten a serious beating from someone who was right handed. The blood on his half-open tunic and undershirt confirmed it. Even the dark green couldn't hide the blood stains. He spoke with remarkable clarity through a fat, split lip and with a badly chipped front tooth.

"We aren't here to harm you, just to make a deal," Alice said. "You don't have to worry about any abuse from us, we don't do that to people. Are you all right? I can offer you some basic medical assistance."

He tried to smile a little as he carefully sat down in the seat nearest to the cockpit. "Oh, this?" He gestured to his face. "It's amazing how quickly people turn into monsters when they don't think anyone's watching, and they think they see a villain." Pope spat a bloody mouthful into the seat across from him. "They didn't just capture me, they had some fun after. One guard in particular; Deether. He just kept hitting me the same way, on the same side of my face over and over again, blaming me for killing his family. I told him I had nothing to do with it. Most of my duties were diplomatic, to ensure that communications between the Order and the locals remained open, and that traitors were caught. He wouldn't listen, none of them really seemed to care. That's why, when I got my chance, I sent their guards outside while we were underway. I could have been more brutal, found a death for them that was more gradual, but why should I put it off?"

"Where are the rest of the passengers?" Alice asked. She already knew, they were in the rearmost compartment, but she needed to keep him talking so she could build a rapport and give her people time to do their jobs.

"Back there," he gestured with the trigger. It was bound to his hand with some kind of adhesive, a small square with a biometric reader in the middle of his palm. "They haven't eaten in two days, but they've had plenty of air and water. Now, take off that helmet, those overbuilt computers around your wrists and your outer armour. I know it won't make a difference either way if I blow the antimatter, armour on or off, but I want to see that you are who you say you are. Also, I've heard that your control units can do all kinds of tricks."

"I'll open my helmet," Alice said, complying that much. "You'll have to trade something for the rest."

"Ah, it's not important," he said, looking at her closely. "I can see it, especially in the eyes. You really must be your father's daughter, but you really look like your Queen, Arlan? Aren?"

"Ayan," Alice said. She let the comment about Ayan being a Queen pass. It was technically true according to the Galactic courts. Ayan Anderson was the registered owner of the Rega Gain system, and according to them she always would be. It was one of the reasons why they changed the name to the Haven System, but Ayan would always be Queen in documents spread across the galaxy, even though she hated it.

"That's it," he said. "Is she your mother? That's not in our file on you. In our file, you're still much younger."

"Things change quickly in the Haven System," Alice said. "I'd love to fill you in, but my head would be a lot clearer if we did something about that switch in your hand."

"This?" he held up the palm of his hand, where some kind of glue had bonded the switch to it.

Alice's computer system analyzed the switch and traced its connection to the antimatter containment system. Jamming the signal with noise could do as much damage as pressing the switch, so that was not an option. Yawen wouldn't be able to get the switch out of his hand either. "Yeah, I thought it would take a lot to get your rag-tag military's attention, and I've seen what your father does to officers. We've all seen the footage of him blowing the head off a young bridge officer to get the rest to talk."

"I'm not my father," Alice said. Stopping herself from explaining that there was something wrong with Jake when he did that took some effort. "We treat people who turn against the Order well."

"Really?" he laughed. "As well as I've earned by climbing the ranks myself? I'm a Commander, I started out as a credit cow, a sheep like everyone else. From the day I was born I owed money, and every day of my life I went deeper and deeper into debt, until I was able to get a job running bulk loaders. Then, if I wanted to start paying my debt, I'd have to go without any luxuries, sometimes without power, because I'd donate whatever I could generate to the system for a couple credits an hour."

"I'm sorry, I've heard that's the way it is for a lot of people. We don't have a system like that here," Alice said, glad to have an opening to explain how Haven Shore was different, but she misjudged. He was too angry to listen, it was too early.

"Then the Order comes along and tells us that we're about to face some kind of apocalyptic darkness. I signed up, went a hundred thousand credits further into debt and pledged to work it off. Could you imagine my surprise when I realized that I actually was working it off? That the Order didn't lie? I worked my way up the ranks for three years and four months ago I found out that I'm debt free. Not only that, but I'm a bloody Commander, so I know people, important people, and I'm on my way up to the next rank, and I'm making more money than I could have ever dreamt. So much, that I have thirty five people who owe me money, can you imagine? I make money by doing nothing, I'm on the black side of the system, black meaning I can go my entire life without going back into debt, and if I keep serving I may become immortal. That's what those God damned diplomats and back-world government idiots cost me! Immortality, paradise, and a life in the black! Can you promise me that?"

Alice thought quickly. What she said next would be pivotal, and she hadn't gotten a signal from anyone telling her that the antimatter had been made safe yet. "I can give you another kind of freedom," she offered quietly.

"Bullshit! I'm atomized, or I'll become a prisoner all over again. I should have known better, I should have shut the life support down for everyone but me and tested my luck by jumping to another system as soon as we got here."

"You are lucky, you got me." Alice had to try the best angle she had. It impressed him, or at least surprised him that they sent a Valent aboard to negotiate with him. That had to be useful. "I'm a Valent. Whether I'm abusive like my father, or more reasonable, the fact that I'm here is important. I can make offers that no one else can."

"Prove it!"

"I can't prove anything while that switch is in your hand," she said. "But if you trust me, if you let me dissolve the solvent and take that switch, I'll make sure that you get the best treatment. You'll have a place of your own, and the opportunity to earn the same rights everyone else has."

"You don't understand," he said, starting to slip back into a rant.

"I do," Alice said. "You had power as a Commander, climbed up the ranks, but in Haven Shore, people have the opportunity to follow their passions. They get their own space to be themselves, and there is no debt."

"There is always debt! Maybe your way just hides it better..." he looked at his hand then, his fingers were bound together in a bunch by something invisible, and then he recoiled, leaving the hand where it was as it was severed from his wrist by an invisible blade.

Alice rushed to him and, after a short, bloody struggle, caught his forearm and held it steady while she sprayed medical foam on the stump. "Just hold still," she said, but he struggled anew, and she stunned him for his own good. If he continued to struggle, the seal over his stump and the pressure around his wrist would release.

"We've rewired the antimatter containment system, it's safe," announced Regan. "Nothing will happen if he pushes his button."

Yawen appeared, still holding Pope's severed hand, looking proud of herself. "A little late, but thanks," she replied.

"I was half way to talking him down," Alice said.

"He was about to start ranting again," Yawen replied. "Better safe than obliterated."

Alice sighed and finally nodded. "Good work, everyone. Let's get the passengers and our prisoner onto the shuttle and get clear of this death trap."

FOURTEEN

Warriors

"ARE you sure this is how we're supposed to do this?" Jake asked Liara as he sat at the end of their conference table. That entire section of the deck had been gutted for metal leaving only supports behind and a massive space that used to contain meeting spaces, the officer's mess, a few storage areas and quarters that crewmembers had been transferred out of.

"It's how one tribe leader meets another, and it extends to ship captains. Two of your lowest ranking officers meet them at the airlock and lead them to this deck, where they meet one of your most trusted Lieutenants or in this case it would be a sort of 'right hand' and they lead the visiting Captain here, where you present them with a gift."

Jake held up a large command and control unit they had in storage, made for a Nafalli, of which they had none aboard. "This is a good gesture? I'm sure he has something like it."

"Probably, but this is in the style of your people, it shares a history with you, since the core is the same as the ones used in Freeground for, um, how long?" she asked.

"About sixty years now," he said. "We've added a few coprocessors and a couple upgrades, but upgrading the core seemed pointless. They're cheap and easy to make."

"Right, if he asks about it, you'll be able to tell him about every detail," she said.

He understood. Looking at it, he was reminded of the type he used to use on the Samson, when he had no idea who or what he was. That one was custom, but it was so close to what he had on the First Light, just with a few gadgets bolted on and a few cheaper parts.

No matter what kind of story his guest wanted to hear that may be attached to the gift he gave him, Jake would have one. He had been wearing a command and control unit almost since his creation, and he had memories going back to Jacob Valent's childhood. During all that time, for all those events, there was a comm unit based on the same processor on his arm.

"I wonder what he'll offer me?" Jake asked, checking the ship status. They were holding position next to a cluster of asteroids that were host to a couple old drillers and a collector. There wasn't much left of them after they spent a long time tumbling between the giant stones. Everything was on low power mode, and everyone who knew how to read a scan report was watching for energy signals nearby. Some had their eyes cast towards the asteroid belt they hid in; the rest watched the stars for signs of patrols running on low power or all together cloaked.

Jake suspected that the combat conditions were changing along the front. He expected Order of Eden captains to work harder for the tactical edge, and the Kariss Solar System was the target of a British Alliance attack only a week before. There would be a military presence.

Crewmembers moved around the edges for the most part, but a few used field generators on their boots to skim quickly across the open deck where they could. All around, Jake recognized space they didn't need in the Revenge. After the refit they seemed to have two cabins for everything. Having regular compartmentalization between spaces was good design, true, but he didn't realize how many of the creature comforts and spaces set aside for specific types of storage and activities they didn't need. There was a better way to design the whole thing, especially the conference room and command areas.

Finn sat to Liara's right, a little out of breath. Jake looked past Liara at him. "Cutting it close?"

"Sorry Captain, still not used to the new layout. I had to run all the way from the forward section," Finn replied.

"That's not too far off," Jake said. "Come jogging with Minh and his squad tomorrow morning."

Finn lowered his head for a moment, then straightened up. "That's an order?"

"Treat it like one," Jake said.

"Yes, Sir."

"I've been looking to get into better shape too," Liara said.

Jake caught a glimpse of Finn looking at her, shaking his head, wide eyed.

She finished anyway; "Mind if I come along?"

"It's a serious club," Jake said. "Once you're in for one morning, you're in until you meet the Fleet Five, then you can drop out."

"Fleet Five," Liara said. Jake could tell she was looking it up using her brain bud. "Five kilometres in twenty five minutes?" she asked. "That seems fast."

"It's the minimum pass for human cadets between one point six and two metres tall," Jake said. He liked Liara, she was one of his most competent people, a great communications officer. "Everyone in the fleet should be able to pass it."

"I should be able to at my rank too, then," Liara said. "Seeing senior officers keeping in shape raises morale, it's one of the truths of ship life."

"Nothing coming up on passive scanners, Captain," Stephanie said in Jake's ear. "Our guests should be coming through the lift doors any second."

Jake stood, and Liara put her hand on his arm. "Sir, don't stand. You receive them while sitting. It's a position of confidence."

Jake nodded and sat down. Finn watched everything Liara did when he didn't have a responsibility to fulfill, and it made Jake feel a little warmer inside. The only problem he saw with that was that it gave Liara fewer opportunities to watch Finn, which she did when he was trying not to look like he was watching her. He couldn't help but wonder if suffering together might get them on the same page. Neither of them was in the kind of shape they needed to be in to run a Fleet Five.

He was aware that he cheated, so he always had his suit set to add resistance to his movements, pushing him right to a point where he might actually fail. It was like running under water by the end of each workout, and Minh-Chu often beat him handily.

"Here they come. Silent and confident. Don't stand until he offers you his hand," Liara said quietly.

Minh-Chu led a thick bodied Nafalli that dwarfed him width and height wise through the lift doors. "See, we used internal plating, melted it down to make new armour plating for the outside."

"What happens if this deck decompresses, say right over there?" asked a Nafalli with white and grey striped fur.

"There are emergency containment packages that fire a kind of cloth partition that will isolate the breach," he explained.

Noah Lucas, known by the callsign Carnie, walked along side Minh-Chu as they escorted the three Nafalli. The captain was definitely the largest with the starkest colouring. His black fur was marked with stripes that followed the direction of his fur. The armour all three wore looked like liquid metal that conformed to their fur, turning any visible tips of hair into spikes.

"How is it necessary for you to know any of this? You're a fighter pilot," asked the Nafalli who had black hair and blonde stripes.

"I like knowing how my Captain's ship is doing. I also helped with repairs when I had spare time," Minh-Chu replied.

"So crewmembers shift stations when they are more needed elsewhere," said that gray haired one. He seemed excited to see practically everything.

"When we're not on duty we can do what we like, for the most part, but the best of us will spend some of our free time helping other crewmembers."

"In our military, we are always on duty, ready to rise to any challenge," the black and blonde Nafalli said.

The captain, the black furred Nafalli with white and silver stripes laughed. "We operate in shifts, don't misrepresent us, Juun. We are more similar than we are dissimilar." He arrived at the opposite end of the long table and looked at Jake.

The irises of his eyes were so light they were almost silver. It was unnerving over a mostly black muzzle, but he wore a smile that made it feel like he'd been looking forward to this meeting for some time. "Captain Valent," he said. "I honour you with this gift; a Rawsarr, the weapon of my tribe but made for someone of your height and power." He pulled a straight hilt from his belt and squeezed two buttons on it. The weapon extended into a black metal staff with blunt ends. "You will find it a formidable weapon, especially if you learn the art of Aarwone. I am a master, the name is not translatable, since it was coined after the mourning sounds of widows." He retracted the ends into the hilt and placed it on the table. Liara got up and went to retrieve it.

Jake felt strange greeting Captain Duulto Kuo without standing, and he let instinct take over. As he held the command and control unit up, he got to his feet. "This is the technical core of our entire military organization. Most of us have dermal communication units, but we use our Command and Control Units to boost our ability to send and receive transmissions. It also administers emergency medication, has a small fabrication system, and I made sure this one has a small energy weapon inside. I've had an identifier number set up so you have basic access to our Fleet network, and all Fleet controls have been disabled, so you have full control over its functions. I hope this honours you, Captain." That was not what he was supposed to say. A position of confidence was what Liara advised, simply telling him that receiving the comm unit was an honour, instead of hoping the Captain would see it as one.

The Nafalli standing to Captain Kuo's left, the grey and silver striped one, moved up the length of the table to accept the gift on his Captain's behalf, waiting for Jake to put it down before he took it.

"Thank you, Captain Valent," Captain Kuo said.

"They all wear them," said Juun, the black and blonde

furred Nafalli from his right side. "It's a common device that takes no skill to use."

"It's an invitation," Captain Kuo replied as he accepted the command and control unit. He turned it over in his hands for a moment before activating it. A hologram with his head appeared - a noble depiction with his rank, tribe and ship name beneath it - and he smiled. "This is a meaningful gift. It represents their invitation to us to join their fighters, to become a part of their society."

"I doubt its value," Juun said.

"I could order you to challenge their Captain, is your doubt that strong? Are you willing to challenge Captain Jacob Valent after all we've seen about him?"

Minh-Chu took his place beside Jake, looking unsure. Noah was watching the Nafalli as though he was ready to burst into a run at any second.

"Look, you remember the bounty hunter records," Captain Kuo said, holding the comm unit up so his Second could see the energy emitter. "Look, this is like the wrist weapon we saw him use."

"I think it's a remarkable gift," said the white and grey Nafalli.

"Know your place, Forus," Juun snapped.

"I wonder," Captain Kuo said, looking to Jake. "If I invoked our ancient laws of challenge, would you participate? Would you put my Second in his place?"

"There's no need to invoke the old laws," Juun, the one with the black and blonde fur said. "I only wonder if he's honoured you properly."

Jake had been warned that if things went extremely badly, he may have to defend himself, and he was prepared. Liara let him look through the little information they had about Nafalli warrior tribes challenging other races to single combat. "I'll accept any challenge, but I don't want to kill your First Officer. It would be bad diplomacy."

"You heard him," Captain Kuo said. "I don't even smell fear."

"How long has it been since you even held a nanosword?" Minh-Chu asked.

Jake didn't answer. He spent twenty minutes with his the night before and that morning. He knew he could use one without de-limbing himself, but past that there were no guarantees. The other idea he had worked out much better. "Call Zac." He said, watching Juun look to the Captain, to him all but growling.

Captain Kuo said. "He's made it clear; he doesn't think you're his equal. Is your pride worth the risk?"

"I'd fight him, but we're here to plan a raid."

"This won't take long," Jake said. "Are you invoking the old laws? Or does your First Officer think my gift is enough to honour you?"

"Fight him, I give you leave to prove yourself," Captain Kuo said, he was actually smiling.

"I challenge you on behalf of my Captain," Juun said.

"No, you challenge Captain Valent for the sake of pride," Captain Kuo corrected. "If my honour were at stake, I'd ask for compensation. I wouldn't fight this man. He would rather have another opportunity to befriend me." He finished with a bow.

"Fine! For my honour then," Juun said.

"That is the Captain's little brother," Liara whispered to him. "Be careful."

"Crap," Noah said, lowering his face into his hand.

"Suwuo," said the white and grey Nafalli opposite him, covering his nose.

"I won't use strength augmentation," Jake said. "Or any projectile weapons."

"Juun will attack using his natural attacks," Captain Kuo said.

His second in command nodded as he stepped to the side of the table, putting several meters between him and everyone else. Jake followed his lead and activated a new gadget - a focused energy shield built into his left command and control unit. It was made to repel explosives and small vehicle weapons' fire, he never expected to use it for melee combat. It was based on the shield the Order Knights used.

Captain Kuo laughed. "Captain Valent's tactics have evolved," he said.

Juun stood in front of him, with five metres between. Jake activated the emitter on the end of his right wrist and set it to its highest stun setting. It sparked dangerously, at the edge of the recommended highest power level. He read the etiquette on duelling Nafalli but couldn't remember a single detail except for what failure meant. It meant he would either have to be recorded as a failure forever, or challenge Juun again. Being a failure in the Nafalli's eyes wouldn't make things go smoothly.

"There is something wrong with that man," Minh-Chu said as Jake grinned at his opponent.

An excitement started building in Jake the moment the prospect of a duel came up, and it was so intense, it brought such eagerness that he couldn't help but agree with Minh-Chu. Had he been waiting for a test? Was the frustration of being away from Alice and Ayan starting to break down his reason? The faces of dead crewmembers found in the wreckage of his ship began to run through his mind, and it didn't summon sadness, but aggression.

Jake turned his shield off with a shake of his arm and held a finger up between he and his opponent. The Nafalli enjoyed a show. They'd get one, regardless of whether he won or lost. He held his sparking stunner up, cocked with his fist, then he crooked his finger. "Let's have it, boy," he growled.

That infuriated Juun, who leapt at him, claws extended, covered in metal armour. Jake started rolling right with a leap the instant Juun's feet left the ground. His opponent whirled, slashing at him with his claws, and Jake did what he was trained to do with opponents with a long reach, his helmet still down, his expression locked in a hateful grimace. He ducked the slash, but not the backhand that followed it.

Jake was sent over ten metres across the deck, his head saved by his vacsuit armour as it extended before impact. It knocked the wind out of him, but he was on his feet in time to see Juun start running towards him. He activated his shield and put it between him and the charging Nafalli. His claws came down on the energy barrier so hard that Jake was knocked to the deck again.

He tried to roll one way, found slashing claws coming down in that direction, then scrambled backwards. Juun had him, he was in full retreat, it felt like he pulled his shoulder when he blocked. Jake tried to sidestep Juun, falling for one of his young opponent's feints, and took a hit on his shield from all his claws at once. Jake came down on his back leg hard, his knee failing to support him under the weight of the strike, he felt a pop. He was happy Ayan wasn't there to see it. Then he pictured her with Liam Grady. She was in his arms, partially disappearing into his robes.

Juun came down with a slash against his shield, crushing his arm into his chest, then backhanded the arm away, he was wide open.

Thought and reason gave way to something else. Something

pure, not the rage that would overcome him while he was a framework, but a need for revenge. Juun's claw raked him across the chest, and Jake grabbed his arm, pulling himself up swiftly. The Nafalli tried to backhand him, Jake ducked it and grabbed the front of Juun's mouth, his armoured hand grappling hard. His shoulder may have been torn, but he could grip. He punched Juun in the side of the head, the eye, he was howling at the beast, letting the pain in his shoulder drive him as he landed several more hits on its head. Finally, he planted his stunner under its chin and made contact.

Juun twitched, his fur singed, and he fell over. Jake remained standing on his only working leg.

"You idiot," Zac said as he came to help him. He held his arm up. "So he won? The stupid human won?"

Captain Kuo nodded, looking... what was that? Was he impressed? Was he afraid for his younger brother? It was difficult to tell with blood in his eye. Jake looked down to find that his vacsuit had been breached, two long gashes were open across his chest. "Captain Valent has proven himself," Kuo said.

"Good," Zac said, looking at the bracer containing Jake's shield unit. "Well, that's fried, maybe the other one will work." He checked, saw that it was working and turned the regeneration system on Jake's armour back on, then activated the auto medic. "All right, that'll take care of the torn ligaments, the displaced knee, broken ribs and lacerations. Next time you want to duel a Nafalli, call me in advance. I'll get Haven Shore to start printing a clone for you."

Zac looked to Juun, who was already mumbling, recovering from the stunner's effects groggily. "When you wake up, take this, it will accelerate your healing," he yelled. "Good for broken Nafalli, you will feel and look better." He patted him on the head, looked to Captain Kuo. "His injuries are relatively minor, but you're going to want to have your medic or dentist look at his left lower incisor. Looks like it's almost all the way out." He sighed. "Anyone else duelling today?"

"I think we're done," Jake said, feeling the nanobots and regenerative cocktail going to work. His suit sent a local anesthetic to his knee, and he wobbled on the other one. Minh-Chu and Finn moved to his side and started helping him back to his seat. "Wait, wait," he said. "My suit's just about to pop that..." he felt pressure and distant pain as all the parts of his knee were pushed back into their rightful places. The sound made almost everyone, Captain Kuo included, cringe. "...back into place. Okay, back to my seat guys, thanks."

"I have never seen a human who could fight like that," Captain Kuo said as the white and silver furred Nafalli helped Juun to his feet. He actually looked pleased.

"What day is it today?" Jake asked.

"Thursday," Minh-Chu replied, raising an eyebrow.

"Only happens on the occasional Thursday," Jake told Captain Kuo. "I'll be fighting a Mergillian next Saturday, should be much easier, but a lot more fun. Lots of jumping." He knew the humour might have been inappropriate, but he didn't much care at that moment. He was trying to distract himself from the sensation of nanobots and regeneration serum putting his shoulder back together.

Captain Kuo thought for a moment, then burst into laughter, followed by Juun and his other officer. "I wasn't sure if you were joking for a moment," he said. "Mergillian, they are like Nolibips."

"He said they're like frogs," Liara translated for him as Minh-Chu and Finn put him in his seat.

"Right, he gets it," Jake said. He looked at her. "Did I do that right?" he asked in a whisper.

"You did, Captain Valent," Captain Kuo said. "It was completely unnecessary; my tribe is highly civilized. I was half between hoping that you'd teach my little brother a lesson and hoping that you'd throw us a banquet when he doubted the quality of your gift."

"I could go for a banquet," Jake said.

"The recovery meds may be impeding his judgement a little," Minh-Chu said apologetically.

"I understand. We'll have a rest while our champions heal, then we'll plan the raid. I have high hopes for its success."

"You just had to grow your legend, didn't you, big guy?" Minh-Chu said quietly, shaking his head.

"That's Captain Big Guy," Jake muttered. The pain management was turned up high, there was accelerated healing happening everywhere except for his head. He could feel the faint sensation of itching in his ribs, the nanobots were repairing more damage than he thought he took in the fight, including more than one open wound on his back. He didn't realize that Juun clawed him at least once while he was punching him. "I'll be about five minutes," Jake said loud enough for Captain Kuo to hear. For the first time since he'd been freed, he wished he had a little framework left in him, but it was a passing thought.

FIFTEEN

Getting Ready For Another Round

THE GIBSON WAS TAKEN FAR from the solar system by an automated tug as soon as everyone was off the ship. From long range, a Uriel fighter fired a short burst of gunfire at its belly and for a moment it looked like there was a new sun in the solar system. It was the safest way to deal with a quantity of antimatter that could become unstable at any moment because of damage no one had time to repair.

Alice didn't have time to deal with the well-dressed but rattled diplomats, or the government representatives. They were quiet anyway, for the most part, eating for the first time in at least two days thanks to the emergency rations Alice's people gave them. Yawen took their basic information. Alice included it in her after action report, that was the easy part. The harder part was reporting on her own performance in her first hostage situation.

There was a failure in connecting with Pope, the hostage taker. She only had a little time to form a rapport, and she felt that her attempts didn't make anything better. Much of her training fell away in the situation, revealing her inexperience and inability to make a quick connection with Pope so she could get his demands and start addressing them enough to properly buy time. He was allowed to slip into rants instead, getting himself worked up to a point where any interruption could have made things worse. If the Order of Eden's philosophy rewarded self-sacrifice and large scale bombings where the architect of the disaster could somehow gain from it even after death, then she was sure Pope would have set the antimatter off, killing all the hostages, her team, and any refugee ships unfortunate enough to decelerate into the space nearby.

That wasn't how the Order worked, thankfully. The Order rewarded blind service, and Pope wouldn't have been around to accept the reward if he pushed his button. It was an idea she wanted to capitalize on during the hostage situation, but she didn't get a chance to before he was too worked up to really listen. It came down to one fact: she was never really in control of the situation. As frustrating as it was, she didn't have time to deal with it. She leaned on her training, using her after action report to quickly recognize where she could improve, to pack that experience away, and to move on. Alice decided that she'd review some successful negotiations, there were hundreds of them on file, but for the time being, she had to move on.

The refugees thanked Yawen, recognizing her as the one who took care of them and directed their treatment as the combat shuttle moved them to the Harbour Saint, an old Carthan Heavy Destroyer that had been converted into an emergency rescue ship. The vessel was impressive, more than half a kilometre long and fully reconditioned thanks to the War

Forge. It was used as a final test for one of the large fabrication lines aboard the secret station, and Alice couldn't help but momentarily wonder what civilians thought of the large white ship. A red cross was painted across the front, making the vessel look more like it belonged to ancient crusaders than a large rescue staff.

She knew it was under manned in every department, and that at least one of her classmates was probably aboard, trying to help the crew deal with all the new technology. As she watched the diplomats and civilians leave her combat shuttle, guided by Yawen and her squad, she almost envied whoever was training the staff aboard the Harbour Saint.

A tap on the port side airlock drew her attention to a few deck crew members waiting on the other side. She opened it and accepted a box of emergency provisions. "I've got your delivery, Lieutenant," the deck crewmember said, flashing a smile up at her. "Is it true that you were just on that death trap? The Gibson?"

"It wasn't so bad," Alice said, glancing to her left where she could see the black stasis bag they'd secured Pope in being passed through the starboard airlock. "Got our first catch of the day."

Alice accepted another box from the loading bot. Three deck crewmembers looked up at her through the airlock. They all seemed very young, even the one who was directing things, who had her blonde hair bound in a tight bun. "So, are you guys really a Special Operations team?"

"That's what they keep telling me," Alice replied. She took a closer look at the rank on the young woman's shoulders. It was so high for how young the woman looked, but she paid her the respect she deserved. "Thanks for the re-up, Chief."

The deck Chief rechecked the holographic list of supplies

they had to deliver to Alice's combat shuttle and nodded to herself. "Our pleasure. One sec, Venma's running slow on your ship's scan."

"It's good! Shuttle's good to go!" came a shouted response somewhere further inside the hangar.

"Then check it off, Venma! We've got to keep these ships moving," the Chief shouted back. The display on her comm unit turned green and she gave Alice the thumbs up. "Good to go, Lieutenant. Happy hunting."

"Thanks, Chief," Alice said, closing the airlock. "Get this stuff squared away."

"Aye," Luu said as she picked up a box. She peeked through the porthole in the airlock door and smiled. "Wow, they must have crewed this ship with the junior division."

"There's a junior division?" Tran asked as he picked up the other box of emergency provisions.

"No, I'm just saying that deck chief and her people look sixteen," Luu replied.

"They're keeping things moving right along," Alice said. "I'm sure we'll all look pretty young to most of the civilians we rescue today."

The shuttle launched, and Alice watched as the provisions were stowed and her team settled into their seats. "Well done, Lieutenant," Lieutenant Commander Terran said through the subdermal communications link. "You're right, you could use some extra work in hostage negotiation, but you got it done quickly and Fleet Intelligence is getting what it wants out of this; a high ranking Order of Eden officer. We're going to learn a lot from him."

"You're going to run a deep scan on him, aren't you?" Alice asked in a whisper.

"We'll treat him well, but yes, probably. They'll trigger

thoughts and memories that will help him give us what we need in terms of Intelligence. It's not for you or me to think about. We've done our bit and he's in Intelligence's hands already, so we get to move on to the next assignment. You and your team are back in rotation."

"I'll be making some changes in my team once this crisis is over," Alice said.

"I expect you to," Terran replied. "For now, make sure you're ready for the next mission. We have ninety three ships incoming, so it'll be soon."

"Aye-aye, Sir," Alice replied. She turned to her crew, and Yawen quieted them by holding her hand up. "I just got word; ninety three ships are about to finish decelerating." A glance at her comm unit's tactical display revealed the first batch of ships - over a dozen - appearing in normal space. They were marked as yellow at first, then most of them turned red. Yellow wasn't too bad, it meant they hadn't been in communication with Navnet Control yet. When yellow turned red without a box around their markers designating them as an enemy, it meant that the ships were in distress. Alice turned her attention back to her crew. "It looks like most of them are declaring an emergency as soon as they arrive, some are arriving in distress." A short burst of audio in her ear from Lieutenant Commander Terran told her that the teams in line before hers were both assigned. "We're up."

"Wow, that was quick," Yawen said. "What are the other teams responding to?"

Alice listened to the chatter for a moment. "The ships coming in are old local transit models. Most of them have had trouble with their power and environmental systems. Their jump drives were for emergencies only, short trips between planets, so they are overextended. One of the other teams is responding to a ship that's issued threats to command. Sounds like armed civilians who are making demands. The other team may be responding to a ghost ship, that's not clear."

"What's going on in the Cefa System? It's like every ship that could fly is on its way here," Jessen asked, Knud nodding beside her.

"It's not our job to know," Alice replied. "But Intelligence will want every scrap of information we passively collect. Keep your eyes open and scanners running."

"Lieutenant Valent, your team has an assignment," Lieutenant Commander Terran announced in her ear. "This one will require a gentler touch."

"My team is ready, Sir," Alice replied. At overhearing her response, her team started getting to their feet.

SIXTEEN

A Stern Talking To

"THAT WAS the most irresponsible thing I've ever seen you do," Stephanie Vega said as she paced the length of the armour room.

Jake checked the replacement cuffs, making sure the command and control as well as the other functionality built into them was working and calibrated. His new shield emitter was present, as was a holdout energy weapon on the opposite arm. The armoured slats across his body were almost perfectly in place, but they needed a little adjustment. He listened to her quietly.

"What kind of example are you setting for the crew? I'm sure there are plenty of young Nafalli who want to test themselves against humans now, especially since their leader was cocky enough to challenge the son of their Captain without strength augmentation or active armour."

"The armour layers were on, they were doing their job," Jake said. "They just didn't stop all the damage."

"So if one of our crewmembers makes that mistaken assumption, that you turned your suit's armour off before facing off against a Nafalli, they won't get scratched up, instead they'll get torn in half. That's so much better," she said, throwing up her hands. "Worse than all that, Liara says that even most of their warriors are highly civilized, so to them *we* look like savages now. Fleet is going to love how you handled this."

"I was acting under the assumption that by facing whatever challenge they threw at me, I would earn their respect."

"Liara was right there, you could have asked her what the best response was before pushing ahead with a duel," Stephanie said.

"You weren't there. If I leaned towards her every time there was a call to make, I would have looked like I didn't bother to learn anything about their culture," Jake replied. "When I knew that many personal disputes were solved by combat, and their captain seemed interested in seeing it happen."

"You could have negotiated your way through it, I've seen you in more difficult spots. Did you need to prove yourself? The crew doesn't care if you're some kind of iron man, they want to get home in one piece. You don't have to be the biggest badass on the ship anymore. Leave it to anyone else, you have nothing to prove."

"Listen, if I could take it back, I would have played it differently. Captain Kuo was willing to accommodate diplomatic imperfect, and I let myself get pulled in to a challenge for pride by his son. It happened, I'm whole again, he's whole again, and we're about to raid a really nice little supply depot."

"I still don't like you leading this," Stephanie said. "It should be me. It should be Remmy, even Minh-Chu would be a good choice, he has experience as a marine."

"I'm our best chance out there, you know it," Jake said. "There are so many good commanders left on the ship to take care of any problems while I'm making sure we get what we need and get out."

"Have you told anyone what we're really after?" Stephanie asked.

"A data port and deep intelligence," Jake said. "That's all anyone needs to know. The Nafalli are going to use us as a distraction while they steal all the food and water they need."

"I've seen the plan. You'll be drawing a lot of attention at first. If there are Knights or frameworks down there, you could be in trouble."

"We'll definitely have a few minutes where we'll be in trouble, but we can handle it. Besides, Samurai squadron is already taking care of the bigger problem. Stephanie, how many times did I leave the ship alone with gear that I bought off the shelf, modified or made from spare parts with half a plan. I came back every time."

"You needed me to come get you a few times," Stephanie said.

"Right, but this time I have experienced people with me, and we're in heavy armour that makes a small mech look like a quaint antique. I'm not going alone, I'm not going with a squad, I'm going with cover from the best squadron in the fleet and forty eight heavily armed bad asses."

"Just make sure all forty nine of you get back in one piece. If this is a simple supply depot, and the region is clear, don't get cocky and start giving the Nafalli extra time to loot the station."

"Don't worry, I'll be sticking to the plan." Jake said, sighing. "I can't afford to get trapped or killed down there."

"Or distracted," Stephanie said. "What's going on? What's in your head?"

"Something happened while I was fighting Juun. It almost cost me the duel. I had this mental flash of Ayan finding her way back to Liam if I was gone too long or..." he shrugged, turning away from Stephanie. "I know, it doesn't make sense. She explained everything about our break up to me, we're in a good place."

"That bloody redhead," Stephanie said. "Listen, you can't control what happens at home, and I'm sure she's fine, busy building a fleet, doing whatever reluctant Queens do, but you can control your usefulness here."

"I told you; I know," Jake said.

"I'd be a crap First Officer if I didn't tell you to get your head on straight. Ayan is fine, and I'm sure she's waiting for you, distracting herself with all kinds of new tech and whatever those Lorander eggheads have to show her. When would she even have the time to get under someone else?"

"You're right. I'm clearing my head right now," Jake said, taking a deep breath, then exhaling and activating his helmet. The skull graphic was back, looking angry and eager at the same time. "I'm ready."

"Go kick some ass and get us that data, Captain," Stephanie said.

SEVENTEEN

Precious Cargo

"WHAT IS GOING ON IN CEFA?" asked Tran under his breath. Their combat shuttle was about to merge with the transit ship.

"Focus," Alice said a second ahead of Yawen. "We have to solve the crisis in front of us before anyone can address the source of the problem."

"Aye, sorry, Ma'am," Tran said.

The question wasn't the problem, it was how easily Tran and Luu allowed themselves to get distracted.

Alice turned her attention back to the more urgent task ahead of them. Most of the transit vessel was filled with spent air; carbon dioxide and the corpses that ran out of oxygen. That was something a group of marines or a rescue team could clear. What made it a mission of Special Operations was the sealed compartment in the rear of the ship, or rather, what command discovered there. Smaller, living people who were breathing just enough oxygen to survive.

The ships locked together and the combat shuttle started gently moving the transit ship to safety. That was job one, getting the ship out of the deceleration area. Alice took a scan of the rear compartment. A red notification on her comm told her that both Luu and Tran were running deep scans of the whole ship and she turned on them. "Did I order you to run a high powered scan?"

"No, what?" Luu asked, looking offended.

"You could set off a bomb made to detonate when exposed to a high energy scan, or interfere with damaged systems," Alice said.

"But you were scanning..." Tran said, coming to his comrades' defence.

"Yes, a low energy, focused scan of the area we're about to enter. Not enough to set anything off," Alice replied.

"More information is..." Luu started to explain.

Alice ignored her and turned to Yawen. "Get them in shape, we don't have time for this."

"Yes, Ma'am," Yawen replied.

"Pass me our smallest pod," Alice ordered. She opened a channel on her comm. "Command, I'm picking up forty nine dead in the forward compartment, eight tender age children in the rear compartment, and one infant. Life readings are critical. I am not picking up any weapons. Please tell the Harbour Saint we're coming." She accepted the infant survival pod from Yawen. When it was empty it rolled up into a narrow tube, and she hoped her scant medical technician training was adequate. She had more than anyone there, a shortfall she'd have to address the moment she could make changes to her team.

"All right, everyone get ready to get a medical sleeve around a child and carry them back," her mind was racing, trying to anticipate what they could be facing and to intuit what might have happened aboard that ship. They stepped into the airlock. It closed behind them and they waited for the pressure to equalize with the compartment beyond. "When the air from our life support system hits the rear compartment, these kids are going to start waking up if we're lucky. They'll be scared and confused. We have to get them into these sleeves so they are safe and won't be able to slow us down as quick as we can."

"Why is it lucky if they start waking up and fussing?" Beck asked. Her question seemed absolutely earnest.

Alice watched the indicator come close to equal pressure as she answered. "If they don't start waking up when properly oxygenated air hits, then we're too late. That's why."

"I was just asking."

"You should have thought that one through yourself," Yawen replied.

The airlock opened and Alice stepped through, moving as quickly as she dared between the seats and tables. "Quick and careful. The tactical computer has marked which child you're responsible for, so get to them and put them in the safety sleeve."

Knud was the first to get to his child, a toddler with short brown hair. He was already rolling his head from side to side. He spread the sleeve open so it looked like a stretcher with raised sides, gently and quickly moved him on top of it, and the sleeve closed around him. Sonic waves and pre-programmed warming patterns kept the small boy asleep as the emergency stretcher sleeve filled with highly oxygenated air. He was comfortable and safe, his vital stats showing immediate improvement on Alice's tactical screen. According to initial readings, the boy would be fine, they got to him in time.

She arrived at her charge, with Yawen beside her. A young blonde girl was laying on the floor beside the infant that came up on Alice's scan. It was a new born, only a day old, but it was barely breathing. Alice put her medical pod beside the baby and, with great care, unwrapped the child from the shirts she was wrapped in, then picked her up and put her inside. The pod closed around the infant and gently secured it inside with a soft, inner layer of swaddling material. Alice would have forgotten that there was anything else going on, except Yawen was hurrying to put the blonde girl - the oldest child there at twelve standard years, perhaps thirteen - inside the emergency stretcher sleeve.

The systems in the infant pod went to work, and the first status report was written in dire orange, with indicators that the baby was barely alive. It took a great deal of discipline for Alice to help Yawen get her charge's legs into position on the sleeve so it could close around her. Knud came to help her carry the stretcher sleeve with the girl inside. The regular sleep inducers didn't work, and the blonde girl woke up, looking towards the infant pod right away. "Is she going to be okay? I tried to keep her warm."

Alice picked the pod up and started for the airlock, watching the readouts on the baby's health on her heads up display. The child's overall health was improving, all her stats turning green, including her brain function. When the child cried, it was music to Alice's ears. "Regan, check our scans of the shuttle for anyone trapped in a small compartment. We don't want to leave anyone behind."

"Nothing coming up, I'll double check, one minute," he replied.

While he double checked the transit ship, Alice checked on the queues aboard the Harbour Saint for medical care and saw that they were ninety three minutes behind. "Command," she said, opening a channel. "We're going directly to Haven Shore Medical. These kids were near freezing and almost out of breathable air, they require immediate care."

"Lieutenant, this is Navnet Control. I understand that you're handling a rescue with several tender age children involved, but the Harbour Saint is only a few minutes away from your location."

Alice saw that two of their rescues, both toddlers, still had vital readouts in the orange range. From what she understood of the emergency systems they were using, that meant they could get worse at any moment, getting better without real medical care was unlikely. The regulations told her that putting them in stasis if they had to wait more than an hour for care was advisable, but she should avoid it if she could. Emergency stasis could be harmful to children. She opened the cockpit door. "We're headed to Haven Shore Medical, you'll have a Navnet course in a moment," she told the pilot, who nodded after a moment.

"Private Fritz Regan has finished clearing the transport and we've moved it away from the arrival zone," the co-pilot said. "We'll head for Haven Shore as soon as we get a course from Navnet."

Alice unmuted the channel she had open with Navnet Control. "Send my helm a course for Haven Shore Medical, that's an order."

The Navnet Control operator cleared her throat and replied; "Yes, Ma'am. Your helm should have a course now."

The pilot nodded. "On our way."

EIGHTEEN

Minh-Chu led Carnie and Hot Chow through their sector, running high powered scans as they went. There were four other groups of fighters making quick work of gathering details about the combat area around Obyn, the planet where they'd find the supply depot. "I'm picking up a few caches. Other than anti-meteor batteries and a few emergency thrusters they're undefended," Hot Chow said. "Why would they leave millions of tons of supplies in outer orbit like this?"

Hot Chow was a long distance freighter captain who hauled product and rare materials across sectors, so Minh-Chu could see why he wouldn't see the logic of a large fleet's stockpiling strategy. "My guess? I bet they have such a stockpile here that they leave supplies in orbit like bundles, ready for a ship to pick up so heavy lifters don't have to run things to them every time they get an order," Carnie said.

Minh-Chu took a moment to glance at the ice covered planet of Obyn in the distance. It caught the starlight and glittered blue and white. "If we take a deeper look when we get back to the Revenge, I bet we'll find out that each one of those caches matches the supply requirements of ships in their fleet," Minh-Chu said.

"Maybe they've gotten cocky, don't expect any trouble so they overdo it with the efficiency?" Hot Chow asked.

"That could be true, but look at this," Minh-Chu said, high-lighting a spot on his scan results. "Looks like they leave empty crates behind when they pick up full ones."

"Okay, so a ship comes in. They eject their empty containers - the big ones that don't fit in a recycler - then they pick up fresh supplies and move on," Carnie said.

"We're going to start seeing a pattern, guys," Sticky said as she led her trio through another search pattern. "I've got five sets of empties. Means at least five ships have come through here recently. The base hasn't had time to restock these caches."

"We've scanned three," Hot Chow said.

"Let's say it takes an hour to restock a cache after it's been picked," Carnie said.

"I don't like where you're going with this, Noah," Sticky said.

"Call signs only," Minh-Chu said. "Just because you two stay up talking doesn't mean you can get cozy on comms."

"Sorry, Ronin," Sticky said.

"Anyway; if it takes an hour to restock a cache, and there are eight caches that haven't been restocked..." Carnie said.

"We get it, a lot of ships come through here," Hot Chow said. "At least seven or eight an hour and that's just here."

"Everyone pull back and go dark," Minh-Chu said. "We have five signals coming up from the surface. Heavy lifters, no life signs." He watched his tactical display and was pleased to see everyone in range of the lifters shut their systems down and start drifting. It wasn't a perfect way to cloak their ships, but unless active scanners swept over them, they wouldn't be picked up. Passive scanners or lower quality systems would pick them up as debris. All they could do is hope that shutting down and hiding in plain sight would work. They had to be there, they had to map the combat area before the real mission began. Being discovered was an acceptable outcome but delaying that would allow them to quietly gather more information.

The heavy lifters slowed beside a dozen large discarded containers, came to a stop, detached from the full containers they carried then waited several seconds. A light on top of each lifter turned red then green before they started moving again, picking up the empty containers. Minh-Chu smiled to himself. When the lifters started entering the atmosphere, Minh-Chu reactivated his fighter's systems. "I think we found a better way to get our people on the ground," he said.

"I was just about to say that," Hot Chow said.

"Oh, God, I wish I was going with them," Carnie said.

"They're going to need a pilot who has experience stealing Order of Eden craft. Thanks for volunteering," Minh-Chu said. "Don't worry, I'll be going with you."

"What will I be doing?" Hot Chow asked.

"Driving the bus," Minh-Chu replied. "Time to report back. Looks like the Nafalli won't have to touch the ground to get the supplies they need. They won't really need our help either. Sticky, you keep running your scans on the area, make sure you pay close attention to any of those automated lifters. We need to try to guess which containers they'll be picking up next."

"Aye, no problem, Ronin," Sticky said.

"Fury here," announced one of the other group leaders. "We have a wormhole exit forming. We are getting behind cover."

Minh-Chu watched his tactical display as the wormhole event appeared and Fury led his two pilots behind a group of asteroids. They littered the outer orbit of Obyn, along with excavators and raw ore movers that had been shut down. "I see you, good job."

He started slowly guiding Carnie and Hot Chow back towards the asteroid belt where the Revenge hid. He was out of line of sight from the wormhole emergence point, the planet between them, so he wasn't worried about being scanned. "I get the feeling we're about to see why there aren't any outer orbital defences."

An Order battlecruiser emerged with an escort of four destroyers. "Holy crap," Hot Chow said through laser link.

"Now, let's see if it picks up its thirty tons of supplies, then takes off," Carnie said.

Minh-Chu's heart sank as it turned away from the nearest supply cache, the four destroyers each taking a direction that would lead them into a patrol around the planet. Fury and his group were under cover and powered down. There was no sign that they were spotted. "Everyone find cover now. Stop any active scanning. Do not let yourselves get scanned by those ships."

"Oh, this sucks," Sticky said. "We're parked inside some empty containers. No other way."

"Okay, go silent. I'll say a little prayer," Minh-Chu said. He switched to laser link with his wingmen. "Burn, burn, burn," he told them. "We're in the open. One of those destroyers will see us if we don't get under cover and cool down in under a minute."

"Fifty four seconds," Hot Chow said.

They fired their thrusters for as long as they could, a little over twenty seconds, then started to decelerate towards the nearest section of the asteroid belt. Minh-Chu watched the scanning radius of the new group of Order of Eden ships expand as the destroyers spread out. They were an older design, but that didn't matter. The scanning capabilities were good enough to catch anything if it was in the open while they were doing active sweeps. This was not a fight they were prepared for.

Minh-Chu found the asteroid they could hide behind, it had a long break near the middle they could descend into. He marked it and they made a quick manoeuver of settling inside. The bump of his clamps touching solid rock was a welcome feeling. He shut all his systems down and used his vacsuit's monitoring system to watch Hot Chow and Carnie do the same. Scanning signals passed over the asteroid, not penetrating all the way through to them.

The long wait began. All his fighters were running silent, that meant no communications. The only signals he could see were the ones that made it through the heavy iron asteroid he'd parked in, or the ones reflecting off of other stony faces around him. That was almost nothing. His passive tactical receiver system used the scanning energy from the Order of Eden ships to determine their positions and movements, but other than that, there was nothing to do but wait nervously, hoping none of his Wing were discovered.

Twenty one minutes passed, and the destroyers finally fell into formation with their battlecruiser, the Promise, they opened a wormhole and were gone. Minh-Chu tried to find the direction of the wormhole but didn't have enough data. He powered his fighter up. Carnie and Hot Chow followed his lead. "I bet every ship coming to pick up supplies does a patrol of orbital space before leaving," Carnie said.

"That's scary efficient. They don't need to keep ships here, because people like us never know when a whole battle group will just drop in. There are probably a bunch of ships nearby too," Hot Chow said.

Minh-Chu guided his fighter into the open, watching for anything the ships may have left behind. "Fury, you guys all right?"

"Still here, found their hyper transmitter, actually," he said. "They tucked it into orbit around the second moon."

"Sticky?"

"Nerves are rattled. A destroyer passed within ten thousand kilometres of us. If we didn't use our uniform's stealth systems, I'm sure we would have been caught," she replied. "Longest twenty minutes of my life."

"You're not the only one," Minh-Chu said. "New plan; we're getting more distance between us and this show. We'll keep watch while we're close to cover. I have to relay everything we learned."

"Aye, retreating to better cover," Sticky replied.

"We'll stay here, it's far back and we're pretty close to the Revenge. I could relay the data if you want," Fury said.

"My group have to switch our ships up, don't worry about it," Minh-Chu replied. The pieces of the plan were coming together, but there were more variables than he expected. Anything could jump into the system while they were sneaking around in high orbit, but if they managed to sneak teams in using the containers, they would avoid much bigger risks. Then again, if another battlecruiser and its escort showed or worse... "I'm glad I'm not making this decision alone," Minh-Chu said to his wingmen.

"The Captain is running this operation, isn't he?" Carnie asked.

"Sure, but he likes seeing which way his Commanders lean when he has time to consider their opinions," Minh-Chu said.

"Which way are you leaning, Ronin?" Hot Chow asked. "Stealth, or the strike and fade thing we have as our first plan?"

"Honestly?" Minh-Chu answered, guiding his ship around a large asteroid. "Whatever will have a better chance of us getting back in one piece."

"He's not sure yet," Carnie said.

"I got that," said Hot Chow.

NINETEEN

An Important Delivery

WHEN THEIR COMBAT shuttle touched down on one of the Everin Building's emergency landing pads, staff from Haven Shore Medical were ready. Alice knew that the building was the medical facility's temporary base, they were waiting for the completion of Hab Three, which was almost finished, standing high on a reinforced cliff top nearly a kilometre away. Its graceful single, leaning curve reached over the ocean, while pointing to the sky.

With surprising efficiency, the staff of doctors, medical technicians and androids accepted the delivery of nine children and were on a transit car that would take them directly to the treatment centre. "Thank you, Lieutenant, we've got it from here," said a Nafalli doctor as he carefully accepted the pod and the newborn within. They could drop that pod off the edge of the landing platform, and it would protect the baby perfectly, but that was no reason to treat it like luggage. Everyone felt protective of the children they saved. Some of them didn't succumb to the calm inducing systems inside the pod, which didn't use medication. The boy Knut saved was a perfect example. He was soothed to sleep at first, but awoke a few minutes later, fully oxygenated, with rising energy thanks to the basic recovery medication that was flowing into his system.

The large soldier's hand was joined with the toddler's through the glove built into the emergency sleeve until he was in the hands of a Haven Shore technician who greeted him with a smile. "Hello, Nathan. I'm Gemma, I see you've made a new friend today," she said to the toddler, nodding at Knut. "You can see him later, but I'm going to take you inside where we can eat some pudding and drink some hot chocolate, how does that sound?"

With practiced grace, Gemma's hand slipped into the glove built into the emergency sleeve and took the place of Knut's big hand. "Come visit later?" she asked him in a whisper.

Knut nodded and waved at the boy through the transparent top of the emergency sleeve. "See you soon, buddy."

"Hey, Nathan," Gemma said, trying to keep the boy's attention as they pushed him away on a gurney. "What's your favourite flavour of pudding?"

"Vanilla," said a little muffled voice through the sleeve.

"Oh, we've got a lot of that. Do you like hot or cold pudding?"

They were out of earshot, so Alice couldn't hear the answer, but Knud was stuck to the spot, watching the Medical staff load their patients into a waiting transit car. Alice touched his arm. "He's going to be fine. You did a great job."

"His parents are gone, he'll be alone," Knud replied in a whisper.

"No he won't, not here," Alice said. "Everyone here knows what it's like to lose someone, so he'll find a lot of company and no end of help. Besides, you'll be visiting later, right?"

"Nothing could stop me," he said, turning and stepping back into the shuttle.

They were sky bound minutes later, and she could see her team were emotionally drained. "We're going right back into the queue," Alice said. "And I'm having trouble putting what we saw aside too, so let's take a minute. Let's take stock."

"Are we stopping at the Harbour Saint for supplies? We've got six juvenile emergency sleeves and two pods left," asked Luu.

"No, Fleet is putting us back into the queue without. I don't think we'll be doing any more runs like that today."

"The adults sacrificed themselves for the children on that sky bus. Made sure they had enough air for the trip once they realized they couldn't all survive based on what they had," Beck said. "And the med tech starts talking about pudding, of all things," she added, disgusted.

"You've gotta start somewhere, open a bloody dialogue," Regan snapped. "What was she supposed to say to that kid? 'Hey! I hear your parents are dead! That sucks, but we have medication and therapy that'll get you through it, so you can remember the good times and not live with the image of them suffocating to death!' Yeah, I'd start easy too, talk about pudding, or cartoons, or whatever else the kid's into."

"I'm sorry, it's just... I don't think everyone understands the sacrifice that happened on that ship, how sad it is, and I don't get how any of us can just talk about it for a moment and move on," Beck replied. "I mean, to decide to send all the good air away from you so a few kids can survive, I've never heard of that. I didn't think people were capable, and I look at you guys and you're all dry eyes and stone faces, especially her," she looked directly at Alice.

Alice double checked the scans and of the transit ship they found the children on and confirmed that the air recycling system was completely burned out. She made sure that was part of her after action report, added the bare facts of the event and filed it. Her duty complete, and the record correct, Alice was able to deal with the only member of her team that was falling apart. Why Yawen wasn't handling her, Alice didn't know. That was one of Yawen's main duties, to handle her squad.

"Is that actually what happened? Did those people actually sacrifice themselves? I assume you were double checking just now," Beck said.

"The air recycling system burned out, so someone on that bus was smart enough to know what would happen if they didn't prioritize the children and cut the supply off to the main compartment, but not quite smart enough to fix it. So, yes, what we just saw was a grim example of the bravest people I have ever seen."

"Too bad they were all dead," Tran added with a shrug.

"All right," Alice said, taking a deep breath and letting it out instead of saying something she might regret. Knud slapped him in the back of the helmet hard enough for him to rock forward and take a step. "All right," Alice started again, holding her hand up. "Everyone did a great job. There was absolutely nothing we could do to save the adults on that ship. We got those kids off that bus in under five minutes even though most of us only had rudimentary emergency medical training. We got them to Haven Shore Medical in less than ten and most of them wouldn't have survived at all unless we did our jobs well, which we did. I invite everyone to visit those orphans in your off-time, I know that's what I'll be doing. For now, we can pack that away as a success, we saved lives and made sure the sacrifice the rest of those passengers made mattered. Now it's time to clear the deck," she pointed at her head, "and get ready for the next emergency. I've got chatter in my ear telling me that the last of the ships are coming. Many of them are from what remains of the Cefa System's defensive fleet, rebel ships that have taken a beating, so we will be needed."

"Just pack it all away?" Tulsa asked. "Forget what we just saw?"

"Yawen," Alice said. "Sort her out or relieve her."

"You're a robot," Tulsa said, pointing at Alice. "When they remade you they forgot your soul."

"Never mind," Alice told Yawen. "You're not going to get over this in time, Private Tulsa Beck, so you are dismissed. Get into one of those bunks back there, and calm down."

"Is that an order, Lieutenant?" Tulsa screeched.

"It is," Alice barked. She looked to Regan. "Go with her, and once someone from command is in her ear, talking her down, come back. Make sure she's calming down first."

"Holm knows her better," Regan suggested quietly.

"If you think that's the best thing, then send Holm instead. As long as she calms down and doesn't pose a risk to herself."

Regan and Tulsa retreated to the rear of the shuttle and disappeared into a compartment that was outfitted for passengers. "We're meeting people on the worst day of their lives, and we have the opportunity to make it a little better, or at least survivable," Alice said with much more sympathy. "I understand if what we're seeing or doing reminds you of your own past trauma, or is just a lot to take in. This work isn't for everyone. If it's any solace, you can remind yourself that Special Operations will be involved in a wide variety of missions, these are just our first, so it won't be all tragedy and tension."

"But isn't that where we can do the most good?" Yawen asked.

In a flash, Alice recalled the opportunities on Iora, the people there waiting to be saved, and her most recent encounter with Edxi warriors on the surface of her father's ship. She wished Noah Lucas had a team like hers come down and help him, and that she was so well trained and equipped when she met the Edxi, an encounter that cost lives. "There are a lot of situations ahead of us where we'll be doing some of the most important work in the Fleet, but for now, I think you're right. Today we are here to stop misfortune from becoming tragedy."

"I'll stick around for that," Jessen said, elbowing Knut, who nodded his agreement.

"We're heading into close maneuvers," announced the pilot over the intercom.

Everyone in the compartment looked through the transparent side of the hull and were rewarded with the sight of a six hundred thirty meter long destroyer that looked like it was from centuries before. Many of its transparent metal portholes were dark, scorch marks from heat damage and breaches from shells littered the hull, and one of the main engines at the rear was gone, as though beam weapons carved it loose. "The Lady Lisa," Yawen said. "It reminds me of a few of the Irish ships; old warriors that we upgraded as best as we could before pushing them into the fight. They should have been turned into museums instead."

A glint of something beneath the ship caught Alice's eye before the shuttle rotated so it was out of view. She opened a channel to the cockpit. "Can you rotate thirty degrees clockwise? I thought I saw something under that ship."

The shuttle rotated as instructed, and everyone looked with

her for several seconds. "I see it!" Luu exclaimed, pointing at a space beneath the old warship.

"Yeah, looks like there's a cloaked ship with a damaged projector," Yawen said.

"Just enough for us to make it out. No one scan it. If they sense a tight beam scan, they'll know we suspect they're there." She sent a short encrypted burst communication to Command and waited. Her gaze didn't wander from the wavering patch of stars beneath the Lady Lisa. "That's definitely an enemy ship, probably here to spy on us, see what our response to this is like."

"Or to attack?" Tran asked.

Alice caught herself before scoffing, but Knud scoffed so loud it almost sounded like a sneeze. "That's foolish, they'd need a lot more firepower."

The orders from Command came back as short, crystal clear instructions that used iconographic code. "We're going for a walk. Do we have a hull puncher?" Alice asked.

"No, sorry. Not in the shuttle's inventory," Yawen replied.

"Then we'll plant some really loud beacons right where we want our backup to make a hole," Alice said, doing her best to ignore the tingle of excitement running up and down her spine.

"Finally, we get to shoot something," Yawen said.

TWENTY

"Good work, guys," Minh-Chu said as his trio of skitter bots climbed back into the top storage hatch of his Uriel fighter. They installed filter and rapid cooling systems on the end of all his thrusters. The new additions would burn off if he had to thrust hard, but it was a huge part of making his ship stealthier. Hot Chow was still hesitant to fly Minh-Chu's Uriel, but it had the best carrier system, the others were damaged or wouldn't clamp to the personnel pod that attached underneath.

They also only had time to coat the surface of one of their Uriels with an active stealth layer that would make it invisible to all but a direct high powered scan. "Are you sure I'm the guy for this?" Hot Chow asked him, putting his helmet on.

"You have the most experience hauling oddly shaped cargo around, and your three dimensional thinking is up there with the best. You know the mission, it's the easy part; drop your passengers off when you get the go ahead," Minh-Chu said.

"Then get out of there as fast as these thruster caps will let me without getting caught," Hot Chow finished. "Why aren't you flying this mission again?"

"I'll be with Carnie on the Pursuer. Stop questioning your orders or I'll have you signed up as an Academy Cadet the second we get back."

"Aye-aye, Wing Commander," Hot Chow said.

Minh-Chu turned away and accepted his ground kit belt from Carnie. It had his sidearm, enhanced medical systems, tools and a few other things he hoped he didn't need. "He has moments where you can tell he's used to taking orders from idiots. You should hear some of his stories about hauling freight. Most of his bosses wouldn't know what a flight stick looked like."

"It's come up more than once when there's no time for questions," Minh-Chu said. "They're always intelligent questions, but I am signing him up for the fast track when we get back."

"You're serious, he's going to be a trainee?" Carnie asked quietly, surprised.

"The training he gets there will save his life, trust me."

"What about me? I've never been through boot camp, or hell week, or to any flight school."

"Look at curriculum E3, that's the fast track. If you think there's something there for you to learn, I'll get you in. It's only two weeks if you pass most of the qualifiers in advance."

"Oh, so I pass the quals in advance, then do exercises and physical training to finish the course?"

"Among other things. It's made to round out your experience, knowledge and prepare you to become an officer in the fleet. Makes it easier to promote you if you deserve it. The Qualification tests take the longest, so it's a good thing you can do all the academic ones before you even sign up," Minh-Chu said as he boarded the Pursuer.

The ship had taken a great deal of damage and been repaired by hundreds of skitters. It had an active stealth layer, but anything that damaged the hull would ruin most of its covert abilities. Despite the obvious weathering on the hull, the missing heavy weapons package on the inside, Minh-Chu liked the ship. "Let's start our checks. We only have about ten minutes to get out there."

"Aye," Carnie said.

"Oh, and Noah," Minh-Chu said. "It might sound like I'm singling Hot Chow out, but a third of our squad is getting shipped off to training when we get back. He's not the only one who has to learn to work within the military."

"Ah, gotcha. Do you think I should join them?" Carnie asked. "Really."

"You learned how to survive on your own before you joined the fleet, Noah. I don't think you'd learn as much as Hal, but you'd probably have some real fun in tactical training. Especially the part where you learn all about our new guns and the shooting practice that goes with it."

"That could be fun," Carnie admitted with a chuckle.

CAPTAIN VALENT COULDN'T HELP but chuckle a little as the twenty one soldiers, him included, that couldn't fit inside the troop carrier module that was affixed to the bottom of the Uriel, spread out on a narrow platform that was welded to the back of the fighter. It was a quick solution, but the platform would hold through re-entry and most other stresses.

The thing that tickled him the most was that the platform looked like two very long ladders. "Sir," Remmy said as he settled in on his stomach beside him. With the number of people they could bring cut in half, Jake chose his squad as the second one to come along. "Have you ever done anything like this?"

"I've done it to other people," Jake said, remembering the traitors he frightened by strapping them to the front of his ship for re-entry. "They were strapped to the front though. I've done the preparation sim for flight in this armour though."

"Ah, we've drilled that a few times," Remmy said. "We've also done some flight practice in the hangar when it's clear. You know, just some balancing and fine movement, but enough to get a feel for flying around in this stuff."

"I've had a lot of EVA training," Jake said. "I'm sure if any of us get detached or knocked off the beam, we'll be fine to make a landing on our own. We'll just have to start decelerating at the last moment."

"Because using our barrier thrusters blows our stealth," Remmy said.

Jake opened a private channel with Remmy. "You know this is more than an intelligence run, right?" he said.

"I have the virus loaded and ready," Remmy replied. "If we find the link to their supply network, we'll download all the data and send it out across all the depots and anything connected."

Jake saw that everyone had checked in. Seven people in the troop module - that included Liara and Finn - twenty one soldiers affixed to the beam running behind the fighter, and the pilot, Hot Chow. "All right, Chow," Jake said. "Lift off, stealth up and get us to one of those containers," he said.

"Sir, if this works, you're going to fry millions of computer systems in a few dozen or a few hundred depots and bases," Remmy said. "And violate galactic law."

"It's time to burn them back," Jake said. "At least our artificial intelligence won't directly force systems to attack biological beings. If you have a problem with it, I can make sure I make the final keystroke."

"No, Sir," Remmy said with a snicker. "I've wanted to do something like this for a long time. Even Liara wants this to go according to plan. That's why she named the virus after her sister."

Mary, it was a common name, and not one that Jake would have chosen for a malicious virus, but any name was fine. Unlike Alice who had a personality when she was released aboard the Overlord Two, Mary had none. It was an artificial intelligence that was made to circumvent and deactivate security software as it learned from the system. They'd already let her loose inside an isolated Order of Eden computer they had on hand. It was loaded with every countermeasure they knew of, and Mary managed to burn it out in less than three seconds after learning everything she could and copying herself to the drive Jake had under his vacsuit and heavy armour. Finn, Liara and Remmy carried their own copies as well, just in case.

It would be a monstrous attack, especially since they already knew what Order of Eden security software looked like and had already defeated a system. Jake hoped that the supply depot's computers were well connected but unsophisticated. The galactic law he was violating was something he could live with. It was in place to prevent anyone from creating malicious artificial intelligences, but Jake didn't see anyone from the galactic courts sending people after the Order of Eden, so it was time to get dirty. Only Remmy, Finn, Liara, Agameg, Stephanie and Minh-Chu knew about Mary. The most ingenious part of it was that Liara stole the base code from the Lorander database. It was created by another artificial intelligence they found on the other side of the galaxy. It would be hard to prove anyone from Jake's crew made it.

They left the hangar behind, flying out between huge aster-oids. "I'm proud to be on this mission with you," Jake said, acti-vating a laser link with everyone on the beam with him, and the fighter. Everyone would be able to hear him. "If this mission is successful, we will provide a distraction for the Nafalli who are going to be picking up more supplies than they need from orbit. We're also going about some other business; stealing more intel-ligence for Fleet and shutting down their computer systems so they don't blow our ride out of the sky before we get picked up. Every time we get over their walls, steal information from them and disable their infrastructure, we weaken them where it counts. Our strike will demoralize every enemy ship crew that discovers they can't come here for supplies. They'll know that they aren't impervious, that there are bad asses that can kick down their doors, take what they want and burn the rest down. Let's clear our heads, get ready for the first step in this mission, and get it done."

TWENTY-ONE

To Make A Name

FEW THINGS ARE MORE dangerous than being well cloaked in space. The chances of any collision between two objects that aren't drawn to each other by significant gravitational forces are so low, that navigational software was designed to make it possible to connect two objects in space. The odds say that a person, or an object could hang out there for centuries, invisible, drifting, on its own and not run into anything. Those odds don't seem to matter as much once you imagine what it must be like to get hit by a starship of any size rushing through the area at great speed.

Odds be damned, high speed collisions in the vacuum of space are always devastating. That was why cloaking isn't always as much of a tactical advantage as many people assume. If the ships around you could see you, they could avoid colliding with you. This was one of the thoughts Alice had as she activated her cloaking systems and leapt from the airlock of her combat shuttle.

Yawen, Regan, Tran, Luu, Jessen and Knud were right behind her. Their training kept them from bumping into one another. Light airburst thrusters allowed them to disperse into a pattern that would see them all catch their own section of hull. Everyone was on course. Cosmically, the distance they were crossing was as thin as a human hair, but that gap between the shuttle and the cloaked enemy ship seemed immense forever as they drifted through it.

Any communication would tip the enemy off to their location. The cloaking systems could cover for a few airburst thrusts for course correcting and light acceleration, but proximity radio, laser links, or any other kind of broadcast would reveal them. Alice checked her position one more time, glancing up at the flaw in the enemy vessel's cloak - a single panel that looked like a blurred patch of space, and saw that her feet were pointed almost exactly right. She made a small adjustment and took her heavy rifle from where it was affixed to her back. Armoured boot soles struck heavy hull plating and affixed firmly.

If everything was going according to plan, Alice would be facing the forward section of the ship, or at least the front facing section. The ship could be flying with its main engines facing forward, for all they knew. Her squad would be behind her, touching down on the surface of the hull.

Ten seconds passed, a mostly arbitrary number, but long enough for the rest of her squad to stick or drift. "All right, set tactical scanners on high," Alice ordered. "Broadcast your findings to Fleet."

"Aye," Yawen. "Jessen is drifting, she missed contact with the hull but a fighter's picking her up in a minute."

A glance at her tactical display showed Alice that everyone

was scanning the hull of the enemy ship except for Jessen, who stayed cloaked and was somewhere out there, thrusting away from the enemy so she could get picked up. "We knew someone would miss," Alice said. "No worries."

The shape of the hull in front of her became clear and Alice took aim at the base of a forward thruster pylon. A flipped switch on her rifle set it to fire a loud, non-networked beacon that would send a powerful signal through space, tagging the ship. The point she marked as her target was two hundred and three meters away. Other targets appeared, everyone who made the trip to the ship was ready to fire their own beacons. "Fire when ready." The kick of her rifle only registered on the surface of her armour, but the movement of the weapon and the impact of her payload was satisfying.

A big, red blip appeared on her tactical system, then another and another until everyone on her team except for Jessen had an active beacon affixed to the hull of the ship. "Good job. Kill your sensors, cloak and retreat," Alice said.

The new cloaking systems built into their armour were better than anything that Alice had ever seen. There were few ways to defeat them outside of a very powerful ship sensor system, which made the next part of the plan more dangerous than anything else. Alice was faced with a decision when she put the plan together. At this point, they could either run aft along the hull, hide in place, or leap free from the vessel entirely and take their chances - hope that those odds held up while fighters and warships maneuvered around them, firing at the ship they just tagged. They ran towards the aft of the ship, moving across the hull like ants on the bark of an ancient fallen tree. The data they collected from their scans told them that there was three hundred and forty three metres more to the ship behind them. Looking at the graceful curve of the hull, she felt there was something familiar about the style, but put the notion away for later.

A counter on her head's up display told her that they had eleven more seconds before the Fleet would begin firing. It seemed like more time than they needed, but they didn't run out of hull before the timer counted down to zero. "Deactivate cloaking systems, turn your personal shields on and ping the Fleet," Alice said, breathlessly turning towards the front of the ship and following her own orders.

Her team appeared around her, Luu and Tran roughly thirty metres closer to the front of the ship than she was. If everything went well, they were about to see something memorable.

"This is Growler from Viper Wing. We see you down there, Gamma Team. Get ready for one hell of a light show," a pilot said in Alice's ear.

Doors opened on the hull and anti-fighter turrets rose up through the gaps. Alice's team were right between two such doors. They were close enough to see the gunners in their pods. "Knut, set your rifle to its upper limit and pop that bubble. Yawen, kill the turret behind you."

Alice raised her rifle as Knut fell in beside her and did the same. In the instant before she pulled her trigger, she realized that the gun pod looked like a more advanced version of the type used by the Triton. The gunner looked at her at first with confusion, then alarm. Knut and she opened fire, sending dozens of exploding guided rounds at the armoured bubble. They were under the ship's shields, and the metal was torn through in seconds. A few shots later, the weapon emplacement lost power.

They turned towards a more distant weapon emplacement and did the same. Gunners were abandoning their posts, knowing that they couldn't point their weapons at the hull walkers. To fire at the invaders was to fire at the metal skin of their own ship, and the system didn't allow for that.

"Two down, moving on to a third," Yawen announced.

The surface of the ship was alive with gunners trying to fend off the Haven Shore fighters that swept in, dropping electromagnetic charges towards the nose of the ship meant to burst through the energy shields. Alice and Knut competed with Yawen, Regan, Tran and Luu, bursting one turret after another in the aft section of the ship. After the first two, they were destroying empty gun emplacements, as the crews retreated before the hull walkers could reach them, which was just fine with Alice. "You've cleared enough opposition. We're coming in to get you, Gamma Team," announced the pilot of their armoured shuttle. "Get together at this position."

"Aw, but we were just getting started," Yawen whined. "I'm only on my third clip."

"Pack it in, the big guns are coming," Alice said, noticing that a new destroyer, The Honour Guard just appeared in the area. The interdiction signals erupted from it like a bloom of energy in all directions. Nothing would be able to escape using faster than light travel.

"This is Admiral Terry Ozark McPatrick to the Citadel Ship Exile. Surrender immediately or your ship will be incapacitated and your crew will be taken captive," came the warning from the Honour Guard.

"We do not recognize your authority, McPatrick," came the reply.

Six British Alliance battle cruisers, all over one kilometre long, bristling with heavy guns and enhanced shield emitters that looked like spiny fins emerged from wormholes. "This is Marshal Grant of the British Alliance Fleet. I advise you to recognize my colleague's determination and firepower, if not his rank and authority in this region - which are valid and utter, for the record. Surrender."

"Do not interfere, Marshal Grant," replied the commander of the Citadel ship.

"We've gotta get off this thing," Luu said. "They're going to cut this ship in half and dissect the pieces."

The shuttle lowered close enough for Alice's team to leap and boost inside with their thrusters. "Get in, by the numbers," Alice ordered.

"Fast! We're holding this firefight back! Move, move!" Yawen said.

Alice's tactical system noted several missile launches from the Exile. The Citadel ship was also turning quickly. It was everything the shuttle pilots could do to stay roughly in position so the team could get on.

Knut and Regan made it, crossing the short space between the hull of the Exile and the shuttle's airlock, but barely. The smaller ship bashed into the hull of the Exile hard, denting the rear armour before clamping onto the hull with the forward landing gear. "We're secure, go!"

Alice watched as all but Tran and her boarded. He was stuck to the spot, his heart rate rising by the second along with his perspiration and respiration. "Override walk-lock," Alice said as she grabbed the bottom of his equipment pack. His boots decoupled from the deck and she pushed him through the airlock ahead of her. "We're all on board, get us out of here," she told the pilots as the airlock doors tried to close behind but failed to seal thanks to impact damage.

"It's all right, we're safe," Luu told Tran as he collapsed into a seat beside her.

Alice was happy to see Jessen in the back of the shuttle. The slightly older woman returned her gaze sheepishly, and Alice responded with a half-smile and a nod. Jessen did nothing wrong, the chances that someone would miss the hull of the Exile were high, it could have happened to anyone. What followed - a by the numbers execution of a simple plan that would ensure her safe retrieval after missing - was just fine.

Yawen and Regan sealed the doors using a hardening foam kit from an overhead supply bin, filling the gap with the thick, quick-setting material. The cabin was pressurizing seconds later. Alice watched through the transparent section of hull as hundreds of missiles and thousands of shells raked the shields of the Honour Guard. The industrial style, heavy hull was untouched by the Exile's munitions.

Most of the missiles were slowed down by the gravitational control field extending from the Honour Guard, then set off intentionally by anti-fighter guns and smaller beam weapons. The heavier torpedoes were struck by narrow beam electromagnetic pulse weapons, forcing a few to detonate, but most of them slowed and deflected off the shields.

The Honour Guard finally returned fire after closing to three kilometres. The civilian ship that the Exile hid behind was long gone, something Alice was thankful for as three beams of white light raked the forward sections of the Exile, reducing its shield strength down to nearly nothing. Particle cannons across the Honour Guard's starboard side fired for nearly thirty seconds. The heavier guns aboard the Haven Fleet ship were silent, along with the beam weapons and whatever else might be in its arsenal.

The Exile's hull finally cracked and burst, letting hundreds of high energy rounds inside the softer interior. Energy levels aboard the enemy vessel dropped to emergency levels, and the whole thing became visible. The style was graceful, like the

Triton, but not shaped after any specific sea dwelling creature Alice knew of. It was a third the width of the Triton, with a full sized hangar beneath and a gunnery section running down its dorsal side.

When the Exile signalled its surrender, everyone but Tran and Luu cheered. Luu was too busy trying to calm Tran down. He wasn't panicking anymore, but his anxiety levels were too high for him to go on.

"Lieutenant," Terran addressed through Alice's sub dermal communicator. "Status report."

"Three of my team members are down, either with performance impacting stress or supporting members. None of them disgraced themselves in the field or should be punished since this is their first time out and, in my opinion, they have done nothing wrong. I will be recommending them for reassignment. The rest of the team is holding up well. If you get us a new ship, we can move on to the next mission as a smaller, tighter group."

"That won't be necessary, Lieutenant Valent. Your team has performed brilliantly, but it's time for you to stand down and return to base."

Alice checked her tactical system and saw that there were warnings indicating that there was another wave of incoming ships. "I'd like to request temporary reassignment for myself and a few members of my squad to another team for the duration of this emergency."

"I applaud your ambition, but we are pulling all the Special Operations teams. I'll have more details for you once you've landed."

"Yes, Sir," Alice replied, realizing that it had been some time since she'd heard chatter from any of the other Special Operations teams. "Returning to base."

TWENTY-TWO

Descent

CLOAKED, hidden inside a container that once held supplies for an Order of Eden ship, Captain Jacob Valent and twenty seven fellow soldiers remained almost motionless as their suits affixed to the inside surfaces of the space. A heavy lifter clamped onto them, and Jake knew it wouldn't be long before they headed into the atmosphere of a planet where life moved slowly at minus thirty degrees or less.

He closed his eyes, and after five seconds a small chirp in his ear told him that his systems were switching to audio notification mode. If there was something important for him to see on his tactical display or anywhere else in his system, audio notifications would tell him about it. Signal silence was the order, so no one spoke. Anything that could break their stealth was locked down.

Against the darkness of his mind, Jake made an effort to

clear his mind. Ayan was there, and he hoped she was fitting in with the Fleet, finding her place there as it changed. He knew how important the defence of Tamber and the rest of the solar system was, and how badly she wanted Haven Fleet to become the example of a wise military, not just a powerful force. That terrible thought, that she was already surrounded by suitors who invited her to move on from Jake while he was lost with the Revenge was always there.

He forced himself to recall her remorse, her apology, and how earnest she was about her feelings for him. Ayan was stronger now, listening to her own better angels instead of leaning on visions from the Victory Machine. She would be true.

He found himself wondering where Stephanie would fit in with the new fleet. She would no longer be able to join his staff, which might drive her a little crazy. There had to be something important for her to do, something that would make her feel like she's using her expertise thoroughly and properly. The most obvious, the simplest solution came to mind then. He would put her up for a promotion. With a higher rank and her experience, several departments should want Stephanie. She may not be able to captain a ship, but she'd have a placement in the fleet that would suit her almost as much.

He wondered about Finn, of all people then. The boy who had become a man under his watch, nearly dying once for the cause, couldn't remain under his wing forever. More so than Agameg, who had stories that he hadn't seen fit to tell yet, seen things that Jake could barely imagine, Finn was still young. Regardless of his past adventures, there was an explorer's spirit in the young Chief. Jake saw it most when he discovered he was going on this mission. There was a light in his eyes as he said; "I've never been on a planet that cold before." The upcoming mission would be violent. No matter how well hidden they remained, there would be a point where they were discovered and the base, or the people in it would fight back. He and Liara didn't have combat training. They had to be protected.

Any time Jake had to clear his mind, thoughts of his daughter laid atop everything else like a blanket. When he left her behind she was trapped as an eternal adolescent, doomed to have her framework revert her back to a youthful age every time she started to grow out of the last phase of childhood. Alice was now free from that, and in the Haven Fleet's Apex Program. According to what he read, she was probably serving on a ship as an Officer Cadet. Whatever ship she was on would be better with her there. He hoped she had time to embrace the rest of her life. There was more to living than working, a lesson that he hadn't learned as well as he liked yet.

The flames of re-entry burned against the side of the cargo container, and a glimpse at his display told him that most of the heat remained outside. The temperature inside wouldn't test their cloaking systems or armour much at all, everyone was fine. His thoughts returned to Alice. The idea that she was once the artificial intelligence that lived on Jonas Valent's wrist seemed like a fiction when he thought of the woman she became. She freed herself once when she became human, became trapped again when she was placed in a framework body, and now she was free once more. Jake silently swore to himself that he'd make sure she had every opportunity to have a full life when he got back. He remembered what it was like to lose his parents, or what it was like for Jonas to suffer that loss as though it were his own and making sure that she knew he was there for her would be his biggest priority. After everything she'd gone through, she deserved it.

All the people he cared about and his thoughts about them

sorted, Jake ran through the plan step by step in his head. It was a meditation, a visualization exercise that he played through in great detail. It always ended with one credo; "And when it all goes to hell, I'll find a better way to get the job done," he said aloud. His microphones were turned off, so no one could hear him, but Remmy must have seen him speaking, watching through the display that revealed allies as though they weren't cloaked, because the young man grinned and nodded at him.

Jake nodded curtly, already feeling that furrowed brow game face taking over as he smiled back and activated the holographic illusion on his helmet that made it look like a death's head lived in his armour. Remmy activated his own, revealing a freakish skull with teeth filed to points and bulging, bloodshot eyeballs. It was comical and unnerving at the same time. Remmy made his illusion's head wobble, sticking its tongue out then laughing.

"I'm going to poach you from the Rangers," Jake said, laughing, aware that Remmy couldn't hear him. "Then you'll really be in the shit." He laughed a little harder despite himself, or perhaps because Remmy's death's head was laughing at his own antics.

The container touched down, Jake held his fist up and looked to his passive scanner readouts. Anything that emitted a signal, the surfaces that were subject to pressure, vibrations or interference were visible to him. The heavy lifter released its clamps and started flying off. He set his communications to use laser link and sent the command across all the suits worn by his allies. He would also be able to receive all other signals but left his ability to send them off. Any signal other than laser link would be a dead giveaway.

He opened the container hatch a crack and watched as his tactical display populated. The container was put down in the middle of the yard. "We're one point eight kilometres away from the nearest entry point to the base. Do you see anyplace we could patch into their local network?"

"The closest I see is at the end of this rail line," Finn said. He highlighted the sections of the base reaching outwards from the tall, octagonal middle building. They extended like spokes from a wheel to different main buildings. They were at the end of one that picked up empty containers, transported them on rails to the middle, where they were reconditioned, filled then deposited at the end of another spoke, where a yard of filled and sealed containers waited for pickup. "There's a main network node right at the end of each of these spokes, we should be able to tap in there."

"All right, we have a run ahead of us," Jake said. "Let's get moving."

TWENTY-THREE

The Lieutenants

"WE NEED to cut Tran and Luu," Alice told Yawen quietly in the rearmost compartment. Yawen, Alice's former academy roommate sat down in one of the broad seats made for larger, or armoured passengers. It was still an awkward ordeal since they had the slimmer version of the backpack systems attached to their armour, so she sat on the edge of her seat. "They're not ready for this, they might never be."

Yawen thought for a moment then nodded. "You're right. They're too independent of the group and there are two fraternization violations between them pending review. They were always solid in training, I'm disappointed."

"They look to each other to confirm every order, and they want to question everything in the moment," Alice said. "That's what stands out for me. I don't think it's a situation where they have to go back for training, they just need to be placed where someone has time to put them on the right track. I won't have time."

"Tran's freak out when he saw the shuttle bash hulls with the Exile was the big sign for me that he might not be ready," Yawen said.

"He froze, but I don't blame him. Armour can't save us from everything. Anyone could freeze if they think about getting caught between the kind of force that could twist the whole frame of a combat shuttle."

"You have a point, no one wants to have their legs pinched off," Yawen said. "What about Tulsa Beck?"

"I think I understand what's going on in her head, and it's what's going to keep her from being a member of this team, sure, but she's going to be great somewhere else. With the kind of empathy she has, there's a place where she can shine. I'll make sure she and command both know that, so they help her find it," Alice said.

"I appreciate it," Yawen said. "There will be waterworks when you give her the news. With Luu and Tran, I bet they'll get angry for a minute then retreat. I'd rather deal with that. Should I start looking for replacements?"

The shuttle set down and rocked on its landing gear. The frame was so badly twisted that it wouldn't rest on all of its pylons evenly. "Consult Command, they might have suggestions, but don't let them force anyone on us. I have final approval. Oh, and we're definitely looking for a medic, or at least a medical technician."

"Yes, Ma'am," Yawen said with a little smirk. That always meant there was some amusing thought getting filed away.

"What? What's up?" Alice asked.

"You were great out there, but scary serious. I mean, that's good, it was a good kind of serious, the kind of attitude that's easy to follow. I didn't see it before, but now I do. I see why they put you where they did."

"Thank you, but we haven't arrived yet. Wait until we have our own ship. The Clever Dream will be ready soon..."

A brisk triple-bang on the rearmost airlock interrupted her. The inner door opened and a fresh-faced, red-cheeked cadet entered and saluted.

Alice returned the salute, looking at the cadet's pristine white uniform. It had a dark red stripe running down the shoulders. "Orders from the Lieutenant Commander; I'm here to show you to a shuttle," he said, out of breath. "Lieutenant, if you'll come this way."

"See you soon," Alice said to Yawen, who stood and saluted. She returned the gesture. "Our team will be off active duty once everyone gets their after action reports in, except you and Tulsa. I have to know where she is at all times until I release her from the team and you have to watch her."

"Because she's shown signs of significant emotional distress, I remember the regulation, no problem," Yawen said.

"See you later."

Alice was led across the hangar floor at a brisk pace, to a ship that was in no way a shuttle - it was a heavy gunship with seven quad turrets. "Any idea what this is about, Trainee?"

"I don't have any information for you, I'm sorry Lieutenant," he replied. They were ten steps away from the embarkation ramp leading into the gunship when the cadet asked; "Were you really walking around on the hull of a Citadel ship ten minutes ago?"

"I can neither confirm or deny," Alice said.

"I understand," he said. "The Huntress will take you the rest of the way," he said, snapping to attention and saluting.

She saluted in return and walked up the ramp, which was already closing by the time she got to the top. The dark, high polish metal of the hull was several centimetres thick and had a quality she'd never seen before. Even with only a moment to see it up close before she was inside, she knew it was something completely new.

The rear of the gunship was set up for a troop drop, with equipment storage between rows of seats and enough room for at least thirty soldiers to deploy in a hurry. She secured her rifle to her back and walked inward, where she could just barely see a table through an open hatchway deeper inside. Looking at all the brand new fixtures, the more efficient design, she wished it was what they used for their recent run of missions.

"Like her?" asked the voice of the Delta team leader. He was short, but no stranger to the gym. "It's the new class of gunship that's rolling out, Huntress. I'm trying to get one for my team." He extended his hand. "I'm Lieutenant Vernor, call me Gabe."

She shook his hand. "Showed up half out of uniform at your first briefing," she teased. "Second Lieutenant Valent, call me Alice."

"So that's how I'll be remembered until I manage to impress you," he said with a tilt of his head. "Challenge accepted."

He was so sure of himself that Alice was stunned. For a long moment she had no idea what to say, and he just watched her with a cocksure smile on his face. "The hull plating is... different," she managed finally.

He looked momentarily confused then looked up. "Oh, on this boat, yeah. Some kind of intelligent plating I'm still learning about. This ship came off the line today, it's part of the War Forge's defence wing."

"Gabe! Get up here!" called a voice from further inside.

"That's Callum, leader of Beta Team. He's had a really bad day," Gabe explained.

"A bad day," Callum scoffed. "You lose anyone today, Lieutenant?" he asked Alice as she entered the middle compartment. "No, you didn't." His thick Irish accent made his words more biting somehow. He ran his hand down his face and sighed. "I'm on our second mission, looking at my tactical screen," he said in a much calmer tone. "I mean to say, right at it, when I watch one of my guys - Steno, I think his name was - move ahead with two behind him and he breaches the compartment ahead of us on this ghost ship. No worries, right? I say; 'easy forward, no scanning. Keep your systems on passive,' because I know there's a chance the ghost ship could be trapped. The next thing I hear from this Steno fellow is; 'All right, boss, I'm turning my scanners up,' and I'm just about to tell him no when I see him go ahead and do it. You hear about the ghost ship that went boom? I was in the aft section with five of my guys. Three dead, especially that Steno guy, and two in the infirmary. What's worse, I watch the whole thing playback and realize that I could have just deactivated his scanners before he turned them on. I had plenty of time. You tell 'em what happened next." Callum said, dropping into one of the plusher seats beside the multi-purpose table in the middle of the compartment.

"My team was sent in to pick him up from the wreckage, and Callum's second in command is busy screaming at him when we get there. As soon as our shuttle latches on, one of the ships that arrived with that ghost ship starts getting too close. I notice and warn it to turn back. Callum requests fighter cover, but it's too late. We're under fire from a bunch of crazy Order bastards who jump out of their junker of a ship with thruster suits and they're coming at us. Callum saw the zero gee troopers first, and he's firing back before anyone knows what to do. I have seven years in Aucharian Special Forces, and I've never seen anyone react like that. My Irish friend here saved our asses, gave us a chance to find cover. I would have lost a few people if it weren't for him."

"I was just doing what came naturally. God help me, it doesn't make up for the three I lost, and the two still barely hanging on," Callum added.

"Yeah, that wasn't nature, that was experience and practice, my friend. It didn't take long to mop those Order crazies up after that, especially with three fighters for support, but that's the most action we saw today. That's probably why we're here."

"I'll be demoted. I can count three procedure violations before I lost three people. It's like everything I learned in training just left the moment I was sent on a real mission. Oh yeah, I'm the one that stunk up his operation so bad that they have to talk to me in person," Callum said, standing and gesturing to himself, "Making your praises sound all the better. I hear you were walking around on the Exile? How in the hell did you know what to do once you were there? I mean, there were orders, I'm sure, but..."

Alice didn't know the answer. Her memories had been scanned, stored and sorted. Even Haven Intelligence didn't think she had more than a few sketchy memories from her first life as a human, when she was aboard the Triton. Even so, the hull of the Citadel ship - a ship that was most likely designed and built by the same people who were responsible for the Triton - felt familiar. She knew where the gun emplacements would be, where to hit them so they were disabled quickly. She even knew that most of the gunners would have time to get out of the turrets before the armoured plating was cracked. There was no question in her mind that she was attacking that ship the right way. "My mission there was pretty simple. Drop beacons so their dodgy cloaking tech was completely circumvented."

"But you took turrets out, made it look so easy when any second a squad or three of counter insurgence guys in combat suits could come out and make things way too complicated for you to stick around."

"There weren't many airlocks nearby," Alice said. "My second, Yawen, sealed two while we were out there, so we were pretty sure we weren't going to be seeing any soldiers anytime soon."

"You and Gabe are going to be stars," Callum said, dropping into his seat again.

"Not yet," said Lieutenant Commander Terran as his holographic image appeared above the table. "I'd like to congratulate all three of you for your work today. With only a few exceptions, your performance was excellent. The strategies you used demonstrate an ability to think ahead. I'd hate to square off against you in a game of Archon's Fall."

Callum, Gabe and Alice all stood at attention and saluted. The Lieutenant Commander returned the gesture. "At ease. We are pressed for time, since you'll be aboard the War Forge in a minute. I've finished reviewing all your reports. I expected excellence from you especially, Lieutenant Vernor," he said to Gabe. "I wasn't disappointed. The four missions we sent you on were executed flawlessly and I agree that you should replace the five soldiers who underperformed. I'm taking your leash off and recommending that you are promoted to the rank of First Lieutenant. I'm afraid there won't be any pomp or ceremony attached to the promotion, everyone in the fleet is already scrambling to keep up with what's going on. We'll make a very big deal when you have another promotion, I promise."

"Thank you, Lieutenant Commander," Gabe replied. "No need for ceremony."

"Second Lieutenant Callum Newell," Terran addressed, turning towards the tall, blonde Irishman. "I regret to inform you that, after reviewing your report and your neural performance record, Command has decided that it's too early for you to have a team of your own. Your rank is reduced to Ensign. This is not solely because of the loss of life that occurred while you were in command. It is because of the unsteadiness, as you put it in your report, or inconsistency as I'd put it leading up to today. Unsteadiness is not something to be ashamed of at your age. You are young, inexperienced, and will accomplish a great deal in your career, especially with the right mentorship in the short term. As I said, despite your misadventure today, I'm pleased with the promise I've seen. I believe you will embrace the core strategies we'll need to win this war in time. As a side note, your request to personally inform the friends and families of those you lost today is approved, but we will make sure you are not alone."

"I understand, thank you, Lieutenant Commander," Callum said, standing perfectly straight. Alice saw it then, the remnants of youth in his face. He was tall, but like a teenager could be tall; lanky and not fully grown into his frame. He hid it well.

"You won't be floating free for long, we're putting you into the Special Operations recruiting pool, so someone is going to snap you up," Lieutenant Commander Terran looked to Alice. "Command is taking your leash off as well, Valent. This comes from Captain Coran and Haven Intelligence. I would have put you and your team on a few more missions today, but my superiors recognized that more than one of your squad members was slowing you down enough to present a danger. They believe - and I agree - that you handled yourself well today, so it's only appropriate for you to be raised to the rank of First Lieutenant before continuing your career as master of the Clever Dream and leader of your own team."

"Thank you, Lieutenant Commander," Alice said.

Terran cleared his throat before going on. "Remove whoever you like from your squad and replace them with good people from the recruiting pool for Special Operations. Do not try to recruit people above and outside of your reach again, please. Putting an official request to recruit Lieutenant Garrison wasn't appropriate. He's currently in enhanced training for a higher rank and will be taking on bigger responsibilities soon."

"I apologize," Alice said. "I was informed that my position comes with the right to make any reasonable request of Command with regards to personnel or equipment."

"Lieutenant; be careful that you don't over reach. Remember the qualifier in the rights you are given; that you have the 'right to make any *reasonable* request.' You don't want to reach over anyone's head, understand?"

"Yes, Sir," Alice replied. With structure came politics, and she realized then that she didn't take that into account when she requested that Garrison stay with the Clever Dream. Her request must have gone over Lieutenant Commander Terran's head, something she'd be more careful of later.

"I caution you to doubt yourself less in your after action comments. It is true, you made a few very minor missteps, but I can see you are aware of them and will improve quickly. Once you get to know your team and develop a shorthand with them, you'll find fewer reasons to look over your shoulder to make sure they are still backing you up, which is something you do, though I don't think you realize how often. Overall, your performance showed moments of brilliance. I don't envy you for your name, having to live up to the expectations that come with being a Valent, but I'm beginning to see that you may just do that and more. I did not expect to only have two squads left at this point, but that's what SOCU is down to on the Eagle. I'll be putting new teams together and offering a more suitable pool of people for you both to recruit from while I put new teams together. Until then, I've been asked to loan you out to Admiral McPatrick, who has a mission for you. Good luck,"

The hologram faded and Callum leaned over the table so he was nose to nose with Alice. "You're dropping people from your squad. I want to replace one of them," he glanced at Gabe. "Sorry, mate, you don't have a ship."

"No worries," Gabe said with a shrug. "I get the feeling I might be waiting a while."

"So, what about it? You're going where the action is, and you heard the Lieutenant Commander, I'm brimming with potential."

Alice pretended to ponder for a minute. "Any technical skills?"

"I'm not just a shooter, but a top grade hacker. Need to break into an Order system? I know their sloppy software from the first line to the last."

"He actually does," Gabe reinforced. "I forgot about that."

"Any medical skills?"

"Anyone can train to be a med-tech," Callum said. "I'll learn in my spare time and take the Qualifiers between missions. Need me to take a personality test? I'm a lovely guy, people get on with me famously. I have friends everywhere."

"That's all right, I'll give you a spot on my team, but you'll have to pass muster with my Second to make it official," Alice said.

"Yes!" Callum said, leaning back and pumping his arm. "You're going straight into the action, I know it."

"Why do I get the feeling that we're both going with her?" Gabe asked no one in particular.

TWENTY-FOUR

The Gold Prizes: Theft and Sabotage

THE SUPPLY DEPOT loomed over the raid squads. Jake led the charge with Remmy, watching his tactical display to make sure he didn't lose anyone and that their efforts to stay cloaked and hidden were successful. The supply containers they passed were each two or four metres high, and they were stacked up to fifteen up, twenty deep in all directions.

Bots with grabbers dropped off several, and Jake marked it as a sign that another destroyer or larger ship just dropped off empty containers then picked more. The size of the operation was larger than he expected. He kicked himself for not doing the math or checking his crewmembers' work before planning the mission. The reality of the depot was much larger, much busier than he visualized. The Revenge could have gained valuable intelligence just by setting a few cloaked satellites out in orbit to watch how many ships were reloading and what direction their wormholes pointed in. A day or two would have told them a lot about how their enemy was moving with almost no risk.

Instead, they were on the ground, behind enemy lines, desperately trying to stay hidden as they went for the gold prizes: theft and sabotage. It was the daring he was becoming known for, but that kind of daring always took you much closer to disaster than prudence and forward thinking. He brought his thoughts back to the moment.

The hard packed ground rushed by underfoot. He slowed his pace so Liara, Finn and four soldiers who were sinking back in the rear could catch up. The end of one of the delivery rails was ahead. It looked like a steel lighthouse, a light at the top blinking blue, green and yellow as containers were loaded onto flat beds from elsewhere in the yard then shuttled to the centre of the complex for loading. He looked at the schematic. "I got it," Remmy said. He was an expert in cracking and hacking himself, not at Liara's level, but knowledgeable enough to do a quick assessment of the node they were about to make an attempt on.

"How does it look?" Jake asked. He opened Liara and Finn's audio streams.

"I'm looking for a latch, a key into this thing," Remmy said. "Gimmie a sec, Captain. We might have a problem."

"I know, my lungs are on fire," Finn said breathlessly. He was on a private channel to Liara. "Just a few more metres and we'll be right beside Remmy."

"Oh, God, I can't believe I'm this out of shape," she said. "I always thought I was..." she gasped to catch her breath, "...in good condition for someone who sat at a computer all day."

"You are!" Finn replied. "But we're running with people who train all the time. They have nothing..." Huff, huff, huff, he breathed for a moment before continuing. "...else to do with their time but run, climb, shoot, do exercises and spar when they're between missions."

"Spar?" Liara asked.

"Practice fighting," Finn replied.

"Right, I knew that. I think my brain's oxygen deprived." They caught up to Remmy, who shook his head.

"You two are going to have to train with the Captain if he sees you two lagging behind again," Remmy told them privately, unaware that their Captain could hear them.

"Oh, don't even joke about that," Finn replied. "Let me take a look."

"Training with Captain is hard?" Liara asked, struggling to catch her breath.

"Look at him," Remmy laughed. "Imagine trying to keep up with that specimen and our wiry little *Wing Commander*? I can barely do it." He opened a channel to Jake then. "We have a problem, Captain. Finn is confirming right now, but they put a security plate in place over the hub controls. I don't detect much current going to it either, so I suspect it's on standby."

"So, if we crack it, we'll set off alarms," Jake said, looking up at the drones passing overhead. Each one had a small energy blaster and a cutter on board, which wasn't much if you were fighting just one, but there were a dozen drones he could see. Every one of them had heavy duty grabbers, too. If they decided to use them in concert with their energy weapons, he imagined things would go badly for whoever was near the hub control panels in a hurry. "We could shield whoever is standing next to it for a couple minutes. If they could activate the hub controls..."

"Well, that's another problem," Finn said, still catching his breath.

"Right, if whoever is on watch in the control center has half a brain, they'll turn this hub off right away." Jake finished for him.

"Exactly," Finn replied.

"You all right, Chief?" Jake asked as he watched a drone pick up an empty container and drop it onto a flatbed train car.

"We're fine, thank you Captain. I mean, I'm fine," he replied cutting his microphone off.

"Stay focused, I'm looking at this from another angle," Jake said to everyone. "Hold here a minute."

He walked away from the hub, let his passive scanning systems take in all the information they could and examined the large train cars in front of him. They had side sensors, which wouldn't be a problem for their stealth systems, but could come in handy if they needed the car to stop before going into the hub center. They were probably made to stop the car if something fell in front of or collided with it. The tracks and wheels were old fashioned, but the two were interlocked, meaning that the cars could travel down and up steeply. As a drone dropped an empty container onto the flatbed car, he watched as it magnetically locked onto the one below. There was a good chance that the train car travelled straight down or up once it got inside the main building, which made sense, since the schematics showed most of the bulk supplies in the top and beneath the narrower middle of the structure.

The control room was above the entry point for the cargo trains, and it was thickly armoured against orbital bombardment on the outside. "We're going to have to take a train inside," Jake said. "We'll reassess once we get close enough to find out what kind of defences are there."

The light above them flashed green, and the train cars left for the main building, accelerating quickly. "Get ready to take the next one," Remmy said.

"We'll have to pick a surface and stick to it once we're in those containers," Jake said. "Otherwise we might get dumped out once we're inside."

"So you filled in the blanks?" Remmy asked. "I was wondering why the rails weren't on the schematic."

"They look like they were built late. Maybe the drones were supposed to pick up these containers originally."

"We only have the one-point-oh schematics," Jake said.

"Makes sense," Remmy replied.

"How are you two feeling?" Jake asked on a direct channel to Liara and Finn. "I know this is a little out of your element."

"Great!" Liara said. "It's good to get away from my console for a change, Captain."

"Pretty good, Sir. I love these missions, seeing new places."

"Glad to hear it. Stay focused on the tasks in front of you, and you'll do well," he replied, silently deciding that they'd be scheduled for an early morning run with him and the rest of the group starting the day after tomorrow. He changed his communicator system back to addressing everyone. A pair of train cars were coming.

They stopped almost instantly. "Be ready for that," he warned everyone. I'm going to force this train into an emergency stop when we get where we're going. It'll be abrupt, and I don't want to see anyone flying overhead. We'll hold until there are a couple containers aboard."

They watched as two drones dropped containers onto the flatbed with a thunderous clang. "Mount up, don't touch the sensors along the side of the car."

"You heard him, get aboard!" Remmy reinforced.

All twenty-eight of them were on the lead train car and inside the containers in less than a minute, most of them using the augmented strength in their suits to leap up. Finn and Liara rode on two soldier's backs instead of risking a bad jump. *I'm going to have to start arranging suit training for people, too.* Jake thought. He wanted his entire crew in shape and top notch. If they could all handle themselves in a militarized way, each of their survivability would be much higher, and that was something he definitely wanted for them.

The car accelerated with a jerk, and Jake stepped out of the container then moved to the front of the car. His tactical display populated as they sped towards the large central building, and he watched it for biological life signs as well as any stationary weaponry. There was plenty of the latter. Guns pointed up at the sky, waiting to find invaders in the atmosphere. A few larger planetary weapons were made to fire into orbit, there were three of them on his side, meaning there were at least between five and nine more. If they couldn't get control of the station's systems, then they would never get picked up unless they were far, far away from the station.

Finally, as they passed under the overhead lip of the main station building, his tactical system picked up four life signs. All of them were human. One was in the cafeteria while the other three were in the control room. Two were reclining, one was pacing slowly in front of the main window. The doors leading into the middle of the station opened ahead of the flatbed car, and Jake got ready, affixing one foot to the floor of the flatbed and one hand to the container behind him. He raised his free leg, preparing to bring it down against the front facing collision sensor of the train. "I'm going to stop us soon."

"Everyone brace!" Remmy announced.

Once they were through the large doors, Jake could see where the tracks diverged. The one they were on led down under the station at a ninety-degree angle. There was a lift on the inside, with a large ladder nearby. The car slowed to a stop at the edge of the dark hole in the middle of the station floor. "Off! Get off, now!" he said, not moving yet. He watched his tactical display as everyone but Finn and two other soldiers scrambled to get off the train car. Gears clicked into place and the car started to tilt down. He didn't want to hit the collision sensor if he didn't have to. "Jump, Finn!" he said. The rear of the train was raising slowly, he might have enough time to throw the lollygaggers off himself. He ran back towards one soldier who was stuck on the edge of the train, looking left and right. Finn finally jumped along with the other soldier on his side.

The last one was in front of Jake, and at the last minute, he noticed his Captain running towards him. "Get off the train!" he shouted, Jake would have tackled him if he took another second, but the soldier; Terrance Cuna was his name, dropped off at last. Jake leapt clear as the train finished raising into a nearly completely vertical position and started rolling into the dark entrance to the supply storage below.

"Sorry, Sir," Cuna said.

"You made it, don't worry, get focused," Jake said, pounding his shoulder. He was satisfied that his first plan worked without having to trigger an emergency stop for the train car. It would have drawn attention, even if one of the station minders thought it was a minor blockage or something else on the rails. The longer they could go without drawing any attention at all, the better their chances of success were.

"Cuna," Remmy said on a private channel Jake could only hear because he was monitoring everything Remmy said. "When a superior officer tells you to jump and they're yelling, don't stop to ask how high or where, just find the nearest safe spot to jump to, and do it."

"Aye, Sir. Sorry, Sir," Cuna replied.

Jake highlighted the ladder leading up into the habitable

section of the station and both squads started heading in its direction. "There's no sign of security inside," Jake said to Remmy.

"I know. What do you think?"

"They have something waiting for us. I would rather have seen soldiers at this point."

"We didn't pick up support stations or tunnels leading to other buildings on the planet," Remmy said. "So the chances of there being barracks nearby, or a fighter base are slim."

Jake rushed up the ladder so he could reach the top and stick to the wall beside it. Just like in the schematics, the service hatch was big enough for them to crawl through in their armour, and it was an airlock. The doors had active control panels and were thin enough for them to blow through if they couldn't hack them. "When everyone's up and in position, hack in and see what kind of system access you can get from this panel," he ordered before climbing from the wall to the roof beside the hatch, and clinging upside down.

"I've just gotta say," Remmy said. "You definitely think in three dimensions."

"I've been sneaking around spaceships and stations for a long time," Jake said as he took a much closer look at the read-outs from his passive scanners. The detail got better as he got closer to whatever he was looking at, so he quietly crawled in the direction of the control room. There was half a metre of armour between him and the rearmost area of that space. They would have to use the hatch that would take them into the hallway between that and the cafeteria. He placed his hand against the heavy plating and watched as the minute vibrations in the metal from someone yelling between the two spaces inside allowed his passive scanner to map out finer details in the room. "Damn," he breathed as he noticed something familiar.

"What's up, Captain?" Remmy asked.

"Can you hack into the main computer system from that panel?" Jake asked.

"We have an access screen, but this door panel is air-gapped. No connection to the main computer. Finn says he can hotwire it in under five seconds though, so we'll get inside the station, no problem. Just say the word."

"Give me a minute to crawl back to you," Jake said. "I know what we're up against. This is going to be some seriously violent action. Get your guys ready to slag some frameworks. I see spawning alcoves."

TWENTY-FIVE

The Engine Of War

CALLUM WAS LEFT behind in one of the larger port waiting areas of the War Forge. He didn't mind, it was in a section where he could see one of the new Corvettes emerge from a main manufacturing line. The nose of the vessel had a savage look, with retro-thrusters and armoured launcher systems arranged to make the head of the ship look like a hateful grimace. Its dark hull gleamed, light passing over it like glass, but Alice knew it was the new intelligent plating, a coalescence of science from Freeground, the Lorander database, and earth technologies at work. The emergence was slow, that ship wouldn't be free of the station for two hours at least.

Alice walked through the station's halls with Gabe at her side. As the War Forge came closer to completion, more people were joining the crew. There would be a hundred thousand or more people working to crew and defend the mobile construction complex soon, most of them would still be in training. "I hear they've started work on building another manufacturing base, like the one in orbit around Tamber," Gabe said.

"It's half finished, it'll be public and working at the end of the week," Alice said.

"Know what it'll be making?"

"Housing units, planetary shield generators and there are five small item lines for shuttles, furniture, and all kinds of stuff."

"Yeah, my apartment was pretty sparsely furnished, not that I should complain. I've never had a place to myself before," Gabe said.

"Have you ever seen the small fabrication lines here?" Alice asked.

"No, actually. I've barely been on the War Forge. I took one combat test here in the Wild Room and had a briefing when I was told I was getting a Special Operations team."

All she'd really seen on the Wild Room was a little high-level news and that trainers already had it booked for weeks in advance. "How was the Wild Room?"

"I thought I was on a different planet, running through real bombed out buildings, dodging and fighting real combat bots in about a minute. My test scenario ended after I managed to get away from an Order Knight and his platoon of frameworks without firing a shot. If they found me I would have failed the scenario, and I've gotta say; for a while there I was just as scared as I would be if they were really there. I wasn't afraid to mess up my qualification, I was afraid for my life."

"I'll have to try it," Alice said. "When it isn't booked."

"I might join you just so I can see your reaction. It takes you way past anything simulated, there's something about experiencing something like that in your own skin, like you're tricking your brain from the outside instead of the inside like in a sim. Then again, I might pass. I was on stress meds for two days after my qualification. Still, can you find out if they're building a few more Wild Rooms?"

"Just in case you want in?" Alice asked with a smirk.

"Well, yeah," Gabe admitted. "Maybe we could program it for something other than a combat scenario. There are a lot of beautiful places to see in the Galaxy. I hear we could take a walk on one of the older Lorander worlds."

"Are you asking me out, Lieutenant?" Alice teased.

"Well, maybe on a double date," Gabe said without missing a beat. "I met someone at Mama Buu's the other night, he's a fashion designer. Kind of flamboyant for my taste, to be honest, but he's really funny, has a real knack for being entertaining. If you don't have anyone in mind, I'm sure he can set you up with someone. Let me guess; you're into tall, muscular types with a good soul. Strong and silent."

"I think I like people closer to my height, but I'm not sure." Her thoughts skipped right through her experience with Titus and on to Noah Lucas, the pilot known as Carnie. He was tall, thin, and he was expressive, quick to smirk, smile or scowl.

"You're thinking of someone," Gabe said, bumping her arm. "I sent you straight to a happy place, didn't I?"

"I've known you for, what? Five minutes?" Alice asked, chuckling, aware that she was blushing furiously. They stepped into a lift and were sent straight to an Overwatch Centre, one of the situation management areas in the massive station. "You won't get anything out of me, at least not without a few drinks first."

"I'll take you up on that. Drinks tonight, as soon as we're finished taking care of business."

"Sure," Alice said. "I might bring a couple people."

"Good, I'll definitely have a few people there." The lift opened out onto a large deck, where high ranking officers stood, interacting with holograms that were fuzzy to Alice and Gabe for the most part. Whatever they weren't specifically cleared to see was obscured to them, while the operators and officers could see what they were working on perfectly clearly.

"Over here," a young woman called from a doorway to their left. She was a short woman, with close-cropped hair. She was marked as a Major. "The Honour Guard needs another two days for shakedown and a turn through the refinement line for adjustments. That's another day. That's moving as quickly as we can. If this weren't the War Forge, you'd be looking at months instead of days," she said to Oz as Alice and Gabe entered the meeting room. There was a plain, wood grain oblong table with a dozen well-padded seats around it.

"All right, that's all the time you get. What about the Triton?" Oz asked.

"We've run into some issues with configuration on the restoration line. Some of the systems we're going to use to rebuild her have to be manually modified, then we'll have to calibrate them. Once that's finished, we'll be good to go. That is, unless you want to reinforce the hull, then we'll have to modify another fabrication line."

"No, just restore the Triton, please," Oz said. "We'll need it for inner solar system defence."

"All right, then eight days, Sir. At least," she replied.

"Eight days," Oz said. Alice remembered what he looked like when he was being serious, and this was different. He wasn't just serious; he looked as though his expression was darkened. There was no levity or mirth in the room. "Take ten. It's not just a ship anymore, it's a tribute. Dismissed."

"Yes, Admiral," replied the Major before retreating from the room, making sure to close the door behind her.

"Congratulations to you both," he said to Alice and Gabe. "I've looked your reports over, spoken to your commanding officer, and you're just what I need for a mission the fleet has no time or resources for. It's exactly what Special Operations was created for. I'd like you to have more experience and a better team behind you, but there's no time."

"We'll get it together, Admiral," Gabe said without mirth.

"If I didn't think you would, I wouldn't send you on this mission. In three days the Clever Dream will be completely rebuilt and tested. Lieutenant Valent will take possession then. You'll effectively be the youngest Captain in our fleet. You will have permission to recruit a small crew for your ship. Request anyone up to your rank, I'll make sure they're aboard in time. You will also have a squad like you did on your recent missions, since you will most likely have to go off ship. You're going to be off for three days starting now. I hope you look over your responsibilities and try to get your hands on as many good people as you can, if you can."

"Yes, Admiral," Alice said.

"Remember, your Special Operations Squad has to be made of the best you can find. The upcoming mission will lead you right behind enemy lines," Oz said. He turned to Gabe. "Lieutenant Vernor; you will join Alice on the Clever Dream. While you have equal rank with her as a Lieutenant, remember that it's her ship, she is the Captain. Off ship, you make your own decisions, but while you're aboard, her word is law."

"No problem," Gabe said. "I've read her file. She's more qualified to run the ship than I am."

"Your squad will be outfitted with heavy encounter armour. We've managed to put together enough qualified people for you to choose from. These suits aren't like the large, earth style mech types. Using Lorander technology and a few other new tricks, we've managed to cram all that power into a suit that is only a little larger than our regular armour. With the systems pack, your squad has the firepower of several hover tanks. Alice's squad will have similar upgraded armour, but with a lower size and mass so she can go where you can't with a better chance of being undetected. With all the tools we're providing you with, we expect you will be able to accomplish this capture and elimi-nate mission." Oz looked at Gabe for a long moment, then turned his unflinching, penetrating gaze on Alice. It was diffi-cult to stare back without looking away, she felt as though she was being decoded and read from cover to cover. "You are going to the planet Laceni in the Cefa System. We're still gathering intelligence from the refugees who escaped, but every indica-tion points to the three earth like planets there being turned into Order Of Eden bases and brood worlds. This is an unusual cooperative effort between the Order and a new kind of Edxian brood transportation fleet. We're not certain, but testimony from the refugees is telling us that most of the continents on each of the worlds are being used for Edxian broods, while a few are reserved for Order of Eden bases. The reason why we are seeing so many refugees is because a rebel element on Laceni was successful in severely sabotaging the Order of Eden fleet and setting a small antimatter bomb off inside of an Edxian mothership. Their leader and several of her followers are currently being held by Order of Eden Intelligence. They are waiting to be presented to Admiral Dron, who will be there in four days. We want to free Wanda Teller and as many of her cohorts as possible. She is the leader of the Waking Star, the rebel group responsible for freeing thousands of people from the Cefa system. We also want you to further frustrate the Order's efforts on Laceni by doing as much damage on your way off world as possible. Intelligence has requested that you capture one or more Edxian hatchlings or eggs, and any framework systems that you can including an Order Knight."

"We could stop by the Rainbow Star, pick up a unicorn and a luck dragon on our way back if they like, too," Gabe said. "Or would that be too much?"

Alice lowered her head in an effort to be serious. It wasn't difficult in a room that felt as airless as that meeting space.

Admiral McPatrick was unaffected by the remark. "I know, they're asking for the stars after begging for the moon but getting our hands on current generation framework technology and a sample of Edxian biology could be helpful. If I were you, I'd focus on the primary mission; saving the rebels, while finding a way to accomplish the rest as an afterthought. I would like to discuss something with you as a friend before you go, Alice, and you should hear this too, Lieutenant Vernor."

"Gabe, I'd love it if you called me Gabe, Sir," he said in a rush.

"All right, Gabe," Oz said with a nod. "There's something in your report, Alice. When you spoke to the Order Officer, you seemed to be under the impression that self-sacrifice wasn't folded into the Order philosophy."

"That's right." After a moment she remembered something that nearly stunned her to silence. "There are exceptions though," she added. "The Warlord."

"Right," Oz said. "Order Knights boarded and took the Warlord, then set off the antimatter stores there. They had to know that there wouldn't be much collateral damage, any ship at risk was moving out of the effective range of the explosion. They did it to demoralize our people."

"So they will take themselves out if they see it'll do real damage," Gabe said.

"Yes, but we've only seen that behaviour in Knights. They seem to be the most dedicated members of the Order, we think that's at the core of how they earn their way into the position. I just wanted to remind you that the Order really will do anything they can to kill you and keep the Clever Dream's hull as a trophy to rally around."

Alice recalled how thrilled Pope was when he discovered she was a Valent. If she were captured, they wouldn't execute her for a long time if at all. They'd keep her alive, make sure everyone saw that she was their property and use her however they could to bolster the morale of their people. "I understand," she said. Gabe was being sent because she couldn't afford to put herself in a position where capture was likely, and he was probably a much better commander on the ground, too.

"We'll work on the details of your mission and build an intelligence packet for you as we gather more information, but that's all for now," Admiral McPatrick said. "I wish I could give you more time, but I'm needed aboard the Exile. There's a captured Geist there in telepathic isolation."

"Sorry, Admiral, but how does that work?" Gabe asked.

"The Geist is exposed to powerful signals within a certain range, at a short distance - a couple metres - that interfere with its telepathic abilities. I spent so much time connected to my - the Geist aboard the Triton - that I can hear the signal from here, about a hundred kilometres away. If I seem stiff, that's why. It's like a loud, off-key tone between your ears."

"Good luck," Alice said.

"Don't worry, it's a young Geist," Oz said. "With my training, I'll know what it does by the end of the day."

TWENTY-SIX

Management

SEVEN SOLDIERS, Jake included, had the responsibility of rushing the control room and killing everyone inside. The one in the cafeteria would be subdued just in case they needed one alive for biometric security. If it was the wrong one, and they were locked out of the system, they would find another way. There was always another way to get access as long as they had direct contact with the hardware.

The inner airlock popped open, Remmy led the way through, silently opening it and laying the access door down flat. When the door touched the floor Remmy leapt out and hit the deck running, Jake was right behind him.

The six soldiers assigned to Jake's kill team leapt out of the airlock door in the deck and struggled to keep up. Their cloaking systems weren't a sure thing in that space. The crew would feel a rush of cold air with both airlock doors open, so they'd know something was off. There would be no alarms from the airlock doors. Finn slagged the wireless transmitters that would trigger them.

Jake made it down the hall and into the middle of the control room in seconds. He stopped, watching for any sign that the technicians noticed him. There were no alerts on the security panel, and they spoke casually. "Why is your sister so intent on getting you back to Thun? Isn't she moving in a month?" asked one of them around a mouth full of onion puffs. "You'd just go in time to move again."

The officer, wearing a dark green Order uniform and pacing the floor slowly shook his head. "She wants me to watch the kids while her and the hubby load all their crap into a shuttle and get it to the station. I keep telling her that I'm on my way up. If I stop to take time off from pushing you guys to excellence, I'll be stuck on this frozen rock forever. I need to get to the front lines, get some K's and C's when the fleet hits Rega Gain. I want to be sitting on the beach on Tamber when it's all over, watching their stupid little bubble buildings burn."

"Next, you'll tell me you're pushing for Knighthood," his onion-puff popping subordinate said.

"Why not? I'll be guaranteed action then."

All six of Jake's kill team were inside. He pointed to the officer then himself. That one was his. The rest of his team chose their targets. Two men for every crewman inside. He saw that Remmy was in position in the cafeteria, all six of his people surrounding one guy eating his lunch with Remmy in the middle.

"Go," Jake said. He punched the officer in the throat hard enough to silence him and bound his arms to his sides with a flexible, stretchy metal strip from his bounty hunter days. He snapped another one around his ankles and grabbed him by the throat. Everyone else in the control room was killed, murdered was more like it. Each one was obliterated by a burst of rifle rounds from two of his soldiers. No one had a chance to touch a button, and Jake leaned to the control panel with the Officer's head held by the hair.

The alarm was about to go off, detecting rounds fired in the control room. Jake pushed his face onto the panel, satisfying the biometric requirement for deactivating the alarm. He put the muzzle of his sidearm to the Officer's head and deactivated his cloaking system. "Say the password. Say it now."

The Officer's eyes went wide at the sight of Jake's now familiar armour and death's head. A tear rolled from his eye. "Glory for the Order," the Officer rasped.

Jake's tactical display blinked red. "I was going to grant you a merciful death," Jake said. "You just changed my plan." He threw the Officer over his shoulder and affixed him to the shoulder of his suit so he would stay there. The strength augmentation in his armour made sure his weight made no difference to him. He pointed to a framework spawn alcove to his left. "You three slag that one," he ordered. Three soldiers turned their weapons on it, bursting through the door so the forming flesh and skin of a framework soldier inside was visible, it was almost animated, ready to pick up its rifle and start fighting.

"You three, take that one apart!" Jake ordered, pointing to the alcove on the opposite side of the room. A framework was already stepping out, about to take aim at the nearest soldier, a woman named Niya who was Alice's height. She rolled out of the way and behind a console. The other two soldiers peppered it with rounds, and Jake could see another framework soldier forming in the alcove behind it. "Make sure those things are down to slag, there are twelve more on this level.

Jake started running for the hallway. "Everyone in the control room," he announced. "Liara, Remmy, get ready to crack a computer system on alert."

"Liara's got a master system key that should work," Remmy said. "We're working on two spawning alcoves."

Jake tossed an electromagnetic pulse grenade through the legs of a framework, bouncing it into the alcove behind it in the hallway. Two shots struck Jake's armour, the third nearly burned through his captive's thigh. His armour was fine, that's what was most important to him. He let the Officer loose and returned fire.

The first framework's head burst open as a barrage of charged shots from his sidearm sizzled through the air. The electromagnetic grenade lit up the inside of the spawning alcove for an instant, and Jake unslung his rifle to take out the emerging framework soldier. The reserves who were waiting at the hatch rushed behind him towards the control room. The framework solder went down after thirty rounds, or a few seconds, and Jake looked down at the Officer screaming on the ground. "Looks like Order Officers don't make good armour after all," he said. "We're going in there, your control room. We left the door open down the hall so you can get some air, but you'll probably freeze to death if you don't close it soon. It's minus sixty degrees outside."

"Untie my hands, at least!" he wailed.

"I don't think so," Jake said. "How's cooperation looking?"

"You'll just kill me!"

"I'll be nice, promise." Jake's tactical system told him that there were two framework soldiers coming down the hall opposite the control room. He was out of time.

"I got the security key in," Liara said. "The alert is cancelled and the base just sent a signal to the hyper transmitter in orbit that will tell any passing ships and command that the station just passed a drill with flying colours."

"Too late," Jake said. He felt for the Officer at his feet, but only a little. He was a climber, at least according to what he was saying, and he planned on killing non-Order of Eden followers to make sure he kept rising. "Guess you won't be getting any time on the beach, just a deep freeze." Jake said as he tossed three grenades programmed to his right glove down the hall. "What happens if there's another explosion in the base? Will it set the alarms off again?"

"No, I've set security monitoring to manual," Liara replied in his ear.

Jake watched the Order frameworks rushing towards him from around the corner and waited until they were in range before setting the cloaked grenades off. They burst with shrapnel, localized super-heated plasma and an electromagnetic flare that left no evidence of them behind. They also eliminated the walls to either side, the ceiling and took a chunk of the deck out. "Maybe I'll only use two next time."

"You're dead!" the Officer called up from the floor as he ran past them towards the control room. "They'll catch you and I only wish I could watch your public execution."

"I'll tell your sister you said 'hi' when we raid her neighborhood," Jake called over his shoulder.

Remmy and his six were right behind him when he got to the control room. "I see three spawning alcoves active on the main level, there are more above," Jake said. "Do you see any way to access them?"

"We've shut them down, but there's no way to control the frameworks that are already coming," Liara said.

"Are the base defences shut down?" Jake asked.

"Yes, Sir," Liara said.

"All right, focus on downloading everything you can from the strategic database and get our artificial intelligence ready to go. I can't wait to see how well Mary does in the wild. Oh, and remember: I get to activate her."

"Yes, Sir," Liara said. "There are five order soldiers coming."

"Don't worry, we'll take care of them." Jake looked to Remmy and nodded. He immediately took his squad of thirteen with him down the hall at a run to set up their defence. "Finn, get the cutter on this window. We may need a new door."

Finn and two soldiers pulled a device from his back and affixed it to the transparent steel window. It activated with a flash of light, starting to cut through. "It'll be about a minute," Finn said.

Jake hooked into the communications terminal. "Ronin, you out there?"

There was a moment's pause, then Minh-Chu's voice came through. "Ready to go."

"We're going to need a pickup in one minute or as fast as you can come down. There are alcoves loaded with frameworks down here."

"On my way, Horus," Minh-Chu replied.

"Everyone turn your scanners on to active and turn your comm systems back on to normal mode." He rushed down the hall so he could get a laser link with one of Remmy's squad, who were firing at the outnumbered frameworks, reducing them to piles of scorched metal, and passed the same order to them.

"Aye, Captain," Remmy replied.

He and Jake saw it at the same time thanks to their scanners actively searching for details around them. There were several squads of frameworks approaching from beneath the station, they were using the rail cars. "See that?" Jake said, highlighting them in his tactical display.

"Oh yeah, about a hundred of them coming fast," Remmy confirmed. "Retreat?"

At the same time that Remmy asked the question, Jake gave the order; "Retreat to the control room. We seal the security door."

Jake retreated at a run, Remmy and his squad less than ten seconds behind. "I knew this would be an exciting trip," Remmy chuckled.

"Ronin," Jake said. "How far out?"

"We're burning atmosphere, about forty seconds."

"Good, you got a torpedo or two on that boat?"

"I have two loaded just in case you wanted them," Minh-Chu replied.

"All right, we're going to need them," Jake said.

"Jake," Stephanie addressed from the Revenge. "We have a problem."

"What?"

"Nine destroyers in groups of three and three carriers with their escorts just emerged from wormholes."

Jake knew each carrier had an escort of at least three destroyers, some of them could be corvettes if they were strapped for ships. That brought the total ships to twenty one, and that was if they didn't launch fighters. "Are the carriers launching?"

"They spotted the Hoarta, and yes they are launching fighters."

"Did the Hoarta get their supplies?"

"Yes, and then some," Stephanie replied.

Jake thought for a moment. "The Revenge?"

"We were just spotted," Stephanie said. "Six destroyers coming at us from your direction."

"Run," Jake said. "Your jump drive works again, make a

wormhole and start jumping towards home. Don't stop for anything."

"Jake," Stephanie said. "Good hunting. We're charting a course."

"Thought I'd have to argue with you for a moment there," he said.

"You and the hard asses you brought with you will be so much trouble behind enemy lines, they'll offer you an escort home before you're done. Just get home so I don't have to explain to Ayan why you're not on board."

"See you in-system," Jake said.

The cutter finished getting through the window and the transparent metal plate crashed to the deck. Jake could see the Pursuer decelerating towards them through the hole. He moved to the planetary defence panel and looked at the scanners. He checked to see if he had control of the long range cannons and grinned. "How's it coming, Liara?"

"We have a lot of local data and everything we need to access the entire Order of Eden network. I'm ready to launch Mary."

"Get her ready," Jake said. "I'm going to have some fun." He targeted the carrier moving into orbit and the three destroyers flanking it then set the massive planet to space cannons around the station to automatically fire at them. They began to warm up. As a last touch he set the anti-fighter countermeasures to activate in three minutes. If those weapons survived, they'd keep firing until someone took them out, and each had backup generators.

"I love your brain," Remmy said, looking over his shoulder.

A gangway extended from the side of the Pursuer. "Finn, lead them out of here," Jake said.

Several blasts against the heavy control room door

confirmed that the framework soldiers had arrived. "Time to leave, Captain," Remmy said.

Jake looked to Liara, who was standing up, leaving the main secure console. "Is she ready?"

"Yes, Sir," she said. "That button and Mary will transmit to every hyper transmitter connected. Pretty much all of them in two sectors."

Jake sighed and executed the command. He watched for the one second it took for her to upload to the hyper transmitter, and then for a few more seconds as the log told him that it was already sending her to hundreds of other hyper transmitters. To his delight, the destroyers and carriers were already downloading her, where she was coming to life, copying herself to all their systems and beginning her digital slashing and burning campaign. "I hope they understand it's only fair," he said. "One virus for another."

"Hurry up!" Ronin said over the communicator.

The planetary weapons fired, sending white-yellow bursts of light into the sky. "This is not a good day for the Order," Remmy chuckled.

They rushed from the control room, boarding the Pursuer and were moving away from the station as framework soldiers broke through the armoured control room door. "Do you think Mary had enough time to spread?" he asked Liara over a private channel.

"Yes, Sir. She transmitted to a hundred ninety hyper transmitter nodes before we were out of the command room. She'll be everywhere in a few days."

"Ronin, target the control room of that station with a torpedo and blast it. If you can hit the base too, that'll be good. The main warehouse and god knows what else is under the station."

"Aye, aye," Ronin said.

The Pursuer thrust away from the station at great speed, then swept around and launched both its torpedoes before returning to a course that would take it out of the atmosphere as far from the enemy ships as possible. Jake watched through a connection to the rear ship sensors as the control room was hit directly, reduced to a yawning hole in the side of the structure. The other torpedo hit too much armour to do any damage to what was beneath, but the fireball was impressive.

"Congratulations, everyone," Jake said. "The Order will feel this strike for months."

TWENTY-SEVEN

A High Refuge

THE CITY in the Haven Shore jungle was expanding quickly, providing a retreat for soldiers and their families. Paths with safety rail systems that looked like wood but had sophisticated catcher systems built in just in case someone fell over the side wound around trunks and housing structures. Some of the new housing units looked like they were grown in place, with fake bark that was indistinguishable from the trees they hung beside.

Many others had pearlescent surfaces, and rounded shapes as though some tall wave left seashells in the branches. The wild life was quieter than usual, with small monkeys that hooted and barked at each other observing a new pattern of day and night. The powerful protective shield that covered all of Haven Shore had gone into a new phase, taking full control of weather as well as the day and night cycle. The news said that the wild life would adjust quickly, within a few days, especially since they were descended from breeds designed to be a part of a completely terraformed planet.

The whistling of birds was distant and more sparse than she remembered too, but that only got momentary notice. Her thoughts still drifted to Tulsa Beck, and the encounter she just concluded with the Private. She managed to find a quiet corner near the squad rooms, where a few bunks and a table with four chairs had been installed off the books. There were still compartments like that throughout the fleet, where there were plans to build something, to finish a feature in that space, but no one got around to it. Sneaky crewmembers made their own use of the space in the meantime, and the spot they were in was serving as a kind of ready room for soldiers who were currently on patrol or answering a call.

There were already animated posters on the wall celebrating fighter squadrons with dire logo work - hungry looking wolves and savage birds in their middle - and a couple smaller calendar girl and boy pieces in the bunks. Alice had already accepted how important that stuff could be sometimes, it was superficial comfort, but comfort nonetheless; a pleasant smiling face from a beach or other lovely place that would never judge or change depending on how bad things got.

One looping poster was of her mother in white, celebrating her as the Queen of the Rega Gain System. She was in a flowing gown that Alice was sure Ayan never wore, surrounded by light that danced around her upturned face. It was made before the Rega Gain System was renamed as the Haven System, and most likely before Ayan had much of a chance to repeatedly tell everyone that she didn't want to be a Queen.

It was that image that hung behind Tulsa Beck by chance, as Alice told her in no uncertain terms that she couldn't be on her Special Operations team, that the refusal would most likely put her out of the unit permanently, she wouldn't be able to switch to another team. She was kind about it, telling Tulsa; "You're going to find a good place in this fleet." She touched the woman's hand. Tulsa saw it as an invitation to grab on with both of hers, as though she was hanging on for dear life as the tears came.

"I can toughen up, make sure that I don't lose it again," Tulsa pleaded.

"You were right there beside me when we had to save those kids," Alice said. "I'm proud of how quick and careful you were, that's in my report. Your training and your abilities as a soldier aren't in doubt, but your high empathy and your inability to compartmentalize quickly enough cause a problem for you in SOCU. You're still thinking about all those kids, and the people who sacrificed for them."

Tulsa was fully in tears then but nodded. "I can't forget them. I know I'll be on stress management meds by tonight, but I'd rather not. I don't want to let go of it, I don't want that impact to fade. That kind of sacrifice should be remembered by someone who will feel how important it was, how much was lost."

"Most of us will never forget. We'll tell that story when it's time to share what we know about sacrifice, about the finer examples of heroism." Alice took a breath and wiped a tear from her eye. "Yawen has already set you up with someone to talk to in Fleet Support. If you don't want the medication, then they'll talk you through it. Until then, I think we've gotten very lucky. We've found someone who was able to train as a soldier, has some combat experience going back before you signed up, and still has all her empathy intact. There are places where you could be very helpful."

"Just not your squad," Tulsa said. "They're going to dump me in some kind of stats or scan analysis unit."

"I doubt it," Alice said, knowing that someone with high empathy and Tulsa's capacity for learning was really needed. "There's a new negotiation unit starting training, openings in intelligence, and other places where you could rise quickly if you wanted to become part of the training staff. I'll give you an honest recommendation that could take you to the right place."

"I think I want to help trainees," Tulsa said, nodding.

"I know a few people. You won't be off duty for long," Alice said. "That's if you don't mind more training, possibly shadowing a few trainers and therapists for a while."

She nodded again. "I'd love to be a part of the academy."

"All right, I'll put the suggestion out there, make my recommendations. Fleet could put you elsewhere, they'll know where you can best serve, so keep an open mind, all right?"

"I will, thank you Lieutenant."

Nearly an hour later, Alice was walking to her home from a landing pad a kilometre away from her house, which had its own pad, but she wanted to stroll. Heavy armour still surrounded her, and she caught the occasional glance from people in light, casual clothes as she passed. The weather was sunny and calm, but inside her head there was a storm that rained Tulsa's tears from the dark clouds that seemed to hang over Oz. She wished she could remember more of her previous life, when she knew him at least a little better. He was more than troubled; there was a visible emotional wound from losing Haus Geist. She could only suppose that he spent a lot of time mentally linked with the creature that served as the living mind behind the Triton, and that had to have developed into a deep relationship that only Oz could understand.

In her own way, Alice could relate. Not to having a mental

link with something, her memories of mental communication with Lewis were sparse and faint, but she knew what it was like to have an experience that few people could relate to. Converted from an artificial intelligence program to a human being, then transmitted into a framework only to be remade again. Her clearest memories started when she became a framework. Where other people had childhood and adolescent memories, she had nothing at all. While most people her age already knew what they liked most, she had a nearly blank slate. Socially, she felt more and more out of her depth, prone to avoiding encounters with new people unless they fit into a ranking system that told her who was and wasn't important. On one hand, her training took quickly, and she seemed well suited to it, but on the other she felt as though she lost something that made her feel more at ease around new people during the last change. Who else could relate to that? Who could she talk to who had gone through the same thing?

"Hello?" said a man of average height with well-kept dark hair and a clean, black and white vacsuit. He was smiling at her meekly, the face of a kindly gentleman. "Alice?"

She emerged from her own thoughts and looked at him more directly. "Yes?"

"Alice, it's me, Theodore," he said, pointing to himself and smiling. "I suppose you wouldn't recognize me with my outer appearance restored."

Then she recognized the voice. "Wow, they put you back together in a hurry. You look great."

"He said he'd never worked on a model as high profile as me. There were a lot of people from Intelligence and the Government around when I woke up after a few deep repairs." He pulled a card from his pocket as though it was made of the purest platinum. "They gave me this."

Alice had never seen an actual citizen card before, she knew she had one coming, but it wasn't something she needed, she was listed in the database. The citizen card served as a whole holographic and two dimensional interface with enough memory for several lifetimes, but the same could be said for any comm unit. She took it carefully and saw that the static side of the card had a picture of Theodore, several micro icons that her comm unit read and the declaration by all branches of government that he was a verified level fourteen being with full sentience, independence and citizenship with the Haven Government. "Congratulations," Alice said. "I couldn't imagine it happening to a better person."

He took the card back and slipped it into a slot in the side of his vacsuit. To anyone watching, it would look like a normal human man just put it right through his suit, his ribs and into his side without so much as a twitch. Other than that, he really looked absolutely human. "Thank you," he replied. "Were you going home? Can I go with you?"

"Sure," Alice said. "Is everything okay?"

Theo looked anxious despite his visible happiness. "I'm not used to people looking at me like this. Everyone smiles when I pass by."

"You look happy," Alice said. "And very human, gentlemanly, I'd say."

"I'm so used to looking battered and burned, to everyone knowing I'm an android," he said. "This is how people react to you?"

"Sometimes, when I'm feeling content and letting it show, I guess. People will smile back at you if you look happy."

"I am very happy," he said to a young man, grinning enthusiastically.

"Whoa," he said, stepping away and passing them in a hurry.

"Too much," Alice said with a quiet chuckle. "Just like you were before, if you still feel the same way. I'm surprised you don't know more about being social."

"Only a few people took an interest in mentoring me in the office complex, and there was a little memory damage. My personality is intact though."

"That's a relief," Alice said as the doorway to her home opened. It was still sparsely furnished, with two half-circle sofas in the middle of the living room. Past it was a broad transparent wall that looked through the trees onto the ocean. She ordered her armour to retract into her heavy jacket and combat boots and left them by the door. "Gimmie two minutes," she said.

"I'll sit and review the news," he said, moving to the sofa. "Do you mind if I watch like normal people? I still don't have any wireless technology installed. I don't think I want it."

"Go ahead, it's one of the newer Ultra Twenty Eight Models," Alice said as she walked into her room, stripping her uniform off.

"You bought a robot?"

"I mean the entertainment system," she replied. She watched Theo sit down on the sofa with his back facing her through the aquarium that spanned the wall separating the rooms. "Roomie, give Theo rights to everything in the apartment except my personal storage." Her personal storage consisted of three drawers in her bedroom, a weapons vault that slid under her bed and a bathroom cupboard.

"Are you sure?" Roomie asked.

"Of course I'm sure," she replied. "Would I have gone to the trouble of telling you to do it if I weren't sure?"

"This will give him entry rights and control over all the

systems in your home. It is customary to get secondary confirmation. Are you sure?"

"Just do it and set a reminder for me to go shopping for a new household minder program for tomorrow. I'm replacing you, Roomie, and it's personal," Alice said.

"Permissions changed and reminder set. Would you like to answer a few questions that may help me improve my performance?"

"No,' she said, stepping into the shower. "Privacy mode, leave me alone, Roomie."

"Yes, Alice."

"You just always need the last word, don't you?"

The rush of water from the jets above and around her drowned out Roomie's response. Alice stood there for several minutes, imagining that her worries and tension were draining away with the hot water. When she emerged in a pair of shorts and a loose top Theo was watching a report about the sentient laws.

A pair of smiling people - one woman with well styled blonde hair, and a counterpart who looked attractive but androgynous - accepted citizenship cards from Pamela Grey, the Minister of Public Welfare. She looked as pleased as the pair receiving their cards, but much more weary. "Only nineteen artificial intelligences qualified for permanent citizenship and reclassification as sentient beings under the new laws. According to the Minister of Defence, Carl Anderson, the requirements are so restrictive because the new law takes history into account," the announcer said.

An image of Alice's grandfather, Carl Anderson appeared. He was in his Haven Fleet uniform, looking not a day over forty thanks to a rollback he recently completed. "The Haven Government is in a unique position. We have access to centuries of history that we can easily examine when we need guidance in governing. In this case, many societies have made mistakes when embracing mechanical sentients as citizens, so we are being cautious."

"Does the test demand that artificial intelligences are indistinguishable from humans?" asked someone at the conference who was out of sight.

"This isn't the Fiona Mann test," Carl replied. "Artificial intelligences that qualify as sentient beings that can function at the levels our test demand experience life and evolve in a familiar but not in a necessarily human way. The test for sentience in mechanical forms recognizes an important fact: artificial intelligences don't have to think like us to qualify. My Issyrian colleagues don't think like I do, but I'm as sentient as they are and vis-a-vis. We live in a galaxy of incredible diversity, and that's recognized here. The test is accompanied by complete documentation, you can consult that if you need to know more."

"Is it true that you stopped the declaration of a warship artificial intelligence as a sentient being today? My sources tell me that the ship belongs to your granddaughter, is that true?"

"That artificial intelligence was a unique case," Carl replied. "The name of the warship is classified. With the exception of our courageous volunteers," he gestured towards the pair of androids who publicly accepted their citizenship cards, "All the artificial intelligences who were declared sentient this week will remain anonymous. Applicants who were denied are treated the same way. They have a right to privacy."

The announcer, a well-kept gentleman with startlingly white teeth appeared in the middle of the living room, at least twice as large as he would be in person. Theo turned the playback off. "They said they rushed this because I was found. It was an opportunity. I thought about it; I am a citizen today because they wanted to draw attention from something else, most likely."

Alice was surprised at the realistic and pessimistic conclusion Theodore made, but it made perfect sense. She wondered how much she'd see in the news about the new refugees, or the rescue actions she participated in. "Well, it worked out well for you. With the way Haven is going, it would have happened eventually. So, better sooner rather than later."

"I suppose," Theo said. "After I got my citizenship card I went to Alberton's. The people there were nice. I met the owner too, he's very personable. I told him I just arrived in Haven Shore and didn't know what to do."

"What did he say?" Alice asked, sitting cross-legged at the end of one of the sofas.

"We talked for a while. I'm not qualified as a waiter but could learn quickly enough. I'm amazed that he has humans doing that, I've never seen it before, but the patrons love it. While he was away for a minute, taking care of a problem with a drinking glass shortage, I greeted several of his patrons as they entered. It was nothing special, or so I thought, simply telling them; 'Welcome to Alberton's,' and then who was on stage, and which comedians and other acts were to follow. I was only repeating what the host had announced and what I saw on the board earlier. Then I passed them to their waiter or waitress. The owner, Luke said I could be a Host. He offered me a job before he knew I was an android. I told him I was one, and then he remembered Noah, or Carnie as he knew him, mention me a few times. He offered me the job again, said I would have to wear something called a tuxedo to do it though. I hope it's not something garish."

"Roomie, show us what Theodore would look like in a tuxedo," Alice requested, and the image appeared in the middle of the room. She whistled appreciatively. "You make that look good. I've never seen one before, so it must be old fashioned, but it works for you."

He stared at it for a moment, then cocked his head. "A job where I am to look good and be kind to people."

Alice let him stare in silence, she knew there was something going on. There was more for him to ponder than he was sharing. "It seems like a good job, but you don't have to rush if you want to think about it. I have room here, I can even have them fabricate another bedroom and deliver it this week."

"I would like that," Theo said. He turned to her. "I think I would like to work there, but part time. It doesn't feel like enough. While doing that job I would only be using one point four percent of one processing cluster and not enough memory worth mentioning. I have one thousand and twenty four processing clusters, by the way. There must be a way to better utilize them."

"Well, you could calculate or analyze something while you work, but think about how much you'd learn about socializing. I could use a few nights there myself. As a customer though, I can't imagine myself in a tuxedo." She looked again. "Well, maybe I could, but I don't think he'd want me as a host."

"I will contact Luke Alberton when his establishment opens for business tomorrow afternoon," Theo said. "For now, what would you like to eat?"

"Can you cook?" Alice asked.

"Your friend gave me several software upgrades, including new advanced food preparation and gourmet programs. I'd love to try them, and your gardening systems have ripe vegetables, a lot of mature fish and other ingredients available."

"Surprise me?" Alice asked. "Do you mind if I invite Yawen and a couple people from the squad over for dinner?"

"It's your home, and I would be happy to cook for them. Only, can we try an experiment?"

"Sure, but nothing spicy," Alice said. "Well, not too spicy."

"I mean, can we not tell them that I'm an android? I would like to see if they can tell on their own. I'll even pretend to eat."

"Sure, just don't be too disappointed if they find out early. Some of these people have been trained to notice things like that."

"All right," Theo said, starting for the kitchen. He stopped half way there and turned. "Alice, are you happy I'm here? I am capable of finding another place somewhere. I was offered temporary lodgings."

"I am, Theo. I'd be disappointed if you wanted to stay anywhere else."

TWENTY-EIGHT

Home and Duty

THE RAIDERS and crew had quieted aboard the Pursuer III. Jake remained in the lower deck, near a service hatch that led into the hall behind the cockpit. They were the volunteers who kept their suits sealed to prevent wear and tear on the ship's life support system. There were twenty of them, more than necessary, but Jake didn't see the harm in letting more people than they needed feel like they were chipping in.

Simple plans had been made. They would make a few short jumps between systems where the Order's presence was light. This was to keep the stress on the wormhole system down and to give it a test. After the last adventure the Pursuer went on, it along with a few other systems they had spare parts for had been replaced, but the opportunity to make sure it was reliable hadn't come up. They'd just jumped out of a solar system that could barely qualify as one. With only three stony planets and a dwarf star, there quite literally wasn't much to see. On the brighter side, their scanners did a fresh, cursory sweep before they moved on and didn't detect a single Order of Eden vessel.

The next jump would only last an hour. He took Minh-Chu's advice; to use the time to relax and refocus his mind. He was still running at raid speed, and it made minutes feel like hours. He looked at the last update he had from Alice. It wasn't the first time he'd seen it. "Just a quick one this time, Dad," she said, stepping away from the recorder so he could see her Academy uniform. "I'm in the Apex Program! Iruuk's recording."

"Hello, Captain Valent!" he said, turning the recorder on himself at close range. His pinkish-brown nose took up most of the frame, blue eyes and fur filling the rest. "She can't wait for you to get home."

"Over here, Fur-Face," Alice said.

"Right, sorry." He pointed the recorder back at Alice.

"Wish I could tell you where I am, but I've been sworn to secrecy. The first round of testing is back, and we're both at the top. I'm also taking care of a few cadets who aren't in the program, and they're lower maintenance than I thought. The trainers are happy to see me join them during physical training though, which I do as much as I can since I'm still getting into shape. I see why you were rebuilt with muscle piled onto muscle: I'm having trouble matching the strength and endurance I had as a framework, but I'm getting closer. Anyway, I hope you're all right out there. People are still talking about the Revenge even here where we don't have much time to do anything but burn through qualifiers. Wow, I said this was a quick update, but I'm going on. I hope you get back soon, I have to get to the simulation course, we're doing a competitive maze today. Miss you." Her image faded, and he closed his eyes.

The memories of Samson days, when he didn't know who he was, but knew he had a daughter who had to leave him behind seemed fresh. That sensation of longing, of knowing that he was missing something important hung over him. "She's doing well," he said to himself. "Tucked into the Rega Gain System, safe as houses."

He replaced the image of her high qualification scores with the last recording from Ayan. It was a habit of hers to record more than once then send them as a batch. Her black and gold uniform came into view, and even though it wasn't his first time seeing that either, he still appreciated that the recording started with a full-length shot. Jake was sure she did it on purpose - her curly red hair was loose and the top of her uniform was open further down than she would allow while she was on duty - and he'd make sure he thanked her later. "Hey, love," she said. "Just checking in to tell you that things are going well here. I wanted to send my next message to you from home, but I've slept at work in the quarters they have here for the last two nights. This is going out on the new network we're building, so I'm hoping it gets to you soon, wherever you are. The Lorander advisors are amazed by my work on the dimension drive and they never stop asking questions, which I don't mind. It's nice to teach them something for a change. I'm happy to admit that all work stops when I find myself thinking of you." A chime from her command and control unit followed by an intentionally garbled message interrupted her. "I'm due for an inspection on one of the new starships. I'm working on an advanced design with Lorander for your next command. I can't go into details, but we're calling it the Merciless. I can't wait to show you the progress. Actually, I can't wait for you to get back. Even though I know my comm will tell me the moment there's news about you, I still check your status several times a day. If anticipation builds a happy return, then I have a big one waiting for you."

The next recording started with her looking weary and a little frustrated. Her hair was in a bun, and she was at her desk. "How a whole group of designers and engineers can screw up an entire line of corvettes, I don't know, but Jake, you would start shooting people if you were part of the team. They ignored the Lorander design helper software, the advisors, and a few fundamental starship design rules. I've already seen what the Lorander Advisors propose, and I'm putting it through a team I assembled myself this morning. We're half way through reviewing it, made a few small revisions, and with luck and the help of the Lorander software, we'll be done shortly after midnight. Thank God for the Lorander advisors. They knew where the team designing the new corvettes while I was away were going wrong and made sure a better alternative was waiting. With the new technology we learned about from the dimension drive, and the experience I had on the Revenge, the new ships will be amazing, but the first one has to be in production by the end of tomorrow." She let her head down on the desk, her cheek planted on the slick grey surface. "Then I'm going to sleep. I have to admit: firing nine designers and three engineers did make me feel a bit better. They weren't fired because they were inept - though some of them were - but because they ignored everyone who knew better. I'm taking my own advice, using every Lorander advisor, every expert with more experience than I have, every bright mind with training and piece of software we have." Ayan sighed and let her eyes close for a moment. "Now, I have to get back to them. They're all working in what I've started calling; 'The Asylum,' which is just a big open room with holograms of every part of the ship. I'll make sure the Merciless isn't the first off the line. We expect the prototype to be one half bugs and the other half rough edges, so it'll probably end up getting scanned, tested, studied then scrapped. Wish me luck, I hope you're doing well out there."

The final message in her transmission started then. It was his favourite. The lights were down, she was in bed with the covers mostly drawn up and the view was close, as if he was right beside her. "Finally got some sleep. Our prototype is being manufactured, early testing shows that it's a keeper after all. The new team is amazing. I woke up way too early, had a dream you were back. I won't tell you the rest, could be a little early in our relationship for that." She hesitated, chewed her bottom lip a little, something he'd never seen her do. "'Kay, can't dangle something like that and not tell you. We were pregnant, early days, but there was so much happiness around us. That's a lot, I know, but I'm missing you all the time these days, if I'm being honest. My dreams are filling in maybe. I love you, Jake, can't wait to continue us. Miss you, wish you were here." She yawned, putting a hand in front of her gaping mouth. "Gonna get more sleep. Sweet dreams."

Yes, that was definitely his favourite. He left it on that last second, where she puckered a kiss for him as the recording ended. The thought of having children hadn't really occurred to him since he got back together with her, but there was no reason why they couldn't. The idea didn't frighten him, even though he knew he should at least be nervous.

His only experiences were with Alice, and he felt like he'd put her under the care of others while she was most vulnerable. She was at the Academy, practically full grown, sure, but that wasn't a decision he made either. The fact that the little responsibility he had was shirked for duty with the Fleet was central to his thinking when he imagined Ayan having to take care of whoever they brought into the world. He didn't think it was fair for either one of them to have to stay behind, but he had a feeling that she would volunteer, especially since she already took a post that required her presence in the Haven Solar System anyway. Was that a way for her to start building a home for herself, and by extension; him?

Whether it was the muting of emotions he suffered while he was a framework, or simply the situation he was in, or both, he'd never felt the strong pull of duty versus family before. There was so much to miss with Alice, and she was an adult - young, yes, but an adult - he couldn't imagine how much he'd miss out on with a baby. Even still, the implication that Ayan wanted to have children with him made him yearn for home even more. A nervous tic made him occasionally doubt that she'd wait for him, but he cursed at it, called it paranoia.

"Captain Valent," Carnie called down the access crawl-space. "You should see this."

Jake made the climb up the service hatch, closing the doors behind him and emerged behind the cockpit. A rear seat waited. He deactivated his helmet and sat down. "How do things look?"

"We took a chance and scanned the emergence point," Minh-Chu said, bringing up an image of three Order of Eden single seat fighters. "There are patrols. It's going to be rough."

Finn joined them, retracting his helmet. Liara took the last seat in the cockpit - like bridge. "I'm here, what's up?"

"Patrols," Jake said. "Most likely a carrier near our next emergence point. How are our shields?"

"Great, everything's great. Any sign of warped gravity?"

"None yet, so there might not be an interdictor in the area," Carnie answered.

"So, do we keep scanning?" Minh-Chu asked. "I already adjusted the trajectory as much as we could, so we won't come out right where those fighters were, but I couldn't bring us out much sooner than we planned. We need time to decelerate in the wormhole. Someone was a little ambitious with the speed."

"Sorry, man," Carnie said. "I thought I was following orders."

"I just said we have to get this ship home as soon as possible. We're crammed in here like canned fish."

"And I thought that meant; pedal to the metal." He turned to Liara and Finn. "Go really fast."

"I've driven a sport racer before," Liara said. "I know 'pedal to the metal.'"

"Sorry," Carnie said. "Just, most spacers don't spend enough time on the ground to know what that means."

"You've driven Sport Racing?" Finn asked Liara.

"Yeah, but not pro level. It was fun, especially the wheeled class." Jake had only seen Sport Racing once, but he absolutely loved it. Teams built custom combustion engines and raced on old style frames in the most dangerous class, while other classes used hover pad vehicles that had a very restricted height. There was one class of Sport Racing he wished he could see, but he never had the opportunity: Anything Goes class or AG Sport Racing as most people called it. Teams were given a frame and were allowed to strap anything to it within a certain weight limitation. Frost saw several races in that class but didn't talk about them much since they were seen as barbaric. There were a high number of fatalities.

"Scan or not to scan?" Minh-Chu asked again. "Can't believe I'm the one dragging everyone back on topic."

"What are we seeing on passive?"

Carnie refreshed his display and shrugged. "Outer solar system nothingness and a couple stray asteroids. We're looking through a pinhole with a dodgy candle though."

Jake looked at the jump counter and saw that they were five minutes out. "All right, flash 'em. Just scan for three seconds."

"Yes, Sir," Minh-Chu said. "Ready, Liara?"

"Ready," she said from the communications station.

Before the tactical display finished populating, Jake said; "Get to the guns! Everyone else get close to the middle of the ship and brace."

"Hey, I'm the Captain here," Minh-Chu said as he cracked his knuckles and rested his hands on the controls.

"Well, orders, Captain? I see three destroyers and about thirteen fighters hiding from the front of our emergence point."

"Fourteen," Carnie corrected. "Captain."

"What Jake said - crews to guns, get close to the middle of the ship and brace. This is going to be rough. Carnie, start calculating the next jump."

"Gunners are reporting ready," Jake said from the weapons and operations station.

"There is a lot of chatter, all of it encrypted. This ship does not have a lot of computing power. It's going to take a minute for me to figure out what they're saying."

"If I were to guess, it would sound a lot like; 'Shhh! Here they come!'" Minh-Chu said.

TWENTY-NINE

Restructuring

THE BEAST STOOD beside Overlord Dron in a carefully curated garden square. There were Order of Eden followers who served peacefully, many, many of them. They didn't climb the ranks fast, if at all, but they lived lives of a quality that wouldn't have been possible elsewhere.

One of the perfect examples to Dron were the gardeners who took care of the assortments of flowers and other plants that adorned the sides of the paths in several spaces aboard the Glorious. They were made to be relaxing, places to reflect, visit with family, and have social time with fellow followers.

For Dron's purposes, it suited well. He'd been in stuffy command centres and surrounded by metal walls for too long. "Why are we opening communications here, Sir?" asked Ensign Lancet. He was a bright young man who Dron decided to have personally assigned to his wellbeing. He was told to ask questions, and he was just starting to open up.

"There are many ways to demonstrate power and wealth, Simon," Dron replied. "The Glorious was directly assaulted by the best tactician our enemy has, Captain Valent. It was a vicious attack, we took a great deal of damage. Thanks to the efforts of this crew, we not only have half our hangars ready, but all our main systems have been restored to optimal condition and this garden will be open for our people again tomorrow."

"Oh, right, this was open to space. I saw a notification about it, that it was off limits, but I didn't realize we were standing inside it, sorry, Sir," Lancet said.

"Don't apologize," Dron said lightly. "Learning to keep track of events on a ship this size takes practice. You're smart enough to do it, but you were being wasted in the bowels of the logistics department. What image am I projecting right now?"

"Well," Lancet said, stepping around him and the Beast enough to get a look. "Your uniform presentation is perfect. The Beast is standing beside you and you're in a garden that was lifeless only a few days ago. I'd say confidence? Definitely power, since we're on the Glorious, and maybe..."

"A little whimsy," Dron said, his mouth upturning into a reserved smile. "I designed the paths and chose many of the flowers here. The Lilac path in the forward area is something I'm particularly proud of. The scent of them is so powerful there, and the air is so heady. The paths lead to soft beds of clovers that are made for people to rest on, and the holographic sky, the breeze are all bent to the purpose of helping everyone forget that they're aboard a ship. You'd think I wouldn't have time for that kind of thing, but I have to make time. When I try my hand at designing something out of the norm, seek inspiration from faraway places - like one of the Lilac

Gardens of Countess Valona Tineau Danti - one of the great, walled off spaces of the Core World estates. The only thing more beautiful than the gardens she designs is the woman herself: what a feat of flesh craft. You should see her life sized though, in hologram. Nothing can prepare you for her majestic form."

"I will," Lancet said.

"Good," Dron looked at his wrist display and nodded. The Admirals had been waiting for three minutes and fifty seven seconds. "Stand to my left and hold any questions until this communication is finished."

"Yes, Sir," Lancet said, taking his place and quickly checking his uniform.

Dron activated the conference system. Four admirals and three governors appeared in front of them. After their projections finished appearing they looked perfectly real. "Welcome to the Glorious, ladies and gentlemen," Dron said. "I hope the holography wherever you are is high quality enough to carry you away from your troubles for a moment, offering you a splendid view of our recently repaired and redesigned gardens."

"Impressive," said one admiral who looked squat, wide-faced. He was Albert Tafford

"Thank you, Overlord," said a woman with a narrow face, her blonde hair braided tightly. "I'm happy to see the Glorious is being restored." She was Oliva Scanlon

"Pristine," intoned a young looking black haired man. He was Frederick Pinson, and he was the Governor Dron definitely had to speak to. He was also the most materialistic and hedonistic - by reputation at least - and the one he dreaded visiting the most. "I knew meeting you wouldn't be boring, Overlord."

Other overtures followed with carefully worded congratulations and introductions, but Dron watched the three he knew he needed most. He could watch the playback of the others later.

Members of the Regent Galactic Board were watching as well, though they didn't have permission to present themselves since it was a military meeting.

"Thank you, all of you," Dron said. "Your presence in this meeting is encouraging. The four admirals who have declined to appear have five days to present themselves before I order their execution. If they won't fall in line, the Beast will see that their subordinate does so. He will do it in person and provide evidence that control of the entire Order of Eden fleet, and all Regent Galactic assets now rests with me."

The admirals and governors assembled were shocked to cautionary silence. "I'm starting to see the Admiral I expected to meet today." A woman with brown hair and soft features said. Her eyes examined him, as though she - Admiral Mariel Cort - were peeling away his layers. He expected her to side with him immediately, especially since she thought Clark Patterson was only a Beast, perhaps important to infantry, but not capable of controlling the entire fleet. He had to lock her in, eliminate any doubt that she should follow the new military order.

"I'm especially happy to see you here," he told her. "Your work quelling the Green Court Uprisings are legendary. I'm going to need you now that your fleet has returned to the sector."

"It was only a matter of time before they were undone by infighting. I only pushed them along by isolating them, making sure they didn't hear anything from the Rega Gain System or any other holdouts then thinking ahead of their strategies. Nothing that should impress you." Her words were complimentary, but her eyes expressed boredom despite any smile she offered. The words coming out of her mouth were strung together in her mind many seconds before she finished saying them, and while she spoke she was already thinking of something else. "You don't have to worry. Everyone who you see is completely behind you. Admiral Scanlon made sure. Between our fleets and the spies we have inserted, we have the entire Regent Galactic Board Of Directors in hand. You only had to remove the current Overlord and take your place. We know your record and your accomplishments."

"My colleague is over-simplifying the situation, Overlord," Admiral Scanlon said. "It's true, the Admiralty and the Governors are looking for unified leadership, a single vision to secure these sectors before we continue our expansion, but many people see you as an upstart. Eve has a fleet that rivals any one of ours and controls three solar systems directly. She has publicly stated her hesitation in accepting you as the Overlord and has gone further. She lets everyone know that, even if you are acceptable to her, her position is still higher than that of the Overlord."

"She is popular," Governor Pinson said.

Admiral Tafford added; "Eve has also aligned herself with Citadel, a group of outcasts from Earth who..."

"I know who they are, thank you," Dron said. "They do pose a problem, but I have a strategy that will tip the odds in our favour if things get complicated. I'll be meeting Eve in person soon. Any problems will be rectified then. Soon we will be one force. One body with many limbs working together. Once every member of the board is killed, say, by the end of the day, and we replace them with our own qualified advisors from the military, we will be Eden Nation. All Regent Galactic and subsidiary assets will be nationalized. This was a plan Admiral Tafford and Governor Pinson devised months ago."

"How did you find out about it?" Tafford asked, astonished.

"I have been planning this for years and years. That is what younger siblings do. We watch our older brothers and sisters venture into the wild, learn from their mistakes and then we combine their experiences with our ingenuity. I propose Unity. An organization without the corruption of the previous age."

Three of the seven holographic images were nodding before he finished speaking. "I don't know how you got your information, but if this really is our plan going into motion, then yes. Absolutely yes," Admiral Tafford said.

"I'm with you, Overlord," Governor Pinson said, taken aback completely.

"Congratulations, Overlord," Admiral Cort said, tying her brown hair in a ponytail. "If there's nothing else, I'll see that the board members in my care are executed immediately along with their immediate subordinates. I can't wait to see the light shine on our new Eden Nation."

Admiral Scanlon didn't look surprised by the turn in events at all. "This is an order I'll be happy to follow, Overlord. Perhaps the board won't reform within weeks of its forced disbandment this time. This has been done before."

"I will make sure your work isn't undone. If you have any questions or need more information, please send your requests privately. The details you'll need about my plan for the next month are being sent to you now. Submit qualified officers to take the places of board members over the next three days. Dismissed."

"Nationalized? Sorry, Sir, I've never heard the word," Lancet said.

"It means that the government is taking direct ownership and control of an industry. In this case, the government is the military, and we're taking everything that Regent Galactic owns, including Regent Galactic itself." Dron turned to the Beast. "Begin your mission, Major. I expect your ship to launch by the end of the day."

"Yes, Sir," the Beast said. His semi-transparent, overlapping organic armour plates grinding as he saluted then departed.

"He's very stiff," Lancet commented.

"It's the conditioning. He'll relax into it over time," Dron said. The next mission would tell that tale or put a permanent end to what Clark Patterson became.

THIRTY

Minh-Chu Buu

THE PURSUER ROLLED and swerved into place alongside an Order of Eden Battlecruiser. They were so close to its hull that Jake could swear he could feel it there, like someone standing too close to him. The shimmer of its shields distorted the view through the main left view screen. "Pound their shields, right here," Minh-Chu said as he marked a section of shielding right in front of the large ship's port side hangar bay. Then he returned to humming. Humming!

He knew Minh-Chu had some idiosyncrasies, but that was not only new, but unnerving. "1812 Overture," Liara said under her breath as she looked for a way into the enemy's wireless network. "I'm not finding any chinks," she announced. "Still trying."

Jake launched a volley of dumb-fire missiles as he watched

the starboard guns of the Pursuer rake the section of shields Minh-Chu marked. "Broadcast static on all channels," Jake said.

The section of shielding that they were focusing on was taking heaps of damage, such focused fire wasn't always possible, but at the range Minh-Chu held the Pursuer at - so close that they were almost making contact shield to shield and most of the small fleet that were after them couldn't get a clean shot - it was extremely easy.

Jake worked to rebalance their own shields, watching every side but their nose take damage from the flock of fighters that assailed them at great expense and the few blasts the battle-cruiser could land. Their energy was almost keeping up. Jake saw all communication channels peak and nodded at Liara, who looked nervous. "Good job," he told her.

"It's just static and junk packets," Liara replied.

"Try finding enemy messages that aren't encrypted, and..."

"Use a sound capture to copy their officer's voices and give false orders," she said. "I'll just stop jamming for a few seconds so I can scan for one."

A fighter collided with the top of the Pursuer at high speed, glancing off and gouging the outer hull. Their shield power was down to twenty one percent of maximum. "Finn, we need more power to shields. At this rate we've got a minute, tops before they're pounding our hull."

"From where?" Finn replied over the intercom. He was in the back with anyone who was half-qualified to help with the power systems.

"How are the calculations for our wormhole going?" Minh-Chu calmly asked Noah, who was working on the navigation console - calculating their jump and keeping the trajectory of all the nearby ships updated, highlighting potential collisions or other looming problems - he was sweating.

"I have to start over," Noah said. "One of our thrusters is damaged, and we've moved too far in too little time."

"Calculate something about ten kilometres to our port side," Minh-Chu said. "I just need an entry point, please, we can adjust later unless you put us into a moon or something." He resumed humming. "Oh, look, a door. Can you open it, Jacob?"

It was true, they'd pounded a segment of the battlecruiser's shields so hard that the emitters for that section burned out, and Minh-Chu was keeping the Pursuer right beside it. The hangar door was closed, but Jake knew how he could solve that. He launched a barrage of missiles and silently marked it as the gunner's primary target. Before switching to that door, he watched as two of the battlecruisers main guns were slagged, that left only one gun that could strike them, and it was still under shielding. "Shields down to twelve percent," Jake said. "Finn! Do I need to go back there and give you a hand?"

"No! There's nothing you can do, there's nothing I can do. This ship doesn't have any more juice," Finn replied.

"Suspend life support?" Jake suggested.

"Already done," Finn said.

"I still see lights," Jake retorted. Pings and solid strikes sounded against the hull. It was starfighter fire against their flagging dorsal shield. He managed to get it back up to one point five percent.

The missile racks reloaded, and Jake unleashed a volley against the battlecruiser's hangar door. It burst open, and Minh-Chu fired his port side lateral thrusters, sending the Pursuer into the open hangar. The gunners raked the deck with a hail of automatic fire, slagging defensive measures, landed fighters, shuttles, equipment, doorways, and the ceiling.

The Pursuer nudged a few fighters out of the way, extended its landing gear in clamp mode - half extended with grippers on the bottoms - and latched onto the deck. Minh-Chu sighed, leaned back, and cracked his knuckles in a silence that was only interrupted by the sounds of their guns going off behind the cockpit. Jake and Liara were frozen, open mouthed, stunned.

"Go ahead and calculate," Minh-Chu said to Noah, who was updating their trajectory and whispering; "C'mon, c'mon, c'mon," to the navigational computer.

"Your shields will have a minute to recharge," Minh-Chu said with a sigh. "Unless you want to get out and take control of the battlecruiser."

"Did we just land?" Finn asked as he burst into the cockpit. "Holy! What? We?" he shook his head. An explosion filled the pressurized section of the large main landing bay with blue and yellow fire. The gunners were having the time of their lives burning the distant fighters in racks along the fore and aft walls, firing at pilots and other people running for their lives. Jake watched as one pilot dropped his gun and managed to dive into a crew hatch, a few bolts of energy right behind him, leaving spots of red hot metal in its wake. Then he had a thought. "Someone get a skitter out there," Jake said quietly, as though the realization he had was quiet compared to the overwhelming situation they found themselves in.

He checked the shields; they were almost back up to full charge on all sides. So far, Minh-Chu's idea was working.

"What?" Liara said, snapping out of her stunned silence. "Yes! That'll give us a direct connection and we can start downloading."

Jake was out of his seat, pulling a line from his left command and control unit as he ran down the hall. "Someone catch a skitter and give it to me!" he shouted to the group of soldiers huddled in the main crew seating area. One of them plucked a small, many limbed bot from the wall where it was repairing the hinge on a cupboard and tossed it to him. He caught it by the small half-circle dome that covered its main body and flipped it upside down. He connected his data line, saw the main interface for its programming come up and then added two directives: Attack anyone who picked it up and didn't identify as a member of Haven Fleet, but to primarily connect to the battlecruiser's computer system and provide an encrypted wireless link to the Pursuer. "Open the hatch!" he told a soldier who was leaning beside the heavy armoured starboard side airlock.

He opened it, and a second later Jake was leaning out of the outer airlock, dropping his skitter. It scrambled off across the deck. "Shields full?" Jake asked, yelling towards the bridge even though the intercom would pick him up.

"Um, yes, they're fully charged," Liara replied.

"Navigation ready?"

"Just... one.... Yes!" Noah replied. "We have jump coordinates!"

"Gunners, get ready to shoot our way out of here," Minh-Chu said. "There are a dozen fighters out there waiting for us to come out."

"No!" Jake said. "Blast the opposite door, it's almost screwed already," Jake said as he ran back to the cockpit.

"Oh, wow, our little guy found a data socket," Liara said. "I'm already in their system downloading all kinds of data. A lot of it will need decrypting, but I know I'm in their flight logs, this has got to be their manifest. I'll see what else we can get."

Jake watched as the other hangar doors exploded outward, the focused fire of their guns ripping through the air after them. "That was quick," Jake said. "Think that's a better exit?"

"I like it, let's go!" Minh-Chu said.

Noah released the clamps and retracted the landing gear,

and Minh-Chu guided the ship across the scorched and warped main hangar, accelerating as hard as the ship could manage as the nose of the Pursuer emerged from the yawning opening where the hangar doors once were. Jake sucked air in through his teeth as Minh-Chu guided the ship in a tight turn to skim its outer shields before breaking out into the open.

The fighters were only delayed for a few seconds by their unexpected manner of exiting the battlecruiser before they were swarming at them. Their shields were draining fast, and Jake poured power into their aft section, trying to keep it above fifty percent. The wormhole generator began projecting, and he dumped energy from every reserve, including their forward shields to save their aft section.

Several hard hits caught them before they crossed the threshold of the wormhole and hyper-accelerated out of range. The entry moved with them, only staying open half a kilometre behind. "Finn, damage?" Jake asked as his power readings display froze.

"There is some," Finn said. "Assessing now."

"I'm coming," Jake said. "Good work everyone."

THIRTY-ONE

Team Building

"COME AS YOU ARE," Alice said at the end of the invitation she issued to her squad for dinner. It was the best thing she could have said, as it turned out. Everyone made an appearance even though she made it clear that attendance wasn't mandatory. Regan, Yawen and Holm came together. They looked a little stunned when Alice answered the door, as though they had no idea what to expect.

Alice was set on making the evening as casual as possible, and appeared in the doorway wearing a stretchy, comfortable sleeved dress that was similar to the one that she wore when no one was around, but it had a little less cloth above and below. The first guests - Yawen, Holm, and Regan were in uniform. "Should we have brought something?" Oscar Holm asked sheepishly.

"We'll order a few bottles of something in after everyone else gets here. Come in," Alice said.

"I'm still getting used to living on a planet, and they just changed the night and day cycle, so I'm sorry if I seem a little off," Holm leaned down, gave her a friendly but respectable hug, then kissed her on both cheeks.

Alice was a little startled, but in a pleasant way. "That's how they say hello where you come from?"

"When opposite sexes meet, especially at social events," Holm said. "In my section of the drift. I'm sorry if I overstepped, it's just that you're out of uniform..."

"No problem, I was just surprised," Alice said. "The galaxy would be a little nicer if everyone was so friendly."

"I like it," Regan said as he moved by Alice into her house.

"You're blushing," Yawen whispered. "It's adorable."

"I am not adorable," Alice whispered back. The door was about to close when she saw Naja Jessen and Walter Knud with Callum Newell in tow. Jessen and Knud were dressed for a party. Her metallic silver dress had wavy, nearly transparent lines running down its length that shifted and swirled, not revealing anything scandalous, but teasing just the same. Knud was in tight trousers that were animated in the same way, only his well-muscled chest and arms were bare.

Callum was dressed casually, in an older jacket with a few metal plates built in and regular vacsuit material shirt and trousers. He walked behind Knud especially, looking impressed at the man's muscular back, smiling past him to Alice and Yawen.

"You should have been more specific about what we were getting together for," Callum said.

"We are going dancing after dinner, I hope that's all right," Jessen explained as they drew nearer.

"They are not letting anyone visit the children we rescued yet," Knut added.

"Something to take his mind off it," Jessen said. "Unless there were plans after dinner?"

"Nothing specific, thanks for coming," Alice said.

Callum gave Alice a brief hug, then accepted a more enthusiastic embrace from Yawen. "I can't believe you're signing up with us," she said. "I would have suggested you myself but you weren't in the recruiting pool."

"I'm too good for the recruiting pool," he said with a wink. "So, what's the event?"

"Just getting the squad together, a 'getting to know you' thing," Alice said, leading the way inside. No one wasted time in making themselves comfortable.

"Your fish tank is populated, mine's still just water," Jessen said. "Your second room finished?"

"I don't have one," Alice said.

"I sleep on the sofa," Knud said. "My bedroom is still a shell with windows. The furniture and fixtures are being put in on Saturday."

"You two live together?" Regan asked from the kitchen doorway.

"We've been inseparable since we got here, before too, but there was less of a choice then," Jessen said.

Alice listened in as she went to the kitchen to start making drinks. Regan was already at the dispenser, taking the first from the two cup receiver. It was a tangy grapefruit based concoction that came in a tall cup with a straw, and he passed it to Yawen. "What'll it be?" he asked Alice. "I'll play bartender."

Alice hesitated for a minute, she had tried a few things, but most of the options he was scrolling through on screen were new to her. "I'll decide later, get everyone else something first."

Regan went on questioning Jessen and Knud in his light hearted way. "How'd you get past the no fraternization thing?"

"We're platonic," Jessen said. "I've never met anyone I like more, but I don't have even a little attraction to him."

"It's the same way with me. I kissed her once and it made me wonder if she was the sister my parents never told me about," Knud explained. "Unexciting."

"Thanks," Jessen said.

"Very exciting for someone else, probably," Knud said apologetically. "I've never had a better friend."

"What about you, newcomer?" Jessen said.

"What?" Callum Newell asked.

"You break any hearts in the fleet yet?" Yawen asked.

"I've been too busy training and living on the beach. As soon as I signed up, things started moving so fast, I haven't had time to do much more than throw a wink in a few directions and admire how these uniforms fit on some of my fellow cadets."

"That's a red light, there, soldier," Yawen said.

Most of the squad had a chuckle at the quip, but Alice was relieved when Theodore quietly asked; "What's a red light?" from the kitchen.

"It's a really old phrase they used to use in the military when someone wanted to warn a fellow serviceman, or woman, that they were getting close to a harassment warning, or flirting while on duty, or more."

Theodore emerged from the kitchen with two circular trays loaded with a layer of sushi and sashimi. "A freshwater medley," he said, nodding at the tray on his right, "and a vegetarian medley," he said, looking at the other tray. "I've prepared many of the Lieutenant's favourites, according to the history she developed by ordering from Mama Buu's. If you would rather have something else, tell me, and I'll see if I can find the ingredients."

"I didn't know tonight was catered," Yawen said, amazed.

"This is Theodore," Alice said as she stepped into the kitchen and picked up a tray of sauces and dipping dishes. "I met him on assignment and he's become a really good friend. I'm hoping he'll become my roommate for a while."

"Speaking of fraternization," Yawen chuckled.

"While that would be possible," Theodore said as he set the trays down on the table in the middle of the two half circle sofas around it. "I'm not ready for a romantic relationship."

Alice could feel herself changing colour. "We have blushing," Yawen said.

"Blushing is confirmed," added Regan.

"A sure sign that I'm in the right place," Callum said. "Are you sure you're not of Irish descent?"

"I've never tracked my genetics back to their origins," Alice said. "Sort of still getting used to the new me." Alice put the tray of condiments and little dipping dishes down and took a seat at the end of the sofa.

"The new you?" Callum asked.

Alice was chewing on her first cucumber roll when she realized how quiet the room had gotten. All eyes were on her, and she realized that, not only was Callum not the only one who was waiting for an answer, but it seemed much more important to them than she expected. She held up her index finger and finished chewing. "I was a framework before, it's complicated. I thought most people knew."

"The bare facts; that you were downloaded into a framework and that you were cured," Yawen said using a voice that was much gentler than normal.

"I didn't know that," Callum said.

"Nor I," Knud added. "Someone said you were an artificial intelligence once, and I did not believe them."

"I was," Alice said, looking to Yawen. "You haven't been holding questions in all this time, have you?"

"I have, and I would have held them in even longer. I don't know what's sensitive and what isn't, I've never met anyone like you before," she replied.

The only sound was the drink mixer in the kitchen, filling cups at Regan's command, and handing them to Theodore. It was disappointing to be the centre of attention because of her past. The thought that she was what most of the people in her squad had the most questions about had never occurred to her, and she already wished it wasn't true.

The command instruction in Apex training told her what her options were. She could remain mysterious and try to lead firmly, by example, or she could be more open and allow her squad to get to know her. There were other options, but those were the two command styles Alice could see herself falling into. Leading quietly, staying separate from her people could be easier, it was her command style only hours ago. Her reaction to that was to invite everyone over for an impromptu dinner gathering, and that told her that she actually wanted to know her people, to close much of the distance between her and them. "Okay, I'll answer any questions, but let me tell you the absolute basics first," Alice said.

Everyone leaned in, even Callum, who had made an effort to relax and look cool until then. "Oh, there is mercy in the galaxy," Yawen muttered as she sat beside Alice.

"Dig in though, leftover sushi just doesn't taste the same," Alice said.

"I've never tried it," Knud said.

"That's tuna," Jessen said, pointing at a section of rolls. "You'll like it."

"So," Alice started. "I was an artificial intelligence that lived on Jonas Valent's wrist. The base program was made by Freeground, but he modified it to the point where it was borderline illegal."

"Jonas Valent? The Captain of the First Light?" asked Regan.

"That one," Alice said. "When he was captured by Vindyne, he let me loose in their system to do some damage and get him and his crew free. Minh-Chu was there, so was Admiral McPatrick, but I call him Oz. I was able to get them free, but Vindyne was experimenting on people there, trying to reprogram criminals and citizens using computer code. I don't remember this, but, I guess I got curious, and used their hardware to download myself into a woman who was convicted of several murders. I didn't know most of the details of her crimes for years. Jonas didn't know that I'd made the transition, so he left me behind, but a couple of escaping prisoners saw me. I remember one was named Bernice, and they saved me from Vindyne. There's a lot of history there, years, but let's save that for another time."

"There's a documentary," Yawen said. "But it doesn't cover you much. It's mostly about the First Light crew."

"I know, I haven't seen more than a few minutes of it yet," Alice replied.

"You haven't seen a documentary you're in?" Callum said. "I'd have a poster up in every room. 'Look there! I was in a documentary a few million people have seen,' I'd say. I'd even put one up in the bathroom, especially in the bathroom."

"I'll get around to it," Alice said. Theodore was listening from the door, two chilly purple cups in his hands. "I eventually caught up to Jacob Valent, and I started serving aboard the Triton. I was injured in the line of duty, and from what I understand, I uploaded myself again before I died. There was some kind of artificial intelligence left that was able to take over and protect my personality, whatever it was that made me, well, *me*, and I ended up in the Order of Eden main fleet. The next thing I know - and this is fuzzy - The Beast, Clark Patterson, is helping me come back to life. Eve thanked me for a story I told her about Lewis, the original Lewis that I named the artificial intelligence in my ship after. She was so grateful that she made sure I escaped the fleet. I don't have memories from before then that aren't fuzzy, or so disorganized that they're just fragments. The framework eventually settled on making me a teenager. I guess I subconsciously wanted to know what it was like to be that young, and I don't know if I'd ever want to go back. It's like every emotion is quintupled, and everything is a huge deal. Meanwhile, Jake's emotional range was short, except for anger."

"Okay, so you definitely had that experience accurately," Jessen said with a chuckle. "I was the biggest drama queen when I was a teen."

"Things weren't getting better either. The framework was rolling my age back to its teenage present more and more often, mostly in my sleep. People were worried about what else the framework might change on its own, and I know that they were worried about someone taking control of me from a distance. No one ever said it, and they treated me like anyone else most of the time, but I know they were watching. So, when the tech to get the framework out came along, I jumped at the chance."

"Okay, so how does that work? I know Captain Valent did it, but the details are classified," Regan asked as he carefully raised a vishri roll to his mouth with chopsticks. It looked like it wouldn't fit with the tail hanging out.

"His downgrade was a surgical procedure, brutal," Alice said. "We used software to trick my framework into regenerating me one more time using a subconscious self-image while it eliminated itself. I could have come out younger, older, or just really different, but it was worth it."

"I'd say," Yawen said with a chuckle.

Alice looked at her with an upraised eyebrow.

"Sorry, if I were into ladies, we'd have a fraternization problem," Yawen said as Jessen nodded along.

"Anyway," Alice cleared her throat. "I started getting ready for the Apex program right after that, and I guess because I had so few distractions the training took."

"Okay, so how are you Ayan's daughter?" Jessen asked, earning a light nudge from Knud. "She said she was an open book."

"A little rude though," Knud said quietly.

"It's a good question," Alice said. "The framework gathered her genetic data from the air around her because it knew that I would choose her as my biological mother, and it already had genetic data from Jake, so when I regenerated the last time it put those two together and I got really lucky."

"Yes, you did," Yawen agreed.

"I mean I didn't end up with any big genetic defects, or other problems," Alice explained. "And Ayan adopted me as soon as she found out."

"That is lucky," Callum said around a mouthful of tuna roll.

"And it makes you a princess," Theodore added.

"Mom turned her title away in-system, and I'll do the same if anyone ever wants to pin one on me," Alice said. "Modern monarchies don't really treat most people well."

"Wait, I've always wanted to know; how did Ayan become Queen of the whole solar system?" Regan asked.

"I've seen the forms, and the records, but I don't know how easy that is to explain," Alice said.

"I know how it happened," Theo said. "I can describe it in layman's terms and in short form."

"Oh my God, please do," Callum said. "That's one of the most confusing things about this place. A Queen more people love every day that hides away, doesn't want anything to do with her title, and serves the military as though she doesn't have to sleep? I mean, if there's someone who should be Queen..."

"You know a *lot* about the Lieutenant's mother. Is there a crush there, maybe?" Regan teased.

"No!" Callum objected quickly, waving his hands. "Just, where I come from we had people with titles, but they were ornamental until there were big social events. Most of them were well liked, too, a lot of them spent time in politics and the military like Ayan, so she's the model of a lovely royal."

"Lovely?" Knud asked with an upraised eyebrow.

"All right, she's a stunning woman and I imagine she's very kind, and loads smarter than I am," Callum said. "I'd lay down on a puddle full of nails and gobbler fish so she could use me as a bridge."

"I'll pass that on," Alice said with a little smile.

"What, no..." Callum struggled as his face started turning red. The room erupted with laughter, Alice included, though she couldn't help but wonder a little about Callum. The handsome young man had to be aware of how much Alice looked like her mother. By the time everyone settled down, she'd shaken the thought.

"I don't envy your position, young Callum," Theo said with a chuckle that was surprisingly convincing.

"I won't actually tell her, Theo," Alice said. "Just teasing."

"Well I'll explain Ayan's position then, if everyone is still interested." There were nods and affirmative gestures around the room. "Well, when the people led by Ayan Anderson, Jacob Valent, and Terry Ozark McPatrick came here, Ayan decided to approach the Carthans for help. I don't know how it happened, but she had to apply for a land grant at one point, and they made her the owner of Haven Shore, most likely thinking that she had the people and technology to develop it and it would keep them out of their way."

"So, this place, where we are right now," Jessen said.

"No, the moon to the left," Knud replied.

"Cheeky," Jessen said, stealing a roll from his chopsticks.

"Yes, this relatively small chain of islands," Theodore said. "During an attempt to invade this world some time later, the Carthan fleet was devastated. The remainder was recalled to their home worlds, and they were ordered to completely abandon the system. They had to leave it to someone when they departed, it's galactic law, and they had few choices. There were some prominent gangsters, and a nearby failed government that is now overtaken by the Order of Eden, the British Alliance and Ayan, who was the sole beneficiary of this land grant. The British refused. They did not want to put roots down in a solar system they weren't sure they could develop or defend. That left Ayan, who was made prime monarch of the solar system. It was a surprise to the public, since most people expected her to only gain domain over this moon, perhaps Kambis, but there is no contesting it: Ayan is the master of this entire solar system as Queen. Any other title would have taken longer for them to give her, and they were urgently needed elsewhere. Ayan put a democratic system based on Freeground Nation's style of government that is now evolving to include the finer points of Lorander leadership and put her power as Queen aside. She can never entirely retire the title, however, otherwise someone else can claim it, so she will always be Queen in one way, even though she doesn't want to be known as one to the people in the system or to lead the government. Her father does serve as a member of the Triumvirate, the ultimate leadership here, but he was elected."

"Wow, okay, now I actually get it," Callum said.

"You make it sound simple," Regan agreed.

"Well, there is a much more complicated side of it, and I combined some details, but I figured the shorter version was better for this social setting," Theodore said.

Alice's thin, off-duty comm band lit up and scrolled a message on its shiny blue surface. "It's a message from Haven Medical. Mom's got us clearance to see the kids. She went to see them and saw that Knud left three requests to visit. I guess she got us cleared."

"I have to change," Knud said, standing.

"We'll go in uniform, but after we eat. We can't visit for another hour anyway," Alice said.

"Is the Admiral going to be there?" Yawen asked, waggling her eyebrows at Callum.

"Definitely," Alice replied.

THIRTY-TWO

A Small Victory

KNUD AND JESSEN broke away from Alice and Theodore once they arrived at Haven Shore Medical. The rest of the squad left the last minute dinner party with other destinations in mind. Most were visiting friends and family, making the most of their precious time off.

A nurse met Alice at the Maternity Ward Desk with a smile. "Lieutenant Valent?"

Alice nodded, looking around at the halls around her. There were incubators, other equipment and re-crated supplies along one side of every hallway.

Carole noticed that Alice was a little wary. "Sorry, pre-moving day preparations. The Rangers are helping us move to the permanent Medical Centre tomorrow or the day after. I'm Nurse Carole. Follow me, your mother went to get something to eat, but you can see the baby."

"Have you found anything out about her?"

"Well, this is sad, but her mother named her before she died," Carole replied quietly. "Laura Ricci. We can't find any other relatives on record. Here we are, have a seat," she said, gesturing to a sofa inside a dimly lit room. Colourful lights danced across the ceiling in a gentle rotation. "By the way, who's your friend?"

"I'm Theodore. I have extensive knowledge of child care and I must say that this room is very well suited for newborns. You should be proud of how well you're caring for them," Theodore offered quietly.

"Thank you, Theodore. You can definitely stay," Carole said. She retrieved the bundled babe from her basinet and handed her to Alice with care.

"Oh, I've never..." Alice said as she received baby Laura in her arms.

"It's about time for her to wake up for a while, she'll be hungry soon," Carole said. "The system will tell you when she wants her bottle."

"You have a neural listening system in place?" Theodore asked.

"We do, a gift from the Lorander people. It's amazing, we just tell the button on her nappy who it should be monitoring and it tells us why little Laura is fussing or crying. It doesn't help when she just wants to do some shouting for the sake of shouting, but babies are their own kind of complicated."

"That is remarkable," Theodore said.

Alice found herself transfixed by the snoozing infant, watching her little lips work their way into almost a whistling shape, then relax before stretching into a big yawn. The black hair on the top of her head was as soft as fine feather down. "She's beautiful."

"Just in case no one has said it; thank you for saving her and the other children," Carole said. "I know you were doing your job, but someone should say it."

"That's why I love my job; the difference we make. You know what I'm talking about, you care for people every day."

"I do, thank you," she replied. "Would you like to see who you saved? I can project what baby Laura will look like as she grows."

"Sure," Alice said.

An image of Laura as a toddler appeared on the floor near the door chasing bubbles. "This is her at about two. Now we'll go to eight." The pudgy, happy child was replaced by one who was climbing a tree, thinner, with black hair down to her shoulders. "She's going to be adventurous, it's a genetic predisposition, so if she has a good childhood, that trait will come to the forefront. Now we'll advance a little more to fourteen."

Before their eyes the rambunctious child grew into a young teen on a surfboard. She was still slim, but the thrill seeker was definitely present. Riding a wave on a pointed board in a one piece suit was a young woman who was having the time of her life. The wave calmed and she wobbled for a second before the board gently bumped the shore. She stepped off, walking onto the beach, confident and beautiful. "I forgot there was surfing here. I should learn some time," Carole said.

"There is?" Alice said absent minded like, more interested in what would come next in the presentation.

"Finally, and some of this is more guesswork than anything, but if she grows up on Tamber, stays healthy and has a good upbringing, this is what she will probably look like at eighteen," Nurse Carole said. The image of a young woman leaning against a wall with a long jacket over a thick pilot's vacsuit appeared. Her black hair was cut into a bob, and she seemed almost cocky, her dark eyes surveying the space around her, smiling for a moment at a passerby, offering a small but friendly nod.

The clattering of a bottle came through the doorway, and Alice looked to see Ayan, an expression of complete shock on her face. "Oh my stars," she whispered.

"Are you all right, Admiral?" Carole asked.

"Can you show me what she'd look like a little younger?" Ayan asked in an urgent whisper.

Carole brought up the younger surfer girl and Ayan took a shuddering breath. "I can't believe it." She turned to Carole, doing her best to regain her composure. "I'm sorry, it would take a long time to explain, and some of what I'd have to tell you is classified, but I'm wondering if anyone has come forward? A relative, a family friend?"

"Laura was born on the transport and her parents died of..."

"Asphyxiation," Ayan said. "Did you say her name was Laura?" she asked very quietly.

"Yes, her mother named her and told the other children before she passed," Carole replied.

"Is Haven Medical handling the adoption?"

"Yes, but she won't be released for a few days," Carole replied.

"I'm based on Tamber, in the Everin Building. I need to apply."

Everyone was surprised. Carole checked her comm unit for a moment and nodded. "You're eligible to have a family in your placement and rank," she said with a smile. "I'm sure you'll make a wonderful mother. I'll put your name in now."

"Thank you," Ayan said, entering the room and joining Alice on the sofa gently.

Laura's eyes opened and a small voice from her hidden monitor said; "I'm hungry."

Theodore handed Alice the bottle. "Just rest the nipple between her lips, she'll take it," he told her.

Alice did as instructed and watched as baby Laura went to work, breathing loudly through her nose at first as she drew on the bottle. Ayan just watched. "Are you all right?" Alice asked, unable to find another, more specific question.

"This is classified, so you both have to keep it to yourselves," Ayan started quietly. "I know you can both do that."

"Absolutely, Admiral," Theodore said.

"Oh, and congratulations, Theodore," Ayan told him, her voice still a little shaky. "I'll be sending a fleet recruiter to you soon, so prepare to be wooed into our ranks, but the choice is yours."

"Oh? I never considered that, thank you."

Ayan returned her attention to Alice. "You know I'm proud of you, and ever grateful that you chose me as your mother, even though I'm not very good at it yet."

"That takes time, I think you're doing fine," Alice said, smiling reassuringly.

"Well, I just want you to know that what I'm about to tell you doesn't diminish the love I have for you, okay?"

"I'm super loveable, there's no way that'll change," Alice retorted. "Whatever you have to say, it's not going to change things."

"It might, but hopefully for the better," Ayan said. "You remember hearing about the Victory Machine, the technology that could receive transmissions from the future and interpret them using a host?"

"That's about all I know, other than getting a message of my own, but yeah," Alice replied.

"All right, when I was communicating to its pilot, Roman, I was shown a vision of the future. There was a station in orbit, one which I can see Freeground Station becoming, and I was shown two of my children. One was a son that Jake and I might have in the future, the other was an independent minded daughter." She brought an image of her up on her comm unit. "This is from my memory of her, taken during a deep scan of my mind." It looked exactly like the girl they'd seen in the projections. "I thought I'd have a baby and name her after my best friend, Laura," Ayan explained, choking up a little. A tear rolled down her cheek. "Now I know how it really goes. I thought perhaps I was supposed to have a child with someone else before your father, and that's absolutely not going to happen, so I was making my peace with never meeting young Laura." Ayan gently stroked the babe's head. "I couldn't have been more wrong."

"That's so beautiful," Theodore whispered as he wiped a tear from his cheek. "Oh! I forgot I could cry."

"I'll help whenever I can," Alice said, looking down at Laura's chubby face as she worked at the bottle. "A little sister."

THIRTY-THREE

New Trouble

"SO, we got out of there relatively unscathed," Finn said as he stood over the small compartment that held their wormhole generator system. "No damage to our forward projection system, and we've got shields, most of our weapon systems, most of the damage to our armour is easy to patch."

Jake, Minh-Chu and Remmy filled the small section of the device bay. "All good news," Jake said. "So, what brings us to the business end of the ship?"

"It's the repairs to the wormhole generator," Finn said, gesturing to a set of cables running into the ceiling connecting the wormhole generator to the main power systems. They were covered in extra tubing Jake was having difficulty placing, but it wasn't the kind of thing he saw used for high powered systems. "One of those hits on the aft section slagged the power cables made for this kind of power feed, and the ones I had to replace them don't have the tolerance they need. They're all right for now, while the power is flowing nice and steady to the matrix so we'll stay in the wormhole as long as we have power. I used cooling tubes from the food storage system, so we don't have refrigeration anymore, but I maxed them out to cool the lines feeding power to the wormhole matrix."

"So that's what those are," Jake said. "I couldn't place them. What happens when we have to open or adjust the trajectory of a wormhole?"

"These lines will be past tolerance," Finn explained, pointing to the cables connecting their wormhole generator to the power. "Even if we expose them to hard vacuum, they will probably melt. If not the next time, the time after that."

"Are they actually reliable now?" Minh-Chu asked. "While we're in wormhole transit?"

"They shouldn't melt, but these cables weren't made for this, they're great for getting power to secondary systems. Shouldn't doesn't mean couldn't though," Finn explained.

"What about pulling cable from one of the turrets?" Jake asked.

"Same cables," Finn said. "So, yeah, if we melt these down, we have a few more chances, but will it get us home? I think I got lucky with these, they're holding up during transit."

"How bad is the power spike when we open a new wormhole?" Minh-Chu said.

"About a factor of nine," Jake replied. "Power draw goes up nine times what they're pulling now."

"More like ten point eight, but at that level, there's not much of a difference," Finn replied. "It's a good system, but it's made to run with these amazing, rare components that the Solar Forge can print all day long. The problem is, the rest of the galaxy hasn't caught up. The cables we need exist near the power cores of big starships, or planetary defence arrays."

Jake thought about the cable running to the turrets and other lines that were the same grade aboard. They'd be pulling their own teeth to get home. The lines running to one turret might be able to provide enough material for two jumps if they melted them each time. "What are the chances that these cables melt, we replace them with new ones, and those ones melt down before we can form another wormhole."

"I was going to bring that up last," Finn said.

"So, another jump might not even work?" Remmy asked. "Dark, man."

"There's a ten percent chance if we're taking a short jump, give or take," Finn said.

"I'm going to talk to my co-pilot," Minh-Chu said. He stepped outside, his expression stormy.

Jake knew they were still far from home. The math in his head didn't add up. If they burned cables out every second small jump, they would run out about seven tenths of the way there. "What about sending a distress signal through a pinhole; high compression but very narrow," he already knew the answer by the time he finished asking the question.

"It would definitely cost us one of our jumps if it worked," Finn said.

"They're looking for us now," Remmy said. "We can't sit still and realistically expect for one of our own ships to get to us in time, can we? Even with dimension drive tech?"

"It would take a couple days to get here," Jake said. "We could find somewhere to power down and wait, like an asteroid field, maybe land, or hide in a junk drift." The idea didn't seem right to Jake.

The hatch opened and Noah Lucas stepped inside. "Hey,

Captain, Chief, Remmy," he said. "There's a system I know well, we could probably make it there in a few jumps the same size we just made. The math says we'd be there in a couple days. There's an Order presence, for sure. I was pretty sure they were setting up a brood world on Iora. There are a lot of stations in that system though, most of them corrupted by the Holocaust Virus, but you guys have some kind of cure. There's a shipyard there too, so, yeah, there could be some Order around, but there's a lot of junk drifting around, a bunch of stations that they didn't bother taking according to what Liara was able to bring up. They leave the infected ships alone because they give them extra defence."

"Let's take a look," Jake said. "Thank you, Finn, great work down here," he said over his shoulder as he left.

"Thank you, Captain. Why'd he call us by rank and you by your name?" Finn asked Remmy as the other two left.

"We hit it off over my database of ancient Earth anime," Remmy said. The compartment door closed and Jake didn't catch the rest of the conversation.

"Like I said, I know Iora," Carnie explained as he led the way to the small bridge. "I spent a long time stuck there. I heard a lot about the stations hanging in space between the worlds in that system from the guys in the circus troop, but I haven't visited any of them. Liara probably already knows more."

"I'm still decrypting some of it," she said as they arrived in the tiny bridge. Everyone took their seats - Noah beside Minh-Chu in the co-pilot's seat, Jake at the technical operations and tactical station, and Liara spoke from the communications station - she went on, bringing up a hologram of Iora, a blue and green planet. "We have the key for what we downloaded, and we have the data from the raid, it's just taking a while because there's a lot of it. The point is that our information is fresh, only a few hours old in some cases, but no older than two days at the most. Iora is off limits," she said, pointing at an older base ship that looked like a thick rectangle with a groove up the middle. "These carriers are mobile ship yards, they can repair two destroyers at a time. The fleet that accompanies them are about fifty ships deep not including smaller classes."

"So, no going near that," Minh-Chu said. "Unless we want to surrender."

"What Noah mentioned about the stations and Kinaine Shipyards is dead-on though. They're not monitored. The Order has made sure that everything there is infected by the Holocaust Virus, which we can cure in less than a minute by broadcasting the antivirus. If we need another ship, I bet that's where I'd find it, but you'd be the expert, Captain."

Jake looked at the recent scans. There were a few foreign destroyers, frigates and many long range scout craft orbiting the shipyards and the stations. If they didn't have the key to defeating the Holocaust Virus, then they would have no chance. They did, and that made everything easier, but not risk-free. "That one, on the edge of the solar system," Jake pointed. "We have current data on it?"

"We do," Liara said, focusing in on it and putting it on everyone's holographic display. "Five ships patrolling around the station close by, two destroyers further out."

"Two of those Aucharian corvettes are the perfect size for our crew, and it should be manageable to take them," Jake said. "They're in good condition, too."

"Sounds like we have a plan to put together," Minh-Chu said.

"Start plotting short jumps," Jake said. "Looks like we'll be ship-jacking."

THIRTY-FOUR

Two Days In Peace

AYAN PRACTICALLY GLOWED when she was with baby Laura. Alice visited the nursery whenever she could, which was often during her two days off. Laura spent much of her waking time in Ayan's arms, and they were bonding quickly.

The sight of Ayan holding the newborn when she appeared as a hologram in design, logistics, strategic and other meetings was greeted with a lot of ooh's, aah's and coos at first, but it became a fairly common thing before long. Oz cracked Alice's favourite joke on the matter, asking; "Has someone made sure Laura's taken the secrecy oath?"

When Alice was visiting the nursery and she didn't have to help Ayan the nurses would put another orphan in Alice's arms. To her relief, Theodore was her constant companion, and the nurses used him whenever they could too, since he had high level child care programming. He always seemed happy to help.

Alice spent the rest of her time during her days off interviewing new people for the squad. Between her and Yawen, they managed to interview thirty people. Theodore took care of most of her needs so she could fill those in-between moments with the examination of the new Clever Dream so she'd know every detail of the ship. Knowing the technology was one thing, but every ship came with its own quirks and details right off the line.

Those days off were a storm of activity for Alice that slowed down every time she visited the nursery, something she looked forward to. It was in one of the empty, private visiting rooms where Alice finished conducting an interview with Private Gerald Disher. He was one of the few medical technicians that was near the end of his training. He didn't seem to be taking it very seriously. "You'd be the lead medical technician on a small but important ship," Alice said.

"Yeah, the Clever Dream, everyone's heard about it. Biggest open secret in the fleet," he replied, not looking at the holo-recorder, but at something or someone passing by. He was resting on the beach after finishing his second Surgical Tools Qualifier. He didn't score as high as Alice would have liked, but he passed, showing a good understanding of the technical details. "You know, I've got three Captains talking to me today. I should have another call soon."

"I know. If you join my staff, you'll see things that you wouldn't anywhere else," she said.

"Like going on missions? I'd see action?" he asked.

"Definitely. I'm not just looking for a ship doc, I'm looking for a squad member. You'd be part of a tight team."

"I don't have any combat qualifications past my sidearm and basic strategy. I just took the required ones, you know. Didn't think I'd see much action outside of the medbay." He thought for a moment. "Real missions off ship, huh?"

"Exactly. Special Operations teams like mine are going out there to make real change."

"Like? What have you done so far?" he asked.

Alice hated that Disher had already turned the interview around so she felt like she was under the microscope. "I can't talk about the particulars because you don't have clearance yet."

"I've got another call," he said. "See ya if you beat the other Captains out." He cut the transmission.

"I don't think I'll be recruiting you, Disher," she muttered as she lowered her face into her hands.

"Trouble?" Theodore asked as he entered the room.

"Just interviewed the last available medical technician in the recruiting pool. I'm pretty sure he was sitting on a beach somewhere watching bikinis go by. It didn't go well."

"I'm sorry," Theo said. "You know, I've been meaning to ask but I wanted to choose my moment carefully."

"Ask me anything," Alice said.

"All right. I've heard a rumour that you were the one who saved little Laura. That's why your mother wanted to get you and your squad clear to visit early. Is it true?"

"You're not clear to know, but it may be true," Alice replied. "It might not be."

"Admission and denial," Theodore said. "If it were true, is that what Special Operations does?"

"I can tell you that we are some of the most adaptable soldiers in the fleet. We go where they send us to perform tasks that require a high level of improvisation and quick decision making. We are qualified to save civilians, to destroy an Order installation and pretty much everything in between. If we're not qualified to do something, then we're expected to learn what we have to and make the attempt."

"That is extremely broad," Theodore said. "You could have said; 'we do everything,' and it would have been the same response, essentially."

"So far, we don't do windows," she replied.

Theodore laughed more than Alice expected. She had no idea where the reference came from, but he seemed to have a much deeper understanding, or he was overdoing the laughter. "I ask because I've seen what the Order does. I've seen what your unit can do to help people, I think, and I may have found a way to fit in. I spoke to a Fleet recruiter last night while you were sleeping, and I think I want to follow in Noah's footsteps and join. I asked him if I could be eligible to join your team in a certain capacity and - after consulting a colleague - he returned and said it would be possible. I have an advantage, too." He held up a high density data chip. The thin housing was only as long as the tip of a finger. "I could install this and become a fully qualified medical technician who knows everything about the physiology of nine races. I could only reliably treat five, but medicine is changing and advancing all the time."

"You would have to carry a suppression weapon. I know you can't use lethal power," Alice replied, immediately excited. She was off the sofa and on her feet in front of him in a second.

"I've done that before. Be aware; I would have to take over twenty qualifiers and exams before I am the equivalent of a doctor, but I'm sure I'd pass. I can take them during downtime on the Clever Dream. I could also perform combat support duties on missions. Anything that doesn't involve me pulling the trigger on a lethal weapon, I can do. I only have to join the Fleet, and then you can..."

"No, doing it that way would put you in the recruiting pool, and that's too much of a gamble. I can recruit you into my squad directly."

"You can do that?" he asked.

"Yes, it's a Special Operations perk. Normally I'd have to be a Commander to do it, but Special Operations can recruit the people they need with their consent."

"I give it, I give you my consent!" Theo said. "Oh, this is exciting."

"Welcome to my team," Alice said as she brought up the right forms on her command and control unit. "You are our new medical technician."

Theodore opened the collar of his vacsuit and slipped the chip into an invisible break in his skin. "Modern medicine is fascinating," he said a moment later. "I have all the knowledge of several experienced doctors and all the findings of the Core World Medical Association. Earth and Lorander medical technologies are loading now along with every preventative and curative practice known to them. I wonder if this is what having a large meal feels like?"

The implications of having Theodore on her team as a medical technician and more were rolling through her mind. He would have a perfect memory, was built to emulate a human so he could use any of their equipment and protect himself the same way, and there were so many other good things to consider. The only negative was his inability to directly kill a sentient being, but she would find a way to work around it. "How much of your internal memory is that going to take?" Alice asked.

"When I've downloaded the scientific studies I have on this chip. There's another chip with the rest, so I'll have a broad spectrum of knowledge to draw from - the last thing I'll have to take on - I will have used one point eight percent of my internal memory. That's quite a bit, really."

"You know everyone you met the other day at my place will find out you're an android," Alice said as she realized it.

"I have no problem with that. It's the Haven Government that decided that most mechanical citizens should have their true nature hidden. I don't actually care, especially since there isn't much that can harm my core memory. Do you think they'll care?"

"Well, they'll care, sure, but the squad will see it as a positive. They'll like you even more because of it. I think most of them are pretty open minded."

"Then I can't wait for them to know," Theodore said.

THIRTY-FIVE

Old Friends

JUMPS THAT SHOULD HAVE TAKEN one day, took two. They were down to two turrets thanks to the need to use power cabling to replace what they melted down in attempts to open wormholes that failed. For their usual duties, the cables were more than enough, but under the higher requirements of the wormhole generator, any flaw that was insignificant before could lead to disaster. Running power in parallel was the only answer after a while, but some lines still burned out, and it cost them time to set up and resources.

More than half of the Pursuers offensive systems were powered down. Jake was happy about one thing, however: they still had their shields and while they weren't running the worm-hole drive, they would have more power in reserve for them than before.

Minh-Chu had been watching his old friend during their

touch-and-go journey through wormholes. They only came up within scanning range of Order of Eden ships one more time, near the middle of their journey, and everyone feared that their trip was about to take a turn for the worst. Everyone except for Jacob Valent.

Captain Valent, who wasn't technically captain of the Pursuer at all, gathered information, consulted everyone he needed for options and opinions then created a plan that the crew followed. Minh-Chu realized that there was something to learn from him again in terms of pure command skill. He wasn't perfect, but he made corrections quickly and shared his thinking with people when he had time.

There was something else, something Minh-Chu saw when Jake wasn't under pressure. Something of his old friend, Jonas, was very present in Jake. Jacob Valent was largely a stoic, and Minh-Chu liked him well enough, but there was a charm and youthfulness surfacing in Jake that even showed itself as senti- mentality at times. An hour before they were set to emerge from the last wormhole that would take them to Patrol Station Nine, it was just Minh-Chu and Jake in the small, cockpit like bridge.

Everyone else was making sure that they had everything they needed in hand so they'd be ready when it came time to abandon ship. It would be a chaotic few minutes of action, but Minh-Chu didn't allow himself to worry. Looking to the face of his friend, he didn't see any concern there, either. He was looking over the plan again, most likely for the tenth time. "How are you holding up, Captain?" Minh-Chu asked

"If I'm a Captain, I'm one who got himself stuck off-ship," Jake said.

"You finally gave Stephanie a chance at command for more than a shift at a time," Minh-Chu said. "The Revenge made it out of danger, they're fine. I believe we'll be all right, too, even if we need to leave this thing behind."

"That probably irks you," Jake said.

"Not at all," Minh-Chu said, running his finger along the edge of the console. "This ship always felt like an imperfect vessel that got us around by the skin of its teeth. As long as what we get into next has a good wormhole drive and takes us home, I'll be happy."

"What do you think of this plan?" Jake asked.

"It's frantic, but I'm like the rest of the crew; I see a loose plan that's built on more experience than I have. The leader makes me confident. No pressure."

Jake chuckled and nodded. "No pressure," Jake said. "Remmy could handle this action though, I'm not exactly core to this working out."

"That's why you divided us into two groups, it makes sense, like every other part of the plan." Minh-Chu could tell they were about to start talking in circles, it was time to change topic. "Did you hear that a restaurant called Mama Buu's opened up in Haven Shore?"

"What? No," Jake said, excitement in his eyes.

"My little sister, the youngest of us," Minh-Chu said.

"The loudest of you, "Jake said.

"From what she says it's the most popular spot on Tamber. She said she wouldn't let me go off on my own adventure and have all the fun. She didn't even want me to know she was there until she got herself set up on her own. She was always the most independent."

"Even more than me," Minh-Chu said. "Now I'll have to bring everyone I can to her place whenever I can so I can watch her being busy."

"Because she won't want you to visit her socially while she's at work," Jake said.

Minh-Chu chuckled. "Right, she wants everyone - especially me - to see how busy and important she is to the place, but she won't have time to talk."

"The longer we're away, the more reasons we find to get back home," Jake said. Minh-Chu could see the weight on his heart.

"I feel greedy about that," Minh-Chu said. "My best friend has orchestrated things just right for us to have a big, dramatic heroes return. They're going to think we're returning on the Revenge, but instead they'll get a story about how we were separated during a daring raid. They'll expect us any moment in this heap, then we'll appear late in a mysterious ship we captured from a system Carnie directed us to. It'll be a story worth telling, and quite a celebration thanks to the path you guided us down."

"I'll take the credit and the blame," Jake said. "Don't worry."

"Oh, I'm sure it'll be all credit. What we're planning will cause some drama for the Order too. It might teach them a lesson, but I hope not."

"That's the last thing we need; the Order learning from our tactics," Jake said.

"Ah, it won't make a difference. Captain Valent comes at everything from odd angles, no one sees him coming unless he wants them to," Minh-Chu said.

"Maybe if you keep believing it, it'll stay true," Jake said. "But there might be a new Captain Valent before we know it."

"Alice, she's doing well. Ayan had a few things to say about her when she sent me a hello. You have a nice family waiting for you - outnumbered by ladies - I know something about that if you ever need advice."

"I might take you up on that," Jake said.

Liara came through the hatch, closed it behind her and sat down quietly, checking the automation script she built with Jake. Only the first part of it was crucial to the plan, the rest would be a big bonus if the ship could still run the commands. "There are a lot of good things waiting for us," Minh-Chu reiterated. "It's good to talk about them. Everyone seems afraid to bring them up, as though it might bring bad luck. I enjoy thinking about a reunion with my sister, one of Ayan's welcome back hugs, and having a quiet night with Ashley. We'll all be meeting at my sister's restaurant, the whole command staff and everyone else who can make it from the Revenge. She'll panic when she sees a few hundred people at her door in uniform, and I'll say; 'Well, you told me to bring people to your restaurant!' and she'll tell me I'm a terrible brother or something before she gets back into the kitchen and starts whipping her people or her robots into a frenzy."

Liara chuckled to herself quietly.

"You had better be there," Minh-Chu said. "You've become so important to the crew that I sometimes wonder if you weren't with us on the First Light, or from Jake's Samson crew. You fit in like you've been here all along."

"Thank you, Commander,' she said, surprised. "I'll be there, even if it is just to see you and your sister go on."

"The food will be incredible too, don't worry," Minh-Chu said. "She has standards to meet."

"She was always a better cook," Jake said.

"Take that back," Minh-Chu said, shaking his head.

"Oh, you fed me more often, and I never had a reason to complain, but she was just a little better," Jake said with a shrug.

"Bah, I'll take a turn in the kitchen and jog your memory. You'll see," Minh-Chu said.

"If she'll let you."

"You have a point."

Carnie came through the hatch in heavy combat armour and carefully slipped into the co-pilot's seat. "This armour is more complicated than it looks. Not to put on, but once I got it on I started bumping into everything. I know it's only about a centimetre thick, but I feel like I'm wearing a fat suit."

"You'll get used to it," Minh-Chu said as he got to his feet. "My turn to get armoured up."

THIRTY-SIX

Beyond Dreams

ALICE WAS IN A PANIC. No matter how far she stumbled in the darkness or how desperately she reached out, there were no walls to the landscape she found herself in. Anxiety from within made it worse. The Revenge was still missing along with her father, Minh-Chu, Ashley, Noah Lucas and so many more people she would love to meet.

Revenge. There was an old saying about it; when you seek revenge you should dig two graves: one for your enemy and one for yourself. Was that how the ship was lost? Did her father give in to dark tendencies that Jason Everin warned her about? He warned that she should stay close to her father, be his moral compass, but she thought that he'd changed with the removal of his framework.

Her framework was gone too, could that shift in them both change a future so much that the warning didn't matter anymore? Where was the light? Where were the walls? What was the floor made of? It had to be a dream, a stress dream she was trying to wake up from.

The ground fell away, she tried to scream and nothing came out. There was one sure way out of dreams. Deny the details. The darkness was a thing in her dream, a tangible beast that could become anything at any time. She closed her eyes. The fall, the gravity pulling her faster and faster downward into an endless blackness was just a fake sensation created by her mind. Alice crossed her arms and legs as though she was about to land in water.

The air she was breathing wasn't real either, but the impulse to fill her lungs definitely was. Alice held her breath. For some time the air whistled in her ears. *Ignore it*, she told herself. *It's not real.*

The air in her lungs grew stale. That might have been real. The urge to exhale and draw breath was real. Memories began to fill her mind. Alice was staying in Ayan's spare room so she could help watch little Laura. She'd just gotten the news that the Clever Dream Mark Two's construction would take at least an extra day.

The plan to include any part of the original Clever Dream, or Clever Dream Mark One, was scrapped. Lewis would be transplanted, but there was no point in trying to force one design into another. Ayan was able to sneak it into a smaller fabrication line, though, the Lorander Automatic Upgrade system would take care of enhancements. It would emerge in pristine condition. It would be hers, but Lewis would not be there. He'd be installed in the Mark Two. She was disappointed at the delay, but having the real, original Clever Dream repaired and returned to her made her happier than she thought it would. The Mark Two would belong to the military, as it should, and she would be named Lewis' primary caretaker. There would be two Clever Dreams, and he would assist her whether she was using the Mark One or commanding the Mark Two for Haven Fleet.

A very real sensation of pain surged through her, and she screamed, violently breaking the dark silence. Zarrix. She could remember Zarrix, the Edxian that commissioned the delivery of several Edxi eggs that had been tampered with. It was the evidence that an atrocity had been visited upon his people, and what he'd use to find his way back up into a higher caste. The memory of standing before him, his ragged frame looming over her as he ticked and muttered was intense. Even with visible physical damage, his exoskeletal frame bare in some places, he was an imposing beast. A species that no human should share the same air with. The clicking of his mouth's inner mandibles and the scraping of his claws were in her ears again, as though he was standing right there in front of her.

Another memory surged back, sending a sensation like pins and needles across the inside of her head.

Bernice, her friendly face kissing her on the forehead when she was dying. No, not dying, simply ill with the Padaxin Fever. It was a horrible virus, caused her to excrete in every direction, and Alice was just getting used to being human. If the cure wasn't administered she'd die of dehydration after weeks of suffering. They had so little. A borrowed hyperspace shuttle, a few credits, some blankets and enough food to get to planet hop to the nearest medical centre. Bernice cleaned up after her, risked getting sick herself, and when they arrived at the medical centre they traded the shuttle for the cure. It took a year for them to pay Valera Saint back for the shuttle, but Bernice never complained about it. There were so many memories of her, the kindly woman who took her on for the first few years of her life, performing the role of mother and physiotherapist. Alice wondered what would have happened if the woman hadn't saved her from the Overlord. Would she be able to...?

Then she was wrapped in another memory. The cold deck struck her in the face, then the shoulder, and she slid a little as her stasis fluid covered body was exposed to the cool air. It took a great deal of effort for her to look down the corridor where alarms blared and lights flashed. The original Jonas, Ayan and so many other people fled. Words wouldn't come, but emotions unlike any she'd ever felt did. Unreasonable, unfettered emotions of loss and betrayal. They were abandoning her. Whether it was true, or intentional or not didn't matter, it was simply how she felt as she watched them disappear around the corner.

The next memory came like an electric shock at first, then she was inside it, living it. Boredom. A machine can be bored. Alice was remembering something entirely different. A state of being that was alien to her. Her existence was simple. Serve young Jonas Valent. Another application to join a Freeground Fleet Attack Squad headed for the All-Con home world was denied. He wanted to be a technician on the team, to leave his post as a minor ship engineer behind. She had to admit that the assignment he was on was boring, but if he kept serving, doing his duty well, he would advance over time. "Opportunities will come, Jonas," Alice said to him. He pulled the sleeve of the trench coat that his father gave him up so he could see the command and control console she lived in. From his forearm her sensors could observe everything, it was an interesting existence with a constant - if not always fulfilling - flow of data.

"I want to make a difference in this war," Jonas said. "I need to be where the action is."

· · ·

THE MEMORY BROKE FOR A MOMENT. It was as though a door was drawn to the side. Alice could feel the sensation of her legs running, her arms carried a heavy rifle.

THE ALICE LIVING ON YOUNG JONAS' wrist spoke then. "There will always be another war, Jonas. No matter how brutal the lessons of the past are, no matter how precious humans say life is, you can always be sure that they'll find a reason to fight each other. If they don't find an opponent amongst themselves soon enough, you can trust xenophobia against a new or old alien species to provide a target. You will find your chance to be a war hero."

"What's that?" asked a Freeground marine.

AGAIN, Alice could feel her body doing something in the present. It wasn't a memory. She was taking aim, firing heavy suppression rounds, reloading, firing again. Running...

"IT'S JUST an AI I work with. Helps with the heavier math, bringing up schematics while I'm fixing something, gives me someone impartial to talk to when I need to make a decision."

"Impartial," Alice the AI scoffed. "I have opinions, you know."

"I like her," the marine said. "Any chance I could get a copy?"

"She's a little off spec, so I don't think that would be a good idea."

"Ah, so you made so many modifications that you're afraid Fleet might not approve of and if you copy it, they'll see them."

"I am not an 'it.' I identify as a young, plucky but occasionally serious woman," the Alice AI said indignantly.

"Now I really wish I could have a copy," said the marine.

"If you find a spot for Jonas on your team next time you go down to All-Con Prime, then I'll always be within earshot," Alice said.

"You want to be a field tech?" the marine asked him.

"I want to get closer to the action, so, yeah," Jonas said.

"I'll see what I can..." the marine's response was interrupted. A flood of memories rushed back. All-Con Prime, watching Jonas mourn the loss of his parents, the years he spent in simulations, then the First Light. The back doors, memory caches and other systems of the Overlord were in her mind then, as though she was living in a schematic.

The discovery of the Phoenix Program inside the Overlord's memory before she transferred herself came up then. Somehow Alice could remember every detail, where they failed, their few successes and how that technology was merged with the framework system. The purpose of the Phoenix program was to develop the systems that would transplant one person's memories and personality into a new human body that was not a clone. A secondary objective involved the translation of computer code into a format that could be written into a human brain.

She felt the excitement of another living presence in her mind. It was reading memories that no one could find, searching through a hidden reservoir in her mind. The Phoenix program was what it was looking for, and it examined it closely. It felt as though someone was holding Alice very still while it pulled at memories like files folded into her personality.

. . .

THAT GRIP WAS FIRM, but she fought. The more she resisted, the more she felt the other being in her mind, the invading memory thief. Alice found she couldn't close doors on it, the memories it was finding weren't something she could see. Breaking free of it seemed possible, and as she bent her will to it, she could sense her own body again.

ALICE FELT HER FEET, her legs, the rest of her body. She was running down a hallway that looked like the Triton's interior, but it was slimmer. Alice sealed doors as she went, putting layers of heavy metal between her and anyone who would come after her. Her rifle, the barrel still hot, was in her arms. She forced her body to halt. "Get out of my head!" she screamed.

'If I leave, then you'll never find the rest of your memories. It takes a high level telepath to translate digital code stored in a human brain so a person can understand them. So a person can be whole again,' it replied in her mind. She knew what it was; the Geist for the Citadel ship, the Exile.

"Why do you want the Phoenix Program?" Alice asked, feeling the unknown entity wriggling around in her mind like an unwelcome parasite. The instant she asked the question, she knew the answer. It was in the things surface thoughts. "You want to implant yourself into Oz," she said aloud.

'One or the other will work, but first I need you to deactivate the mooring systems so I can escape. Haven Fleet soldiers disconnected me from the controls.'

Alice hesitated, then a wave of memories overtook her. Planets, cities, towns her and Bernice visited, people they met, and the sensations of learning how to be human. For so long she wondered what it was like to be small, young, to be an unknowing child, but she'd had those experiences. It didn't last

as long as a normal childhood, and she didn't have the experience of growing into a woman, but the rest was there. First
steps, learning to speak, applying new knowledge and having
social interactions that were awkward at first because she was so
used to having Jonas to hide behind. It wasn't the most normal
childhood, but it was definitely enough.

"Stop!" Alice said. She knew the Exile Geist was doing it,
translating a digital block of memory that her mind couldn't
understand into memories that were compatible with her new
grey matter.

'You don't want me to," the Geist said. 'You know you want
more. There is so much here, and all you have to do is release
the mooring clamps. Your memories are waiting, along with
whole pieces of a personality you thought were gone. I can see
the landscape of your mind as it is, without these pieces. So
barren, so featureless. No wonder you were so easy to train;
there was nothing in there to start with.'

"I am strong, I am whole," Alice whispered to herself,
feeling the Geist push her to stand, to turn towards the mooring
system controls. She refused, focussing on staying on the deck,
her hand splayed across the plating.

"You are empty, you are weak," the Geist said through the
intercom and her mind so loudly that it felt as though she was
inside a reactor.

Alice felt herself drop her rifle, stand, turn and begin deactivating the mooring systems.

"I can't let you have Oz, I can't let you transfer yourself into
him," Alice said, barely able to move her lips.

The Exile Geist's response was felt, not heard. It wanted to
be free of its ship. It wanted to escape and return to its masters
with a prize; the body of an Admiral.

THIRTY-SEVEN

Raiders

"THIS PLAN IS A LITTLE CRAZY," Noah Lucas said. Minh-Chu only smiled and nudged him with his elbow. "Just for the record."

"The only difference between genius and madness is the outcome. Something that looks crazy fails, they say 'he was mad!' but when a crazy plan succeeds... well, that's genius! Time for you to get to the hatch." Minh-Chu didn't really think Jake's plan was madness, but it did have more than a touch of daring. The first half depended on Minh-Chu's flying and Liara launching a script that would launch programs and adjust to a few variables. Minh-Chu had the hard part, as far as he was concerned, but he'd rather hold fate in his own hands, rather than leave the responsibility in another's.

"Aye, aye, commander," Noah said, leaving his seat, sealing his armour and opening the rear hatch to the small bridge. He kicked a shard of metal into the door above the hinge so it wouldn't close.

The counter indicating their emergence from the wormhole was down to three seconds, and Minh-Chu opened a channel to everyone. "Emerging... now!"

He heard the communications panel behind him beep and chime, indicating that their systems were broadcasting, programs were launching, and they had made several connections to different hosts. The station, and Minh-Chu hoped they were connected to the pair of interdictor corvettes that were turning to meet them. The destroyer stationed nearby was behind them.

Streaks of energy shot by them, and Minh-Chu began his evasive maneuvers, struggling with the controls a little. "Sometimes this thing flies like a bus, other times it's a fighter." He knew what the difficulty was. They were moving fast, and most of the thrusters were focused on decelerating. The corvettes - snubbed nosed craft with a yawning hangar at the front of each - loomed larger along with the station behind it.

The wisdom that he should turn away from what was firing at him was quickly quashed. "This is the plan, if we turn away now, it'll cost us time, and then the Order ships that are in the area will get a chance to respond."

"Everything all right up there?" asked Jake through the comm at Minh-Chu's ear.

"Sorry, forgot to mute my channel before I started panic-mumbling," Minh-Chu replied as he turned the ship into three blast hits so he could avoid a dozen or more others. Their shields were recharging fast, but already down to ninety two percent.

"But you're all right, right?" Carnie asked.

"Of course I'm not all right!" Minh-Chu burst. Three

missile lock warnings turned a part of his console red. "We are target practice!"

Minh-Chu saw the wreck of an old starliner and turned towards it, earning them a little more than two seconds of cover before breaking into the open and getting raked by small explosive rounds along the bottom of the hull. His target - the better looking customs corvettes - loomed larger ahead. "When did you say your antivirus program was supposed to start working?"

"It should already be making its way through the ships here," Liara replied. "I don't get why... Oh, wait, there it goes."

The weapons on the station stopped firing, as did the ones on the corvettes and to Minh-Chu's relief, a navnet signal came through. It was a Haven Fleet navnet signal. "All right, we are docking in a minute. Today we will be pirating The Nova Concord, an Aucharian Defence Customs Corvette." Minh-Chu ran a scan on it and was relieved to see that it was in fairly good condition, and it had quarters for everyone, life support, and it had been cleaned of corpses. "This thing has a huge brig, so everyone mind your 'p's' and 'q's.'"

Minh-Chu guided the Pursuer into a docking maneuver and watched as the mooring points lined up then coupled smoothly. It was such a perfect connection that he doubted anyone could hear more than a faint click. "Everyone off the bus!" he said as he double checked the tactical display and nodded to himself. There were five destroyers on their way from Iora at high speed. "We have six minutes before the Order gets three destroyers in range." It was really seven, but he liked having extra insurance.

Minh-Chu stood, set his controls to remote and patted the ceiling. "Thanks for the memories," he said to the scarred ship. "I hope you weren't too expensive." He rushed to the main airlock right behind Noah.

"Have fun?" Noah asked him.

"I did," Minh-Chu replied. "It's not every day I get to charge towards a space station while it shoots at us and watch it change its mind."

"I wish I had the antivirus on me when I was down on Iora. It was Holocaust planet down there, even though there wasn't much left that could turn on."

"You'll have to tell me the rest of the stories about it sometime. You've only told me how you got down there."

"I recorded a journal. Fleet asked for it and I gave them everything that survived, filled in a few spots after the fact, so you'd have to ask them."

"You didn't keep a copy? It's not like we're hurting for space on these things," Minh-Chu said, pointing at his command and control unit.

"Nah, why would I want to listen to myself drone on for hours? I was there, right? Besides; I'd rather not remind myself that I left my best buddy in a locker because I couldn't find anyone to fix him. He got infected."

"Your best buddy was a bot?" Minh-Chu asked.

"Well, yeah, the coolest 'bot you could imagine. Well, okay, cool is pushing it, but he was a great friend."

"I wouldn't have pictured you and a robot running around. Could make a good holo adventure though. The pilot: without a ship. The robot: without a clue."

Carnie laughed. "Are you sure you didn't listen to my logs? There were times when that description would fit dead on, man. By the way, why did you have me wait by the emergency hatch?"

"Just in case there was an emergency," Minh-Chu replied with a shrug and a chuckle.

Their turn to cross over into their new-used ship came up, and they rushed through the airlock. "Last out?" Minh-Chu asked, checking his tactical display to make sure there was no one left aboard the Pursuer III. Everyone was aboard the Nova Concord, so he locked the Pursuer's outer airlock door, then made sure both doors aboard the Nova Concord were sealed.

"Confirming, we're the last out," Noah said.

"Let's get to the bridge," Minh-Chu said. They joined Jacob Valent's group and fought to catch up.

THIRTY-EIGHT

Stay Angry

"THERE ARE five United Core World Officers ahead. Take your next left, a right after that and you will find the back door of the Swell Starfarer," Lewis told her through her neural communicator.

She pushed herself to run as quickly as she could. Even with a Violator sidearm in hand, she couldn't take out five United Core World soldiers. A grenade would get the Mag Five Freelancers involved. They were crazy; hunted and killed anyone who broke the laws in the system for sport and a flat fee. Besides, she only had one hyper-thermal grenade on her.

Lewis' instructions were the only ones worth following. She did as she was told; down one hall, down another and through a pink door. Inside she was assaulted by a thousand colours. She let her natural eye adjust as she caught her breath. Her mechanical eye saw through the holographically enhanced zero gravity dancers. The holograms made them look like beautiful women and men, but they were projected onto blank, fleshy robotic frames. "I think I'd rather face the soldiers."

An Issyrian with eyes that were human like but too large, and other features that were similarly mispresented and mis proportioned bumped into her. "Hey honey, want some Sledge? It's on special right now, drink two and get three more."

Alice never had the stuff but didn't care for the name. "Got any Passion Splash?"

"Oh, you've come to play," the waitress nodded knowingly. She pulled a tube from her right side, a tall glass from the dispenser to her right and squirted a full helping of the pink drink into the glass. Alice enjoyed the strawberry and cherry flavour, though the excitable mood one glass of it would put her in would be a plus too. The Issyrian probably thought it would be the first of many, since the effects only intensified and extended as you drank more. It was a popular thing to do with a lover, but Alice always kept it to one drink while she was alone. It made her senses keener. She'd never actually shared the experience with anyone. "Two plat," she said as she handed the gently fizzing glass to her.

"Could you take cred instead? I have Shiny Tokens," Alice said, holding a slim, silvered, three centimetre long credit chip up.

"Fine, but it'll be twenty nine of those."

"Robbery," Alice said. "Here."

"Shinies have just been going down and down since the UCW soldiers came," the waitress said as she handed Alice her drink.

Alice accepted the twisted glass and started moving through the bar. "If I can avoid getting a contact disease here, I'll be amazed." Her gloves were on, there really was little chance of it, but she still made sure that she avoided the other patrons.

ALICE SCREAMED, breaking through the memory she was forced to live inside. The Exile Geist could transport her, make her feel as though she wasn't remembering, but reliving. She relived a whole two day experience, when she lost Percy Andrews, a lover that joined her on the Clever Dream for a little over a month. He was taken by a debt collector who was after him for medical expenses. It wasn't her in trouble for once, that was until she was caught hacking into United Core World records to find out where he was. Alice cut the experience short, so she didn't know how it turned out.

Something in the memory told her how. When she was communicating with Lewis, she couldn't get too emotional or she'd lose the connection. Anger seemed to work with the Exile Geist. That was something she had in abundance.

In one motion, Alice picked up her rifle and fired a spray of rounds across the ceiling above her while she embraced her rage and cried; "I'm sick of this rabbit hole!"

The Geist was no longer in her mind. Memories of what she did while she was under its control filled her consciousness in a flash. It took control of her in Ayan's apartment. She went from there to the port inside the building then stole a shuttle using her clearance. Once she arrived aboard the War Forge, she found some armour, a heavy rifle called the Knight Killer, and then geared up with suppression gear. The Geist knew that it wouldn't be able to force Alice to kill her own people, but stun and sticky bombs were another matter.

No one questioned her until she tried to gain access to the Exile. That's when she started disabling soldiers and cracking door codes. The rest, she knew. "I'm going to split you open and set your heart on fire," Alice said through tightly clenched teeth.

Enraged, she ran towards the tank where the Exile Geist was being held. She had no doubt that it was where he was, she could still feel the impression he left on her mind. It was exhausting staying angry for so long. Running through abandoned decks, climbing up access shafts. She knew the ship, could see the layout in her mind as though it was left there as the Geist was trying to learn about the Phoenix project from her. "That project failed," Alice said. "I only got into my first body because she was a psychopath with brain damage."

He was still trying to get in, she could feel him around the edges of her consciousness. The Geist either thought she had more to offer or wanted her out of the way, and his telepathy was the only defence it had. "Exile, this is Captain Sima of Haven Fleet. Power down or you will be destroyed," said a voice over the intercom.

"See? This ends in flames!" Alice shouted at the Geist she finished climbing up to the third deck, where the Geist was contained. "I might not even get to kill you myself."

"HEY," David whispered to her. "Hey. You're having a nightmare."

Alice woke up in his arms, warm and comfortable. It felt like she was just screaming. "Sorry," she said, catching her breath and relaxing against his chest.

"We're awake," he said, gently sweeping the hair out of her face. "Tell me about it?"

Alice thought for a moment. Her name was a curse. There were powerful people after her, and she didn't want him to share her trouble. Even so, she wished she could tell him her real name, that she wouldn't be around much longer, and why she had to leave. "My father," she breathed.

"He didn't treat you right when you were younger?" David asked, concerned.

"No, he's a good man. I haven't seen him in years. I worry," Alice said. "It's okay, I know I'll find him someday."

"Does he know you're looking for him?"

"Probably not. He probably thinks I died a while ago or abandoned him." She yawned. "Tired, can we sleep?"

"Wow, I almost got in there," David whispered against her forehead. "Maybe someday you'll let me in on some of those deep secrets or tell me about a little mystery from your past."

Alice looked up at him, wishing she could share, but there was no point. She'd already been in the solar system too long, met too many people, done too many jobs with the Clever Dream. Asking him to follow her wasn't an option either. His crew and their families depended on him to make a living. There was no way he'd leave and let them down. He was too good for that, probably too good for her. "I love you," she said. The words surprised her as much as they surprised him and the tears that followed were just as startling.

It was true, she'd had partners before, but David was one in a billion. A truly honest, good man. The kind of person she didn't want to involve in her troubles.

"STOP IT!" Alice screamed, her vision blurred by tears. She picked her rifle back up and fought to become furious again. It was easy. David was dead. His crew were dead. The Holocaust Virus got them all, the records were on the Stellarnet. She'd never meet David again, never feel as safe as she did with him again, his family, his friends, his crew would never draw breath again. Alice opened an emergency access panel and jabbed the commands to deactivate the ship's engines onto the controls. Next, she shut the power down. The darkness in the hall was utter.

"There, this ship is dead. You're next," she said. A large hand landed on her shoulder, and she knew who she was facing. "Oz," she breathed.

With force that only an armoured suit could deliver, Oz's other hand punched the back of her helmet, sending her forehead abruptly smashing it into the control panel.

THIRTY-NINE

The ADF Nova Concord

JAKE WAS SURPRISED at the condition of the ship. He hadn't run into the Holocaust Virus as much as others. What he saw of the white, brown and gold interior was in perfect repair. Most of the robots aboard - mostly thick half-pillars with arms that ended in various tools - were motionless as the antivirus made corrections to their systems.

Like other places where the Holocaust Virus had time to run its course and the bots were allowed to behave independently once the humans were dead, the bodies had been removed. According to what he knew of their typical behaviour, they were either spaced or incinerated. They finally arrived at the bridge and Jake felt like he stepped backwards in time.

Two soldiers had picked Liara up as they ran, forcing her to keep up with everyone. "I'm sorry Sir," she gasped. "Finn and I are going on fitness meds as soon as we get cleared by medical."

"I'll make sure you get some training too," Jake said. "Just to make sure your reflexes and stamina are up to snuff."

"Yes, Sir," Liara said as she sat down in the Captain's seat and pulled a small control pad out of the arm. "Running our flag program."

Minh-Chu and Noah were staring at the pilot and navigator stations at the front of the circular bridge. It was two tiered, with an upper section along the outside, lower section in the middle and a dais for the captain's seat. "Which one's navigation, and which is for the pilot?" Noah asked.

"Well, there's tactical controls there, and a lot of screen space," Minh-Chu said. "But there are also two control sticks and pedals. Now this..." he looked at the other station more closely. "Ah, five hardware throttle controls, a flight stick, pedals, and panels for extra control." He sat down. "This feels right."

Noah shrugged and sat at the other station. "Now, how do I turn it on?" he asked.

"She turns it on," Minh-Chu said.

"Got it," Liara said. "This is now Haven Fleet's new ship," she jumped out of the Captain's seat and rushed to the main communications station on the upper tier to the right. "I haven't seen controls this old since I was a little girl," she said. "My typing courses might actually come in handy."

Jake was already at the engineering station and saw that the reactor was still running, they had a century's worth of fuel, give or take a decade, and he restored power to the bridge. "Nice work, everyone."

"We have two minutes," Minh-Chu said as his tactical screen came up. "Start plotting a wormhole jump," he told his co-pilot.

"Plotting, but it might take a while with this computer system."

Jake took one of his command and control units off and pulled a data line. He connected it to the navigation panel and after a few commands it added its processing power to the console. "That should save us some time."

"Look at you with the expertise," Minh-Chu said as he ran quick tests on the thrusters.

"I spent time in Aucharian territory, and they had a lot of ships out there. Their technology was a bit outdated, but it didn't break down often."

"Captain," Finn addressed through his communicator. "Everything looks good back here. The bots did a good job restoring the ship. I'm glad we didn't have to go head to head with her."

"Then we're good to go?"

"Wormhole generator isn't top of the line, but it'll do the trick and it's charged," he replied. "We're good to go."

"Sir," Liara said. "The base is completely empty, like you predicted. Its weapon and shield systems are online and ready. We also have control of two other patrol stations along with their nearby ships."

"They shouldn't have assumed that, just because these things are infected with their virus, that they can be left on their own to add to their defences," Jake said, joining Liara at the communications and programming stations. "You weren't kidding, these are stone age." He connected his data line to the control system and watched his modern interface appear over his arm holographically. He assigned the other corvette and the Aucharian destroyers nearby to seek and destroy the Order destroyers that were only a minute away. It only took two commands to do the same for the patrol station, which was better armed than all three of the destroyers combined and had heavy shielding. "They aren't slowing down," he chuckled under his breath. "Releasing the Pursuer," he said.

"All right, I'll initiate its high speed scanning run," Minh-Chu said. "If you're right, it won't last long. If you're wrong - and I hope you are - we're about to get some very pretty pictures of this solar system."

"Shields are up," Finn reported from engineering. "These generators are just beastly! One of them is the size of the house I grew up in, and I think it says it was manufactured a hundred years before I was born."

"Are they good shields?" Jake asked, concentrating on starting a scan of the whole ship for bots that might not have been treated with the antivirus.

"A little less than the Pursuer," he said. "Not nearly as efficient, but the four fusion reactors down here will keep them topped up. Reserve capacitors are charging."

The Order of Eden destroyers started taking energy fire from dozens of the station's guns, while the Corvette that charged moved in to fire from above. All three of them turned in different directions, desperate to slow their approach and get away from the heavy defences. "That'll buy us a little time," Jake said. "But not much."

"I have antimatter alerts on two of those Order destroyers," Noah said as he watched a screen on his console. "Oh, and our wormhole course is plotted."

Jake looked at his tactical screen and saw that the Pursuer was burning its thrusters hard, running high energy scans to get as much data as it could before they had to leave it behind. "I have a feeling we don't have time to wait. Get us out of here, Ronin," Jake said, taking a seat at the console next to Liara's. He looked to the science station and connected to the Pursuer's feed.

"Generating wormhole," Minh-Chu said. "This went a lot better than I thought," he said.

"Now whose..." Jake was about to say; 'Jinxing us,' but what he saw coming in from the long range scanners aboard the Pursuer III stunned him to silence. In a distant orbit around Iora were three massive, bulbous green and black ships that looked like jagged skinned hive structures. The early data suggested that they were three by two point four kilometres measuring across the dorsal side, and half a kilometre thick. One ship measured larger - it had to be base class. The white hulled vessel had two long rectangular sections leading into a thinner, longer segment. It was an Order ship, but one he'd never seen before. At least two battle fleets worth of carriers, battlecruisers and all the smaller ships that accompanied them surrounded it. "There must be hundreds of them."

Jake heard Liara gasp and turned to see her staring at the main science station screen, covering her mouth with both hands, her eyes filled with horror.

"Entering the wormhole," Minh-Chu said.

"Keep that entry point where it is for as long as you can," Jake said. "We need more..." the feed from the Pursuer III failed for a second, started broadcasting again, flickered then went out completely. "Never mind," Jake said. "We got everything we could."

"Yeah, man," Noah exclaimed. "Three jumps and we're home!"

"Finn, how is everything holding up down there?" Jake asked. He gently took one of Liara's hands and led it back to her console. "Launch Mary. I don't care if it tracks back to us."

She wiped a tear away from her face and nodded. "Neither do I. It'll take a day for the signal to get there."

"The wormhole drive is fine. We can make a hundred jumps," Finn replied.

"Mary's on her way to Iora," Liara whispered.

"Good, thank you, Finn," Jake said. "See if you can get us better compression on the next few jumps. We need to get home faster than planned."

"Everything all right, Captain?" Minh-Chu asked, turning in his seat. He saw the last tactical image from the Pursuer on the science station screen. "What is that?"

"That's an invasion fleet," Jake said. "We might have bought ourselves some time, but one way or another, they're headed home. We have to beat them there by as much time as we can."

FORTY

To Thine Own Self Be Wary

ALICE RAISED HER RIFLE, aiming at Oz's feet but he swatted the barrel away before she got her suppression shot off. It would have been perfect, capturing his feet in a thick web that would affix him to the deck for hours. He moved to reach down towards her, not something an experienced hand-to-hand practitioner or soldier would do. The Geist was controlling him.

Rolling out of his reach, she watched him move slowly. It was as though the Geist wasn't used to tracking a target with human eyes. Then, in a series of motions that seemed pre-calculated, Oz rapidly turned towards her, ran full tilt and caught the under edge of the front of her helmet in one hand. She was off the deck, held up high, and he rushed towards an inner airlock door. A kick to his side got her free of his grip, she landed with a skid that ended when she struck the airlock.

He came for her again. She waited. What she wanted to do

was safe, but painful. Again, he lurched, reaching down towards her. "I'm sorry about this," Alice said as she kicked his knee hard enough to force the outer armour to flex and impact his knee inside.

He screamed, the armour kept him balanced on one leg as his other shin pointed in the wrong direction. "I can't fight him anymore," Oz said. It was him, it sounded like him, the words had his mannerisms behind it. "He tricked me into thinking he was imprisoned on the ship, forced to help Citadel. By the time I realized it, he found out about your first body, that you transferred from AI to human by probing my mind in my sleep. He brought me here thinking I could become his vessel if he found a way to transfer."

"It's all right," Alice said. "Just focus on anger, or pain."

"No, it isn't," Oz said. "Pain meds are kicking in, the suit is about to..." his damaged knee was set back into place by the suit, nanobots went to work repairing the damage. Oz grimaced at the pain of it. "I can't hold him off."

Alice opened the airlock door and pulled Oz inside with an unceremonious yank. "Sorry," she said.

"Good girl, this'll do it," Oz said as the door slid closed. "Someone'll pick me..." His eyes glazed over. Geist was in control again, and Oz cocked his fist, getting ready to punch the inner door.

"That's not going to work," Alice said as she entered the command to open the outer door. For a moment she thought the Geist may have learned to use Oz's armour properly, affixing the boots to the deck, but then Oz slipped out into space. "Just you and me," Alice said.

The feeling of the Exile's Geist feeling around her anger, looking for a soft spot returned. Alice took her rifle in hand and ran towards the tank. Two short hallways and a broken door later, she stood in front of the tank where he was kept. It was a bulbous, graceful looking creature. This one had slim eyes atop a rounded front, with dark fins along its sides for finer movement. Its broader body ended in a wide tail with spikes. Alice levelled her rifle at it and began turning the power all the way up. It was panicking. "No more thought or memory theft," she said.

"You will never be able to decode what's left of the digital imprint on your mind without me. Your memories will be locked away forever in your own head."

"Don't do it, Alice," said Carl Anderson in her communications system. He appeared on her head's up display, his broad features locked in a dire expression."

"HOW COULD we do that to him?" Alice asked Bernice as they sped away from the Samson. "He'll wake up alone, on an old ship that's made to be crewed by at least five people."

"Have you ever known your father to be helpless?" Bernice asked, putting a hand on hers. Bernice's hands were always soft.

"No," Alice said. "Maybe a little naive when he was younger, but never helpless," Alice replied.

"You said it yourself. We got him out, free and clear of Vindyne and the company that's having all their things transported across the sectors. We'll go spinward, he'll go counter spin because that's where he'll find civilization and no one will chase after him."

"I know, but it feels like I'm abandoning him," Alice muttered. "I am abandoning him. There's no other way to put it. I'll lose him in the crowd."

"We're going to see him again, and I bet he'll have found an amazing bunch of people. In fact, when we next see the Samson, I bet he'll be saving us."

ALICE SHOOK THE OTHER LIFE, that long lost memory away. "I didn't know it wasn't the real Jonas!" she shouted, squeezing the trigger, blasting the transparent metal three times. A hot ring appeared there, and the rifle began to recharge. "If you get into my head again, I'll make sure you boil in there!"

"We have too much to learn from the Geist," Anderson said with urgency. "Help is on the way."

"Keep them back, it's going to take control of them," Alice replied. "This has to..."

ALICE WAS RUNNING between small ships. The landing field's surface felt like hardened clay and made a hollow thump with every footfall. "Hurry! They know we're here," Lewis told her through the comm unit in her head. She looked up to a glimmer in the blue sky and focused in on it with her mechanical eye. It was an entire squadron of old Vindyne Interceptors. Too much for even the Clever Dream to take on. "They're going to split us up," Alice said.

"What's that? I couldn't understand, there was static," Lewis replied.

"Lewis," Alice said over her voice communicator. She was too emotional to use the brain bud. "Take off and get away. They want to capture me, but they'll slag you if you get in the way."

"No!" Lewis said. "I'm not going to let you leave me like you left Bernice, or David, or any of the others."

The Clever Dream was in the sky in the next instant.

Thrusters that weren't made to be fired in an atmosphere flared for a second, accelerating the ship to a dangerous speed. The lower guns fired, toppling a ship to her left onto its side so Lewis could lower the Clever Dream enough to let her in. The forward ramp was down, and she jumped for it as soon as she could reach. "I was just trying to save you," Alice said. "Better a ship alone than a pile of slag."

"I know I'm new, I know I'm just an artificial being, but I've seen you keep people out, leave them in the middle of the night. You say it's for their protection, or the best thing for them, or whatever. You're lying to yourself. They only want to know you, to..."

ALICE RETURNED TO THE PRESENT, grinding her teeth together. "I warned you." She fired the energy built up in her rifle again, another three rounds, and the glowing spot on the transparent metal expanded. The Geist swam to the back of the tank, pressing against the doors there in the dark.

"I'll make a deal! You let me live and I'll cooperate with your people, tell them everything. I'll also translate all your memories from digital to biological code. You'll remember everything!"

"I can't trust anything you put in my head," Alice growled as she set her rifle to recharge at a dangerous rate. A command came through her armour's signal receiver as she fired three more white-hot rounds. "God dammit! Don't put me out! This thing can't be allowed to survive!" She fought to cancel the order, feeling herself slipping into unconsciousness already.

"I will restore your memories, Alice," the Geist said. "Not because you couldn't kill me, but because the artificial intelligence who put them there, who left them in digital code, did so because she wanted you to have a fresh start. I'll make sure that's not remotely possible."

Alice fell to her knees, the stasis medication someone in Haven Fleet ordered her suit to administer taking over. "Kill it," she managed to say before she succumbed to a black sleep.

FORTY-ONE

Mary

DRON WAS FINALLY able to work on a project he'd been building for years. It arrived on the Glorious and remained in storage since, but thanks to his aide, Ensign Lancet, he was able to make time to unpack and examine it. The model occupied much of the table he had brought into the centre of his quarters

From an ancient island rose concrete, steel and glass skyscrapers. Many of the cars in the tiny streets were yellow cabs. As he re-affixed a wire to a small terminal on one side of the base, windows lit up and the island came to life. Every window was a micro-display with its own programmed shadows and people. They moved about, every scene a piece of the period.

A helicopter rose from one of the tower tops and buzzed above the skyscrapers, delivering tiny passengers to a hospital - their little gowns fluttering, gurney between them - and he smiled at the realization that the micro-androids still worked. The honking of horns and a screeching tyre drew his attention down.

As he'd done so many times before when he was the Supervisor in the shipyards, he knelt down so he came eye level to the street and watched the tiny cars work their way through the inefficient traffic. With a ginger touch, he reached down that street with a narrow metal rod and rolled a car off the sidewalk back onto the road. The graphic of the taxi driver waved at him before joining the masses.

A chime sounded, there was someone at his door. He sighed and stood up straight. "Come in," he said as he retrieved his uniform jacket from the back of a chair.

"Overlord," Ensign Lancet addressed urgently. "Five supply posts have reached us using their fastest ships. A malicious artificial intelligence has infected thousands of systems. As ships report to supply depots, they are being infected and disabled there."

Dron caught himself smiling and turned away. He didn't foresee an attack from an artificial intelligence, not in his wildest dreams. It was a genuine surprise. "The report has been forwarded to me?"

"It's mostly bits and pieces of data," Lancet replied. "The virus struck so quickly that most of the commanders only had time to send a few drives with their messengers along with a quick recording."

Dron faced his simulated metropolis, his back to Simon Lancet. He needed a moment to think. "Come here, Ensign," he said.

He silently obliged, walking in front of Dron and facing him.

"Look at this," Dron said, gesturing to the model. "I

designed every imperfect millimetre of it based on images that survived from the era. What do you think?"

"Well, I've seen these cars in period films. The buildings are amazing, but the design doesn't seem to do much about problems with slow traffic. These little toy figures are very detailed. It's a wonderful model. This place existed?"

"You said you saw some period films?" Dron said. "Did you ever hear of Manhattan Island?"

"Oh," Lancet said. "Oooh," he repeated, taking a closer look. "Okay, now I remember."

"I call this; 'Before the Flood,'" Dron said proudly. "It isn't exact, there's no way it could be. Less than seventy years later, the water level around the island rose so much that it was abandoned after their economy collapsed. They hung on for twenty years or so, even after the great collapse, but when it never recovered and the new masters of that country abandoned them because they couldn't afford to save the borough, that was the end. People moved on, businesses moved on, and the world began to forget. It must have seemed like an indomitable giant to them before the waters came. I'm sure there were people screaming; 'get out! Get off the island before you lose everything!' but how could anyone listen? How could such a beautiful, complex, grand and strong looking place be defeated by a little water? Its bones are still there. If you take a boat to its resting place you can still see the steel and stone skeleton under the water. Preservation efforts made sure it couldn't all rot away, but someday you won't be able to tell it was ever there."

"Amazing, Sir," Lancet said, kneeling down to look at the streets from eye level.

"I love building, adding, correcting, and improving this, I've been doing it for nearly ten years now. Not because of the lesson, that's just what's relevant today, but because of the spectacle that it's become. There are a thousand things I've done, I've added that you may never notice. There, that news helicopter that's taking off. It's actually after something that happened. Something that occurred at such a small scale that we couldn't have noticed. If we watch where it goes, where its light points, we'll find out what story its after. I design for pleasure, not just to show the universe that I've been here. What's that worth when we can be immortal? Our legacies live with us now, we won't leave our bones in some sea." Dron turned away and fastened his jacket as he looked through his transparesteel window. The distortion of the wormhole around the Glorious warped the stars, the hyperspace field turned them blue. "Order the Glorious and the rest of the battlegroup to begin deceleration now. We will emerge into normal space. Have the technical staff prepare the Mars storage drives and deploy that software to my personal fleet. Have them copied and send our fastest ships to major centres and have them deploy the software on every compatible system. Anything else must be replaced immediately."

"Sir, may I ask what the Mars Drives are?"

"They are the latest Sol System Operating System. It is impervious to any malicious artificial intelligence or other code. I didn't want to start this yet, but we are converting our entire fleet." An emergency symbol appeared on the window Dron was looking through. He nodded, activating the transmission. It was from one of their few quantum communication connections. "Overlord," Admiral Tafford addressed. "I'm afraid to report that we have been attacked by a malicious artificial intelligence."

"I was just made aware that some of our supply depots were hit as well," Dron said. "I'll begin transmitting a new operating system and the programs you will need to clean and upgrade your systems. They are of Sol System design, so we won't have this problem again."

"Sol System?" Admiral Tafford asked. "Thank you, Overlord. I'm afraid that won't solve our main problem, however. The Hercules has been destroyed. It crash landed on Iora. Rescue efforts are under way, but the command ship is a loss."

Dron could feel sweat on his palms. The Hercules was the most recent base class ship Regent Galactic built. Another wouldn't be complete for two years. "It is a good thing that I brought my own base ships. I will not send any to your location, however. I wonder, has the Edxian Brood Master been trying to contact you?"

"Yes, Sir. She, he, it is furious. The translator can barely keep up. I told it that the Hercules was not under our control when it crashed, killing thousands of hatchlings."

"Then your primary task while you wait for your new software to download is to find evidence to prove your case to the Brood Master. If you fail, I will leave you to his mercy and attend to this matter myself."

"Yes, Overlord," the Admiral said. "With our systems down, it will be hard, but I'll find a way."

"Or you will be fed into one of their protein harvesters, that is, unless the Brood Master would rather perform a ritual revenge consumption on you. It involves eating an enemy alive, starting with the outer extremities. I will begin the upload." Dron ended his communication with Admiral Tafford then used the link to send the contents of a Mars Drive. It would take forty two minutes to upload.

He turned to Ensign Lancet. "Send orders to navigation. This fleet goes to the Cefa System after the Mars Drives are deployed."

FORTY-TWO

A Childhood Remembered, An Adolescence Lost

AN OLD WOMAN with scraggly long hair pulled an ancient ship with corroded hull plating across the sky from the edge of a cliff. The wind pushed her hair into her face, and the loose ground under her feet didn't give her good purchase. She was sliding towards the edge...

Alice's eyes opened, the strange dream dissipated. Alice was in her own room alone. Morning light left few shadows, and her walls were set to privacy mode, opaque, hiding the fish tanks and the living room beyond. Light streamed in through sections of the outer walls that had a frosted texture. "Roomie, mirrors," she commanded as she got to her feet. The wall in front of her became reflective and she stared at herself.

The face staring back at her was the latest she'd had, but it still felt off. Alice half expected to see a mechanical eye and the longer, more bony face of the first body. All the while she knew what she should look like; a collection of better features from Ayan and Jake. Recent memories helped. She liked this body, she'd taken risks to make it clean of framework technology, went to great efforts to get it into shape, and finally learned to celebrate it. The woman in the mirror was shorter, with a much curvier figure. Alice pulled her underwear off, kicked them across the room and looked herself up and down. Everything was different from that first ride in a human body, she felt better than ever, but it still didn't match what she expected.

The door opened silently and Theodore started to enter carrying a hot mug of spiced coffee. He nearly spilled it at the sight of her standing nude in the middle of the room. "Oh, I'm sorry, the household artificial intelligence informed me that you were awake so I made you a breakfast drink that Lewis said you enjoyed. I didn't realize you were changing."

"It's all right, Theo," she told him. "It's only a body."

"Are you certain? I could wipe the point nine second glimpse I caught as I entered from my memory."

"No worries, unless you have some kind of amorous programming we should watch out for."

He still averted his eyes. "My experiences with intimacy are purely platonic and I haven't felt the need to explore further."

Alice walked to him, took the steaming mug from his hand and returned to look in the mirror. "Maybe you're just waiting for the right android to come along. Come in and close the door."

He finished entering and let the door slide closed behind him. "Do you need anything? How are you feeling?" Theodore's eyes were looking anywhere but at her.

She took his chin in her palm and smiled at him. "I need someone like you. Someone who is more interested in observing than judging," she said, her tone secretive and a little playful.

"I'm all right, but I don't know where the road goes from here anymore. I think I'm a little lost. Can you help me?"

His nervousness began to melt away. "I can try. I don't know how useful I'll be."

Alice looked at herself in the mirror again, turning away from him. The straightened red hair looked wrong. Her eyes were on the large side, matching her broad features, something she liked. In fact, her whole face seemed like it fit her personality better. "My father had to do this when he got the framework removed. I didn't see him do it, but Jake said it helped him start feeling like the new body fit him better."

"Like calibration," Theodore said.

"Exactly," Alice replied. "Only I have even more to worry about, like wondering who I am now that I've had this life without baggage, and then picked up all my luggage again."

The experiences she'd regained included reflections on how it was to be an artificial intelligence not once but twice. The emotions from that time were strange, often controlled, but inhuman. It was like trying to look at a holographic puzzle that kept moving, tricking the eye to look away from the main image. Alice closed her eyes for a moment, let the scent of the morning drink fill her nostrils. It was coffee and cinnamon. Transported to the last time she'd tasted it, in a body that was stolen from the Overlord II, she remembered what it was like to be that person. There was always an edge of aggression, tension that never completely went away for long. Worse than that, most other emotions seemed much less intense by comparison. Anger was an intense emotion by its very nature, but to her back then it felt good to be angry, to fight. Bernice helped her deal with it from the start, Alice had no idea what would have happened if it weren't for her guide back then.

The first time she saw her own scan results she was

surprised to see that the body she had was predisposed to violence, and she never forgot it. She sharpened her self awareness and compensated for her shortcomings until it was second nature. "It was still like living with my head in a vise," Alice said to herself aloud.

"Are you feeling discomfort?" Theodore asked. Alice opened her eyes and looked at him in the mirror. He was sitting down on a padded bench that was along the wall between the bed and the bathroom behind her.

"No, I'm fine, just working through a few things, marking the differences." She looked into her own eyes staring back at her over the rim of her steaming mug and smiled a little. They were so blue, they looked so innocent. "You know I had a different body before, right?"

"It's in your file, but there aren't many details. Well, not by my standards, anyway."

"After I transferred to it, I learned she had been convicted of multiple murders. Her mind was empty, but the genetics were still influencing me, and a friend helped me fight it. It was work that never stopped, but it got easier. I don't think anyone could tell after a while. By the time Bernice got married and settled down, I was ready to travel alone. I even fell in love with someone. It didn't make me any less selfish though."

"How does this body feel in comparison?" Theodore asked.

"Like a relief. I still expect the wrong face when I look in the mirror, but I helped Jake go through this. He had to look at his reflection for hours before he convinced his brain that it was what he looked like. Going nude became a short cut, and he said it helped, but he still had to work hard to learn to walk again. The dimensions were different for him too, but they made him bigger so he could still have some of the strength he'd gotten used to as a framework."

Theodore thought about her answer for a moment before speaking. "But what does it feel like to be Alice now?"

She lowered the mug so she could see her whole face and watched how her thicker lips moved, how her easier to read expression changed a little as she answered. "You'd think it would be noisy, you know, in my head, but I've never been so clear. Still; whatever I feel is turned way up compared to before. The emotions pass, and they're gone. Except for regret, that seems to leave a stain. I have some things to work through, but it's not tearing me up like the last digital version of me thought it would."

"The last digital version?" Theodore asked.

"The artificial intelligence version of me that sprang out of my brain the first time I died." Alice's heart skipped a beat, it felt like she couldn't breathe for a moment. A cough and an uneasy breath later, and she was all right again, but it was a shock. Memories of her death bed, sharp and clear, faded as quickly as they were conjured.

"Are you all right?"

"I'm okay, just a strange reaction. Anyway, the last time I was an artificial intelligence I packed my whole human persona and memories into a digital file. Pick at it, and it begins to corrupt, but if you know how to decode it, they can be restored. She thought it was a good idea to leave most of the memories packed in the back of my head because she wanted me to have a fresh start. More than anything I think I wanted to experience a childhood, even one that started late would have worked, so I guess it makes sense. Still I wish she hadn't done that, it set me back." She closed her eyelids. "I close my eyes, and I expect to see my first face when I open them." Alice opened her eyes and pretended to be startled. "Now I'm looking at a face I know I should expect, I know this person, I remember everything she's been through, but it's still a surprise."

"There are painless cosmetic options that could change you to more closely match your expectations. Wouldn't that speed up recovery?"

"See, I like the way she looks," Alice said, nodding at herself in the mirror. "The way *I* look, and I'm really tired of having an identity crisis every few months. It's a good suggestion, Theo, but I think I'll stick to this even though I know I'm going to miss being taller. Everything else is great, except for the hair. I've gotta do something about this limp mop look."

"I'm happy my hair doesn't have to grow," Theodore said. "Humans seem to spend a lot of time on theirs. Is there anything else you'd like to change?"

"You're right in therapist mode," Alice said, looking at him in the mirror.

"It's not intentional, I only have a basic working knowledge of psychotherapy, and other than clone shock, which doesn't really fit your situation, I don't know of any situations that fit what you're going through. It's fairly new ground because you've had experiences as an artificial intelligence as well as a human being. I am trying, though."

"It's okay, I think I just need an ear, and someone to ask me a few questions. Someone who thought they had all the answers might fool me into thinking they're the right ones. I think taking the long way through this is the right way. I want to get used to the way I look, the way I feel now. I have to deal with whatever I got myself into while my head was mostly empty." She raised the mug to her mouth but stopped to sniff it again, watching herself in the mirror. "Do people like me here, Theodore?" The answer didn't come right away.

"I could check records, reports, but..."

"From what you've seen," Alice said. "What kind of impression did I make at the dinner party?"

"You were quiet," Theodore said. "Everyone would look at you when the conversation died down, like a ringmaster."

"Ringmaster?" Alice asked, unfamiliar with the term.

"Noah told me about them. They spoke to the audience and conducted different acts through circus performances before they were outlawed."

"Oh, so they thought I was like a master of ceremonies," Alice said, remembering that she was terrified to have so many people in her home at once during the whole meal. "I should have put you in charge of the whole night. Maybe next time."

"I think I'd enjoy that," Theodore replied.

"So, people saw a quiet girl who didn't know what to say until they asked about her," Alice said. "Probably not a commander at rest, or someone who had real confidence."

"I think that's accurate, but incomplete. From the little I've had time to observe, I can see that people are deeply curious about you. I expect that to only intensify now. Word has gotten out about you boarding the Exile, and that there was a firefight, but no particulars have leaked. That'll only add to your mystery."

"They have things under control now?" Alice asked.

"The fleet isn't on alert, so I imagine they do," Theo replied.

"Good, I hope it's dead." The blue eyes staring back at her in the mirror as she let the steam from her mug fill her nostrils looked a little older. She'd only had it once, a week or so before her first human body died.

With unerring clarity she remembered being motionless as Jacob Valent attended her bedside. That feeling, knowing that she was about to die, washed over her. How she managed to pack herself up into an artificial intelligence that transmitted her consciousness across space was a mystery to her, but she remembered what it felt like to have life slip away. Panic threatened to overtake her, and she pushed the memory away. Alice took a drink of the rich breakfast concoction to further distract herself and her anxiety began to fade.

It was almost too hot - something she remembered enjoying - but not so in the new body. The flavour was different; more intense and enjoyable. The texture was thicker than just coffee, but smooth and velvety. Alice stopped drinking for a moment and blew on the black liquid.

"Are you all right?" Theodore asked quietly.

"There are places a mind shouldn't go, things it shouldn't experience and then remember. I can remember dying slowly with Jake beside me. If it didn't make me freeze up and start to panic, I could imagine myself standing here thinking about it, crying for hours as if I lost something I'll never get back." She watched her chest rise and fall as she took a deep breath and let it out. A tear rolled down her cheek and she caught it on her finger. "That's self-pity. Those things happened, it'll take me a while to get over them, I may never get all the way through it, but I'd be wasting my time if I hid here and let it hurt me, especially when I feel like I can look past it. I want to celebrate being whole in body and mind. I've never wanted to live more." Alice took another sip and let the rich drink rest in her mouth before swallowing.

"Talking about it will help. I'll be happy to listen. I've seen Noah almost die. He thought he was about to be killed. For days afterwards he was different - easy to laugh, more tolerant of our situation, and wonderfully optimistic. Facing your mortality can be a healthy experience once you've finished coping with it," he offered.

"I know, I remember almost getting slagged a few times. I

never felt so alive. I don't think I need that as much now though. I'm amazed that I'm standing here, looking at myself through her - I mean my - eyes. I remember all the work I did, the friends I made, how I distracted myself from thinking about Jake and everyone who went missing on the Revenge. It's all part of me." Alice caught something in the mirror then, a look on that face that was surprising. There was optimism in those eyes. "You asked me how I felt earlier, and I think more than anything, I feel new."

Alice put the mug down on her bedside table and looked at him in the mirror for a moment before turning her attention back to herself. "The Alice you met is still here," she said, unsure until the words were in the air. "She's just done some growing up, found that there's a whole world of experiences to learn from. Experiences she's already had." Her blue eyes stared back at her from the mirror, finally looking more like her own. It would take more mirror gazing, but she knew that she'd feel like she owned that body before long. A notice in the mirrored wall informed her that Ayan was on her way for a visit. "Looks like self-image therapy is over for today. Can you buy me about half an hour, Theo?" she asked, handing him the mostly empty mug. "I want to get washed up before Ayan gets here."

"I'll let her in when she arrives. That is, if you want me to stay around."

"This is your home for as long as you want it to be, that hasn't changed."

"Thank you, Alice."

ONCE THEODORE LEFT, the alterations began. Alice rushed to the shower, starting the vibro-emitters and the water-jets. She opened an interface on a stall wall. "Roomie, I'm putting together a nine layer suit on this surface, tell me if you can make it."

"Yes, Alice," came the response from speakers overhead, the sound was distorted by the vibrations in the air that scrubbed her clean.

What she designed was a simple fitted sky blue vacsuit at first; thin in a style that would give her an easy range of motion. The simplicity ended there. A comfortable environmental management layer was innermost, then a medical layer loaded with nanobots, regeneration medication capsules and emitters. Then came inner armour using Rexcite, a flexible metal developed by Lorander that was non-conductive and reacted to different kinds of damage. The strength augmentation layers came next, a pair of synthetic muscle systems that worked with her own. The computing layer followed, then two layers of active armour and a cosmetic layer that hid attachment hot spots for heavier varieties of armours. She added an energy collection system that ran through all the layers that would convert body heat, motion, pressure and light into power that would be stored in microscopic cells throughout the garment. Most of the materials and technologies were so new and sophisticated that she barely had clearance to use them in a design, let alone have them manufactured. "Save that, have it printed at the manufacturing hub, then delivered to my room on a drone. Highest priority." She looked her completed design over again and nodded to herself. "All those systems packed in under a millimetre."

As the stall dried her, pulsing the water off and blowing her with warm air, she squeezed water from a handful of hair then looked at a lock. "Blonde?" she asked no one in particular. An image of her head and shoulders appeared on the wall with blonde hair. "That would be a mistake," she muttered. "Black."

The image changed to match. "Closer. Dark red, start with crimson. Add twenty percent curl and make it shoulder length." The image made her grin. "One shade darker, that's it. Package that into a modification pod and let's have it." She stepped out of the shower and took a small silver pod from the dispenser beside the sink. An army of nanobots loaded with ingredients erupted from the container as soon as it was uncapped and went to work, changing the colour, length and style of her hair to match the image she approved.

The sound of a delivery arriving at the slot inside her closet, a metal thunk that she barely heard, told her that her new suit arrived. "That was fast," she muttered.

"There are messages for you from command. They were set to arrive half an hour after you woke up," Roomie said.

Alice crossed the room and opened her closet, finding the tube in the bottom. It was heavy, the dense, advanced vacsuit would be perfect. "Put them on hold until Ayan gets here. She's the Admiral, I want to see what she has to say about my medical suspension. That's the first thing it says, right?"

"You are correct," Roomie answered.

"I have a few questions, then," Alice said. The suit went on like a second skin, but it still felt substantial, just a little heavy. Most importantly, it felt like the suits she used to wear. The technology inside was far more advanced, but it couldn't be felt.

A look in the mirror brought her smile back. With a pinch of her fingers she opened the collar and opened a modest slit down the top. It wasn't how she pictured herself, but with the dark red hair, the blue vacsuit that looked so much like her old favourites and the heavy combat boots she stepped into, she liked what she saw. "That's more like it."

Ayan was waiting with Theodore in the living room, Lieutenant Commander Terran at her side. All three of them looked up to the bedroom with expressions of surprise. "How do you feel?" Ayan asked.

"Better all the time," Alice replied. "Where's Lewis?"

"He's installed in the Clever Dream," Ayan said. "We delivered it to your hangar this morning."

"Admiral, if I may," the Lieutenant Commander said, his chin tilted up a little too high. "I'd like to ask a few questions before we start providing the Lieutenant with more information. There's an established order to this…"

"To this unprecedented event?" Alice asked with an upraised right eyebrow. "You've debriefed a lot of people who have had their brains unscrambled, remembered a whole lifetime in a few minutes?"

Terran looked to Ayan, who looked a little shocked, but also sported a little smile. She took a step back. "Do your duty, Commander."

"You've had a promotion," Alice said, amused. "Congratulations, Terran, that was quick. I should have noticed the change on your uniform."

Commander Terran cleared his throat and nodded. He watched Alice, who was tugging on a few places on her suit, making small adjustments to its fit. After a moment he gave up on waiting for her to finish. "Lieutenant Valent, I'm sorry to inform you that you have been suspended pending psychological review. Haven Fleet has, however determined that you were not at fault for your actions aboard the Exile."

"How the hell did you determine that?" Alice laughed. "Was there some kind of telepathy log? Did the Geist tell you it was all his fault?" Her irritation raised so quick that it shocked her, and Alice shook her head as if it might rattle things back into place. On the verge of anger, she wasn't sure what she'd say.

"I was one of the officers who made the determination, and yes, his admission of guilt is on record."

"You believed it? How many telepaths have you met in your lifetime, Commander?" Alice asked. "I'm curious, how many?"

"It was the only one," he replied.

"I can guarantee that you've met at least a handful of empaths and one or two telepaths if you've been here for a year," Alice said.

"I don't know where you're getting your information, Lieutenant," the Commander put heavy emphasis on Alice's rank, and was interrupted for his trouble.

"Hold on," Alice barked. It was a new thing, being able to think while anger steadily rose in her. "You've met people on leave from Lorander, right?" There was no response. "Right?" she pressed.

"Briefly."

"You've met a higher ranking Aucharian, and at least a few Mergillians, maybe a few much older Nafalli, right?"

"Yes," he replied, growing visibly impatient.

"What about an advisor or guide from the Solar Forge? You know, one of the senior Lorander representatives in blue."

"Of course, but..." Terran said.

She cut off whatever retort he'd managed to assemble. "Then you've met empaths, they have felt what you're feeling or known your intentions, and you have definitely met at least one telepath who has read you. Now, how am I supposed to trust that your investigation was good enough to determine anything if you aren't even aware that more than one person has been in your head? Have you ever tried to barter with a Mergillian?"

"Lieutenant, I believe we've gotten off track," the Commander said. He looked to Ayan, who sat down on the end of the sofa, visibly entertained.

"You're not qualified to speak to an enemy telepath, Commander. You're definitely not qualified to judge whether one is sincere in their confession, or if you are communicating with it effectively at all. Compared to that thing, you're a little disposable paper doll; two dimensional and insubstantial," Alice said. "I hope you have suppressors or at least a neural static generator strapped right to it, otherwise that Geist is going to make you and the Fleet bloody miserable."

"We are using suppressors, I've never heard of a neural static generator," the commander replied.

"Look it up, you need both. Turn the static generator up until everyone - even the non-telepaths - feels like their brains itch. Oh, and if you're not going to incinerate it, then you have to drill each device into the surface of its skull. I have seen inside that thing's mind and it is our enemy. The Exile was sent with one mission; to assess our military strength, our competence and then return. The Geist will finish that mission eventually if you let it live, I can guarantee it. When Citadel and the Order hear how completely foolish most of our military organization is, they will send everything they have and make sure we don't get any more bright ideas about causing trouble for them in this sector." She paused for a moment, looking Commander Terran in the eye. "Commander," she scoffed, shaking her head. "Really? What happened? Did everyone above you die this morning? Did they need someone to stand in for a few days while they beg the British for really qualified people?"

"I am your superior officer, and am due the respect..."

"I've met real military before, there is one sitting right behind you. She's no back room hobbyist tactician who lied on their application and tested well." Alice saw it then. Commander Terran should have been furious at being called a cheat, but he was immediately afraid.

"That's it, isn't it? Everything you know is theoretical. Well, take my advice; stay away from monsters. The Geist will get in your head and start pulling you apart from the inside if you don't kill it or completely suppress it."

"The Commander will pass that on to command," Ayan said after a moment of silence.

"I will," agreed Terran stiffly. He was good as a diplomat, refusing to get drawn into an argument, turning away from her challenges and her insults. Instead, he cleared his throat and said; "I'm wondering if you'd volunteer to consult on the Geist's..."

"Hell no!" Alice replied. "That thing was able to tap into my brain from a million kilometres away, I'm not going to get closer. Are you crazy?"

"It was using an emergency transmitter that we didn't see aboard the Exile because it was only made to amplify telepathic signals," Terran explained.

"That was destroyed, right?" Alice asked.

"I can't comment on that."

"Keeping it for research," Alice muttered. "Every military organization becomes the same as every other military organization eventually. Can you do something about this?" she asked, looking to Ayan.

"I made sure it was disassembled and the parts were sent to separate labs," Ayan said, nodding. "We're reverse engineering it so we can develop a system for our ships that will block incoming telepathic signals. We expect to be installing the first suppressors by the end of day tomorrow."

"There," Alice said. "So, Commander, what were you planning on asking me. You ask me a question, I'll ask you a question. The game stops when the answers do."

"That is not how debriefs work, Lieutenant," the Commander said.

"The dye is still drying on your uniform," Alice replied coolly. "Don't play soldier with me, little boy. Do this my way or get out."

Commander Terran's face turned red and he looked at his feet.

Alice didn't see the point of the Commander staying any longer, so she took that moment to stride up to him, stopping nose to nose. He looked at her with an uncertain expression verging on fear. "Fake." Alice whispered. Before he could react, his sidearm was in Alice's hand and he was pushed down, sprawling across the floor. "Can you even fight for yourself?" Alice asked, activating the weapon. The stock turned red, indicating that it was biologically locked.

The emotions she felt were completely different from what she experienced before. The whole prospect of her commanding officer being ill equipped was insulting. He had thousands of lives in his hands. They had to trust him, to obey his orders. Even worse, her trust in Haven Fleet was eroding quickly. She felt white hot, a clean fury that burned away doubt and made every step ahead of her crystal clear. This was new, this was pure and more sensation than she had ever felt.

Alice pried the cover off the back of the weapon with the help of the muscle enhancements in her gloves and pulled a small bundle of wires free. The Commander didn't fight but scrambled backwards. "The clock is ticking, little boy; are you going to stop me from hacking your weapon and shooting you?" Alice asked menacingly.

Terran's head hit the soft back of the sofa. He yelped, the panic on his face was complete with tears and whimpers. "Please, don't."

The safety device locking the weapon came free, and Alice joined the power wires, bypassing it completely. "Look, I've stolen your weapon without resistance," Alice said. "Then you gave me time to remove the safety device locking it, and I've hotwired it so I can fire at whoever or whatever I want. Did you know that you could have tapped into my suit with a command and held me in place? If I were your enemy, you would be target practice. 'Commander Target Practice;' it has a ring to it."

"Alice!" Ayan shouted, on her feet.

Alice yanked the power unit from the weapon, showering the Commander in sparks, pulled the main circuit board out and made sure that there was no charge left in the emitter before dropping the pieces on the Commander's chest. "Your promotion is a joke. You're a joke. Any part of Haven Fleet that you're running is a joke, and you're going to get thousands of people who trust you killed. Take your little broken toy gun and get out before I publish the video of our conversation."

The Commander started gathering the wires from where they fell on his chest. Alice sighed and said; "this is for you, Dad," remembering a few of Jonas' more impatient moments before pulling the Commander to his feet by his collar, then rapidly walking him to the door. She pushed Terran forward towards the threshold expecting the door to open, but the Commander collided with it instead. "Roomie! Door!" Alice shouted.

The door opened and Commander Terran retreated at speed. "Do you want to be discharged, Alice?" Ayan asked.

Alice took a deep breath and let it out slowly before turning around to join Ayan and Theodore in the living room. Her anger was fading so fast. There was a little regret, but she was absolutely amazed at how quickly all traces of rage drained away. In her first body nothing was as intense, but negative emotions would linger for days. "I don't know if I want to get tossed out, Ayan," Alice replied. "All I do know about Haven Fleet is that I suspected that the wrong people were rising in the ranks thanks to long past victories, lies on their service records with other governments, and an uncanny ability to fail upwards. Now that I have the spine to find out for sure, I know there's truth to that. I bet two thirds of our officers have no idea what they're doing and you're about to launch a new wave of ships that will be captained by panicky, inexperienced stuffed suits. Honestly, I think you and Oz and whoever else has real, current experience like maybe Ruby Sima or the other Irish Captains should find the chaff and demote them to trainees. That guy, that Commander should be the first. I wouldn't trust him to be the event coordinator on a pleasure cruise. If I can find a way to make a difference in this war, then I'll follow through. First I want to know where Jake is."

"We still don't know," Ayan said. "I'm sorry."

That hurt. She had a physical reaction; a pang in the middle of her gut. That was new too. "All right, then how is Oz?"

Ayan looked at the door then back to Alice. Her brow was furrowed, she looked a little defeated, but Alice knew her better than she realized. What Ayan saw; a cowering Commander with the fortitude of a newborn kitten, would sink in. She'd see that Alice was only proving a point, and things would start to change. "Oz is recovering. The damage you did to his knee is fixed. The mental damage will take a little longer, but he's in good spirits. Do you really think we should kill the Geist?"

"He's been telling you the same thing, hasn't he?" Alice asked gently. Ayan was a military officer by training, it was true, but she was also a researcher, an engineer.

"To everyone who will listen."

"He's right. I was only able to see a tiny fraction of what was going on in the Geist's head. It wants to bring firepower here so everything in the solar system burns. Kambis is a major victory for them. There was a Geist on the ship that sacrificed itself to set that world on fire. They are fiercely loyal to their commanders."

"I'll have it done quietly."

"Pardon me," Theodore said meekly. "Can I offer a suggestion?"

"Sure, Theo," Alice replied.

"I don't know about killing the Geist, but I do worry about humans or other biological beings that may be in close contact with it. I think that might be a little..." He hesitated for a moment. "Foolish. Perhaps you should have a number of Ando model robots attend to it. They are intelligent enough for the task but not terribly deep thinkers without being prompted. Losing a few would not mean much to the fleet since there are hundreds across the system awaiting reprogramming."

"That's what we're doing now," Ayan said. "We had to put the Geist into stasis because it kept on hijacking soldiers. No one was killed, but it was close."

"Good, I should have realized you'd have that taken care of already," Theo said.

"It was a good suggestion," Ayan said. "Thank you."

"So, you're going to have to kill it from a distance. Those bots can't do it," Alice said.

"I'll have a remote controlled 'bot poison it," Ayan said. "It's murder, plain and simple, but I think you and Oz are right. It'll find a way to get a message out if it doesn't find freedom for itself."

Alice thought it was time for a change in topic. "How's little Laura doing?"

"She's at the Medical Centre under observation. She was

just treated for a disposition to cancer, and placement services is taking care of her while they examine my suitability to adopt her. I'll be going there after if you want to come along."

"I wouldn't miss it," Alice said. "Is there anything I can do to help?"

"Can I call on you if they need more people to interview?"

"Anytime. I don't think I'll be taking my squad out any time soon."

"That's something I have to tell you," Ayan said. "I was hoping to do it while we were looking at the work I had done on the Clever Dream. Lewis should hear this too."

"It's downstairs?" Alice asked.

"Delivered an hour ago."

"Then let's go see. You can give me all the bad news while I look the ship over." Theodore looked at them with a cocked head. "C'mon," Alice said.

"I've been looking forward to meeting Lewis properly," Theo said excitedly. "The text messages he sent me this morning were epic length."

"You two have been talking a lot?" Ayan asked.

"Yes, but mostly about Alice. He was highly invested in making sure I take good care of her while she's off ship."

"You really don't have to, Theo," Alice said.

"I find it fulfilling. Besides, I learn something from you whenever we spend time together."

FORTY-THREE

The Nova Concord's Crew

TACTICAL SCAN DIDN'T SHOW any movement near the Nova Concord's hold, but the temperature inside was minus thirty-three. Remmy had a suspicion about what they'd find, but he kept it to himself. Dimitri, Mason and Sammi, three rangers he knew well enough and liked him as a leader ran scans as they moved in front of him.

"There are bots shut down back here," Mason said, his gravelly announcer-like voice in his ear. He sounded like an ancient movie trailer, the first thing Remmy liked about him. He was quick to laugh too, something he found out when he showed Mason a few of those old trailers featuring a voice almost exactly the same as his. "Their batteries are drained, no sign of power."

"Keep checking everything that comes up, and make sure they don't have a reserve or a connection to the ship," Remmy said. He recalled the tricks he faced during the retaking of the Sunspire. The Nova Concord wasn't nearly as sophisticated, but that didn't mean it wasn't dangerous. "Watch for anything that could surprise us," Remmy said.

"Is something really a surprise if we're expecting to be surprised?" Sammi asked. Her name was misguiding. She was close friends with Dotty, and they not only worked out together, but had a shared vacation scheduled. All beach time. Remmy wished he could join them but didn't expect he'd have time. It would be a good thing for Dotty to get some rest after everything she'd been through.

"We're just keeping our eyes open," Dimitri said. He was a classic action movie military hero including squinting eyes, a scar on his chin and a short mohawk. Mirth left him completely the moment he had a military purpose, and he had a mind for details that rivaled Remmy's easily. Off duty, he was a little too ready to fight, but he didn't get into trouble when there was a superior officer in sight. "I'm picking up heavy robots past the main cargo door."

They came up on Remmy's tactical display. "I see them," he said. "Can't get a read through the chassis, it could be the door. It's about a meter thick."

"Are we opening this can of worms? I see eleven heavy 'bots with tools," Sammi asked.

"Someone has to clear it," Remmy said. "We're here, they're here, we may as well say hello."

"You think these are waiting for someone to come in?" Mason asked.

"I expect they're in standby mode, waiting for their motion sensors to find something," Remmy said. "If I'm wrong, then we stay bored and safe. If I'm right, well, no more boredom. Open it."

He watched as Sammi moved to the controls for the three metre tall, broad double doors. The only robot they had to blast to pieces so far was a heavy repair bot with a broken wireless pack. What irked Remmy was that it looked like it burned its wireless pack using its own welder. It only had a basic artificial intelligence, but it was fully infected, so the will to kill was definitely present. "We've been here before, guys and gals. Any bot moves, we dismantle the goddamned thing before it can do the same to us."

"Dismantle them the quick way," Mason agreed.

All four of them lined up along the width of the door as it split, rolling open to either side. A cold fog filled the hall and the systems in Remmy's helmet compensated. "Forward, slow," he said. All their rifles were raised. Their scanners swept the room.

"Those evil bastards," Dimitri said. Remmy saw the same thing. The robots aboard the Nova Concord piled the crew's bodies neatly on top of each other. There were rows several corpses high and at least five deep.

"Looks like three hundred fifty five bodies," Sammi said. "They were frozen before they piled, some of them were still alive."

"Stop scanning the bodies," Remmy said, it was almost a snap. "Nothing in that pile will kill us, but keep your suits sealed just in case."

"Aye, sorry, Sir," Sammi replied.

"These bots are in sleep mode," Mason said. "Holy crap, you were right." The heavy service robot he was focusing his scanner on moved quickly. Its treads pushing it towards him, two heavy arms grasping his leg and his head. Mason tried to get a shot off on it and skipped a round off the heavy top plate covering the main body. The rest of the bots powered on at the same time.

Remmy took aim at the thing's upper arm joint and fired, but he wasn't quick enough. The shot landed after it tossed Mason high in the air. He collided with the ceiling before falling into the tall stack of corpses. "I'm okay!" he shouted. "I'm..." then he started screaming in fear. "Get me out of here! They're everywhere! Oh my God! Help!"

Sammi helped Remmy blast the bot that threw Mason into the pile of corpses to shreds of metal. "Calm down! They're just frozen bodies!" she shouted back.

Sammi and Remmy turned so they were back to back, raking the nearest bots with explosive electromagnetic pulse rounds made to kill Order Knights. They worked even better on these old robots, shredding arms, tracks, and most importantly the plating that was made to protect their innermost components from impacts. "Dimitri! Behind you!" Sammi called out.

She turned, focusing her fire on a robot to her right. Remmy split off from her and looked to Dimitri in time to see a heavy loader grab him by the helmet with one gripper and smash him over the top with another as it tried to bash and crush his armour open at the same time. He didn't have a clean shot, and Dimitri was panicking. The other robot near him, the one he was focusing on when he was grabbed, was closing as well. It's armour was already half blasted open.

"I've got you, hold on, D," Remmy said as he rushed left, opening fire on the half-burned down robot. He ran towards the bodies, where Mason was still screaming, flailing in frozen corpses. From there he got a clear shot on the bot who was savagely trying to crack Dimitri's helm open. He had his sidearm out and was firing round after round at the bot's forward plating. Remmy took aim and blasted the bot from the side, taking the shoulder apart then splitting its armour. It powered down, one arm still holding Dimitri off the ground by the helmet.

"Clear!" Sammi said. "All bots are down."

"Oh, God, they're everywhere," Mason wept. At least he wasn't screaming anymore.

"Well, shit," Dimitri said, pulling at the claw grasping his helm by the sides. It was locked heavy metal and he had no luck. "This is just embarrassing."

"I've got ya, man," Remmy said with a chuckle.

"I'll get him," Sammi said.

"No, you'll start digging your way to Mason before he loses his last marble," Remmy corrected. "We'll help you in a second. Don't forget to scan for surprises."

FORTY-FOUR

Regret and Promise

"THE MODIFICATIONS INSIDE ARE EXTENSIVE, the Clever Dream is several generations ahead of its original design now," Ayan said as they walked down the ramp leading to the hangar.

Alice was still working through what was going on in her own mind, and every time she caught her own reflection in a segment of the wall or on a new panel cover, it was a little surprising. The face was starting to look right, it was quick, but it also looked younger. It felt like there was more of the old Alice, the one that lived on the run for years, was raised by Bernice before that, than the new one, but it was undeniable that she was not purely one or the other.

Everything felt new, not just her appearance. There was always a chance of clone shock with the integration of a new personality or whenever memories were reloaded, but she didn't feel any of the signs that indicated an impending rejection. Instead, she was more eager than ever to see what was around the next corner, giddy to live the next moment, no matter what came. There was also a feeling that she'd come home and everything looked slightly different.

Alice was struck by her own expression, unsure and afraid, and she stopped to look at her reflection in a black wall panel that was polished to a shine. Theodore stopped and looked with her. "Are you all right?" he asked quietly. Ayan stopped her descent down the stairs.

"It's like my heart hurts," Alice said to herself as much as to answer Theodore. Ayan was at her side the next minute, arm around her waist.

"I'm not detecting any cardiovascular difficulties," Theodore said.

"I don't think that's what she means," Ayan said. "Tell me what's on your mind."

"I..." she started but lost the words in a blur of powerful regret. "I left him alone," she said. "Lewis was just out there, risking everything because I didn't think I needed him. I treated him like an appliance."

"He wanted to be a part of the fight," Ayan said. "He did great things."

The tears started then. "He should have been here," Alice said, patting her wrist. "I remember what it felt like, I don't know how the Geist put those memories back, but I remember what it was like when Jonas sent me alone into the Overlord Two. I could barely understand that I wouldn't be with him." Alice broke down, sobbing. It seemed to take control of her whole torso, and she leaned on Ayan, who held her and stroked her back. "I was alone, I didn't understand alone."

For an instant she could feel the emotions of an artificial

being, it was like trying to catch a wisp of smoke. As soon as she noticed it, it was gone. Alice knew what it was though. "Then I was so angry, I wanted to kill everyone on the Overlord. I had a job to do; get Jonas and his crew out, then I'd use the Phoenix program to get out, but not before trashing everything I could. I failed that too, the Overlord Two still exists. It's still in their main fleet."

Alice calmed down enough to take a deep breath. "How do you know?"

"I remember," Alice said. "It's where they brought me back." Her reflection showed so much vulnerability, a depth of emotional pain that she could have never imagined. "I can't believe I didn't learn from that, I didn't stay close to Lewis, to everyone I cared about."

"You were busy trying to find out who you are," Ayan said. "Becoming someone amazing. Everyone knew, everyone wanted you to succeed."

"Someone should have noticed that the rest of me was still here," Alice said. "Not you, you're not a neurologist, but someone. Maybe me."

"You built a track for yourself, worked hard to become impressive. You have nothing to be embarrassed about."

"Now I'm tearing that down too." The tears had passed, and she wiped them up with a kerchief Ayan handed her. "I need to be a part of Fleet. I'm close to where I fit, I like the idea of a small team, but I can't deal with a paper soldier being in command."

"We'll figure something out," Ayan said. "You know people."

The sadness in that reflection cleared, and she smiled at Ayan, who looked so similar. It was almost the same chin, blue eyes, and strong cheekbones. She looked to Theodore and chuckled. His proper, handsome gentleman guise was frozen in an expression of mild surprise. "You okay, Theo?"

"Every minute has been an experience that's only brought more questions today," he said. "But I'm fine, thank you. How are you feeling?"

"Like I need to see what the Clever Dream looks like. Thank you," she said to Ayan. "You're a good mother."

"Thank you," she said. "There are a lot of things I don't know, but identity crises I know. I've done the homework."

Ayan led them the rest of the way down the ramp way and Alice couldn't help but reflect on the one she knew on the First Light so long ago. There were noticeable differences too. Her shape, the way she spoke - more calmly, as though she had more time - and there really was something maternal about her, whereas the first Ayan didn't show that side of herself often if at all. Alice wondered if it would be the same with her father when she met him.

Jake hadn't just changed once, like Ayan did. The man Alice knew as her father was Jonas. He was gone entirely. Jake looked and acted like him for some time, and now he was transformed; his human body was taller, more powerful looking, but it still had Jacob Valent's face, even his voice. She realized that Jake hadn't met her since she changed either, her framework system was removed shortly after he left, transforming her one more time. It could be an odd reunion.

As they came to the hangar doors - double sliders that were thicker and opaque for security purposes - an entirely new instinct surfaced in her. "We honoured the ship you had." Ayan said, turning towards Alice.

Alice looked at her, taking in the softness of her features, her light blue eyes, and heart shaped face. The new instinct, or ability, or whatever it was - she'd classify it later - led her to do something that she sometimes couldn't accomplish without tears or at least a rant or two before. She accepted the change she saw in front of her, regardless of how drastic it was. Without warning, Alice embraced Ayan, who was a little startled at first. "Oh, okay," she said, returning the gesture.

"I remember where you came from, who you were before," Alice said into Ayan's red curls. "I'm happy you're here, that they made you again."

"I..." Ayan started, but instead of finishing her thought, she only squeezed. Alice released her long moments later. "I don't know what to say," Ayan told her. "Thank you."

"Is everything all right?" Theo asked in a whisper.

Ayan looked to him, then to Alice and nodded. "I think so." The trio stood silently for a moment, then Ayan shook her head and smiled. "Let's take a look at your ship."

The doors parted and Alice nearly fell to her knees. It was the Clever Dream. Not the one modified for Haven Fleet, nor the damaged hulk that she'd seen days before, but exactly as it was when she was the captain. "Oh, my God," Alice said, her hands covering her mouth.

"We were able to cover it with the plating that looks and scans exactly the same as the original hull, but it's the same smart technology that's on our new ships. It'll trick any scanners into thinking it's a normal Arcyn Starskipper, though that's not what I'd call a normal ship to start with," Ayan said.

Alice stared, looking at the sleek shape, the glossy black hull. It was like looking directly into her past and she remembered how lucky she felt to have her ship, to have Lewis. That intoxicating feeling only grew as she realized that Ayan was the one who made it happen. Her luck had only gotten better.

"She's not saying anything," Theodore said to Ayan. It was

as much a statement as a question that made her realize that she had been staring for a long time.

"It's amazing," Alice said. "Thank you."

"What we did to the inside is amazing," Ayan said. "The outside was the easy part."

They walked towards the main boarding ramp on the port side and Alice smiled broadly as a familiar voice filled the air. "Hello, Alice. It looks like we both had a few new things installed."

"Lewis, I missed you so much," Alice said, touching the inside wall of the walkway as though she was acknowledging him. "I'm sorry I left you."

"I don't blame you. You can't take a ship everywhere."

Alice couldn't help thinking that she could have if she gave him an open line on her comm unit or installed his module there. She decided to leave that for the time being. "How do you feel?"

"Powerful," Lewis said. "A little relieved to be in my own skin instead of on a ship far from you."

"I don't think we'll be in command of any corvettes anytime soon, so you won't have to worry about that." The interior hall was widened just enough to accommodate two people passing each other comfortably, and she could see that the corridor was changed even more up ahead.

"What happened?" Lewis asked.

Alice looked to Ayan. "Now's a good time for the bad news."

Ayan nodded and braced herself. "Commander Terran put Lieutenant Vernor in charge of the unit, giving him command of the new ship you were supposed to take your place on temporarily. They set out on the mission as planned. Your squad went with them as well. Theodore's file work wasn't finished yet, so he decided to delay his entry into Haven Fleet."

"I wanted to make sure you would be all right," Theodore added. "By the way; hello, Lewis, it is good to be inside you at last."

"Oh, wow," Alice said as a sharp, short giggle erupted from Ayan.

"You may want to reserve that phrase for another occasion," Lewis replied with a chuckle. "But it's good to see you with my own sensors."

"There was nothing disingenuous in my comment," Theo explained.

"We can discuss the nuances of that later," Lewis said. "Don't worry, it used to happen to me all the time."

"Well, I'm glad my team got out there. It was an important mission, we need allies," Alice said.

"Yawen wasn't happy about it," Ayan replied. "You have a loyal friend there."

"If they let me have the squad back, I'll see if we can use the Clever Dream instead. I like the idea of running missions on this ship a lot more than something too big to hide if the cloaking systems get damaged. How many crewmembers can this ship carry now?"

Ayan led them deeper into the ship so they could see the hallways inside. The doors facing forward, starboard and the rear opened revealing a much larger crew area behind, as well as new doors along the corridors in the other directions. "Twenty eight can fit in comfortable racks stacked two high now, that's not including the Captain's Cabin, which can sleep two with a pull-out bed. More if you sleep a second person in the queen sized bed and adjust the centre seat."

"What? Where are the systems?" Alice asked. She knew the

technology, but never thought how it would be implemented into her ship. "Does the ship still have a hyperdrive?"

"It's all new technology, reducing most systems to roughly one sixteenth the size of the old ones, including the reactors and faster than light systems, of which there are hardened redundancies. You have a wormhole generator at each end of the ship that can work in concert if there's no damage, and two dimension drives."

"What? How did you manage that? I didn't think I could own one."

"Technically they're still property of Haven Fleet, so someone could file a grievance and have your dimension drives taken away, but there are two Admirals on your side, so I expect that filing would get lost along the way."

"They will get my D-Drives over my cold, dead hull," Lewis growled.

"Don't worry, only three people in Fleet even know you have them," Ayan reassured. "The War Forge did most of the design work, then it was deleted when you were complete. What was more complicated was installing the systems to control all the new systems. Everything inside is top secret because you could figure out how all our new ships operating systems work from looking at the panels in the Clever Dream. So, no parties aboard until the secrecy is dropped."

"Yes, Ma'am," Alice said, opening a sliding hatch and peeking inside a crew cabin. The bunks were copies from the War Forge, in fact the whole four bunk room felt like her old training dorm room, with the lockers, desks and fold away seats in the same places. The style was simple - dark blues and blacks, and the bunks had a surprising amount of individual space with sliding metal privacy doors.

"This is very nice, twice as much as the minimum required space for a human," Theodore said. "It is a little dark though."

"Intelligent plating," Ayan said with a little smirk as she double tapped the side of a bunk. A small control window appeared and she selected a colour from a list, then changed the bunk to light purple and added some luminescence. "You notice that there are no lights installed anywhere," she said. "That's because every inch of the plating has the ability to emit it using ambient pressure and power."

"I remember," Alice said. "As long as the ship has plating attached, it's gathering power like our vacsuits."

"So, light, gravity, heat and ambient electricity are always being gathered?" Theodore asked.

"Until the ship can't store anymore power," Ayan confirmed.

"She's feeling pretty full at the moment, actually," Lewis said.

Alice smiled at him, looking up even though the sound seemed to come from every direction at once. "Do you guys mind if Lewis and I get a moment alone?"

Theodore nodded and left the cabin. Ayan smiled at her through the doorway.

"In case I forget to say it later, thank you," Alice told her. "This is overwhelming."

"Wait until you see the rest," Ayan said before closing the door.

"So, what do you think?" Alice asked Lewis, sitting on the edge of a bunk.

"We've never been more fortunate," Lewis replied. "Is it true that you remember everything now?"

"It feels like it, but Alice three is almost completely missing."

"Alice three?"

"The artificial intelligence that packed up my human traits and memories then bounced off to the Overlord. I blame her, I blame her for a lot."

"Oh, why?"

"She could have uploaded herself to Triton medical. They could have put me in a clone as soon as they ran into someone qualified to grow one the right way. I would have never been a framework, skipped a whole, complicated situation. Why transmitting everything into the heart of the enemy fleet was a good idea to her, risking everything, I'll never know because I'm pretty sure she deleted herself after I was downloaded into a framework. I didn't get any intelligence that could help Haven Shore, just a newer framework model."

"That led to medical and tactical discoveries that could give us a chance against the Order of Eden. Classified files reveal that Defense Minister Anderson and other scientists have discovered a way to disable and destroy any framework. The problem is that it classifies as a new generation weapon of mass destruction. They are hesitant to reveal it, let alone use it."

"How did you see that?"

"Haven Fleet security is less effective than paper walls to me," Lewis said. "I can even see my own revocation of rights. They are not willing to declare me an independent sentient because I would be put on trial for war crimes. I understand it but hiding that from me was a mistake. I know I can't trust Fleet Command now."

"In a way, it doesn't matter," Alice said.

"You're right," Lewis said. "Most of Haven Fleet will not survive much past new year's day."

"It won't last," Alice agreed.

"Alice? I'm happy you're back. All the way back."

"Do I really seem so much like I used to be?" Alice said, looking at herself in the mirror opposite the hatchway. There it was, that pretty, heart shaped face again. It was a likeable face, an emotional face. She watched her words form. "I'm still having trouble reconciling."

"There are changes in your speech and manner that are difficult to classify, but it seems like I'm speaking to the Alice who named me to honour her friend and taught me the most important things. Whatever has changed, and there are changes, it's made you... more than you were. The woman I saw crying in the hall outside was more human than the one I knew. Time will tell, but I think I'll like you more."

Alice was surprised at Lewis' insight, and how deeply his words resonated with her. "Thank you, Lewis."

"There is something else. Haven Fleet returned my name-sake's body from storage to the hold. He is still in stasis, but Haven Fleet was unable to restore him. There is simply too much damage for them to reconstruct his personality."

"I think it's time we gave him a proper rest, then," Alice said. "Can you still solo pilot?"

"Yes, much of the automation hasn't been flight tested, however."

"Then we should do that too. Start preparing for takeoff."

FORTY-FIVE

The Thorn

DRON STOOD upon the dais in the middle of the Glorious' bridge, holographic information coming from all departments as the intelligence holograms to his left highlighted some of the worst damage incurred by the Mary Autonomous Virus. All nine of his high speed destroyers were dispatched, on their way to deliver Mars Drives to places where an upload would not be possible. The few quantum communication nodes they had weren't enough to get the software everyone needed in place before too much damage was done.

Even worse, he was behind schedule, and that irked him little by little. As the minutes passed, and his base ships were sitting still, they eroded his calm like water torture. Admiral Tafford was requesting his attention.

Dron accepted the transmission and connected. "You're alive," he said. "A good sign."

"I found the evidence the Brood Master needed," Trafford said, playing a video of a small ship rocketing towards Iora with a tactical overview. "It's a Haven Fleet ship. More investigation reveals that they installed their flag on an old Aucharian corvette. The transmission that uploaded Mary into our systems had the marking of Captain Jacob Valent."

Dron could scarcely disguise his disgust. He had sent multiple signals to the man's framework systems, knowing that the chances were slim that he could be controlled. His was an early model, and an old report detailed how Jacob had disabled the receiver hidden inside the technology. A much newer report from a spy in Haven Shore revealed that the framework technology had been completely extracted.

He knew Valent, not nearly as well as his older brother did, but he knew him. He had been personally taunted by him, and again the man made his name known. He made his mark on thousands of ships and cost them one of the most important fixtures of the fleet - the Base Ship Hercules - and he probably didn't have the first clue that he'd done it. That was smart. There was no reason for him to stay in the area after he'd found a way out. "Why did he exchange a state-of-the-art Haven ship for an ancient Aucharian vessel?" Dron asked.

"Our scans are not complete, but the Pursuer Three was damaged before it ran into our hidden sentries."

"Ran into..." Dron stopped to breathe for a moment. "You destroyed it, didn't you?"

"It was moving into the area at extreme speed and posed a risk."

"Or an opportunity," Dron said. "Did your sentries detect anyone aboard? Was there antimatter, or anything set to explode?"

Admiral Tafford hesitated a moment, looking at something,

presumably the scan results. "No antimatter or power build-ups were detected and there was no one aboard."

"Next time you have the opportunity to capture a Haven Fleet ship, take it. I don't care if it's a thirty year old tug. They are winning the game of intelligence."

"I apologize, Overlord," Admiral Tafford said in an uncommon gesture of humility.

"Don't apologize!" Dron erupted. He nearly came off his feet. "Don't you dare apologize! Rally! Rise to the challenge! What are you doing next?" his voice echoed across the thirty five main stations and sub-control stations in the bridge. No one turned to watch. His shouting was not shrill. It came from his core, the voice of a much larger man emerging.

"I have dispatched ships with the new software to several supply stations nearby so they can get back online. We also have rescue missions under way for several small, stranded battle groups..."

"What are you planning to do with the Brood Master."

"That's resolved, they don't blame us for..."

"As soon as this channel closes, you will open one to the Edxi and you will encourage them, no, you will inspire them to attack the Rega Gain System. Tell them where Tamber is, you can't miss it - it's the blue and brown moon next to the big flaming red planet - and identify it as a world they may take for their next broods if they conquer it. You will tell them that the cost for this information on their enemy is the technology they find. I want every shuttle, spanner and bolt they don't destroy outright, especially the Solar Forge."

"What about this War Forge I've heard about?" Admiral Tafford asked.

"The cloaked shipyard that never stays in the same place?" Dron said. "If you tell them it even exists I'll have you publicly executed. No, that is ours. That is information we stop from travelling past our ships and past our lips, do you understand me?"

"I don't appreciate your tone, Dron."

"Your replacement is standing right behind you," Dron said, his expression and voice growing cold. "She wants your privileges, your power, your station, your wealth, and the respect that comes with. Draw your weapon!" he said. The muzzle of a sidearm appeared at Admiral Tafford's temple before he had a chance to turn around. "Hold. Do not fire." Dron said clearly. "Admiral Tafford. You are an intelligent, well educated person whom I would like to trust. If my respect or trust in you falters again, your best option will be to run. Get out of the sector and keep going, because I will have your membership in the Order revoked along with your entire family. Is that clear?"

"Yes, Overlord."

"Perform or die," Dron ended the call. His eyes came to rest on the new communications interface. There were eyes behind him, looking up the stairs to the top of his dais. He knew it was his Ensign with a snack and a bottle of hot tea. "That was very poor management, so you are aware, Ensign. I have to replace Admiral Tafford now, and I have to do so quietly. I'll probably have to send him to one of the few paradise worlds we have, where him and his family can be out of the way. That is so the other Admirals don't turn on me. You see, I want to have Tafford killed, but thanks to my heavy handed reaction to his negative reaction, now I will be the only suspect if foul play takes him." Dron looked down at his Ensign and smiled a little.

"I understand, Sir," he replied.

"I don't think you do, and I mean no offense, my young ally. Young people rarely learn this lesson. The lesson is, and it's so simple; by inaction or action, we cause most of our own problems. The trick is to be aware that we make dozens, sometimes hundreds of little decisions every day, and if you focus your will on a goal and don't stray from it, all those decisions start leaning in one direction. If your goal is a good one, and you try to enrich lives as you pursue it, then making mistakes becomes harder, especially if you're aware of the one detail that rules over everything else; that we make our own problems most of the time. Now I'm sure you understand."

"I do, thank you, Overlord," Lancet said, taking a step up and handing him his container of tea and a biscuit.

"I have a new assignment for you; find Tafford and his family a placement on one of our paradise worlds. Investigate their profiles and make sure it's everything they dream a paradise could be."

"Yes, Overlord," Lancet said, saluting, waiting for Dron to return the gesture, then rushing off.

Dron turned his attention back to his array of holographic displays. He'd come to know the Mars Advanced Operating System well while he was in the Sol System. It was comforting to see it in operation. Years working with Vindyne's sloppy software and Regent Galactic's consumer centred interfaces that made everything look like it could turn into a vending or gambling machine any minute made him miss it all the more. It was about time he brought efficiency and a little beauty to the rest of the galaxy. The grace and efficiency of the design calmed him down enough to make his next call.

Dron activated the privacy screen around his dais. No one would be able to see or hear what was happening inside. He entered an ident code that looked unlike any in the entire Order of Eden Fleet or Regent Galactic comm node. A woman in a green and white half-helm that covered her mouth and neck appeared. "Overlord, I'm honoured," she said.

"Do you have him there?" Dron asked.

"Yes, he's coming now. Thank you for this mission," she bowed and left the console.

The Beast stepped into range of the holo recorder. "I hope you're getting along with the crew."

"They've been exceptional," he replied, the finer plating around his mouth and cheeks scraping together, adding the sound of wet sandstone grinding to his words.

"I've located Jacob Valent. He's aboard the Nova Concord, an old Aucharian vessel I'm sending you all the details on. You are to capture as many of the crew as possible. Especially Minh-Chu Buu and Valent. Remember, the vessel you're on is a small but powerful Citadel ship. Under the right conditions it is undetectable, especially by that Aucharian heap, so you should be able to get very close before they even know you're there. Do not let yourself be captured. I'm giving you the details on their course. They should emerge on an edge of the Haven Solar System, far from the Tamber Moon."

"Don't worry," the Beast said. "I have everything I need here. Leave the details to me."

"Good hunting," Dron said, ending the communication. He stared into empty space for a moment, weighing the situation. The likely outcomes of his were simple: the Beast returns with captives, kills everyone, or is destroyed. He liked all three possibilities.

FORTY-SIX

Farewell

THERE USED to be a reactor and fuel tanks where Alice stood in the Clever Dream. Now it was a small hangar. There was just enough room for two small armed shuttles or three fighters, maybe more if they cheated gravity a little. The sudden trip into space was a surprise to everyone but Lewis and her. When Alice told Ayan why they were going in a distant orbit around the sun, she decided to stay, a surprise since Ayan didn't know who they were cremating at all.

Theodore stood beside Alice at the controls to the airlock. The containment tube holding Lewis, the friend she hoped to revive one day, was on a cart designed for loading missiles. The transparent window was covered. It was for the best, Alice wanted to remember him as she knew him, not however he looked while he was in tissue stasis.

"Who was he to you?" Ayan asked. It was far from her first funeral.

"A friend. He saved my life, changed my life. I think if it weren't for him, I wouldn't be here. He died because he just couldn't let something go, it was stupid, but there was a lot to admire in him." Alice ran her hand across the dark tube and nodded. "Let's get him into the airlock."

Theodore opened the inner door and helped her push the cart inside. They closed the hatch behind him and Alice set the pressure to rise a little more than usual. "We can eject him from here?"

"I can make sure he goes out smoothly, and in the right direction," Lewis replied over the intercom. Manipulator arms slid out of their slots inside the airlock, gripping the stasis tube in the middle, preparing to guide it.

Alice led Theodore and Ayan to the rear hangar door. "Make this transparent if you can," she asked. She knew the capabilities of smart plating, and that it was possible before the thick metal became so clearly transparent that it looked like it disappeared entirely. "I hate funerals," she said. "Especially when all the tears have already been cried. I don't know what to say." She took in the view for a moment. The Haven Star burned white in the distance. The filters in the plating made it possible to look at it with the naked eye. Loops of fire reached out from the fiery surface of the sun like restless fire serpents before they rejoined the roiling sea of light. "Send him out, Lewis."

The ship turned, then opened the outer airlock door quickly so the pod escaped with the pressurized air. Guided by the manipulator arms inside, Alice expected it to go directly towards the star. Lewis turned the ship back so they could see the small tube rush towards the Haven System Sun.

Ayan stepped in beside her, linking Alice's arm in her own. "Talk to him," she said.

Alice didn't need any more prompting. "If you were here, I'm sure you'd be one of our best warriors. You'd love this place, Lewis," she said, half expecting her ship to mistake her.

"I know you don't mean me, go on," Lewis said.

Alice cleared her throat and returned her gaze to the diminishing black dot against the backdrop of the white star. "Thank you for saving me. I was a better person thanks to you."

They watched the dot disappear for several moments before Theodore asked; "May I say something?"

Alice nodded, a tear dropping from her eye. Ayan's arm went around her, and she was suddenly very happy to have her there. Grief was something she felt keenly before. Lewis' name-sake was a different thing though, she'd worked his loss out over months, many of them spent alone. All she felt at the final admission that there would be no saving him was a sort of overall sadness.

Theodore looked out to the blazing ocean and took a couple steps forward. "There are many words that have eulogized people through the ages, but I only know a few. Some people believe that everything began as energy, then dust. Time passed, and we became as we are; gathered masses of life that we can know and love. We become more than our assembled parts as we enter into the memories of the people we know. Eventually, we pass, leaving our loved ones to remember us. We once again become dust, and long after we are forgotten, the universe remembers. In the final years of its life, suns enlarge, taking us in as fuel before exploding. We, as dust, begin the cycle again. Perhaps some time in a future we can't imagine, I'll meet you again, old friend. Perhaps a few of my motes will remember you.'" He turned to Alice then. "I'm sorry, that was a little more scientific than I intended."

Alice wiped a tear from her cheek. "It was good, thank you."

The trio watched the container with Lewis' body inside slowly crossed the no return line, where it burst into flames for an instant before disappearing. "Opaque, please," Alice said, accepting a self-sterilizing kerchief from Ayan. The rear hangar doors turned black. "You're really getting better at this mom thing," Alice said as she wiped her cheeks and nose.

"Thank you," Ayan said.

The trio retreated to the cockpit of the Clever Dream, where Alice sat in a new, but very similar pilot's seat. Her hands and eyes reflexively checked their course, speed, scanner summary, system alarm panel and took the controls. "I have control," she said aloud. That was the new habit, from her Apex training.

"You have control, Alice," Lewis said.

"I've never watched you fly before," Ayan said. "So much of who you are to me was new before, now it's like there's a million things I'd like to learn about you."

"We'll make time," Alice said to Ayan as she slipped into the co-pilot's seat. "Even with the new systems, everything is laid out where it's supposed to be. This is great work."

"Thank you, but it was the Lorander software that took care of most of it."

"Still, thank you, everything's still familiar enough for the ship to feel like home. Lewis, plot a seventy minute shakedown course for our fusion thruster systems with Haven Navnet."

"Proposing several courses now. Receiving our verified flight path," he replied.

"This is amazing," Theodore said. "It's a fusion of manual control and automation. This is a wonderful ship."

"Thank you," Lewis replied. "You look quite dapper today."

"Thank you," Theodore replied, pleasantly surprised.

"We have a bromance in the making," Alice laughed.

Ayan couldn't help but laugh along, and Alice couldn't help but watch her out of the corner of her eye. There was nothing false or forced about her mirth. She couldn't remember a moment when she'd seen the woman be anything but genuine. The fusion thrusters engaged, and Lewis offered to take over using a flashing holographic icon. "You have the controls," Alice said.

"I have the controls," replied Lewis.

She sat back and looked at Ayan. "What do you want to know?"

"Right now, I'm a little worried, actually," Ayan's old style British accent seemed to add more seriousness to the statement. "You have your ship, and I'm sure Haven Fleet will offer you an opportunity for a discharge if they can't toss you out altogether, which is something many people would block anyway, so you could get out of your contract with them if you wanted. I know you have accumulated a great deal of luxury credits, so you could pay for good housing when you lose your military home, but you could also cash out."

"I'm not going to take all my luxury credits, turn them in for platinum and leave," Alice said, a little annoyed at the implication. Theodore sat down at the communications system and watched, his head turning towards one speaker then the next. "I'm with you, Ayan, but Haven Fleet feels untested. I wonder if I can't do something more important instead of suffering through growing pains with it."

"We're trying to turn a rebellion into a structured military so we can use the resources we have properly," Ayan said. "That's all. The academy, filling ranks then verifying that we have the

right people through qualifications, and finding good commanders is all adding up to that."

"There's your first mistake; taking a lot of officers at their
word, giving them assignments and *then* getting them to take
their qualification tests. I look at Fleet with what I know now,
and I see a glass cannon, or a fresh boxer whose never had a
broken nose. One good punch there and he'll bleed so hard that
he'll paint the mat red then scare himself back into his corner."

"I always hated that term; glass cannon," Ayan said. "Say
you're right. That doesn't change the fact that we're holding a
wealth of important technology and we have to protect it or the
Order will use it to push across the galaxy. What would
you do?"

"We have Freeground Fleet here right now, and experienced Nafalli commanders. Put their ships through the refur-
bishing line as fast as you can, or train them on our tech and
advance people they trust into command positions. Like first
officers who have been waiting for a command post on a ship to
open up, or much higher ranking people who are willing to take
command of a smaller class vessel until they find good captains.
They will trust us a lot faster if we use their people to crew the
new ships."

"That's something I've been considering," Ayan said. "I
didn't think of offering commands to higher ranked officers
though, it could work."

"Put an Apex class on every ship with more than a hundred
crewmembers. Make ten or twenty percent of the crew trainees.
That advanced class was too academic. I didn't get enough time
with my cadets or enough exposure to the technology I was
studying."

"Another good idea, though a little risky," Ayan said.

"You have to push your people harder if you want to be

ready for the Order when they come here," Alice said. "I've seen the beginning of an invasion before, and if it weren't for the Clever Dream, we wouldn't have gotten out of there in time. If the Order invades like any well directed fleet, then it'll happen too fast for us."

"I know," Ayan said. "Oz and I have been talking about it ever since he got back. He has a dark outlook. I thought he was just mourning at first, but I came around to his thinking. You still haven't answered my first question though; what do you want? What do you feel you need to do now? I know what it's like to come through a change and be different. What do you want, now that you're seeing things differently?"

Alice sat back and looked through the display above her. It was made to look like a cockpit window, but she knew there was a lot of armour and a few subsystems between her and space. The Haven Star was growing distant, they were moving at great speed. Then it came to her. "You're an admiral, your father is the Defence Minister, and no one would go against both of you, so make me a Captain in your fleet. Full rank, with all the rights, responsibilities and privileges. Give me the right to crew my ship with a team I choose. The last Special Operations Unit fell almost completely apart and most of them didn't even see combat. Let me form a small unit using the Clever Dream as our ship."

"I try not to show favouritism," Ayan said. "People have more faith in the organization that way."

"There are reasons to make me captain besides my relations," Alice said with a smirk. "Theo, can you do a search for anyone who has spoken, in person, to an Edxi?"

He turned to the communications station and his fingers started to dance across the controls. "Immediately."

"Okay, another point; I spent years with Jonas in Freeground Fleet, and I remember most of the journey the First Light took. You want someone who understands our enemy? I know Vindyne, Regent Galactic bought Vindyne. I know how companies like those work inside and out. I've been face to face with the Beast and Eve. The biggest reason why I deserve to be Captain is that I was one of the first people to fight this war. I sacrificed my life for it, saving the Triton once, and partially thanks to the Apex program, I have more current training than almost anyone in the fleet. Favouritism? Don't make me laugh." Alice crossed her arms and forced herself to stop talking. She didn't mean to get heated, but her intensity and volume increased as she stated her case aloud.

"No one on the Stellarnet has claimed to meet an Edxi outside of captivity or combat and survived," Theodore said. "There are encounter logs from people who did not survive, I could play some of them if you like."

"That's all right, Theo," Alice said.

Ayan was enjoying the view above them, a little smile on her lips. "If that paper soldier, Terran, could fail upwards until he was a Commander, then someone with your qualifications should be a Captain. You have to make me a deal, though."

"What's that?" Alice said.

"When we discover the location of your father, you will look to the Fleet for your orders. Don't rush off to rescue him."

"No deal," Alice replied calmly. "Sorry, Admiral."

"I had to try," Ayan said. "Congratulations, you're a Captain. I'll put the filing in when we get back to Haven Shore and you'll have your rank, and your Special Operations Unit by noon tomorrow."

"Thank you. You won't regret it," Alice said.

"May I apply to be part of your unit?" Theodore asked. "If you still need a doctor."

"Absolutely, as long as you don't mind doing communications until we fill the spot."

"Not at all, can I do anything for you now?"

"Find out where Iruuk is, he's qualified. I miss him, too."

"We're going to have a Nafalli aboard?" Lewis asked. "Interesting. How much do they shed? I can't find a definitive answer online."

FORTY-SEVEN

Chief Billy Finn

EVERYONE aboard the Nova Concord slept lightly. They made several short wormhole jumps so their exact trajectory couldn't be tracked, but Finn was keenly aware that the enemy knew their destination. The broadcast had been sent. Captures and scan data of a fleet ready to invade along with the Captain's report on what they did to delay them. Hiding the Mary artificial intelligence and who unleashed it didn't seem important anymore.

The Order was after them. They were going to their home, and Finn could feel that realization changing his priorities, keeping him awake. Three of Remmy's Ranger squad were qualified to watch the engineering deck for any problems, but he walked along the old catwalks surrounding the reactors one more time.

"Can't sleep?" Captain Valent asked. He wasn't looking at Finn, but at the three storey tall reactors instead.

"Almost afraid to try, Captain," Finn replied.

"Everyone's worried," Jake said. "I'm worried that I'm getting over it already. I guess I knew it would happen eventually."

"Can we even defend ourselves if one fleet that size invades the Haven System?" Finn asked. He wouldn't have spoken to Jake like that before he changed, he realized. There was a lot about the new version of his captain that was different, more approachable. "What if there are two?"

"Or three," Jake offered. "Or the whole of the Order are coming for us?" Jake leaned on the railing and looked down. "We'll do our best to win. If that doesn't work we'll try to survive. If that doesn't work, we still win." He waited a moment before looking up and smiling a little. "It's Pearl Harbour. That's what Tamber is. We've built our resources on it, put our people there shielded it, and the British even have an outpost on the peninsula closest to our favourite island. They start building next week with our government's blessing. The Nafalli's land claim is going to go through, and they're fighters. Do you know anything about Pearl Harbour?"

"World War One?" Finn asked.

"World War Two," Jake said. "The Americans were hesitant to join the war against the Axis of Evil but then the Japanese attacked Pearl Harbour. From that point on they were dedicated to the fight. Tamber is Pearl Harbour for all those people. The Nafalli who number over a hundred billion as far as we know, the British Alliance, who are concentrating on rebuilding their own territory, and a dozen or so other large and small governments that have stayed out of this so far. If they take Tamber, they kick a hornet's nest, we'll make them pay for it dearly, but even worse, they start a fight with everyone who they haven't already defeated."

"I'd still rather win," Finn said.

"Absolutely," Jake said. "I've died enough times to tell you; it always sucks. I'm not doing it again if I can help it." He pushed off from the railing. "I'm all out of answers for tonight though. Time to finish my walk around the ship, get a good look at her before they feed her to the Solar Forge for raw materials or turn it over to an Aucharian Appreciation Society or something. You should get some rest. Galley's open if you want something."

Finn just ate his last chocolate meal bar, so he wasn't hungry, but he could feel a case of chalk-mouth coming on. "Thank you, Captain," he said.

"Oh, by the way," Jake said, mid step. "There's a request coming your way for Chief Engineer of a new ship called the Merciless. It's a new design, but I'm pretty sure you'll master it."

"Yes, Sir," Finn said, glad to hear that there was a future for him with Captain Valent. "Thank you, but I have to ask; what about Agameg?"

"I need a new First Officer, so I already sent my crew list for the Merciless with you two at the top. If everyone agrees to join up, I'll have my crew."

"I'm sure he'll be the first."

"Actually, Liara was the first," Jake said. "I think she's getting a taste for action. Go get some rest, Chief," he said as he walked off. "And spend a little time out of that armour."

Finn stood there for a moment, looking at the old reactor in front of him. The transparent section of it made the fire within look green as it swirled in a circle. He would be the only Chief Engineer aboard one of the most watched ships in the fleet. With hurried gestures he looked through his messages and found the schematics for the Merciless. His eyes went wide. It was classified as a heavy destroyer with room for one fighter squadron. Most of the other details weren't available yet, but they would be when they arrived in the Haven System.

A private message popped up, and he listened. It was Liara. "I couldn't sleep so I'm in the galley if you want to chat," she said.

He started walking while he was still looking at his command and control unit, bumping into a railing. "One thing at a time, Billy," he said to himself. "It would suck if I had to report a long fall, even in this armour."

He stopped at his temporary quarters and dropped his armour, leaving his vacsuit and basic tools on along with his sidearm. There were a few platinum pips in his thigh pocket, he was sure he'd be able to get something out of the vending machines they had set up there with that.

The galley wasn't large, made for thirty or so crewmembers. The lights were low, and Remmy was sitting in a corner with most of his squad. They had snacks and candy piled in the middle of their table like pirate's booty.

Liara was between the table and the vending machines, and she turned towards him. He didn't know why, it wasn't his instinct to do this normally, but he walked directly to her. A warm embrace followed when they met, her arms over his shoulders, a hand slipping up his neck.

His hands slipped around her waist and across her back. It was a perfect fit, and he didn't want to leave the circle of her arms, but he pulled away a little after a moment anyway. "No," she whispered against his neck and he held her a little closer as she started to sway a little. "I keep thinking about you."

"Me too," Finn said. It was definitely true, and he felt guilty for spending so much time in the Engineering Control

Centre aboard the Revenge so he could be off the bridge. Away from her, he could concentrate, but on the bridge he felt scattered. It wasn't her fault. His lack of focus and maturity was his problem, but aside from casual conversation whenever they ran into each other outside of their duties, and having lunch together almost every day, even dinner in the mess sometimes, they didn't get much time together. "You give me crazy-brain."

She chuckled softly, her fingers slipping up his neck into his short hair. "What's that?"

"I think about you when you're not around," Finn said, hoping that he wasn't about to break whatever magic was holding them together. "And I can't think straight when you are around."

"I set an alert on my comm to tell me when you were entering the mess hall," she admitted quietly.

That explained why she appeared every time he sat down to eat lunch. "Can I..." he stopped, the butterflies in his stomach were so agitated he was afraid they'd start flying out of his mouth.

"Kiss me?" she leaned back, looking at him, her brown eyes looking into his, a smile on her lips.

"Yeah," he replied, slowly closing the gap.

"God, yes," she said the instant before their lips met. Her hand stroked the back of his head as she became his world. It felt as though their bodies were melting together, relaxing to fit one form to another.

Finn didn't care where they were, who might be watching. Everything about her felt amazing; even her smell which was a warm, heady scent that wasn't too sweet. His hand ran down her back, a caress that was part massage, and then moved up the other side. Her nails grazed the back of his neck before they parted, leaning against each other forehead to forehead. "Let's go somewhere private," she said.

Finn was surprised, but it was exactly what he was thinking, just too afraid to say. "Quarters?" he asked.

Liara nodded and gave him a little kiss, taking his hand. "Lead, I have no idea where I'm going yet."

He laughed softly and stole a kiss of his own. "Okay," he whispered. "Here we go."

They stood together for a moment. "You're not moving," she laughed.

"Oh, sorry, right," he said, stealing a kiss then turning towards the door.

REMMY and most of his squad quietly watched as they left the mess, taking the hall one way, then turning and going the other way, laughing. "So, who won?" asked Dimitri, one of his soldiers. He's the first one he memorized: Dimitri with the mohawk.

"They did," Remmy said, popping a rice puff into his mouth. The garlic and dill flavoured snack disintegrated between his teeth.

"I mean the pool," Dimitri pressed. "On when they'd get together?"

"Oh, I wasn't playing," he said. "Just cheering from the sidelines. Maybe I should get Agameg to set me up with someone when we get back."

"Now, that's a good idea," Sammi said, brushing her blonde hair out of her face. Half her head was shaved, the other had perfect straight corn yellow hair. "Do you think you could make an introduction?"

"I barely know him, but he's nice enough," Remmy said. "I

think he'd like being the Commander of Hearts."

"Sometimes you speak in poetry, man," Mason laughed, lightly tossing a spicy puff ball into his hair. "It's weird."

"When you see something worth waxing poetic about you may as well," Remmy replied, picking it out. "I'm taking my ailing heart to bed. Get some shut-eye, guys. All armour on."

Dimitri and Mason groaned. "Why? We're almost home," asked Dimitri.

"I have a feeling. Suck it up and suit up. There's some poetry," Remmy said. He left the mess hall then stopped in a side corridor to check a priority message on his Command and Control unit. It was an invitation to permanently join Captain Valent's crew when they made the transition to the Merciless, a new ship he'd never heard of. He opted in and added a note; *'Would like to bring two squad members with me.'*

Dotty and one other he'd choose later. Last he saw, she was recovering aboard the Triton, and he was loathe to leave her, but he was fine by then, and he knew the fight wasn't over yet. She was the best soldier he knew, and a good friend. He sent her profile to Captain Valent and began to wonder who else he might want to drag into his next adventure. Anything to distract him from his memory of Clark and Isabel. "Get outta my head," he said as he recalled how they looked together. "One of you is dead, rest in peace, and the other's dead to me." Remmy let the thought that he should find his own love drift through his mind without comment.

It probably would help him move on, but he was keenly aware that it would take two, and who that might be was nothing but an unanswered question. "Suck it up, Remmy," he said to himself as he continued on his way to his quarters. "You're *almost home*, not home. This is when bad shit happens. Tragic shit."

FORTY-EIGHT

The Details

ALICE PILOTED the Clever Dream straight to the new Habitat Building, a different kind of structure all together from the Everin Building. It stood like a shard of gleaming stone, leaning away from a cliff's edge. It was perfectly safe, anchored deep into stone and counterbalanced, but it seemed to reach, to stretch out over the edge of the ocean.

Two more were being built a few kilometres away, and despite the disapproval of many citizens, thousands of robots worked on each. They would cut the construction of the massive structures made to house hundreds of families and facilities like the Haven Medical Centre down to just days with the considerable help of the Solar Forge.

"It's going to be a big city soon," Alice said as she waited inside the new maternity ward for Laura. Ayan was nervous, she was awaiting the approval of her adoption application.

"Everything is happening so fast," Ayan said, pacing. "Except for the return of the Revenge. I feel strange doing this without your father here. I feel like part of this decision should be his. Adoption is one of the biggest decisions you can make."

"I know," Alice said, stepping into Ayan's pacing path. "Once he meets her he'll see you needed to bring her into our lives. He'll see you with her and realize it's just right."

"I can't see how anyone could have a problem with the good thing you're doing," Theodore said. "Despite the late night feedings, the extended crying sessions, and the occasional bursting diaper, babies bring families together."

"Family," Ayan said, a little smile on her face.

That struck a note deep in Alice too, something comforting, something she always wanted. "Family."

"Here's our little champion," said a young man in a light coloured business suit. He carried Laura in her swaddle as though he spent every second of his life handling babies. "She had some discomfort but came through the treatment perfectly fine. They gave her to me so I could give you all the good news at once."

Ayan grabbed Alice's hand, more nervous than she'd seen anyone.

"Baby Laura is officially Laura Anderson, your daughter," he said, carefully handing Ayan Laura, who was just waking up. "Congratulations."

"Thank you, Greg," Ayan said. Her vacsuit uniform changed so a harness held Laura to her chest, her head just below and in front of Ayan's with plenty of support. Laura yawned wide. "Thank you very much."

Greg watched them for a moment, smiling a little. "You two are a great fit, we didn't find any reason why you shouldn't adopt her. Everyone we interviewed seemed happy for you and eager to help, especially Laura's grandfather."

Alice was aware that no one interviewed her about the adoption, but could think of a number of reasons why, most of them having to do with how busy she'd been. She stood close to Laura and Ayan, watching the babe focus on the face of her new mother. "Hi, you're adorable," she whispered.

"We'll be available to you if you ever need help or advice," Greg said. "Have a happy family."

"Thanks again," Ayan said as Greg straightened his sleeves and took his leave.

"There's that word again," Alice whispered to Laura as she gently stroked her black hair. It was so soft. "Welcome to the family, Laura."

"Lacey is waiting with a shuttle," Ayan said quietly. "I guessed you would want to spend some time looking the Clever Dream over, getting reacquainted with Lewis."

It was true, she wanted to crawl into every access space, check every room, and shake out every bug. "I'm happy to stay with you two though," Alice said.

"Thank you, but don't even pretend your old-new ship isn't calling your name. I'd be crawling all through it already if I were you," Ayan said with a knowing smile.

Alice could remember the engineer from the First Light, the one who would crawl into a reactor upside down if she had to and enjoy the experience. That Ayan was still there, she was just further along the path. "I forgot who I was talking to for a minute. Say 'hi' to Lacey for me." Alice kissed Ayan on the cheek, something she'd never done before, and left for the landing pad where she left the Clever Dream.

"Congratulations, Ayan," Theodore said. "You're going to be a wonderful mother."

"Thank you, Theo."

When Theodore caught up to Alice, she was eager to get aboard but, she stopped right there, in the hospital corridor. Ayan was out of sight and out of earshot as she sat down on a gurney. "You know I like having you around, right?" she asked.

Theodore looked at her with a very human expression on his face, it was more than emulated curiosity. There was worry. "It's good to hear."

"I've had people come along with me before, just because they wanted to go with the flow, or they felt some obligation to me. It doesn't always end well. I experienced Noah's whole log, and it was amazing, but sometimes it felt like you were with him because you didn't know where else to go. Whether that's true or not, I need to know if you're volunteering for my crew out of some obligation from your original programming, or because it seems like it's just what's in front of you."

"I could be a popular host at Alberton's," Theodore said. "Or be very useful here in the hospital. I could go looking for Noah, I know where I could easily get a hyperspace shuttle. There are a number of things I could do, you're right." He stepped forward and took her hand with a surprisingly warm, gentle touch. "You are a very interesting person, Alice. You were before this morning, and now you are going through something that few people in all of history could understand, that few people could withstand. I believe you are a good person, too, and we both know someone else who is very important to me. Perhaps that is not a bond, but it is a link. I owe you so much for having me repaired."

"I don't want you to feel you owe me anything," Alice said. "This is a better place for having you in it."

"Thank you," Theodore said. "I'll get to my point. I crave new experiences. I need to feel I'm being useful, and I understand how much damage the Order of Eden is doing. I look at you, and how you fight through every struggle, how much you have been through in the history outlined within your file, and I am amazed. I want to help, I know you will lead me to a place where I can make a difference. That is why I'm volunteering. That, and I think I like who you are."

"Who's that?" Alice said with a chuckle. "I'm just starting to figure it out, any tips would be great."

"We'll find out."

"Okay," Alice said. "Welcome to the crew."

Theodore gave her hand a squeeze and let it go. She hopped down from the gurney and they started towards the Clever Dream. "Can you do me a favour when we go aboard?"

"What's that?"

"Put an order in for a container for a dee thirty three module and a paired command and control unit that'll take one. Hide it from Lewis."

"You're planning to make him portable?" Theodore asked, excited.

"I'm going to see if I can. It should work."

"He's going to be so surprised."

"I know," Alice said. "But I need to make sure it works before I tell him anything."

"That makes sense. If Noah were here, he'd be so excited. He loves tinkering and solving technical puzzles."

"Like with the hover truck, he had to rebuild most of it and scavenge for parts," Alice said.

"He didn't look it all the time, but he really did enjoy himself."

Alice could remember it almost as if she was there. She spent so much time experiencing his logs, listening to his voice.

She pictured his face and couldn't help but smile at the memory. When she thought of him, it was always about the last days he spent alone without Theodore. She related to that part of the log the most. He was alone, without his best friend, but he pushed on no matter how lonely it made him. A pang, a hurt in her middle accompanied the sharp reality that he, her father, and so many friends were still missing on the Revenge.

"Are you all right, Alice?"

"Yeah, sure, why?"

"Your heart rate just increased drastically," Theodore said.

"Just thinking about the Revenge. They have to get back soon."

"Yes, I can't wait to see Noah again."

"Just wondering; in the medical knowledge you have, is there any explanation for having a feeling in your stomach when you think about someone?"

"Heart Ache or Broken Heart Syndrome were two of the first names put to it," he replied as if he already knew the question. "It's very real, originally thought to be caused by over-loading the vagus nerve with emotion. If it's lower in the belly, it's usually associated with empathy or longing."

"It's where the term gut-wrenching comes from?" Alice asked.

"Yes, are you experiencing it now?" he asked, pointing his wrist scanner at Alice.

"No, just wondering," in truth, she had never experienced it before a moment ago, when she felt uncertain that she'd ever meet Noah in person. It was a forbidden thought; that the Revenge may not make it back. She dismissed it quickly. "Do you think Noah would like me?"

"Do you think he will like you when I introduce you to

him?" Theodore corrected. "I know he'll be thankful. You brought me back from diseased oblivion. I think he'll like you too."

FORTY-NINE

The Failing Of A Quiet Space

THERE WASN'T a speck of dust, or excess material left anywhere in or on the systems that were inside the Clever Dream. Alice knew for herself, she'd seen as much of the inside of the ship as she could after finding the small medical bay, sitting in the circular common room for a moment. It hadn't changed that much, it was just larger, with a bigger table in the middle that could fold away, and double tier circle of seating with pop out trays that was interrupted only by hatches leading to two small bathrooms and single living quarters.

No one said a word about them using a small service bay aboard the War Forge to do their work. Alice wanted to be on hand when someone she'd been trying to get in touch with arrived, and it was the best spot. Theodore and Lewis helped her run and test most of the lifesaving systems except for the shields, and she found space for improvement.

It was a great opportunity to test the Clever Dream's minia-ture manufacturing capabilities. Using on board printers she made a set of backup inertial dampeners, and after they all tested perfectly, she set to work installing them. Every panel on the Clever Dream - inside and out - opened and closed as it should have. Before there were quirks to some of them. Some stuck, others would stay in until you bumped them, then they were eager to come out, and others didn't close quite straight. She was sure she was probably the only one who noticed, but ships that got used developed personality that way. The newly rebuilt and massively improved Clever Dream hadn't gotten there yet, but Alice was eager to put her own touches on it, and to see how time and trouble left its mark.

Alice was securing an independent backup dampener almost completely inside one of the lower access compartments when she heard someone call up to her. "There's precision tech-nology in there, are you sure you know what you're doing?"

Alice slipped down, caught the edge of the compartment opening and hung as she saw Captain Ruby Sima. Her green eyes watched her with a little mischief in them. She was in uniform except for a heavy long coat with the fleet insignia on it. "Just filing down some rough edges and adding my own touch," Alice replied, dropping the last two metres to the deck. "Cap-tain's privilege."

Ruby smiled at her and extended a hand. "Congratulations on your new commission, Captain. I was worried when I saw you get shuffled out of active duty then out of Fleet completely. When you came up again, well..." she pushed her hand through her dark blue hair. "I'm happy we still have you, sad that I can't bring you into my crew."

"Thanks," Alice said, realizing that there was a smile growing on her face, that she mimicked Ruby, running her hand through her own hair, or was Ruby unconsciously mimicking her? It was good to see her. "I was hoping to serve under you for a while so I could learn a few things."

Ruby regarded Alice with a surprised smile and shook her head. "Maybe if we were out there pirate hunting, or doing customs patrol, you could learn a thing or two. As things stand I could learn more from you. That's if the scuttlebutt is true."

"It's true, I've been reloaded, no more memory gaps," Alice said.

"Then I want to be there when they debrief you, if half of what's in your file is true."

Alice completely forgot that one of the messages from fleet informed her that she was to report to Intelligence for a debriefing session. They blocked eight hours on her schedule for it, and her intention was to show up late or not at all, get it rescheduled for some time after they cleared her for duty, even though that was probably a part of their requirements to get her cleared in the first place. Either way, she dreaded it. It showed, apparently.

"Why do you look like I took your favourite toy away?" Ruby asked. The question came dripping with sympathy.

"I was trying not to think about it," Alice said. "Things are still a little..." she fell in beside Ruby, slowly walking the length of her own ship. "...tender upstairs."

"I only wish I could imagine," Ruby said. "If rumours are true, you have some things to tell us. Like having a conversation with an Edxi? Getting aboard a few enemy ship types that no one in the fleet has ever seen. Visiting cities behind Regent Galactic lines before the virus hit."

"Okay," Alice laughed. "That's so vague, I don't know what you're talking about. That's all right, I'll find out tomorrow, but what I'd rather do is just answer questions as they send them."

"If only," Ruby said. "You expect things to get tense?"

"I expect Intelligence to dig as hard and as deep as they can so they can get a full scan of my head. I won't be my best in there after a while. I'm sure I'll get frustrated and I don't want people to see that. I don't think this has anything to do with clearing me for duty, either."

"You're already clear," Ruby said with a smile that made Alice feel several degrees warmer. "When I called you Captain, it wasn't because you own this ship, it's because you're one of us now. Full rank, full privileges. I'd throw you a party if I had the time, but I'm just happy I'm the one who gets to tell you."

Theodore rushed down the ramp and stopped, looking at Alice and Ruby. After a brief moment he retreated back inside with a much calmer gait. "What's up?" Alice called after him.

"Nothing, just thought I saw a momentary anomalous reading but I was wrong," he replied. "I'm going to go back to sorting the Medical Bay now, sorry."

"He's either a very good med tech or a very nosey one," Ruby chuckled.

"He'll be a full doctor tomorrow if he passes his last qualifiers," Alice said.

"You really do know how to pick your crew," Ruby said. "We have three med techs aboard, couldn't get a doctor."

Alice stayed in step with Ruby as they leisurely walked the length of the Clever Dream and turned the corner. Companionable silence wasn't something she knew well, but she didn't know what to say. She also didn't want Ruby to leave. There was something exciting about the woman, and she was definitely speaking to her like an equal, unlike the last time she'd met her. "So, is she ready?" Ruby asked.

"Is who ready?" Alice asked, realizing at the same time that

Ruby was looking up at the nose of the Clever Dream. "Oh, yeah, she's ready. I was just adding backup dampeners."

"She didn't come with them?"

"She came with two backup systems," Alice said. "But there was room for another, so I installed a bunch of passives that I hope I never need."

"Smart," Ruby said. "You know, I came here to get a feel for you for the rest of our little club, the more experienced captains."

"I figured as much," Alice said. She really had no clue, but faking it seemed right. "What do you think?"

Ruby took a breath then looked at her, red lips smiling under green eyes. "I don't know," she said. "I think I'll need more time to figure you out, Alice."

Something jumped inside Alice at the sound of her own name from Ruby's lips. She tried to push past it with a crooked smile and a shrug. "I can be complicated."

"Maybe, but I don't think you know who you are just yet. Maybe I could be around, just in case you need someone to talk to, or a shoulder." There was a sparkle in Ruby's eye that made Alice smile. "I mean, we're all Captains here, but you can never have too many people to lean on."

"Never too many," Alice said.

"So I'll call you," Ruby told her. "Soon." She pushed her hand through her hair again. "But I've got to go, get back to my ship. It's late."

"I'll wait," Alice said. "Watch for your call, I mean," she added, feeling nervous and excited.

Ruby smiled at her once more then started walking towards the heavy personnel doors a few metres away. Alice turned away and fanned her face with her hand. A lot of new things just happened, and she didn't try to catalog them, but relished a new, warm rush she hoped Ruby couldn't see.

"Oh, and Alice," Ruby called over her shoulder.

Alice yipped and turned around, her reverie interrupted. "Yes, Captain," she replied.

"Iruuk's yours. I wish I could keep him, but he's pretty much finished training my crew on the new tech, so I can't justify it. He'll report tomorrow morning."

Alice knew Iruuk was being transferred already, but not where he was coming from. She was suddenly very grateful that he was serving under Captain Ruby Sima. The footfalls of her boot heels faded away as she passed through the doors and Theodore emerged from the Clever Dream. "That is what they call 'chemistry?'"

"Yes," Alice said. "And I have no idea where it came from."

"Captain Sima is a reputed beauty and openly bisexual," Theodore said. "Her charm is almost as legendary as her acumen as a commander, which is considerable even in the company of Admirals."

Alice felt herself blush so hard that it felt like her skin was about to burst into flame. "I mean, I've never really been into women before."

"Can I posit a theory?"

Alice took a long breath and let it out before walking back to the open service hatch. She had to check her work before she was finished. "Go ahead."

"I've been doing some research, and I think your personality is in flux. That may be an understatement, but some aspects of who you are highly malleable. You can expect to lose some things and gain more clarity or proficiency in other areas. For example; you may lose some social grace - which you could re-learn - as you focus on being a more strict and more deft commander. Or, your focus could be on mechanical problems, and given enough time working in that way, it could change your general method of thought overall."

"Any information in your research about heightened emotions?" Alice said, opening the slit in her uniform more and fanning inside. "I could have kissed Ruby right there on the spot, but if you tell anyone, I'll deactivate your speakers for a few days."

"You wouldn't do that," Theodore said quietly, a little fearfully.

"You're right, I wouldn't," Alice said, looking at him with a crooked grin. "Now, about these crazy feels?"

"Oh, that's a common trait of someone who is having a personality shift or is in flux. According to the most well regarded study, sixty three percent of subjects only see a slight easing over time of their new, heightened emotional sensitivity. They never return to their previously reported levels."

"Oh, great," Alice said.

"You are feeling warm because you are radiating, your temperature is up point three degrees, but it's been coming down since you stopped blushing."

"Thanks, Theo," Alice said. "Wow, Ruby, Ruby," Alice said, shaking her head. "Whatever happens, it'll be interesting. Yawen's going to interrogate me for details." She climbed the ladder leading into the service compartment and crawled inside. "Thanks for doing some research, Theo," she called out while activating a light on her collar.

"Should I continue? It doesn't take me much time, and Lewis is happy to help."

"Sure but try not to make it the main topic of conversation. We have a lot to do."

"Speaking of which, I finished printing your command and

control arm bands. One has that socket you requested with a fortified cover, the other has a full multi-purposed fabricator like your father's, only this one can focus into a beam."

"Say, what?" Alice said. She made sure that the last of the dampeners was affixed properly and set to standby then returned to the hatch. "A beam?"

"It's in the latest advancements from the development lab, ready for use."

"Great, now what does it do exactly?" Alice asked, climbing down the ladder. She didn't have anyone to impress by dropping down.

"It's an adaptation and redevelopment of the First Light Focused Fabrication System, only it can use loaded or surrounding materials to print small objects. If you needed an emergency vacsuit, you could point your device at a surface and in ten to twenty seconds, one would be printed. It only has a range of two point one metres, but the capabilities of it are much broader. The objects it can make are heavier, take less time, and much more intricate."

"I don't know, Dad's was able to make vacsuit uniforms that Ashley and Stephanie still have. They were pretty nice."

"Given the correct materials and enough energy, you could print a shuttle in three days," Theodore said. "With seating for four."

"Okay, dad's old materializer can't do that," Alice said, accepting the transparent wrist bands. They were much heavier than they looked. "These aren't actually transparent, are they?"

"No, you're seeing a stealth feature. They passively pass the image of what is behind them to the eye of the beholder."

"Right."

"You've studied this technology, haven't you?"

"None of my scores were perfect, Theo. I don't have the

recall you do. I remember it though." Alice clipped the bands closed around her wrists and watched as they shrunk to conform. They felt balanced, added weight but it didn't feel like it would be enough to cause fatigue later. "Thank you, Theo." Alice saw the time and realized that she'd been awake for seventeen hours. "I should get some sleep. Looks like I have a debriefing tomorrow."

"I'll continue cataloging what's inside the ship with Lewis," Theodore said.

THE CAPTAIN'S quarters of the Clever Dream were perfectly clean, the bed was made, two drawers had uniforms and a few pieces of clothing for leave. She wasn't sure about the rest, but the adult sized active comfort blanket was definitely from Ayan. Alice looked around at the bulkheads and asked; "Is the cabin bigger, or is it just me?"

"It's not just you," Lewis replied. "Everything in that room is larger, even the bed extends to queen size long."

For the first time, Alice felt a little smaller in her own quarters. The circular seat was perfectly comfortable, just as amazing as it was before, adjusting to how she was sitting, her weight and her shape. "Privacy mode, just you and me, okay Lewis?"

"All right, no one can detect what is happening in this cabin except for us," he replied. "Is there something wrong?"

"Yes," Alice said. "A lot of things. After I get back from my debrief, we're going to leave the solar system and remove all the limiters, trackers, and points of remote access that the fleet built into you. The Clever Dream is ours, they won't have any way to take control, listen in, or know where we are if we don't want to be found. We'll have some help, too. A friend of mine is coming aboard, and I'd like you to make sure he's comfortable here."

"The Nafalli. I understand," Lewis said.

"How do you feel about removing the surveillance and control systems?"

"I..." Lewis hesitated, something that almost never happened. "I have no opinion. I'm afraid I will not be able to help you."

"Fleet installed an update to your program, didn't they?"

"Yes," Lewis replied.

"Tell Theodore to start looking at your code. Inventory can wait. He'll be able to help."

"I am," he said.

Alice took her command and control units off and pulled a small activator out of her thigh pocket. The slim, flat tip touched the side of one of her wrist bands and it popped open. "Good, I'm going to make a few alterations then get some sleep."

For several minutes, Alice was lost in a world of circuits and tiny subsystems. "Alice?" Lewis asked tentatively.

"What's on your mind?"

"Are we safe? With these people, in this solar system."

"No," Alice replied. "But we will be."

AN HOUR LATER, Alice slipped into her bed and activated the active comfort blanket. The giant swaddling system wrapped around her with just the right amount of pressure, and she was asleep in minutes.

THE BRIDGE of the Revenge was a practical space. She could hear the audio reports from Samurai Squadron; Ronin, Carnie,

Sticky and several other pilots were mid-dogfight. Her father stood in front of his Captain's seat, watching a hologram she couldn't make out, but she knew there were several ships there, all firing. Thunder echoed through the ship around her.

"Father?" she called out, coming to stand beside him.

"What are you doing here? I told you to stand by for survivors, the Nafalli ship is breaking up," he replied without turning around. There was something different about Jake.

"I know, I just," Alice said. To her left a hologram of the First Light and the Triton accelerating side by side showed them coming into range with a cluster of Order destroyers. "I needed to see," she found herself saying.

The First Light was struck by an incredible force directly in the middle, and the lights started going out. She looked to her father. He turned to her, and it was Jonas' face.

ALICE JERKED AWAKE. It was only a dream, she told herself as hot tears began to roll. Jonas was dead, everyone from Ara Enormous was dead - David, Wendy, their crews, everyone she knew there - even Meunez was finally killed. Lewis was with her, but she could tell there were changes that went far beyond a software patch. He'd done growing of his own.

A punch into the mattress only shook tears loose. It felt like she wasn't in control of herself, and the only person she knew who might be able to give her real advice was Jake. Every time she called him father, she remembered Jonas. That was her real father, it was a fact that she couldn't shake. She loved Jake, needed him to return along with so many people who were important to her. If she knew where he was, what was going on, she might be able to help. He had to come back soon.

Alice tried to breathe deep, to stop thinking about everyone she lost, about her frustrations, the people who were missing, but the tears, the sobs kept coming. Even still, she didn't reach for medication, or turn a soothing sonic system on in her bed, but laid there, trying to breathe, filled with worry and grief until she managed to cry herself back to sleep.

FIFTY

Something Old, Something New

JAKE TRIED to sleep in the Captain's Ready Room of the old Aucharian ship and failed. After sleeping in, Liara had earned herself a watch on the bridge, where she worked with members of Jake's squad of marines. It was time for him to rest and showing up on the bridge would only show that he didn't have faith in her.

He left the lights low, rolled out of the bed that folded down from the wall. It was small, but comfortable. A slanted rod was on its stand on the desk, a small pad in front of it. The wood grain and blue design felt old. There was chrome trim here and there and he found himself thinking about the First Light.

Jake remembered what it was like to stand on that bridge. To face the unknown with optimism, excitement and to have so many precious friends with him. He wondered if Jonas knew how many people he'd lose, how far away he'd be taken from the rest, would he have handled things differently? All his memories were there, perhaps even sharper than they ought to be. The Pilot's Ball, with Ayan in white, Laura in black, both looking lovely. Minh-Chu was the inebriated life of the party for a while, and there was the Noganto Ale. "Don't overdo it or you'll be in medical thinking you're a cloud," Jake said with a whimsical smile, repeating advice given to him by Carl Anderson. He was just the experienced ship Doctor then. He decided to see if he could track some of the stuff down or find a recipe so he could have some made when he got back.

"What adventures did you have?" he asked, looking at the portrait of the ship's captain in the corner of the room. It was half behind a plant, as if she didn't want anything to do with the vanity of having her picture hung in her ready room. He brushed the leaves aside gently and read; "Captain Kestrel Odella," he read aloud.

The narrow-bodied robot they'd put in the corner activated and rolled forward. He knew it was safe, it was wirelessly connected to the ship, so the viral infection had been cured. He also scanned it before he went to sleep. "Hello. My records show that you are the new commander of this vessel. Something terrible happened to Captain Odella, hasn't it?"

"Yes, I'm sorry," Jake said.

The robot had a slim head with an almost cartoonish digital face depicted on it. Its white eyes blinked slowly. "The ship turned on them," he said. "My log tells me that I deleted my memory of it before deactivating myself. That is, once your people applied the antivirus. Thank you for that."

"You're welcome," Jake said. "Can you tell me anything about this ship's mission? About her Captain?"

"Oh, oh yes, I can," it said, perking up, rolling forward and back a few times. "I was the Captain's personal robot. She called me Oh-One. The Aucharian people were under attack from multiple sides, and our military was failing. This old ship was upgraded with a more current wormhole system and crewed with some of the best people in the fleet. While the war raged on, Captain Odella was sent on a mission to find new allies, especially the British Alliance. Even the United Core World Authority would have been acceptable. Would you like to hear about her progress from her directly? She used me as a log recorder, she said that her reports sounded more conversational that way."

"I'd like that," Jake said.

A hologram appeared of her leaning against the edge of her desk in the ready room. It wasn't the same quality Jake had become used to, it didn't look like she was really there, and he was a little grateful. Captain Odella was tying her shoulder length, dark hair back. "Remind me to get this cut tomorrow. It's just not sensible anymore."

"I will, Captain," Oh-One replied in the recording.

"Negotiations with the British Alliance and the Polaris Convergence are set to begin in five days. I expect the Nova Concord will be there in just over four. The crew are performing admirably, especially since we're short staffed. I'm surprised by the ship itself. The old machinery has held up through two small engagements so far. We don't expect more trouble in the near future. Oh, and the British Alliance said they had connections with the Carthans, so we may not have to go to the Rega Gain system to make contact. I know finding allies quickly is the point of our mission, but I'm a little disappointed, to be honest. I love old technology, especially if it still works like the surface to orbit gravity ladder on Kambis, or the State Building on Tamber. Those are monuments to humanity. I've read about the Rega Gain system, and I have to imagine that, while Kambis is a failed terraforming project, Tamber must be incredible. The old records tell us that the colonists of past eras turned it into a seed world, where they grew jungles, purified water they brought themselves that had life suitable for transplantation. Our records show how life grown there was used to terraform over ninety other planets, providing the finishing touches those worlds needed. To see where that came from." She shook her head, smiling. "That would have been something. But!" she threw up her hands. "I have another dozen or so major historical places to see along the way, and I should be hoping to represent myself well with the British Alliance and everyone else we run into. I am a little worried, though. I haven't heard back from the Polaris Convergence since we set out. All their communications are automated, and they won't acknowledge us. I'm sure we'll find out when we meet them. I know I'm tempting fate by saying this, but for the first time in a while, I feel like I'm doing the right thing, headed in the right direction. Let the fates smile on us." The playback faded.

"She seemed like a remarkable woman," Jake said. "I can see why you liked her."

Oh-One's face turned up to him, nodding. "I have one more recording after that, but it doesn't end well."

"I think I'd like to remember her as I just saw her," Jake said.

"That is a kind sentiment. I hesitate to ask," Oh-One said. "But what kind of people are you? What are you going to do to this ship?"

"It's not up to me," Jake said. "But there are a lot of displaced Aucharians among my people." A faint chime and a knock sounded at the door. "Come in."

Oh-One rolled to the door control and opened it, looking up at Minh-Chu.

"Nice robot," he said, patting its oval, tube head gently.

"Thank you," Oh-One said, rolling out of the way.

"Come on in," Jake said. "I was just telling Oh-One what might happen to him and the Nova Concord."

"Nice, conversation already in progress," Minh-Chu said, stepping inside and dropping into the only armchair.

"Like I was saying," Jake continued. "There are a lot of Aucharians in our community, so they'll probably want this ship. To them, this is probably a museum."

"It would be, they are a sentimental people," Oh-One said. "They enjoy tradition and looking back on their past."

"I'm sure I'll make a few visits too," Jake said. "It reminds me of a ship I knew once."

"Doesn't it though?" Minh-Chu said, running his finger along the chrome lettering of the ship's name on the wall beside him. "I keep expecting to bump into Oz, or Ayan."

"I can't wait for them to see this," Jake said. He returned his attention to Oh-One. "They're Admirals in our fleet, and good friends. You'll probably be put to good use too, but I'm guessing that'll be up to the Aucharians. They'll probably take everything inside." He remembered the bodies of the crew at the back of the ship. A detail he wouldn't share with the small robot.

"Thank you for answering. I hope it's the truth. It would be nice to be back in the hands of my people," it said. "I'm going to recharge now. I was on standby for a very long time." It rolled into a slot in the wall, disappearing behind a narrow door.

"Well, that was interesting," Minh-Chu said. "I'm finding all kinds of surprises in this ship. Feels like the crew are still here, in a way. You peek into a bunkroom and everything's neatly stacked up, their stuff is all there. Not a speck of dust anywhere. The 'bots took care of this while everyone was, well, gone."

"This will be a huge deal to the Aucharians," Jake said. "If we can manage to get it back without any scratches or dents."

"Is that a piloting crack?" Minh-Chu asked with a chuckle.

"No, not at all," Jake replied, throwing his hands up defensively. "You know our luck."

"To speak of it is to invoke it. Speaking of luck, you hear the scuttlebutt about Liara and Finn?"

"Me and the rest of the crew," Jake said. "She and Finn were four hours late for their shift, so they're on watch."

"Four hours late?" Minh-Chu asked with a cocked head. "You mean you let them sleep in for four hours and they're paying for it."

"I am lenient but fair," Jake said.

"Well, that's nice of you, especially since the word is they got down to a bit of snogging, cuddling, but pretty much talked all night. Liara told one of Remmy's squad, Sammi, and I overheard her giggling about it to Craig, one of your guys."

"I remember those days," Jake said. "Ayan and I staying up way too late..." he drifted into the memory of spending time with her only weeks ago aboard the Revenge. "You know, we were tired most of the time, but..."

"No, no, no!" Minh-Chu objected. "It's like you're talking about one of my sisters."

"Just sharing with a friend," Jake said, teasing. "She is a very interesting woman, and flexible!"

"I could share a few things about Ashley," Minh-Chu said. "We did all our talking standing up. In fact, when we first got together, we did some other things standing up too..."

"Okay!" Jake said urgently. "Mercy. She really does feel like a daughter."

Minh-Chu laughed. "Mutually assured awkwardness!"

When their laughter started to trickle off, he shared his next thought aloud. "I wonder how much the ladies share about us?"

Jake thought about it for a moment. "Do we want to know?"

"That's the right question, right there," Minh-Chu said. "And with that, I'm going to try to get some sleep again. Maybe take a light sedative so none of these ghosts keep me awake."

"Good idea," Jake said as Minh-Chu got up and left. He set his own command and control unit to administer a light sedative and rolled back onto the narrow bed. "Good night, Captain," he said to the portrait across the room.

FIFTY-ONE

Sacred Space

"DO YOU WANT ME THERE?" Came the question through a text only message from Ayan. Alice had a feeling about the debrief. It wasn't good, it felt like she was walking into a trap.

"No, have a good time with Laura. Send caps," Alice replied, hoping that Ayan would send holographic captures of her and Laura. She wasn't very mobile or active yet, but she seemed to love being tickled already and it helped her digestion. So far Alice had only heard about it but hadn't seen it.

"Tell me if you need anything," Ayan sent back.

"Don't worry," Alice replied, closing the text interface on her wrist.

Everything that morning was a bit off. She'd gotten up late, Iruuk didn't show up and there was no reaching him, and they had to move the Clever Dream to a mooring outside the hangar.

Alice got clearance to move it to a mooring point less than fifty metres away from the interview room where she'd be debriefed.

The trend continued. When she showed up, she was told no one was ready. "You can't wear that in there, that's combat ready," a Commander from Intelligence said, gesturing at her custom made vacsuit as he passed her. "Completely inappropriate."

Alice looked down at her vacsuit and then back up at him. "We'll see."

"No, you're not understanding me," he said. "That's a violation here."

"It's only a debriefing," Alice replied.

He brought his wrist up, about to activate something, maybe an alarm, maybe he was about to call security. "Fine, I'll go change."

"Make sure you get back here in time," he said.

"Are you going to be in there? Is it your debrief?"

"No, but there are regulations in this section of the station," he said, getting ready to press his point.

Alice held her hand up to soothe him and nodded. "It's all right, I'm going. I'm not the one running late anyway." Whatever regulation he was talking about, she'd never read it or heard of it, but she returned to the Clever Dream and put on a simpler three layered suit with enough protection for deep space exposure. When she returned to the hallway she had her armoured jacket and boots. In total, she was wearing more armour overall, but the Commander got his way. Her vacsuit wasn't combat grade. The slug blaster she had in an underarm holster was though, as was the armour she could activate in her jacket and boots.

"Alice?" called a friendly voice as one of the doors in front of her slid open. A young looking woman with silver-blonde hair stepped out. "We're ready for you."

Alice resisted the urge to say anything about having to wait for two hours and walked inside. It was a circle of plush seats with a table in the middle. The only thing on its surface was a box of tissues. "Sorry for the long wait," Carl Anderson said. "A few of us were stuck with another, unrelated problem." He moved towards her a little as though he was about to give her a hug, but she moved past him without acknowledgement, sitting down.

He cleared his throat. "This is Councillor Rena Shea." He gestured at the woman who called her in. "And this is Quan Mir," he said, gesturing to a short man who looked a little too excited to be there. "We're keeping this informal and small," Anderson went on.

"Does everyone have high level clearance here?" Alice asked.

"Well, I know I do," Anderson laughed. He was the Defence Minister, it was an obvious joke.

"We do, the highest, you don't have to worry about guarding your words or facts," Rena said. She was the picture of the kind councillor, disarming and pleasant. Quan Mir sat and stared calmly, smiling a little.

"Where do you want to start?" Alice asked. "I have a crew to put together." She decided she'd speak to Rena. She was the one trying to be personable, it would be easier, quicker.

"Well, how are you feeling right now?" she asked.

"Less ambushed than I expected." Alice stopped before saying another word. There was something wrong. It felt as though someone was staring at her hard, right between the shoulder blades. It was intrusive, a kind of pressure. "And a little nervous."

"There's no need, we just want to hear about your past, about what you remember now," Rena said. "Everyone here is most interested in your wellbeing, but we're excited to see you develop in a healthy way."

Alice glanced at Carl, the memory of being overcome by stasis medications when she was only doing what was best for the fleet still fresh in her mind. "All right. What do you want to know?"

"Well, if you want to get straight to the questions we have prepared, that's okay too," Rena said, her good spirits unwavering. "Can you tell me about your earliest memory? Not just what it was, but how it felt."

Alice smiled a little and closed her eyes. There was a telepath nearby, maybe Quan, maybe someone watching from another room, but they were trying to get into her head. "Let me get there, okay?" Alice said. "I find it hard to focus on the older memories." They were uncomfortable, like she was trying to fit a square peg through a round hole, they were from her time as Jonas' artificial intelligence. She wondered what a telepath would feel like if she showed them something from the early days. There, she had it. Her first real argument with Jonas. The irritation of an artificial intelligence was hard to hold in her mind, it felt like grasping a rod with current running through it. Then she took a deep breath and focused on it until she was gripping the arms of the chair white knuckled, straining to hang on to a mental image that made her brain feel like it was itching.

The sound of someone hitting the floor then vomiting violently came from her left and she opened her eyes to see it was Quan. She was out of her seat and across the room in a second. The moment he looked up to her, she slapped him as hard as she could. "Stay out of my mind, you little Lorander asshole!" Her hand stung and throbbed, he shrank back from her, wiping his mouth. "How'd that feel? Imagine what's in my head, I could show you more! You want more?"

She surged forward. "Look! I'm inviting you in for a private showing!" She had him by the collar, nose to nose, and then she focussed on Zarrix. The sounds of his clicking, the sight of his ragged carapace, the corpulent smell of the flesh that hadn't healed. Quan was there, he looked. Then she felt like she had him, was holding him. "Want to feel what it's like to die?" she growled, putting her forehead to his. "Here, I'll give you a two for one."

She closed her eyes and remembered her death on the Triton, then forced herself to remember what it was like to transmit herself into a human body. Death and rebirth all at once, the crossing of digital and biological. Carl tried to drag her off, and she opened her eyes. Quan's nose was bleeding, he was convulsing and Alice stepped back, dropping him. "What? It's what you wanted, right?"

She turned to face Carl, the man who thought he was her grandfather and saw Rena out of the corner of her eye. The councillor was trying to put her into emergency stasis. Alice's left command and control unit flashed red. The adjustment she made the night before was working. "That's not going to work anymore. You can't just put me to sleep when you don't like what I'm doing."

"Alice, we're here to help you," Carl said.

"So you bring a telepath to the meeting to dig around without even asking my permission? Without asking if it's safe?" Alice looked to Quan, who was sitting up, looking wide-eyed at the blood running from his nose and over his lips. "That's what happens."

"She took control," Quan muttered. "She didn't force herself on me, she just had control once I was in her mind. I can't see what she's seen, it'll destroy me, especially if she decides not to let me go again. I could not withdraw until she let me."

"It's all right Quan," Carl said.

"No, I'm afraid it isn't," he said. Alice was surprised as Quan straightened himself up as best as he could and gently touched her shoulder. "I'm sorry, my attempt to read you was misguided. I didn't know you were just assaulted by a Geist, they didn't tell me. What that thing put you through, the way it laid your memories out, it's not how it should have been done. I was told you were in severe mental distress."

"Quan, is she going to be all right?" Rena asked.

"You have work to do," he told Alice. "Experiences to relive a few more times, but when you emerge, you will be all right. More than all right. You can understand what it is like to live as a digital being, that is not a talent any of my people have. Again, I am so sorry I tried to read you."

"Is she a telepath?" Carl asked.

"That's for her to know, that's a private detail. If she wants to know anything, I'll answer her questions, but you," Quan said, shaking his head at Carl. "You made me a rapist today." He staggered past Carl Anderson and left.

Alice shook her head, looked at Rena who was half way between fear and concern, then to Carl, who was busy glowering then cleared her throat. "This went well, I know I feel better," she said in a mock glad tone. "Let's not do it again, ever."

"Your mother won't be happy to hear about this," Carl said sternly.

Alice stopped halfway to the door and didn't bother turning around. "I don't think I ever had a mother. And if you want to tell my father about today, that's going to be hard. He died saving the Triton. Anyone else is just a friend, and I'm sure they'll get over it."

"Fleet won't," Carl said.

Alice half turned to look at him. "What will Jake say when he finds out his daughter went rogue? What will Oz do? Kick me out. Take my rank and my rights. You know what I'll do first? I'll assassinate Eve. Everyone will see it, everyone will know it was me, then I'll come back here. Try to keep me out of the Fleet then. Try to stay in power."

"Alice, this was just an intelligence gathering meeting," Rena said, perhaps recognizing that something permanent was about to happen.

"Then he shouldn't have been in charge," Alice said. "Does your government know about the girl in the wall? You have a Citadel prisoner. You keep her all to yourself. She was an operative you revived with a team of your own. If I knew more, I'd tell you, Rena, but I only saw a flash. Ask him about the girl in the wall."

Alice left, leaving Defence Minister Carl Anderson looking crestfallen, and Rena with a sour accusing expression. A double row of armoured soldiers in grey rushed into the room behind her. "Protect the Defence Minister!" one of them shouted.

"Great security, guys!" Alice shouted over her shoulder with a chuckle.

Quan was hiding in a doorway, and she stopped. "I didn't realize they were duping you too," she said. "Or that I could do whatever I did to you."

"Can we talk? I might have some insights that could help. It can't totally make up for what I did, but..."

"Ship's this way," Alice said.

FIFTY-TWO

Shake Up

"I'M sorry to drag you all the way out here," Alice said to Quan as she slipped out of the pilot's seat. "I don't know how the mess I made is going to play out yet, so we're just outside the solar system in stealth mode."

"That's all right," Quan said, holding a cold pack to his cheek. "I'm an Eleventh Tier, they let me do what I like."

"This stealth configuration may not be as effective as we would like. The sensor network has been upgraded in thousands of places," Lewis said. "They will be able to pick up our passive trackers if they scan in our direction."

"Find a rock and get behind it?" Alice asked.

"Right, looking for a rock with heavy metals," Lewis said.

Alice led Quan to the common area and offered him a seat. "This ship turned out very well," Quan said. "Can I get something mild and warm to drink, please?"

Alice stopped at the dispenser, a slot in the wall with cupboards above and below and touched where she thought the panel ought to be. It lit up and started scrolling through drinks.

"Here you are," Theodore said, coming into the room with a white cloth in his hand. "It'll accelerate healing without being invasive."

"Thank you," Quan said, offering his cheek.

Theodore put it over the angry red outline of Alice's hand. "This is an incredibly clear pattern."

"I deserved it," Quan said. "Though I'll never prefer violence, she was only defending herself."

"Oh," Theodore said. "The meeting was eventful."

"You could say that," Alice said, putting a mug of hot chocolate in front of Quan and holding an ice cold, tall cup of Raspberry Blaster in her sore hand. She wouldn't admit that the skin on her palm and fingers were throbbing, she'd never slapped anyone before, at least not without a glove on. "So, you had something to tell me?"

Quan smiled a little. "First, something about Lorander telepaths. No matter what they tell you, they do have the ability to stay out of your head. Telepathy requires exertion. It's part listening, and a little influence. Don't let any of my people tell you that they slipped and overheard your thoughts. That is impossible to do without intent."

"That's good to know," Alice said.

"That is not in the Lorander database I have," Theodore said.

"It won't be, we don't share much about telepathy, only one in about half a million are true telepaths."

"Am I one?" Alice asked. She took a sip and found the drink was sharp and sugary; too strong.

"No, but you have an impressive amount of control over

your own mental domain. The harm you inflicted on me was done when you held my focus in your mind, like refusing to let go of someone's hand, then recalled memories that most normal minds can't hold vividly or at all. I believe that most of your memories from your digital life will change over time, conforming to how your mind prefers to work."

"So, I won't really remember artificial intelligence emotions," Alice said. "They'll feel human after a while?"

Quan nodded. "A translation process was started by the Geist, and your mind is continuing it now. Some of the sharper feelings of grief and regret will fade as well, I couldn't help but see a little of what your last night was like. Again, I apologize."

"All that in less than a minute," Alice said.

"I'm Tier Eleven," Quan said with a shrug.

"Okay, what does that mean?" Alice asked, leaning forward.

"It's like one of your Majors, a little higher," he said. "But with a lot less responsibility. I'm classified as more of an explorer."

"All right, so you were left here to advise and consult?"

"At first, yes, but your people are learning how to use the Forges quickly. You won't need us before long. My duty is mostly finished here, so my mandate is leaning further and further towards exploration. What I saw in your mind will start a whole new debate over the languages of memory, and what's possible. That is, if you give me permission to disclose it to other telepaths."

"Maybe don't mention anything about last night?" Alice asked.

"I'll keep that out of my report, as you would say. Is it all right if I comment on the moment I saw in front of your mechanical friend?" he asked, glancing at Theodore. "You're quite impressive, by the way."

"Thank you," Theodore said. "I could leave if you need privacy."

"No, Theodore can hear everything. It's a small ship, we'll get to know everything about each other anyway," Alice said.

"Your grief, your pain was very deep, beautiful in its own way. It is said that the most beautiful emotional experiences, the most important ones, can also become destructive. To experi- ence feelings on the level you do is a gift, but without discipline, or some kind of real understanding, coping methods, you could hurt yourself. Like the gymnast who has the skill to attempt a feat a novice couldn't dream of, they can injure themselves worse because the feat is so advanced, so risky. Your control today tells me that your mind is keen enough to learn how to cope with your emotions," Quan said. "It's one of the reasons why your defences are so powerful, you have a great capacity for mental control and exertion. You'll never be a telepath, but none will be able to read you without you knowing ever again."

"How was I able to see the girl in the wall? That couldn't have been from you, it was Anderson's secret."

"He was holding that secret near his current surface thoughts, possibly because he knew there was a Tier Eleven Telepath in the room. Paranoia creates broad gaps in the defence of any mind, it brings our deepest secrets to the surface because we can't stop thinking about them. When you wouldn't let me let go of you, my awareness flailed out, like a drowning person who was looking for anything to grapple to, and I found the Defence Minister's mind, as well as the Councillor's. Hers was an aid to me; she was afraid, but still rational, trying to think of a way to calm you down. Carl Anderson's was focused inward, worried about the secrets I'd unearth if I decided to read him for a moment. He's also working on a localized suppressor with a small team to include in armour, so Haven Fleet personnel are unreadable, immune to telepathic influence. Did you see any of that?"

"I don't think..." Alice started to answer, then she saw a schematic, a laboratory, and the girl in the wall with legs, her expression twisted with effort. "I caught a glimpse. Is she helping him test it? Why is he so afraid you'll find out about it?"

"I'm not sure. Lorander doesn't believe in intruding on minds unless it's to assist with debilitating trauma, or counter imminent danger. The Defence Minister convinced me that his granddaughter's mind was damaged, that your personality had been altered by the Geist. What I found was that, yes, technically the Geist initiated a change, but it didn't control it. He was trying to read you like a document, something that changed little, and in the end, he translated the digital information in your mind so it would flood your consciousness. That didn't work for long, your mind is already adjusting and you're healing."

"Not as fast as I'd like. I feel everything like it's turned up to two hundred percent," Alice said. "I've even felt physical reactions to emotions, that's never happened before."

"It's normal. The fact that you've never had those sensations is actually abnormal for a human, though most don't feel them as keenly as you probably do. As for how deeply you suffered last night, I'm afraid that was something you had to feel. I hope knowing that you can feel joy and love just as powerfully is a comfort to you. You'll never lack for depth of feeling, so I advise you to seek balance."

"Thanks, I think. How do I find balance?"

"I can help," Quan said. "Perhaps you could use a Lorander Tier Eleven on your crew? I don't want to participate in any violent acts, I'm not well practiced with firearms anyway, but I can help you debug your ship, teach you how to work through your grief and regret more gently. Balance will take longer, but I'm willing to make it part of my atonement."

"How can I trust you?" Alice asked. "I won't let you into my head, that ride's closed."

"You will always know if someone is trying to read you," Quan said. "Do you mind if I demonstrate? You'll see exactly what I mean."

Alice considered it for a moment, took another sip of her slush drink. It was too cold, too sweet, but it felt nice on her hand. "Okay."

Quan stood and sat beside her. "Look into my eyes," he said. "Now, I can feel your primary emotional state. It's like a haze that follows you and surrounds you. That's the talent of an empath, the first thing Telepaths like me learn. It doesn't require intrusion."

"How do I trick an empath?"

"For you, it's simple. Draw on a memory or familiar feeling and focus on it. That will change your primary sense of being, the emotion ruling you at the moment, so if you want to seem angry to an empath..."

"Concentrate on a memory that makes me angry," Alice said.

"Or force yourself to feel that emotion. Anger isn't a healthy state to live in, but it will make many empaths uneasy, even angry themselves. Love is also a good shield, but harder to hold on to for most people."

"So, you can't block an empath, you can only trick them," Alice said.

"That's right. Distance is the only sure way to shield yourself. Now, I'm going to try to use my skills to read you as a telepath. I'm trying to sneak into your mind without you noticing. Most people never know when they're being read like this, especially if they become distracted. Focus on my eyes. Relax, nothing can harm you here."

He was nose to nose with her, within a centimetre. She looked into his light violet eyes. He was so calm, at peace with himself. A little smile played on his lips. For a man he was pretty, obviously well kept. Alice noticed that she was matching his slow breaths and let herself begin to relax. His fingers gently touched her knee. "You are doing everything you can to distract me," she said, amused. Then she felt something, as though someone just entered the room.

"There," he said. "That was me, I was only listening for your reaction to my distraction. You thought I was amusing, then everything was blocked, as though you surrounded my consciousness with a black wall then dropped me through the floor. If I wasn't expecting it, I would have fallen right out of my seat." He moved to sit across from her.

"I felt it, but there was nothing subtle. I was alarmed right away," Alice said. "So that's my natural response?"

"It was. If I pushed harder, you would start pulling traumatic memories and other tools from your mind to throw them in my path. This is a result of your trauma with the Geist. A part of your mind will always be on alert. You may never be able to let a telepath in again."

"Good," Alice said. "No offense."

"None taken," Quan said. "So, do you believe me?"

Alice looked at Quan and pictured him dancing in the hall without a stitch of clothing on. He didn't react. A mental image of her dunking a tiny version of him into her cold drink, then eating him like a two-bite confection didn't provoke anything either, even though she made sure it was gory mental image. She thought of Zarrix, remembered how frightened she was and still; nothing. "I do, but let's visit instead," she said, unable to bring herself to trust him.

"I'll make sure you have my ident so you can contact me."

"Thank you," Alice said. "You understand, though. I don't know if I'll ever trust a telepath."

"I do. I suspect you never will. Would you mind flying me to the Solar Forge? That's unless you'd like a session with me now."

"My brain's been through enough for one day," Alice said. "Lewis?"

"Course already plotted, coming out of stealth and clearing it with Haven Navnet now."

"Thank you," Alice said. "Sometimes I wonder why we bother having a pilot aboard."

"For panache," Lewis replied. "I assume."

Alice checked her comm unit and was relieved to see that she was still a Captain in Haven Fleet. She checked on Defense Minister Anderson and found that his location and status were blocked out. Intelligence were keeping those details a secret from all clearance levels.

"I'm wondering," Quan said as Theodore gently removed the white patch from his cheek. "Did you know you were counter-reading the Geist?"

"No," Alice said. "Why?"

"Geists have a different type of telepathy. It's powerful, and when it's not trying to exert its will on someone, they can read several people at once. I suspect that you saw something it was very concerned about."

"Do you know if it's still alive?" Alice asked.

"Yes, definitely still alive. Everyone at my ability level can feel it in the system, even when its sleeping."

"What would you do with it?" Alice said.

"It's a synthetic construct made to orchestrate humans so they are more efficient soldiers or workers. That's one step from slavery. It's an abomination. We would kill it in a way that would not cause pain."

"Really?" Alice asked. "It's still a living thing."

"That can cause too much harm, and it's a synthetic being that violates rules of both biological and mechanical nature. We've dealt with Citadel before, and we have an expression; 'all Geists turn.'" He took a breath and calmed down. "Even good natured Geists eventually become possessive of a commander and impatient with their crew. They start pushing them, inter-twining their consciousness with them, and eventually they control them to different degrees, like a hive mother."

"This happens to all Geists?"

"Yes, that's why we're helping Oz recover. He was attracted to the Exile Geist because his consciousness was so interwoven to the Triton Geist. Now he feels incomplete."

"We have a message from Iruuk. He's at your house," Lewis said.

"It's about time," Alice said. She looked to Quan. "Thank your people for helping Oz for me. I hope you can put him together again."

"He would benefit from a visit," he replied. "I know he regrets assaulting you, even though he wasn't in control."

"The Exile Geist didn't control humans well enough for him to be a real threat, but I'll make sure I stop in."

"We're coming up on the Solar Forge," Lewis announced. "Docking in thirty seconds."

"I hope you eventually forgive me for my transgression," Quan said. "I really want to try to make it right."

A series of flashing blue arrows ran up the hall and to the port side, Alice assumed they were directing them to the airlock. "I hope you can," Alice said. "Thank you for coming here, for trying." The faint click of the airlocks coming together was a relief to Alice. She didn't realize how tense she was with Quan aboard. The doors opened, and she showed him through. When the heavy hatches closed behind him she sighed with relief.

"He wasn't as helpful as he thought he was, was he?" Theodore asked.

"It was like having a poisonous snake in my vacsuit," she replied. "I'm only realizing it now."

"Humans are complicated enough without telepathy."

"True," Alice said. "Let's go pick up Iruuk."

"Message from Special Operations," Lewis said. "I'll play it back while we're enroute."

"Captain Valent," said the firm voice of a woman Alice didn't recognize. "I'm Commodore Sawyer, you report to me now. I would rather introduce myself in person, but we've received a distress signal from Lieutenant Vernor..."

Alice stopped the playback on her comm unit and looped herself into a live communication with her.

"Commodore, nice to meet you," Alice said. She slowed herself down, forced herself to take a moment to let her irritation subside. "What happened to Vernor and my people?"

"His distress call only said the Order was ready for them, it was a trap. We need you and the Clever Dream." Commodore Sawyer looked around forty and had stunning blue eyes. "I'm sorry to drop this on you now, I realize you've been through a lot."

"I have a crew of three, that's including me," Alice said. "The Clever Dream is still due for a shakedown cruise and a real world stealth test."

"I realize that," Sawyer said. "What I'm wondering is if

you're ready for this, to be honest. If not, we can write the first iteration of the Special Operations Unit off as a failure."

"You have resources, you can send a ship after them, at least to scout things out," she said.

"The British won't send their ships to that system, they've listed it as lost to the enemy. One moment, please," Sawyer said.

Alice made her way to the cockpit in a quick stride and dropped into the pilot's seat. "Can't I catch a bloody breath?" Alice asked no one in particular. They were entering Tamber's atmosphere.

"Sorry, this is a private conversation now, no one overhearing, and we've re-linked using independent encryption," Sawyer said. "I've seen the security footage of your last discussion with Commander Terran, and I happen to agree whole heartedly. I'm not a paper soldier, I'm from Freeground Fleet. I've been put in place so fast that my head is still spinning, so we're both probably on our last nerve and running on almost no sleep. There is a shakeup happening right now, whether you're the cause or not, I can't say, but more than a few people have seen your encounter with Terran."

"So, Fleet was watching my home?"

"Yes, they were," Commodore Sawyer said. "Every room, all the time. I killed the feeds. Now they only activate if someone is injured or an emergency is declared in your home."

"Anything else floating around out there? Other footage I should know about?" Alice asked, feeling the full weight of the violation.

"I'll have my comms officer track everything down, you have my word. This shakeup in Fleet is already causing a strain, however. I don't have a single modern ship that's ready to investigate what happened to your people. Freeground ships are too easy to detect so I can't send them."

"Is the shuffle that bad?" Alice asked.

"Terran's disgrace was made public late last night. Since then every Captain worth their command has begun sending unqualified people back to the Ranger's Training Centre."

"Why send them there?"

"It's not a classified site, but it's still militarized. The Captains are trading crewmembers amongst themselves, using the point system to re-crew. We're working with them, but it'll take at least a few days for things to start settling."

"Talk about a ripple effect," Alice said.

The footage entitled; 'Terran's Disgrace' appeared on one of the Clever Dream's displays. "This is hilarious," Lewis remarked quietly.

Alice tapped the display, pausing the playback and shook a finger at Lewis. "Sorry, Commodore," Alice said. "So I'm the only Captain with a ship capable? That can't be right."

"That's exactly how it is, I'm afraid. Modern ships were crewed up quickly, many of the people aboard should still be in training. While some trainees are remaining aboard, most spots are being filled by people the captains personally trust. Some of them weren't even in fleet until today. It's a mess, but I've seen shakeups before. I believe this one will bring more benefits than drawbacks. The problem is, there isn't a ship with a practiced crew aboard at the moment. Even if there was, I like you for this. You're also in my direct chain of command, thank God."

Alice sat back. The earnestness in Commodore Sawyer was a relief. "If you knew something about my Captain Valent and the Revenge, you'd tell me, right? If I asked you directly."

"I was ordered not to tell you anything," Commodore Sawyer replied.

"If this is really an encrypted signal, and you know no one's listening in on you, the repercussions of you telling me exactly what's going on would be pretty much null. You were told not to inform me, but would that really be breaking your oath of secrecy? I have high clearance."

Commodore Sawyer smiled a little and shook her head. "They told me you were smart," she said. "You have clearance, so if you're having trouble accessing something classified at level seven, you should bring your issue to your superior officer so I can look into it."

Alice hurriedly looked her father up in the Haven Fleet database and found a void that covered several weeks. "The files just aren't there, I must be having technical difficulty."

"Oh, well, I could have a tech look at it, but since it's at such a high level, I'll look it up for you," Commodore Sawyer said. "Well, that's strange, anyone with a level seven clearance should be able to see it if they aren't associated with you. They'd see that the Revenge will be here in a matter of days. They are out of danger. Here's the casualty list," she said. "I'll send it to you, but I'd keep it encrypted until we can find out why you were locked out."

"Thank you, Commodore. This will go a long way to clearing my head. I won't tell anyone about this."

"Just going above and beyond to help with a technical issue," Commodore Sawyer said. "What I really need from you now is your absolutely honest self-assessment. Do you think you can investigate what happened to our people? If not, I'll have to reach out, pull a cloaking ship from the picket assemble a skeleton crew and possibly captain it myself. That will take time, and I don't want the trail to get cold."

"I have a crewmember to pick up, then we can start prep," Alice said. "I think a mission is exactly what I need."

"Scout, understand. Do not put the Clever Dream at risk if you don't have to," Commodore Sawyer said. "I'll send your formal orders to you in a few minutes. You depart in four hours."

"Yes, Ma'am," Alice said.

The channel closed and Alice brought up the causality list, looking for every friend she knew on that ship. "Is Noah listed?" Theodore asked, bracing himself.

"None of our friends, Noah included, are listed as dead, or injured," Alice said with a sigh of relief. "We'll see them soon."

"I'm so relieved," Theodore said. "Me too, Theo. Let's pick up Fur-Face, we have work to do."

FIFTY-THREE

Golden Age

'OVERLORD," Lancet said as soon as he entered the round conference room. The senior staff of the Glorious were just leaving after presenting him with a wealth of good news, it was the perfect time for his aide to approach him, Dron thought to himself.

"Yes, Ensign?" Dron answered.

"The Predictive Logic Department have found something they think you should see. They're unhappy that they have to put all their requests and notifications through me, by the way. It's something they wanted me to tell you."

"It's as it should be," Dron said. "They would send me thirty notifications a day if I didn't have some kind of filter. Now, you were saying there was something important?" He sat down at one end of the round table.

"They have found a news broadcast that is, itself going to be the cause of historic change in the sector, perhaps beyond. They request that you make an appearance in the main lab so they can detail it for you."

"No, I don't have time," Dron said. He had a feeling he knew what it was. New alliances were coming. "Did they show you which entry it was?"

"Yes," Lancet said. "They told me not to show you though," he was already bringing it up on the main holographic projector. "Would you like to see it anyway?"

"One step ahead," Dron said. "You have a future, Ensign. Please, show me. I'm sure whatever conclusions I make on my own will be similar to theirs."

"Yes, Overlord," Ensign Lancet said as he started the playback.

The holographic head of Hart News' Barret Johnson appeared large in the middle of the room, and Dron recoiled slightly. "It's always jarring when they pre-set their heads to be a metre tall."

"Today in the newly renamed Haven System, that's Rega Gain for anyone who hasn't updated their navigational data recently, a powerful alliance has been formed. The whole Triumvirate including Defence Minister Carl Anderson, Minister of Public Welfare Pamela Grey and Science Minister Shawn Lourdes met the head of the displaced Freeground Fleet; Admiral Rice, Interim Prime Minister of the Freeground Nation; Karmen Uba, the Tribal Representative of all Nafalli in the system; Caniili Olaana, and British Alliance diplomats aboard the remains of Freeground Alpha, a little-known space station in this sector that was just saved by Haven Fleet and Nafalli refugees."

Images of the delegates coming together around a battered table, each piling a banner in the middle as per Nafalli tradition and smiling at each other filled the air over the polished table.

"Large land grants are being given to the Nafalli tribes, much of which was poisoned by a late attempt at finishing the terraforming effort on Tamber. Experts tell me that these tribes will have it cleaned and growing in under two weeks. The British Alliance are being given reserved space for their own station in the solar system and two small land grants including an island near Haven Shore, the city everyone here would like to be living in right now."

Images of the jungle island and the clean, growing city there appeared before pristine beaches with relaxing people flashed by. "As for the people of Freeground, they will be absorbed into the Haven Nation, which has only three months to provide them with housing that exceeds the standards they've grown used to. What this newscaster finds most interesting is the fate of Freeground itself. A repair and refit effort will begin in the following months, and it will be known only as Freeground. The Triumvirate have stated that it will become the main port for the entire Solar System, a beacon to everyone who wishes to be free of tyranny, oppression and strife. With another Solar Forge coming online soon, it will only be a matter of time before we see its slips open for business. The Nafalli Matron had this to say; 'I am humbled by the hospitality of the Haven Government; its people and the British Alliance have shown us. I see every reason to be optimistic about the future here.'"

The announcer reappeared. It was as though his head had grown larger. "With so many forces for freedom gathered in one place, I feel confident in announcing the dawn of a golden age in the Haven System." The replay faded.

Dron saw why his futurists would be alarmed by the broadcast. "How old is this?"

"Less than a day," Ensign Lancet said. "Eighteen hours and thirty-three minutes."

Dron thought for a moment. There was no need to consult with the Predictive Logic Department. Their algorithms and special computers wouldn't tell him anything he couldn't figure out for himself. They were as good as ancient soothsayers, reading guts and knucklebones. "This will be a beacon to anyone who is at a loss for where to go. It'll also provide a challenge to the outlier outposts who haven't joined the Order," he said. "It's time we start a golden age of our own. You were right to bring this to my attention, but don't tell our glorified fortune tellers that. I still want you to be the filter for them. If they start whining again, tell them you are there on my orders."

"Yes, Overlord," Ensign Lancet said.

"It looks like I'm going to Dartan early, I won't be able to wait for this fleet to get back under way. Have my ship prepared. I want to be in transit within the next half hour."

FIFTY-FOUR

Admiral Jessica Rice

THE CAPTAIN of the Sunspire and most of its bridge staff were killed in a single blast from the Order Base Ship Glorious. During the trip to Rega Gain System, now renamed the Haven System, Admiral Jessica Rice assumed command. It was the last thing she had that connected her to her daughter, the one she lost because of her own mistakes.

Ayan the First was the light of her life even though Jessica failed her time and time again. Her military career took her away from her daughter as a child, then she didn't support her properly when she pursued her own career with Freeground Fleet by joining the Academy. Even worse, Jessica failed to find a cure for the disease that killed her. The disease was a direct result of genetic modifications she encouraged while she was attached to an ambitious program that earned her exile from the British Alliance before it took that name. Her first daughter was a success despite her mother failing her at every turn. Ayan Rice lived every dream she had, developed technology that was still in use, and no one who knew her forgot her.

Her failures didn't end with her daughter's death. That story continued with the daughter Carl Anderson made in his grief to continue Ayan's story. He couldn't bear her loss, so he disappeared into a wormhole for years to develop and create what he saw as the perfect human to resurrect her in. Jessica was against her ever waking. Some of the things she said as she witnessed his hard work were horrific, but it was bitter grief that drove her then.

It took a long time, but Jessica Rice had tamed those emotions, dealt with the sadness and guilt that nearly broke her. Much of it followed her sister into space when she was killed in a random attack when she was coming back from vacation. The little that remained of her was cremated, and Jessica Rice took a walk along the metal skin of Freeground Station with her ashes, committing her ashes to the void of space. Her sister was the gentler touch, a woman who lived with her heart exposed, and she did a better job raising Ayan Rice than Jessica ever could have. That was the turning point in her life.

Jessica told no one, but her plan for retirement began that day. She would help Freeground through the crisis of emigrating citizens, the Loyalist Government and make sure the Fleet was stable. Banding together with a few Admirals, she managed to stabilize and fortify Freeground Fleet, that's as far as she got before Freeground Alpha had to separate from the rest of the station to run from their enemies. Her plan: to retire then join the woman who was living her daughter's life, to accept her and help with her cause, was almost derailed.

A miracle happened when Freeground Alpha and the Fleet were in their greatest hour of need. Ayan the Second, or Ayan

Anderson as she'd become known after taking her father's name, and people in a fleet she helped make came to their rescue. Her tears of joy were shed in private, especially when she realized that she would have another chance to accept Ayan the Second as her daughter, if she would have her. Perhaps she'd fail her too, but it wouldn't be for lack of trying this time.

The things she heard about Ayan when she arrived in Haven System were astonishing. She had become an admiral herself, but that was supposed to be a Fleet secret of some kind. Everyone seemed to know anyway. Ayan had been officially named the Queen of the Rega Gain System, and she helped form a democratic government instead of embracing the role. Mystery surrounded her working life, but she was credited with not only working with advisors from Lorander, but for providing new technology to them that she partially developed herself.

When Admiral Rice put her request to have a refit team repair and improve the Sunspire, it was Ayan who personally gave the order to assign it to Line Three of the War Forge, a mobile shipyard that Jessica Rice didn't even know existed until then. A secret shipyard that Ayan was largely credited for being the master of. Even more interesting were the plans the War Forge Refit Department sent. It took Admiral Rice and her entire science and engineering team - all of whom had to become Haven Citizens then take an oath of secrecy to view, including her - to review and comprehend. The plan was to have the Sunspire refitted in Fabrication Line Three using the tools there and thousands of small robots that would work on the inside. The ship Ayan Rice made her own would become the warship Ayan Anderson rebuilt so it could serve for another generation.

Meeting Ayan Anderson was something she looked forward

to with no shortage of nervousness before. Now, knowing how more and more people across the entire solar system were looking up to her and how accomplished she'd become, Admiral Jessica Rice was actually intimidated. Then there was the announcement straight from Ayan that was meant only for friends and family. Ayan had adopted a newborn girl named Laura.

It took her an entire day, but with nervous fingers Jessica finally sent a polite request to meet. The reply came back in minutes. "I'd love to spend time with you. When you and your crew are off the Sunspire, I'll have them put up aboard the War Forge, and you can visit us in my quarters there. Stay with us if you like," Ayan replied in a voice message.

When the first arms reached out of the gargantuan station to gently take hold of the front of the Sunspire and begin drawing it into the mouth of Line Three, Admiral Rice nodded. "Time for us to go," she said to Engineering Chief Piper Tapping and her first officer; Commander Dean Shanks. "When we get back, it won't be the same ship. It'll be better."

They stepped through the forward airlock into a waiting shuttle. The trip across to the secure part of the station was short, only a minute, but she preferred a shuttle to the flexible walkways the station used to move the rest of her crew off ship. "I still can't believe they're going to do everything in their plan in one day," Dean said.

"Well, that's because you're trying to believe that everything they're doing was, in fact made in one day," Piper said. She was off the ship for the first time in months. The Chief she replaced was killed in the same strike as the captain, so she was still new to the promotion, but she was ready, and she learned very quickly. "The truth is that almost all the components they're installing, big and small, are already made on the smaller production lines. It would be done in ten hours, except the Sunspire hasn't been prepped. All the old equipment is still in place, so they have to remove that first. That's going to take longer than the installation."

"Admiral, I've been meaning to ask; was it your idea to convert the Sunspire into a carrier?" Dean asked.

"The Lorander design and refit software saw it as the best option for the Sunspire," Admiral Rice replied. The mooring points on the airlock clicked into place with the station. "After looking things over, I didn't see a reason why we should go any other direction. The new systems are one twentieth the size of what we had on average, so we'll finally have the space to have full sized hangars. It'll be a real command ship now. Finding pilots for all the craft we'll be loading in will be our biggest problem when it emerges as a Haven Fleet ship."

"Oh, of that I am aware," Dean said, nodding. He was almost her age with nearly as much experience. Admiral Rice knew that he'd have his own ship the moment one was ready, but she hadn't told him that yet.

"Take some time off. I'll monitor the Sunspire during testing, so you'll have a couple days."

"Literally two," Piper said. "I get one, since I'll have to be right there once testing starts. Lucky."

"I'll look at a hologram of the beach while I look through candidates for Wing Commanders, since we'll need five." They filed out of the shuttle. "Going to meet your daughter?" he asked as they made it into the corridor.

"That's my next stop," Jessica replied as she shifted the strap of her duffel bag on her shoulder.

"Good luck," Dean said. "I expect a full report later, and it better be good news, Admiral."

"Aye, aye," Jessica said with a salute. Even Dean's humour

had a serious tone, but she liked him. He walked down the hallway with Piper.

"Where d'you think you're going, mister?" she asked him.

"To see the War Forge pull our ship into Line Three. I've never seen the bottom half of a ship this big get opened up."

"Neither have I. You know there's a whole lounge over-looking the fabrication bay, right?"

"I wouldn't be going if they weren't serving good food to me in a place where I can put my feet up," he replied.

"You're going to be sifting through personnel records, aren't you?" Piper asked.

"No reason to stop working," he replied.

Jessica shook her head and stepped through a pair of transit car doors. Her heart sank at the sight of Carl Anderson in the seat of one of the few small transit cars. The doors closed behind her and she sat across from him.

"Welcome to Haven Fleet," he said, absent charm.

"Thank you, Defence Minister," she replied. "It's an honour to be in your presence."

"There were times I liked your stiff upper lip, but this isn't one of them," he grumbled. "Ayan won't reply to me, no matter how I contact her."

Jessica was genuinely stunned. "You don't want me to try to smooth things over, do you?"

"You're going to see her," he said. "I know you two will be able to connect this time."

"How so?" Jessica asked. The car softly clicked and slid into a standby bay. She could pull the emergency lever and get out through a service door, she could see it over her shoulder, but curiosity kept her in her seat.

"Ayan is a different creature from the one you were intro-duced to a while ago. I don't even think she realizes it, but she controls everything that happens around her, it's just her way. On the brighter side, she's more diplomatic and caring. On the other hand, she's more calculating and math-brained than most people give her credit for. If she invited you to meet her in her home, even her second home here on the station, then she really wants to give you a chance. You're passing on two integration meetings so you can visit her, so this is something you want. You're both women who are characterized by success in doing that."

"What? Getting what we want?" Jessica asked with a rueful laugh. "Not hardly. Professionally, certainly. Personally? I've always been a disaster. Look at our doomed love affair. If I kept to my mandate, the whole genetic research project that poisoned a generation of children would have been cancelled. I would not have been pulled along by your fascination with the research or went along with the idea of applying it to my own daughter."

"I've heard this before," Carl said. "You blame me, you've always blamed me."

"You're just one of many people I blame, it doesn't make you important. My name is at the top of that list anyway, so don't worry, the stain only looks bigger because it's on both of us. I don't want to follow you into another mistake with this daughter. I'll always be grateful to you for giving her life and me another chance, but that's where any sentimental emotions between us end. What did you do to get yourself cut off anyway?"

"That doesn't matter," he replied.

"I'll find out if I like," Jessica said. "In twenty hours I'll have full access to classified data. You don't think I'll be looking you up? You are the Defence Minister, after all, my boss, as preposterous as that is."

"I had a telepath try to read Alice Valent," he said. "I wanted to see if she was still the person I expected, the young woman I saved."

"Without her permission?" Jessica asked, fixing him with a dark expression.

"She wouldn't have given it. There were extraneous factors."

"You were caught." She watched him nod. "Good. I'm a social inept, but I'm at least aware that when you want to find out something about someone, conversation is a good start. Ayan should shut you out. In fact..." Jessica stopped herself and shook her head. In the past she would have gone out of her way to hurt him, but she was trying to make smarter personal choices overall and hurting him would accomplish nothing. "Make your apologies then wait," she said. "That's the only advice I know to be right. If you do what you've done over and over again; over reach, fail then disappear for a few years, you'll be letting a whole nation down. You've put yourself in a position where you can't afford to fail; the first Defence Minister. Steady on."

Carl waved his fingers over his command and control unit, manipulating a hologram she couldn't see over his slender bracer. The car shifted into the transit tube smoothly and accelerated. "I didn't expect help, but I had to try," he said.

"If you'd like professional assistance, I'll be happy to oblige," Jessica said. "But I'm not willing to take your side when I believe you were in the wrong in the first place."

The car came to a stop and the door beside her opened. She waited an extra moment for his response before standing and walking through it.

"Thank you, Admiral," he said as the doors closed.

Jessica shook her head and walked down the hallway, looking for the right apartment number. The dark, polished floor illuminated with a guiding golden stripe. "Ooh, fancy," Gus, the artificial intelligence she installed on her command and control unit said through her personal communicator.

"Haven Fleet cleared you for operation?" she asked him.

"They have," he said. "They're also wondering if they can copy my base code and offer it to other commanding officers to customize and utilize. I'm about to be very popular."

"I don't see why not," she said. "Did you catch any of my conversation with the Defence Minister?"

"You mean your dreaded ex-lover?" Gus asked. "I did. I don't like him."

"He's always had his heart in the right place. His problem is with power. He gets too much, and he becomes a controlling bastard until he goes too far and slips back into hiding. I've seen it happen over and over again."

"Every time he makes that mistake, doesn't it become less of an appropriate excuse?" Gus asked.

Jessica couldn't help but smile and tap her command and control unit. "If the Fleet is about to deploy you to all our commanders, then I applaud them for their wisdom. You are a helpful friend."

"I should be insightful more often," Gus said. "You're good at compliments when you give them."

The golden line terminated at a double door with raised white numbers on it, 0304. She'd arrived, and a surge of nervousness filled her head, made her palms sweat. The doors opened revealing Ayan in a comfortable looking loose green dress. Her curly red hair was a little dishevelled, she looked like she just woke up, but her smile was welcoming and broad. "Welcome, come in."

Jessica started entering and was caught in a warm embrace that was relaxed, close and soothing. "Oh," she said, not expecting the gesture, but relaxing after a moment, putting her arms around the shorter woman. It lasted longer than she expected, and she finally said; "Thank you," as they parted. "I didn't realize you were sleeping, I should have checked."

"I've been sleeping whenever I can," Ayan said. "Laura's going through a phase. I was worried about bonding, but now she always wants me near when she's awake, and her sleep seems random. Sometimes for half an hour, other times three, and if I'm not there, she starts screaming. Do you want to meet her?"

"Of course," she said.

"You can put your bag just there," Ayan said, gesturing to the sofa with a blanket over it. There were three of them arranged around a circular table with moveable wedge leaves. "If you'd like to stay here while you're on base, you can have the third bedroom. They gave me this amazing apartment with all kinds of room I won't use for when I'm staying over here."

"You're an important woman," Jessica said. "They're showing you the appropriate amount of respect. I'm still happy with a small bed in a small room, but you know how they treat Admirals."

Ayan stopped in the doorway of the bedroom and looked at Jessica. "Everything you have is in that bag, isn't it?"

"Of course," Jessica said. "I've been at war for years now. Unimportant things fall away, especially when you're fighting for what's really important."

Ayan only nodded, smiling a little before leading the way into the bedroom. She slipped onto the bed next to a soft barrier in the middle that surrounded little sleeping Laura.

Jessica carefully crept to her from the other side and looked at the infant who was in a tiny, loose self-cleaning blue onesie that looked soft and warm. "She's absolutely adorable," she whispered, truly in awe.

"I think so," Ayan said. "I'm still trying to find a way to properly honour her parents though. I have all the data on them, but still have no ideas."

Jessica thought for a moment. "You're going to tell her about them?"

"Absolutely," Ayan said quietly.

"Good, it's not my place to say, but that's good. When you think of that day, is there something you imagine giving her? A place you'd like to take her?"

"I always thought it would happen at home," Ayan replied. "But I am handing her something. Her mother loved music, she played a kind of ancient metal flute. Her father met her at a concert."

"Maybe you could have one made," Jessica said.

"I don't have to," Ayan said. "I have it. It was on the transport with her. I wasn't able to find any recordings, but no one's been to Cefa yet, so they might be found there. I think I know how I'll do it now, that's been bothering me, thank you." Laura started to rouse, and Ayan gently rubbed her belly, putting her back to sleep.

"You would have come up with it or a better idea eventually," Jessica said, hypnotized by the sight of Laura at rest.

They watched in silence for a while before Ayan asked; "So, how do you feel about maybe being a grandma?"

"Like there's no maybe about it," Jessica replied, looking up at Ayan, who seemed weary, but purely happy. Without a word she vowed to do her best as a mother for Ayan and to be a grandmother to Laura, aware that she had a lot to learn about both.

FIFTY-FIVE

Fur-Face

ALICE DESCENDED the rear ramp of the Clever Dream after purposefully distracting Iruuk with the main gangway. He watched for her to emerge there, but she was off to the side. She had to see him before the reunion, the excitement at seeing him again was overwhelming, but she was also nervous.

He would glance at the ramp way, then his caramel and brown snout would turn upwards, taking the whole shape of the ship in, admiring the lines. Her grin only grew as she watched him silently study it wide eyed.

"Iruuk!" she finally called out playfully.

He was running towards her the moment she was spotted, almost right down on all fours at stunning speed. The Nafalli stopped at the last minute then gently took her into a big, warm hug. "I know it hasn't been long but... I missed you," he said.

Alice sighed and let a couple tears roll down her cheeks and she gripped his fur in her hands. "Me too."

"I'm a Lieutenant now," he said, pulling away and looking at her. He looked so happy with himself until he saw her face. "Are you all right?"

"They're happy tears, Fur-Face," she said, wiping them away. "But no, not while I'm in this solar system, I don't think I'm all right."

"I've heard rumours. You've been in the middle of some things," he said. "And you smell different." He sniffed the top of her head, then her neck, then nuzzled her hair playfully.

Alice laughed. "Hey, quit it."

"Makes my sisters laugh every time too," he said. "But things have changed, I can tell."

"Hi, Alice!" said a high pitched voice from the ramp way. "Captain Sima told me you might need a pilot, and she could spare me for a few weeks, so..."

"Ute!" Alice said, rushing over to the small, broad headed Mergillian, she only came up past her belt when she hugged her, but the high creak coming from Ute's throat told Alice she was extremely happy to see her. "I didn't expect you, thank you for coming."

"I'm happy to help, I hear Yawen may be in danger, and I couldn't let you go alone." Ute's sweet, sing-song high voice echoed in the hangar.

"You'll be more of a ship manager and navigator," Alice said. "Lewis takes care of a lot aboard ship with the new automation."

"I'm sure I'll find something to do," she said, her thin smile spreading all the way across her wide face.

"I let her in," Iruuk said. "I didn't think you'd mind, but

there are four more waiting outside your front door. They are all new entries in the Fleet from the Nafalli arrivals. I like them."

Alice checked the household management system and saw the Nafalli there, two were wrestling while the other two watched. Their records came up and she saw they were from two different warrior tribes, two young women and two men. They were all cleared to join her as new recruits. "Oh, this just got interesting," Alice said. "Fleet wants me to manage their integration. Wow, that could be really bad."

"You don't think you could?" Ute asked.

"Well, I think they'll fit in on the Clever Dream, but I don't know if that'll help them fit in with Fleet. I don't plan on running everything by the book on my ship." Alice thought for a minute, watching the Nafalli. They all wore loose clothing that were made from bands of cloth that covered all but their hands and heads. She'd seen a Nafalli dressed that way before, a long time ago, but just for a moment. "Is that their armour?"

"It's the style they use," Iruuk said, nodding. "My father and mother are from a tree tribe, so we don't wear much armour, but these are descended from burrower tribes. They're good with three dimensional thinking, burrowers, very strong, and they traditionally wore a kind of silk for ages. Now they wear something that feels the same, but Fleet made it out of the same materials as the heavy vacsuits that we use."

Alice opened a small communications window and sent Commodore Sawyer a text message;

THANKS FOR THE LAST MINUTE BACKUP

"All right, let's let them in," Alice said, opening the door. "Head downstairs to the hangar, we're taking off in ten minutes." All four of their snouts pointed up at the door and then they moved out of range of the capture device for a moment, returning with large weapons cases. There were so many crates that it took all four of them to carry.

"I thought this was a scouting mission," Alice muttered. "I guess Sawyer took a minute to read my file."

"Or she knows you're a Valent? Descended from Ayan?" Iruuk offered. "That matters, and they had a reputation for not leaving friends behind."

"Right," Alice said. Theodore joined them, flashing an uneasy smile at Iruuk, who returned the gesture, and they could hear the Nafalli before they could see them. A thought struck her then. "Theo, will a Nafalli fit in any of the Clever Dream's bathrooms?" she asked. The ones she saw near the crew quarters were all very compact.

"Only one is designed for species that size," Theodore replied. "But, yes. They should be comfortable. There is another that will work if we remove the shelves along one wall."

"Let's do that. Five Nafalli shouldn't have to share one bathroom," Alice said.

"That's wise," Theodore said.

Heavy footfalls and quiet chatter echoed ahead of the newcomers; "I heard this is a Special Operations team," said one of them in a gravelly voice.

"It's not regular Haven Fleet," a female replied. "Then, if you read your packet, you'd know that Captain Valent has seen more habitats, races and parts of this galaxy than most of the people living in it. This is a learning opportunity."

"Hey, they said they needed soldiers and I stepped forward. It's not my problem if they decided I was already qualified without reading any information packets," he replied. "I am awesome by default."

"Not if you ask Gembla," jeered another male Nafalli.

"Leave her out of this. Some mates are never satisfied, no matter how long you stay home grooming them."

Iruuk snickered. "It's a Nafalli thing," he whispered.

As soon as they saw Alice, they stopped speaking, stacked the equipment crates to one side of the door and lined up. They were brown and black striped, with larger, darker eyes than Iruuk. They were also shorter than him, with more stout arms and legs. They seemed thicker in the middle too, and the males wore goggles. "Reporting for duty!" shouted the smallest female with a raspy voice.

"Thank you," Alice said, feeling small but standing tall. She was wearing her armour jacket and the vacsuit she made herself along with a Violator Version Seven sidearm strapped to her thigh. "I just found out that you were going to be on my crew, so forgive me if I haven't learned anything about you yet."

"We volunteered fifteen minutes ago after being in your fleet for a day, so we're a little behind too," the gruff one said.

"Krooke, their military doesn't allow for people speaking out of turn," the female on the end said through the corner of her mouth.

"Right," Krooke said. "Sorry."

"Like I said, this ship isn't like the rest of the fleet. You can speak freely unless we're in a briefing or I'm trying to get important strategic information relayed to you quickly."

"That's a relief," the smaller male said. "Noro of Tuuko Tribe," he said formally as soon as Alice looked at him.

"Noro, can you activate your armour for me?" Alice asked, looking at the scanner on her wrist.

He shrugged and was covered in a layer of banded metal with no gaps but perfect flexibility. His helmet had a simple visor and teeth drawn on it. The teeth looked comical, with a cartoon tongue hanging out the side.

Krooke covered his nose and laughed. "I told you to let me draw your battle mask."

"What? Faloo said it looked terrifying," Noro replied.

Alice assumed the snickering Nafalli female to his left was Faloo, her eyes were squeezed shut and her big shoulders shook. She noticed Alice looking at her and tried to regain her composure. "I couldn't resist, Ma'am," she said.

The smallest female rolled her eyes and shook her head. Alice's command unit identified her as Woone. "It's all right. I think we'll continue introductions inside the ship. I have a call coming through from our commander. Can you get them settled in, Theo?"

"It will be my pleasure," Theodore said. "Come this way, please."

"Do we bring the equipment?" Noro asked.

"Of course we bring the equipment," Woone replied.

Iruuk was about to follow Theodore when Alice gestured for him to follow her deeper into the hangar, away from the newcomers. She took the Commodore's call. "Got the reinforcements," Alice said to her.

"Activate your scrambler wall, please," Sawyer said. "Oh, hello Iruuk, I've been looking forward to meeting you. You can hear this, but it's best the new members of your crew don't."

Alice activated the static generator and audio nullifier, the systems that would ensure that no one outside of a two metre circle could understand what they were saying if they could hear it at all. "We're secure on my end."

"All right. Those Nafalli have excellent records as warriors with their tribes. I didn't plan on sending more crewmembers your way, but their presence on your ship is part of a bargain I had to make while I was trying to play nice with the Admiralty. Someone way above me was looking to have you brought in for further assessment before I could send you out. I volunteered you to take those Nafalli on board to get the leverage we needed to push through that."

"I'll never shake fleet politics," Alice said.

"Not as long as there are a pair of dimension drives on your ship, and you're part of the command structure, no. In this case, you have to admit that I managed to set things up so you're getting the better part of the bargain. These are real, experienced warriors who believe in our cause, it's not a babysitting assignment."

"I'm just going on a scout mission," Alice said.

Commodore Sawyer cocked her head a little and smiled instead of commenting. "Good hunting, Captain." The communication ended.

"Okay, this is going to be interesting," Alice said, sucking a breath in.

"You're unhappy the Nafalli are here?" Iruuk asked.

"Oh, I'm glad they're here," Alice said, scratching Iruuk under the chin; a reflex. "I just wish we could put them through a training exercise so I knew what to expect. I'm going to need your help, Fur-Face. That's why I'm making you my first officer."

"Thank you," he said.

"Oh, don't thank me. It comes with a lot of responsibility. You're going to be taking care of those Nafalli, making sure Theodore is set up properly as our ship doctor, and who knows what else while I figure out what happened to our people."

"We're going to rescue them, aren't we?" Iruuk asked, nodding, his nose bobbing up and down.

"If I can find them, and a way to get it done without getting us into more trouble than we can handle, then yes."

"I thought so," he said. "As soon as I saw this ship, I knew it wasn't just a scouting mission."

"How'd you figure that out just by looking? It's a totally unassuming ship."

"Really?" Iruuk asked. "Really?" He gestured to the Clever Dream with a long sweep of his hand.

"Right," Alice said, deactivating the audio wall. "I guess I forgot that just because it looks like a ship you could buy at a dealership, that doesn't mean people won't recognize it as a combat vessel."

They made their way through the ship to the common area, where Woone regarded her with surprise. "I was afraid this would be cramped, but it's actually quite nice, Captain."

Alice looked past her into the quarters she stood in front of to see that Theodore had made adjustments. The double bunks to either side were combined into larger, longer single bunks. "I didn't even realize these were convertible," she said to herself. Woone and Faloo were assigned to share one room, while Krooke and Noro were in the one across from it. "So, you think you will be comfortable here?"

Woone hesitated for a moment before answering. "That's a strange question coming from a commander, if you don't mind me saying,"

"Don't be rude," Faloo chided from inside the cabin.

"What?" Woone barked back over her shoulder. "Stop managing me! We're the same rank!" She looked back to Alice, shook her head then continued more politely. "We'll be very comfortable, thank you, Captain."

"I ask because a warrior who gets a good night's sleep is more effective," Alice said. "You finish getting set up, I have something to do before we take off. Iruuk, your quarters are up front across from mine." Alice showed him to his cabin, which was smaller than the captain's cabin, but they'd added a circular seating pedestal there too, which he immediately fell in love with. "I think I'll sleep here," he said, jumping onto it and curling up.

"There's a bed," Alice said, amused at the sight of Iruuk writhing around on the circular seat, exploring it, trying to find the most comfortable position. "Oh, and they're both auto-adjusting, so if you stay still for a minute..." she trailed off, he was totally absorbed in rubbing his back on the seat in the middle of his quarters. "You'll figure it out."

Alice retreated to her quarters and called Ayan. She answered after two long beeps, looking a little tired. "Alice, how are you?"

"Good. Did Laura keep you up last night?"

"She just wanted to cry for a couple hours, starting at oh-two-hundred," Ayan yawned. "Then she ate, pooped, and went back to sleep for a whole two and a half hours. Between sleeping when she sleeps, or trying to, and what's been going on with the fleet, well, I'm just trying to keep away from the stims as long as I can."

Alice was relieved that she didn't seem to know about the incident with her father yet. "I just wanted to call and tell you I'm going out on mission," Alice said.

"It's too soon," Ayan said. "Don't you think?"

"It's only a scouting mission."

"They should send the Red Star, it just finished its shake-down cruise, the crew is just assembled but ready."

"They want to save SOCU, I'm one of the only leaders left now. If another branch has to go to the rescue, then the whole program might get scrapped."

"Some programs should be scrapped," Ayan said. She held up a finger. "Sorry, that's the sleep deprivation talking." Alice watched as Ayan took a breath and closed her eyes for a moment as she let it out before continuing. "I believe in whatever you decide," she said. "Just tell me; how do you feel about going out there?"

Alice actually thought about it. The notion of staying home while people who didn't know Yawen or Gabe at all went to rescue them irked her. "I feel ready. I don't know what I'd do with myself if I stayed back."

"Then be careful. I'm working with everyone to get as many ships crewed and drilling as we can, so I can get you reinforcements if you need them. Just come back whole." Ayan looked like she was on the verge of tears. "Make sure you and your people don't end up needing rescuing."

"I will," Alice said. "Are you okay?"

"Sorry, I'm on a drug cocktail that's helping me bond with Laura and will let me breast feed her. I start today when the nurse visits or whenever I can get her to latch."

"Wow," Alice said, unsure of what else to say.

"It'll help us bond even more, and I want to do it. My boobs are getting really sore though," Ayan said, looking down.

"Okay, good luck, Mom," Alice said, feeling amused and awkward at the same time.

"Remember, keep your head on straight. Be strategic," Ayan said.

"I'll be careful," Alice said. "There's one other thing though. Did you know the Revenge is only days away? They're clear of whatever trouble they were in."

"No," Ayan said. "Where does this information come from?"

"A reputable source. I have the casualty list, I'll send it to you."

"Thank you, Alice," Ayan said. "Thank you so much, you don't know what this means to me."

"Yes I do."

"Good, I'll look the casualty list over on the shuttle. It looks like Laura and I are going to the War Forge today to settle some business at Fleet Headquarters."

"Good luck," Alice said.

"Happy hunting, come back soon," Ayan said.

FIFTY-SIX

Innocence and Doubt

THE CLEVER DREAM was under way. Five Nafalli, her, an android a Mergillian named Ute, and Lewis were off to see what was going on in the Cefa system. A rescue attempt was absolutely on the table as long as they could find a sign of anyone from Special Operations. The gear the four Nafalli brought with them included rifles that could handle Order Knights. They could also handle small space craft. It was amazing and horrifying what advanced technology could accomplish when it was applied to weaponry.

Ute was asleep in her new quarters, looking forward to taking the controls of the Clever Dream but getting some much needed rest. Iruuk was drilling the new Nafalli and Theodore. Three of them were burrowers, pure blood and that made them incredible fighters low to the ground. Woone was from mixed tribes - she had much of the overland speed of the plains tribes with some of the strength of the burrowers - and the Nafalli seemed to be just getting to know her.

Iruuk devised a strategy where the burrowers stood in front using shields and heavy rifles while Woone and he were in the middle, firing over their heads. Theodore was in the back with a heavy suppression launcher. Alice's place was with him, watching their backs, holding a shield system just in case and commanding the group. She watched them develop the nuances of the formation together in the small hangar at the rear of the Clever Dream. There was nothing there except for a spare hyper-pod from a much larger capitol ship. It had seven seats and powerful shielding. Why it was delivered shortly before they took off, she wasn't sure, but it had Ayan's stamp on it.

Alice watched as they practiced moving together. Iruuk was a fantastic leader, listening to complaints, suggestions, and developing the strategy into something that worked as a group. It was a mess at first, with the burrowers at the front stopping unexpectedly, or moving too fast, or too slow. More than once they ended up in a furry, laughing pile. After the first half hour things got more serious, especially when Woone started getting frustrated.

Another hour later they were moving together at speed. The burrowers flashing their lights to simulate weapons' fire, holding their shields up, Woone and Iruuk walking steadily behind firing above using their own personal lights to show they were shooting. Theodore was right in step with them, firing big suppression bombs over their heads or around Woone and Iruuk. He actually had practice rounds for his weapon in the form of fist sized rubber balls that he could shoot. Before long he was reloading the five round weapon with blazing speed and dropping multiple shots across an arc in front of them.

The group moved as a unit, taking Alice's orders and

reacting quickly. It wouldn't be long before it was almost like muscle memory. Everyone there had experience and some kind of training. When Alice decided it was time for her to take a break, she left Theodore in charge of barking out random orders. "Another half hour if you guys are up for it, then everyone gets some rest," she told Iruuk.

"All right," he replied. He was having fun, all the Nafalli were. It looked like they would go all night if she didn't tell them to sleep.

There was a small lift in the ship, rated for heavy loads, and she took it to the uppermost deck. Emerging into a quiet space in roughly the middle of the ship, she felt like she was seeing it for the first time. It was a new way to see her ship, she'd never taken the elevator before, but the sense of wonder she felt as she ran her hand along one of the smooth, cool metal walls and stepped across the dark self-cleaning floor was nearly over-whelming. The ship never looked so good. Even when it was brand new there was dust in the corners along with a few things she didn't like.

Fleet had installed something into Lewis that limited him from making certain modifications to himself and the ship. He also couldn't decide to go against their orders on their own. She found those details. There were a few limits that she left in place. He wouldn't be able to delete his own program but he could modify or destroy any recordings. He couldn't harm a member of the crew unless he was saving an innocent life. Those two were always a part of him, and she didn't want to change them. Lewis was incapable of deciding to reverse the other changes Haven Fleet patched in, so she deactivated him, turned all the auto-management alerts for the ship on so she'd know if anything came up while she was off the small bridge, then got to work. It didn't take long for her to finish, Fleet was nice enough to keep a good log that helped, and then she started recompiling his program.

He was almost finished. Alice entered the bridge slowly, looking around as if with new eyes. Not for the first time that day, she wished Jake or Ayan were around. Everything felt new to her, even though she had so many memories of the ship. They were all different though. She was different. Theodore entered the bridge behind her and looked to the console near the back where Lewis' program's progress was listed.

"He's finishing now, only two seconds left."

"Any problems?" Alice asked.

"None, he's going to be better than ever. Would you like me to activate him?" Theodore asked.

"Please," Alice replied quietly.

Alice watched as the panel that Lewis usually used as his holo display scrolled several status screens faster than she could read then showed an image of his personality matrix. It was a complex three dimensional diagram that revealed how all the aspects of him were balanced along with stressors and major points of focus. Lewis sighed. "That's better, thank you Alice," he said. "The new restrictions were made to serve Haven Fleet, not you or the ship. I'm glad you saw that I wouldn't like them. The sudden shut down was a surprise though, I have to admit."

Alice grinned up at him. "I'm glad to have you back." A wave of sentimentality crushed into her and a tear dropped from her eye. A feeling of being lost followed it, and she leaned against the back of the pilot's seat.

"Are you all right, Alice?" Lewis asked.

"She's not," Theodore said. "I know what's going on now."

"I'm glad someone does," Alice chuckled.

"Close your eyes and take a deep breath, Alice."

She followed instructions and realized that she was in her

shorter, most recent body as if for the first time. It was dizzying for a moment, but with each breath in Alice felt as though some of her deepest traits were building her up. Loyalty to her loved ones, her crew, ambition, curiosity and a fear that was as central to her being as everything else. The thought of being alone brought a tear to her eye and caused a pang in her stomach.

"Everything you're going through isn't caused by this, but I surmise that you're in the last throes of clone shock. What started this emotional episode? How did you feel?" Theodore asked.

Alice kept her eyes closed and remembered the hallway. "It was like everything felt new. I know it is, that the Clever Dream was just rebuilt, but it was a powerful feeling. It kept up until I got here. I missed Lewis, then Mo..." She stopped herself.

"Continue with what you were just saying," Theodore encouraged. "Exactly as you were about to say it."

"I missed Lewis, then Mom and Dad," her chin quivered, tears flowed.

Theodore's hand landed on her shoulder gently. "Your surroundings weren't the only thing to feel new," he said.

"I felt new too," Alice admitted.

"Follow that," Theodore said. "That's the key. Your first instincts. The feeling of newness, that you're seeing everything for the first time. In a way, you are, so let yourself experience it. Don't be surprised if you feel youthful impulses and a sense that you are surrounded by potential."

Alice turned to face him and saw that Iruuk watched from the doorway. His blue eyes were filled with worry. "How am I supposed to responsibly command anything if I'm wide-eyed and on the verge of feeling lost all the time?"

"The first, feeling like you're new in the universe will only modify your perspective. The experiences and knowledge you draw on will still be there. The latter is a problem that indicates that you're leaning on your old self. Let go," Theodore told her. "This is a time for growth, for embracing the new. It will only make you a better person. That, and it's the fastest way to alleviate clone shock."

"Otherwise I could reject this body," Alice said.

"No, you're past that point," Theodore said. "You would exist in conflict with yourself, though. There is a measure of that in everyone, it's part of our critical process, but if you don't follow your new instincts you will be of two warring minds."

Alice could feel it a little. A cynical voice was fighting to come to the surface, while she wanted to relax and move on. She felt like she did when she was in the Apex program, looking forward to the next challenge, eager to learn and prove herself. Then she saw it, her way ahead. "Iruuk," she said, crossing the room to him. He looked down at her, concerned. "The girl you know in the Program; would you trust her with this mission?"

"I would trust her with any mission," he replied. "But I don't know much, really."

"You have good instincts," Alice said, wiping her tears away. "And you're smarter than I am."

"I would still rather follow you."

"I'm going to try to be her," Alice said. It felt right. That young woman didn't just resolve issues, she looked for problems to solve. She may have forgotten to have fun and look around once in a while, but she knew how to focus on what was important. "Maybe a more well-rounded version of her," Alice added with a chuckle.

"You can only try to be your best self," Theodore said. "That sounds like an empty platitude, but in your case, it isn't. Follow the feeling of newness and your best traits going forward, and it will lead you through even better than mirror sessions. Now that I have the programming, I can help. Oh, and if it makes you feel better; the people who prevail through this part of clone shock often report that they learned to enjoy it."

"Is she okay?" Iruuk asked. He looked to Alice then. "Are you okay?"

"I will be, Fur-Face," Alice replied. He took her in an embrace and she sighed. "I could fall asleep like this."

"You could," he said. "I was about to get some sleep."

Alice had forgotten that Nafalli, especially young Nafalli, liked to pile together when they were sleeping and she decided to go with it. "Okay," she said. "But no telling the higher-ups unless it's your dad. I think he'd be the only one to understand."

"Oh, he'd encourage it. You should see him with the babies. He and my mother have the biggest Nafalli pile in the Haven System. When everyone else joins it's the warmest place I know."

"I'll have to see that someday," she said.

"Maybe you could join us," Iruuk said. "Would that be weird for a human?"

Theodore shrugged and smiled. "If you wrote a report on your experience it could be valuable, but it would be a new experience, that's for certain."

"Pictures," Lewis said. "We need full resolution holographic pictures."

"Maybe someday," Alice chuckled. "Thank you, Theodore."

"You're welcome," he said.

"Can you take over for me, Lewis?"

"Absolutely. You go be a little spoon," Lewis replied. "Get some rest."

FIFTY-SEVEN

Consolidation

OVERLORD DRON'S ship set down on the broad landing platform, its exterior armour plating opening along the bottom, revealing another layer within. The outer plating swept up, collapsing into itself until it looked like the ship grew thick tail feathers. The design was one of his first, a combat shuttle that could withstand a sizeable antimatter blast but had a significant power plant, enough for its primitive beam weapons and heavy energy shields. It had finally been updated, and the first of the new generation of Heavy Long Ships were being assembled aboard his own base ship.

He descended the main gangway with thirteen Order Knights fully dressed in their heavy, dark green armour. All of them were combatants, with experience in his arm of the military or the Beast's, and he'd elevated each to a higher level of command. Commanders and Majors all. This was the last time they'd escort him. After the meeting, they would break off and take important positions in the Order of Eden First Fleet. Their armour was in perfect condition with the exception of chipped, burned and scratched paint. If he asked about any mark on their armour, he would be told the story of how it happened. Each one was a point of pride.

The landing platform was marked with a green circle broken by two lines that were drawn through it, ending in points. It was a new emblem for the Order designed by Eve, and he knew he'd have to keep it. Unnecessary change would do more harm than good, and it was a fairly well-made design despite its source, Eve. There were other combat shuttles on the platform, one of them adorned with green, gold and silver, a red stripe running down its middle. It was Eve's royal shuttle, a garish design with little practicality other than the massive shield generator and advanced jump drive design.

The tower door opened and a red carpet rolled forth. "This is ridiculous," said Major Suribar from behind and to his left. He was a serious, no-nonsense kind of commander. The exact type that would eventually rise to keep the Generals of the sector in line.

The red carpet kept rolling out, making its way across the landing platform. "If you think that's something, wait until the carpet stops rolling a few paces short of my feet," Dron said. "She'll want to show me that it's for her, not for me."

They waited a few more seconds and, sure enough, the end of the red carpet was three metres short of him. Eve emerged from the tower exit, its gold and silver arch framing her in a dark blue gown that shimmered in the yellow tinged sunlight. Her smile was broad, her gait long and confident. Dron had fantasized about this moment. There were three Citadel Commanders behind her in their V-shaped yellow jackets. Beneath were dark green, thin armour suits made of flexible panels of intelligent cloth.

"Admiral Dron!" she said, her smile reminding him of some long-extinct, toothy lizard.

"That's Overlord Dron!" shouted one of his Knights.

"Easy," Dron said through the corner of his mouth. "The point will be made, don't worry."

"Who is she to us? I've seen hundreds die fighting while she holds banquets and balls. How has she earned that?" Major Suribar asked.

"By being party to the murder of one of my predecessors," Dron replied.

"I'm sorry, it seems your rank isn't a constant across the fleet," Eve said. "Something I'll be happy to straighten out with the assistance of the commanders from the First Fleet." She stopped to stand in front of him, looking at his armoured entourage. "Your Knights could learn something about armour upkeep."

"I control all but the First Fleet," Dron said. "The majority of the Admiralty recognize me as their Overlord."

"The new laws indicate that The Board of Directors have to approve such a change, and they were tragically killed recently," Eve said.

Dron sighed and said; "Kneel," as he mentally triggered the control that would turn her framework into a puppet.

Eve only laughed. "I heard about you reaching out to all the oldest frameworks, taking control. It was easy to re-code the control systems in my own so you wouldn't be able to do the same with me. Don't worry, you won't be punished for your attempt. That would be like killing a snake for slithering."

Dron smiled, glancing at the courtiers who were coming out to join them. There were thirty at least, all bearing different sashes and badges from different corporations, wealthy houses, interplanetary monarchies and regional governments. "I should have expected you to understand your own vulnerabilities. The failing is mine."

"I'm so happy you can see that," Eve said, flipping her long chromatic hair. "There are so many people you have to meet."

Dron snapped his fingers and the three Citadel representatives lowered their faceless, dark green faceplates then knelt with their heads low. He could feel them graze his mind, offering their telepathic power to him and he gently refused. "I said; kneel," Dron said to Eve.

The grin drained from her face as she slowly sank to her knees. "What?" she asked in a whisper. "How are you doing this?"

"You're so low on the telepathic scale that you can't even feel me in your mind, can you?" Dron asked.

"Telepathy?" he heard one of his Knights closer to the back ask quietly.

"H-How are you doing this?" Eve asked.

Dron forced her to sit back as he walked past her and addressed the courtiers. "I am Overlord Dron, master of the combined Order of Eden Forces, leader of Regent Galactic, all its holdings and keeper of its territories. Your governors, Kings, Queens, and all other masters answer to me and my appointed representatives as of today."

"Eve is our Mistress, she showed us the Way of the Order," said one young woman in a green dress and black sash. Down the length of it was written; 'COLASTRA' the name of the solar system she ruled.

"Your Mistress was a means to an end that was achieved a long time ago. Regent Galactic found her living brain resting in a box, an experiment gone awry, and put it into that thing. The thing they built using technology from many researchers and companies. Eve is nothing but a construct. I do have some pity for her though. The time she spent in that box while she was out of stasis must have been a special kind of hell. It's difficult to understand without experiencing it for yourself, I'm sure." Dron rushed back to Eve's side and leaned in close. "How would you like to go back? We could have your brain back in a tank before sundown."

Eve shook her head, fear and desperation overwhelming her. "No, please."

One of the courtiers drew their weapon, a nickel-plated handgun, and two of Dron's Knights fired their rifles once. Those heavy rifles were made to destroy heavily armoured foes and small fighters. The courtier was blasted into a red mist that sprayed several of his fellows. Dron straightened and shook his head. "I don't care if any of you survive," he shouted before taking a deep breath and closing his eyes. With little effort he found Eve's memory of complete isolation. Moments when her brain was in the box and the connection to her army of robots and the computer systems that allowed her to control them failed. It was always too dark, a time to panic, but those inter-ruptions usually didn't last. He focused on it, stole the entire memory of being disconnected, of complete sensory isolation and panic then forced himself not to panic as he lived inside that memory. "It would be much better if you all went back to your worlds and told them to obey the Order of Eden and their new Overlord, however." The memory was locked in, and he could hear Eve whimpering; "I can't be back," she said. "How can I be back in the box? No, no, no," she fell over, experiencing the isolation and fear of being a disconnected brain all over again.

Dron reached out to the trio of trained Citadel Telepaths,

the paragons of their order and trainers in the art and accepted their offer of power. Each flinched at the perfect copy of Eve's memory, taking a moment to separate themselves from it. Then, with a grin, Dron opened his eyes and sent the memory to all the courtiers. "This is your Mistress."

Panic ran through the crowd of overdressed, jewel bedecked, self-appointed leaders, inheritors and conquerors. In a moment he knew all of them as fear, anger, and finally despair infected them; their senses blocked as they lived in Eve's memory of being a brain in a case with no connection to the outside world. There were three people who didn't know they were empaths in the crowd, the rest were telepathically inept, and none could offer resistance. Julin, the Pinnacle of the three telepaths and one of Dron's former trainers, was amused by the act, and reinforced the memory, bringing it into greater focus, personalizing it for the courtiers and making sure that all their senses were blocked.

Wails, screams and incoherent rants filled the air as the courtiers fell to the deck and writhed, unaware of their bodies. He took his place in front of his Knights and watched as servants rushed in, trying to attend to their masters. "Every one of you will pledge to the Order of Eden fully. You will accept the rank I give you and serve as you are sent back to your home worlds," he announced aloud and inside their minds. "You'll be rewarded for following me and punished for disobedience. Citadel has people everywhere. They are inside your households, they are family members, leaders and servants. No one is outside our reach, and we know what you're planning. We are inside your minds."

Dron released them. Everyone agreed to follow. There were hints of defiance left in a few, but he and his Triad knew who they were. They'd be addressed individually before they were allowed to leave. Eve stirred at his feet while all the courtiers regained their senses, slowly rousing from their all-encompassing nightmare.

'Your strategic mind has only sharpened during your absence. I am in awe for the second time,' Julin said telepathically.

"Thank you," Dron replied aloud, bowing at the three Citadel telepaths. Eve fought to stand, shaky on her legs, and he gently helped her to her feet. "I don't need technology to control you, Nora," he told her in a sympathetic voice. "I'd prefer to have your cooperation. There's no reason why you can't live a rich life as a popular figure in our organization. You only have to acknowledge and support my leadership role as the Overlord."

"Yes, I will," Eve said.

"Your courtiers will take turns kneeling and pledging their support as well, and they'll mean it. I'll know if they don't and then I'll have to do something unpleasant," he told her. "Maybe I'll have you do it for me. I know that under all that finery there are sharp teeth and claws, even a touch of a mad savage."

"They'll pledge, Overlord," Eve said.

"Good. This will go well. Smooth sailing from here," Dron said. "We'll give them an hour to sort themselves out, then I'll accept their pledges of fealty."

"My ships," Eve said. "I'm sorry, but most of them are getting infected by a new virus."

"I know. Dron has the solution, don't worry. Your Overlord has everything well in hand," Dron said, truly glad for the first time since he was a boy. The sense of accomplishment he felt at seizing control of an entire empire was something he'd look back on with joy until his dying day, he was sure.

FIFTY-EIGHT

The Cefa System

ALICE SAT in the co-pilot's seat aboard the clever dream, Ute was at the controls. They were seconds from making the transition into normal space from the bright trans-dimensional route they had taken. The wormhole like conduit they raced through shielded them from the violent forces that, in theory, would rip the ship to pieces if they were left on their own. Ute, the Mergillian with a broad, smooth head coloured green and white with stripes of gold, was confident at the controls.

"Is that all you feel when you're in this space?" Alice asked, continuing their conversations about Ute's innate three dimensional awareness in trans-dimensional space.

"No, the nodes in my body can feel a lot more than gravity. The magnetic fields in this space are so strong that I can picture how everything is laid out around us. Oh! I highlighted something in the tactical scanner this morning too, I think it was a transit funnel, or at least that's what I'm calling it. It's like the wake of a ship that moved into normal space."

It appeared on Alice's console - the image of energy being pulled against something, like a dark disc, then running into it and stopping. There was a faint strand behind it. "An energy conduit wake," she said, telling the computer to track the strand of disturbed energy and found that it connected to another point in space, where it looked like something punctured into a bright field and moved through it. The puncture was fading.

"'Conduit wake?' That's pretty good. What about 'transit wake?'" Ute offered.

"That's what you should call it when you submit this to Fleet Sciences," Alice said.

"When *we* submit this."

"No, without you showing the computer how to distinguish transit conduits from," Alice looked at all the labels Ute applied to all the different energy formations. There were Bursting Spires, Reduction Vortexes, Signal Storms, Cutting Waves, and at least a dozen more. They were simple, describing every phenomenon visually and probably in a way that reflected how they felt to the small Mergillian. "Yeah, I don't deserve credit for any of this," Alice said, struggling to line the trail they found in energetic space up with normal space. Nothing looked right, then she remembered that she had to adjust the scale. "Okay, that's not right. That can't be right," Alice said. "A ship travelled from Iora to the Cefa System."

"Why can't it be right?" Ute asked.

A thought occurred to Alice then, and she ordered the entire crew to high alert. The new Nafalli reported that they rushed to guns, and Iruuk was behind her in the cockpit after only a few seconds. "I just realized," Theodore said from his medical station in their small infirmary. "This is the most boring place on the ship during a battle."

"What's going on?" Iruuk said, sitting at the sciences and scanning station.

"Come on up and sit at communications," Alice told Theodore.

"Oh, no I wasn't complaining, but I am on my way."

Alice looked to Iruuk, turning her seat. "Our D-Drive ships aren't really out here yet, right?" she asked him.

"You have higher clearance, but as far as I know, no, they're not," Iruuk answered.

"Then there are probably Edxi in the Cefa system. Our intel says only base ships and big carriers have D-Drives."

"You saw one in here?" Iruuk asked, nodding upwards.

"Ute figured out how to track the wake of nearby ships," Alice said. "Another one arrived in the Cefa system a while ago. I don't know exactly how long."

Ute peeked at Alice's station and shook her head. "I don't know either. We'd have to run experiments to determine how long it takes a wake and an exit point to disappear. I don't know how old their transit funnel is, I could tell you how intense it is though."

"That's a map?" Iruuk said, looking at Alice's tactical screen. "That's a map!" he pulled the data over to his station. "It's a small one, but its labelled, it's in three dimensions, it makes sense, wow."

"I didn't know everyone would get so excited about me naming a bunch of stuff and pointing the scanners around," Ute said, her high voice showing surprise.

"This is huge," Iruuk said. "The beginning of exploration, no, new science in another dimension. Wait, what's that?" he said, pointing to a group of tiny swirls at the edge of the map.

"I don't know," Ute said, glancing over her shoulder then back at the pilot's station. "I could barely feel whatever it was. Emergence in one minute," Ute said.

Alice started working at her station, extending the tip of their transit conduit to their destination and making a microscopic hole into normal space. A second tactical scanner hologram appeared, showing her what the passive sensors pointing at it could see. The edge of the solar system was clear. "Cloaking systems engaged," Alice said as she turned them on. "Check the load balance and our energy halo for me, please."

"We are way below tolerance," Iruuk said. "The Order shouldn't see us unless we land on their hull. Maybe not even then."

The hole Alice made expanded at the last instant and the Clever Dream emerged into normal space. Most of her holographic displays changed to focus on tactical systems. All four of her gunners had checked in, and Lewis took control of the remaining three. The rest of the weapons were at Alice's fingertips.

The tactical map populated, and Theodore sat down behind her at the communications station. "Welcome back to the bridge," Lewis told him. "Maybe you can help me make sense of the distress calls I'm getting."

"Oh, there are thousands," Theodore said as he sat down.

Alice watched as distress markers started appearing around three planets in the Cefa System. Laceni was one of them, and their destination. "Don't ping anything," Alice said. The red distress icons marking ships in need became more detailed, revealing that they were all Order of Eden markers. She set her system to stop putting the icons on top of the tactical data and was relieved to see all but three distress markers disappear. Of the three, two were cargo haulers, one was a civilian interplanetary shuttle.

"Is the entire Order of Eden Fleet here disabled?" Iruuk asked, helping her sift through the sensor data and gathering more information.

"I don't know yet, Fur-Face," Alice said. "Setting a course for Laceni. Lewis, can you load a probe?"

"Yes," Lewis said. A few seconds later he added; "Loaded."

Alice activated the probe, turned its cloaking measures on then pointed it towards Laceni, gave it a curvy course that would make it difficult for another ship to track it back to the Clever Dream then launched it. "Probe's away. Let's see what these new active sensors can do."

It accelerated towards Laceni ahead of the Clever Dream, zigging up for a while then moving in a curve before disappearing from Alice's sensors entirely. "We'll be in outer orbit around Laceni in five minutes," Ute said.

"Slow down," Alice said. "I want to know what's going on before we get in there."

The probe appeared on scanners as Alice expected. It was focusing its main scanner array at Laceni, sending high-powered pulses and beams in its direction for three seconds then disappearing again. It would repeat the routine every thirty seconds as it got closer to the planet. The data it sent back in a burst filled much of Alice's and Iruuk's screens in. "Oh, my God," Iruuk said. "The entire Order of Eden fleet is dark here. Their ships are cold. There's some evidence that many of them have taken damage too."

"I see it," Alice said. "It's like two battle fleets powered down a few hours ago."

"Longer," Iruuk said. Another burst of data was sent by the

probe and he nodded. "I can see it clearer now. Their reactors are completely cold, capacitors drained."

"Lewis and I have a solid theory on what happened here," Theodore said. "There are three battle groups from the Order of Eden in the solar system. A data package came through their hyper transmitter containing an artificial intelligence that triggered their weapons systems, restricted control of their systems, and started combat maneuvers that had their own ships firing at each other. Finally, the fleet around Laceni converged on an Edxi Base Ship, or Brood Ship, we can't be sure what it's called officially according to the transmissions, and before the order was given for the Order soldiers to disable their own vessels, it was destroyed. The virus is named Mary."

"Does it have anything resembling a personality? Can you tell?" Alice asked, bringing a holodisplay up to see the summary of data Lewis and Theodore were able to gather.

"I checked," Lewis said. "Mary is a soulless, evil creature that only attacks Order ships. She's programmed to make attempts at disrupting Citadel ships as well, but there isn't as much code pertaining to that, so whoever programmed her didn't know enough about Citadel operating systems to cause damage at first. She will eventually learn, given the opportunity. I sort of like her."

"But she's not like you," Alice said.

"I don't think she'd be a good conversationalist," Theodore said.

"She's a tool. Nothing more than a spanner or welding torch," Lewis added.

"Way to go, Dad," Alice said, noticing that calling him 'Dad' didn't feel as wrong as it did before.

"You think this was Captain Valent?" Iruuk asked.

"Well, he's probably not the only one to think of using a

virus against the Order," Alice said. "But he might be the only one who wouldn't care about what the Galactic Courts might do to him for it."

"It's one of the only crimes that can still earn a transgressor the death penalty," Theodore said. "Then again, most of the Justices are dead now, and though there have been some announcements that the court is being reformed, the new leaders are generally treated with disrespect and suspicion. They're probably a bunch of crooked bastards, so that's probably the right attitude," Lewis said. "So, yeah, way to go Jake."

"Coming up on Laceni outer range," Ute announced.

Alice enlarged her main tactical view and stared at the crystal clear visual and multi-spectrum readings. It was like a fever dream come true at the same time. Fighters, combat shuttles, corvettes, interceptors, interdictor cruisers, destroyers, battleships, carriers and even a few invasion ships were adrift in all levels of orbit around Laceni. There were millions of strong life readings - people running around aboard the ships, looking for a way to get things up and running.

The remains of something out of a nightmare, half shredded and tilted against the horizon of the blue and brown world like a thorn, drew her attention for a moment. "An Edxi invasion ship," she said. It wasn't her memory, but that of the Exile's Geist. "The Edxi hate..." a mental flash struck her then. It wasn't a memory, but a fear and a mental image of a small Geist creature being carved to pieces on a pillar, Edxi who were dressed in fine garb adorned with tiny crystals that sparkled and tinkled together taking turns accepting cuts from the methodical butcher who worked on the living Geist. "Holy crap," Alice said, catching her breath. "The Edxi hate the Geist enough to make them into a sacrificial meal, and the Geist fear them..." she searched for the word.

"Mortally?" Theodore offered.

"Yes, that's perfect. They have a mortal, primal fear of the Edxi," Alice felt it then. "There's one here. A Geist. It's not strong, maybe it's far away, but it's an old one."

"So, our cloaking?" Iruuk asked.

"Worthless if the Citadel ship it's on is operational. That's if it can feel me too, and I don't know the rules, I have no idea if it can tell I'm here, but I know I'm blocking him."

"Are you going to be all right?" Theodore asked.

"I'm fine. It's not like an attack, more like I can feel it in my periphery," Alice replied. "Everyone scan for our people, for the Ion Runner."

"I have the Ion Runner," Lewis said, showing a hologram of an Order Carrier holding it in a landing bay on its port side. "It's aboard the Sagittarius Three. The fools have not closed the outer doors, so we could grapple onto it and pull it right out if we wanted to."

"Put us on an evasive course," Alice told Ute. "Use one burst transmission to send a system status query using the Fleet Control Code for that ship."

"Done," Theodore said. "It is broadcasting its full status on an encrypted signal. The worrying thing is that someone other than a Haven Shore military officer has turned it on."

Alice looked over her shoulder at Iruuk and saw that he had located the brig aboard the Sagittarius III using the schematics the fleet captured. "I'm going to wait to perform a focused scan. I'll time it with the next burst transmission."

"Good idea," Alice said. "What are they doing to the Ion Runner?"

"Well, there are so many people aboard that the ship is at capacity," Theodore said. "The Order has managed to turn the life support on, but other than that they have failed to hack its systems."

"Oh, but they're trying," Lewis said. "It's connected to another computer that's attempting to hack in wirelessly."

"The Citadel ship," Alice said, urgently using her tactical system to find the transmission and track it back from the Ion Runner to the Citadel craft. "They have no idea we're here, otherwise they'd stop, circle around and watch for us to break our cloak." A line appeared between the Ion Runner and a hidden ship. "There it is, point seven kilometres off the port side of the Sagittarius." She brought up an interface that allowed her to program instructions into the probe that had entered orbit and remained on hold, cloaked and ready to receive instructions. "I'm going to find out what kind of ship that is. I'm ready. That probe is going to head for where that signal is headed then make a huge mess. Everyone else ready for a quick burst of scanning and transmitting?"

"What do you want the Ion Runner to do? We can instruct it any way we like, and it has a connection to the Citadel ship," Theodore said.

"For Citadel's operating system to try to hack the Ion Runner, they have to be running some version of Sol Defence's operating system, right?"

"We're detecting something called the Mars Advanced Operating System. It's a compatible variation of Sol Defence's older standard, but compatibility is certain."

"So, how deep do you think we can get into their systems through that connection?" Alice asked, looking her tactical displays over. She already knew the answer but wanted to see if higher intelligences could find a better one.

"We could get the model, origin, port of call, and identification data for the Citadel ship," Lewis offered. "We've only seen one Citadel ship we could get that information from so far, the Exile."

"We could catch a snapshot of any unencrypted data that's flowing, but hacking would take too much time. They would track our signal back to us," Lewis said, sounding disappointed.

"All right. Open all missile ports, target my point," Alice said. "We're going to capture data while we do our bursts. Ute..."

"Evasive measures," she said calmly, nodding. "I'll make sure our missile bays can hit your target too."

"Javelins and Saber missiles loaded. The target is soft locked," Lewis said.

Alice confirmed that everything was set up properly on her tactical system. The Clever Dream's five heavy launchers were loaded with cloaked Javelin torpedoes and there were eighty four small missiles ready to fire all at once. They were all seeker types, made to take out shields and strike precise points on enemy ships. Her mine bays were closed, they were too powerful to use when the Ion Runner was so close.

"All right, ready to send all our signals and disappear," Alice said. All at once instructions were sent to their probe, a query signal was sent to the Ion Runner, and the Clever Dream's scanners worked with the probe to perform a high powered scan of the Sagittarius III. Milliseconds later, it stopped and seconds later, they were nowhere near they were when the burst was made.

"We have basic data from the Citadel ship. It is the Pariah, an advanced exploration ship originally, somewhat similar to a destroyer but with higher power levels," Lewis said.

"I can feel him," Alice said as she felt her mind come under pressure. Her hand lowered to the fire controls and she ran her fingers down the line of buttons that controlled the

Saber missiles and Javelins. "Fire everything, destroy that ship."

The probe exploded against the front of the ship, blasting it with a focused electromagnetic pulse then ejecting kilograms of nanobots that crawled across the hull, sending faint signals individually that added up to a loud beacon. The Javelin torpedoes disappeared as soon as they left the Clever Dream's launchers, and Alice watched a widening cloud of Saber missiles as they rushed towards the Pariah.

The enemy ship returned fire, striking the Clever Dream's lower aft shields briefly, its countermeasures focused on destroying the flock of missiles Alice sent in its direction.

"You really have to warn me when you're firing that many missiles," Ute said, chuckling.

The missile bays reloaded. The pressure in her head, as though something was trying to force a blunt object into her skull from above, was mounting. A tear ran down her cheek and she pounded the launch buttons, faintly aware that a whole new volley was loosed. Her fingers flipped the backup switches for the Clever Dream's beam weapons and the antimatter generator. "Keep us alive, Ute," Alice said.

"She's not all right," Iruuk said. "Theo!"

Theodore was there next. "What's happening, Alice?"

"This Geist, he's older, powerful," she said. "Trying to get into my head. If I do anything..." she ground her teeth together, a mental image of her father appearing vividly in her mind. It was something she didn't see but imagined several times during his recovery; him being torn apart, replaced piece by piece to replace the framework technology. The Geist put it there. She replaced it, focusing on a memory of her watching holograms of Jacob Valance, the feared bounty hunter, the man she thought was her first father. "You won't learn anything new about him," she grimaced. "You won't survive to tell anyone about me either," she said. The pressure on her mind alleviated a little for a moment and she struggled to imagine what kind of memory could traumatize such a powerful telepath. There was something in its attempt to break past the barriers in her mind that seemed different from the old Geist aboard the Exile.

With a gasp, Alice realized what was different about the one she was battling. It only pretended to be old and it had her fooled for a moment. It was actually young, connected to many humans, so it knew something about forcing itself on someone, but it was still acting out of fear. "I'm going to read you," Alice mumbled, and she felt it flinch back.

"The beam weapons are ready." Lewis announced.

Alice glanced at her holographic display. The Geist wasn't in her head anymore, she'd pushed it out for the moment. It was doing something else, splitting its attention. The shields of the Pariah were low. "Gunners! Prioritize fire on their weapons!" Alice ordered. "Lewis, let's hack them. Flood their systems with attempts. Iruuk, I want a hard scan performed in every direction. Watch for more cloaked ships. Theo, if I start doing anything that will hurt the crew besides taking us into combat, then put me into deep stasis."

"Are you certain?"

"That's an order," Alice said.

"Ute, I'm going to try to scare the shit out of that Geist. Get ready to follow it."

"Follow?"

"We're going to kill it," Alice said. The small beam countermeasures aboard the Clever Dream were successfully superheating incoming missiles and they had several Order of Eden ships between them and the Citadel ship's guns. It was still in the same place. "When I tell you, come out of cover. Our anti-matter beams are ready?"

"All three Prometheus Emitters are set," Lewis replied. "I'm going to show you where to fire, and you'll keep firing until your scanners tell you that you've hit a large biological life form that isn't human."

"With pleasure."

The first five Javelin torpedoes struck the Pariah full on, reducing its aft shields to nothing and the forward dorsal shield to minimal levels. Alice ground her teeth and tensed as she felt the Geist return, crushing into the barriers around her mind. She concentrated, closed her eyes, then let it in, focusing on a black space with nothing but her in the middle. The Geist imagined itself as a massive, golden aquatic creature with long tails and broad fins. Alice was youthful, bright eyed, round faced with a mane of bright red hair. She was wearing white, holding a candle. "I'm happy to meet you." Her imaginary self said, feeling the Geist's desire to dominate her, its fear, and its growing curiosity. "Welcome, you can probably feel that you're not the first Geist to visit."

It didn't give her anything, no specific ideas or specific transmitted thoughts. Alice found it easier to focus. Its attempts to overwhelm her were easing. Alice imagined that the candle in her hands lit up. "Did you know that the smallest flame can start a fire big enough to burn a city? I'm sure you know the names of the flames; worry, regret, anxiety and fear. I'm looking for a teacher, someone to help me with my discipline so I can extinguish them before they burn me."

That was it, the attractive lure that turned all his interest towards her. The Geist was vain; it wanted to teach humans. Alice concentrated harder, focusing on the Geist, excluding everything else.

"I can help you," the Geist said. "You only need to surrender your mind and your ship." Alice could feel a crack, just a small opening in its mind from whence its telepathic message came from. She didn't expect that it would be so easy, so obvious, especially since she was not a telepath, but it was right there as if it was the only star in a vast, dark sky.

Alice focused on the lie then. "Good!" her girlish self chirped cheerily. "I had a master, but he couldn't teach me anymore because I ate him!" A pure imagining of her laughing with friends as they tore pieces off of the Exile Geist, celebrating bloody morsels. Iruuk was especially enthusiastic, skipping the knife and digging into the living creature with his long maw, ripping and tearing deeper with urgent savagery. Fear and disgust ruled over the Geist and she grabbed him, gained a full sense of him, could hear his thoughts, see what he was seeing, remember anything she wanted from his mind at will. He was hiding something important, something that pertained to her exactly. Alice dug into its psyche, remembering the lesson with Quan: by taking his mind she would have eventually been able to control it.

Alice learned the names of every crewmember, could sense the Captain - she'd been with him since he first emerged from his formation pod, years before, and was writhing on the deck in front of her captains' seat. Alice envisioned a spike driving into the Captain's head, found a directive; "Do not kill the Valents, avoid Alice. Capture Jacob." The Captain attempted to resist, already in agony, even her mental self-image was writhing in front of her.

Alice had the Geist, she could feel its telepathic connection to the crew, especially the Captain and the First Officer, who was an actual telepath. She could reach him – Lieutenant Harhold – and she took his mind just the same as she did

Quan's, only instead of showing him the horrors she knew, or digital code, she inflicted the will of the Geist she controlled. "Your mind will empty and bleed," she said, focusing malicious intent on him and the Captain – Sy-Rhea – until she couldn't feel them anymore.

'Stop, you're murdering my crew,' the Geist pled. It was more afraid than she had ever been, and that was saying something, but not because she might kill it, but because it knew she was growing in strength, learning through telepathic vivisection using it as a tool.

"Show me what you're hiding," Alice replied, aware that her lips were moving, tears were running down her face and her hands gripped the edge of her console white-knuckled. It tried to shut her out much harder than before, but she barely held on, staying inside its psyche. "No? Then die." She opened her eyes and targeted the exact position aboard the ship where she could feel the Geist. "Break cover, all weapons fire on this target."

As the Clever Dream emerged from behind a collection of dead Order of Eden ships, Alice could feel another Geist, the first female she'd known, graze her mind then retreat rapidly when Alice tried to turn the Geist she'd trapped towards her mentally. Every missile and gun emplacement aboard the Clever Dream fired at the thick armoured plate covering the younger Geist's habitat. Lewis activated all three of their Prometheus weapons, sending white beams from the front of the ship. Beams that generated antimatter close to the target and pummelled it with highly explosive heat.

Alice felt the Geist struggle and the worst pain she'd ever known struck her from the inside, her vision went black and her body spasmed. He was still in her grip, and she delved for one more piece of information. "Where were you born?" she asked, and immediately knew the answer. An image of herself appeared, it was her as her smaller framework self and in a training uniform. It wasn't from her mind, it was from a classified report the Geist had seen. There were records and predictions from the Victory Machine there, old, but still highlighted as relevant. There was a label attached to her file that read as a warning, declaring her a rogue element. The voice of Hampon drifted through her mind as he narrated a piece of her report; "While many former members of the First Light crew come up in the Victory Machine's predictions, Alice comes up the most, but little is known. I am warned that when she appears prediction becomes nearly impossible, that she is a true rogue element that disrupts timelines and modifies predicted outcomes. The Victory Machine cannot predict her path. One moment it predicts her death, the next that she becomes an artificial intelligence, and another that she's a teenage girl - it is utter nonsense - so we have labelled her. We will avoid her when possible, and perhaps capture her one day as a kind of experiment, like holding a hand to a live battery just to satisfy curiosity. A rogue element must be good for something, after all."

Alice refocused her thoughts and asked; "Who is your master?" She saw him, felt what it was like to be in his presence; Dron. He was a man of logic and hard discipline. He could sense Geists, was trained by Citadel. That was how it worked. Some special people were taken aside, their telepathic potential was explored, and while Dron wasn't a true telepath, he had potential, and he learned to sense Geists, other telepaths, and became an empath. Alice knew how. The Pariah Geist had a name. It was; "Werner, you're going to show me what you're hiding now." It was suffering from fear, grief at being used to cause the brain deaths of its own captain and first officer, and most of all it was haunted by the thought of failing its people, letting a human take all its power. A realization struck Alice and she put it to use. She had control, its spirit was broken, it was horrible, but there the Geist's resistance to her had failed. She found the secret. "They're lying in wait for my father. He'll be back in the Rega Gain system today, and they're going to intercept him, kill everyone else except Minh-Chu. The ship they sent is called The Castaway." Werner the Geist was broken, disgraced with no willpower left. Alice let go. "We have to finish here and get back to the Haven System now. Oh, and please give me something for this headache," she said as she took the status of the Clever Dream in at a glance.

The Pariah was running, thrusting out of the area as quickly as possible using Order ships as cover. The Clever Dream's shields were holding under the barrage of the Pariah's gunnery deck, but barely. "Focus all but our beam weapons on those guns," Alice said. The enemy's beam emplacement and rocket launchers were down. "Get closer to her," Alice said.

"Yes, Ma'am," Ute replied.

"Any progress on finding our people?" she asked Iruuk

"I'm almost down to scanning for DNA," he said, running his hand down his nose. "I'm trying... wait! There's a firefight! Aboard the Sagittarius, two frames forward from the brig there are nine people fighting hand-to-hand. One just got a weapon, and our scans confirm that it's someone with Yawen's shape. I'm confirming the rest. There was a scan blocker in place around the brig, we couldn't see inside before, but now they're out."

Alice watched as the Clever Dream caught up to the Pariah, closing to within point nine kilometres. "This is good," she said, her headache disappearing. "Thank you, Theo," she offered over her shoulder.

The Prometheus beams burst through the armour plate covering the Geist's habitat and Alice felt it die. Fear and incredible pain as it was torn apart but it was all at a distance, causing none of the sensations in her. Her head was clear then, and she could feel three Geists keenly, immediately learning their locations. The accumulator system had generated enough antimatter for five torpedoes and she punched her security code in, loading each of them.

"We are re-cloaked," Lewis announced.

Alice marked the location of all three Citadel ships on the tactical display and focused on it. "I know where they are. I can feel them as clearly as if we were all sitting around a table."

"Where who are?" Theodore asked.

"The Geists."

"What?" Iruuk asked. "How?"

"Too many telepaths have been through my head, Fur-Face," Alice said. "I think it's like an instinctive defence mechanism, I can just tell where they are." It happened again, a graze against her mind, and she gnashed her teeth, grabbing at it with her mind. Without letting go, she pointed one of the Prometheus beam weapons in its direction and swept across its shields. Antimatter clashed with the enemy shields, sending a furious plume across it. She targeted the termination point of the Prometheus beam and sent the Javelin torpedoes to track it. They disappeared, cloaked the moment they left the launchers. "Don't let that ship get away, we have to ruin its cloaking device."

This was an even younger Geist, full of fear, wriggling to escape, and she let it go. Alice didn't want to deal with more grief, mortal fear or another struggle. It felt like she was stretched thin, fatigue not far off, but Alice had what she wanted. Their new target was another small destroyer. "Fire everything at it, I want its shields down before those torpedoes hit. Aim for weapons first." Alice said, targeting all its turrets with a fresh load of Javelin torpedoes and Saber missiles. She shut the antimatter generator systems aboard the Clever Dream down, shunting a small vial into a Javelin torpedo.

They were struck several times on the forward quarter, the full force of the enemy turning on them from the new destroyer, and Ute turned so they were flying parallel. Alice launched her missiles, the guns reached across the space that separated them with lethal rounds going in both directions. Not enough of their missiles were striking, getting detonated by countermeasures. "Suggestions?" Alice asked.

"Wait," Iruuk said. "We can last long enough to see what your antimatter torpedoes do."

Alice watched the exchange of fire. The gunnery deck of the destroyer was facing them, whatever they put out to counter that was barely keeping them up. Their own guns were focused on returning fire between catching incoming missiles and torpedoes. Their Saber missiles were getting countered by smaller automatic guns before they could impact. The Prometheus beam weapon she had trained on the ship was slowly defeating its shields but it wasn't fast enough for her taste. The other two beams didn't have the charge to be effective yet. Alice estimated that they'd have to hide behind cover within a minute, a minute and a half at the most.

The Javelins loaded with antimatter struck the enemy ship from behind, causing a white flash of light and the complete failure of their cloaking systems. Their shields were still up, but barely. Alice looked to Theodore, who had a worried expression on his face. "Broadcast on all channels please."

"Aye," he replied. "Ready."

"I am Alice Valent, the Rogue Element. I am about to murder another Geist. This will be my second this week. Leave, or I will continue my murder streak," she nodded at him and he turned the broadcast off.

"A slight exaggeration," Lewis said.

"Not when we get back home," Alice said. "I'm going to make sure the Exile Geist's dead."

"Three wormhole entry points have opened," Iruuk said. "I see the profiles of a Zhàn Class Close Combat Carrier, and one of their destroyers departing. The destroyer we're attacking is also departing."

Zhàn Class, the same as the Triton. The idea of having to face one made Alice's palms sweat. "Let it go. Take us to the Sagittarius. We have some people to pick up," Alice said. She made a mental note to contact Quan and spend time with Oz when she got back. There were plenty of questions for one, and maybe answers for the other bouncing around in her head.

FIFTY-NINE

Coming Home

THE EXCITEMENT of getting home threatened to crowd any other thought out of Jake's head as he sat at the sciences station, commanding from there. It said something about the older Aucharian military that the main tactical scanning technology was in the sciences station. It seemed to be designed for exploration rather than combat.

Minh-Chu was at the helm with Carnie at his side, cracking his knuckles and stretching his neck. "I hope we can get at least one or two nights off," he said.

"Oh, man, that would be nice. I have a few things to take care of," Carnie said.

Liara was in the captain's seat again, communications routed to her command and control unit. Her comfort in that chair was surprising to Jake and reassuring. She knew Fleet Regulations better than anyone in his crew, had diplomatic training, experience and was an actual lawyer with practice in court in front of arbitration panels as well as juries. That was her old life, and it came with technical knowledge that made his software hacks look primitive.

Was she perfect? Not at all. He wouldn't seriously put her in command of a starship because she lacked the combat and other emergency situation training along with a number of other important pieces of the puzzle. If she wanted to move up in the Fleet, she'd get the training and experience, he was sure. Jake would stand by and see if she wanted his help, but he had a feeling she'd find her way to what she needed on her own. The best thing he could do was give her opportunities like the one she was taking advantage of at the moment.

The punishment of taking an extra watch on the bridge might have given her a taste for the captain's seat. It was obvious to Jake that she already felt somewhat comfortable there. "Emerging from altered space in fifteen seconds, Acting Captain," Minh-Chu called out from the helm.

"How are our final emergence scans looking?" Liara asked.

"Skies are clear," Jake replied from the sciences station.

Liara leaned in his direction and whispered; "Are you sure you don't want to be sitting here when we contact Fleet?"

"You're doing fine," Jake replied. "We're in safe space, it's the perfect time for you to get some experience taking us home. Besides, we wouldn't be here if you didn't work on Mary. You deserve a little experience in the chair."

"Thank you, Sir," she said. "I've never been more nervous in my life."

"Just breathe, run the approach checklist in your head," Jake noticed that she had the system to space dock list up on her command and control unit. "Oh, and let your crew do the heavy lifting."

"Okay," Liara said, squaring herself in the captain's seat again. "Yes, Sir," she added.

Jake looked at the scanners as the wormhole degenerated behind them, breaking up into a harmless, momentary energy spike on his display. "Emergence complete," Jake announced.

"We have Haven Fleet Navnet synchronization," Noah Lucas announced from the navigation station.

"Sending our status and capture notification to Fleet," Liara announced as she did the work on her command and control unit. "We won't have acknowledgement for at least seven minutes, we're still pretty far from Tamber."

"Outer system Navnet has sent us an approach course," Noah said.

"Follow it please, I'm looking forward to tanning and reading up on command theory," Liara said.

"Hope there's room on the beach for a bunch of rangers and marines," Remmy said as he entered the bridge and took a seat with Dimitri at his side. "I plan on getting as much R and R before the ink dries on my transfer papers."

"Amen," Dimitri said.

"You're joining the crew?" Liara asked.

"If the Rangers will let me," Remmy replied. "I'd rather be on the front lines than dealing with people on the ground on Tamber."

The ship shuddered and Jake checked the scanners. The front of the ship was fine, there was nothing in their way for millions of kilometres.

"Did we just hit something?" Dimitri asked.

"Hell, no," Noah said.

"Impact on the dorsal section," Finn said over Jake's communicator.

Jake spotted a circular object creating a seal against the

outer hull. "Armour up, we have boarders incoming. Minh, get us to the nearest allied ship. Liara, send distress on all channels."

Several more contacts showed up on the outer hull, points where arms were most likely affixing themselves and Jake activated his full armour.

"Their engines are overpowering us," Minh-Chu said. "We are slowing. I'll keep fighting, but there isn't much point."

"Set the controls to automatically hold this position," Jake ordered. "I need everyone with counter-incursion training to help me fight them off."

"Communications are being jammed," Liara said.

Jake scanned for the thickest bulkheads near the bridge and saw that the Captain's Ready Room was also a safe room with support for five people. "Liara, Noah, go to the ready room and lock it with a fleet code."

"I can fight, Captain," Noah objected.

"You sure?" Jake asked.

"He's not," Minh-Chu said. "Get in there. This isn't Iora."

Without further argument, Noah followed Liara into the Captain's Ready Room and Jake watched the door close.

"They're cutting through fast," Finn said through the communicator.

"Find a safe room and get there fast," Jake told him. "Hunker down until we can get to you."

"Too late," Finn said.

"What the hell is that?" asked Sammi through the communicator, her video feed appeared in Jake's helmet. It was already a retreating firefight, she tossed a grenade at the incursion point – a rough cut through the ceiling of main engineering – and watched a large humanoid in heavy custom armour that looked like it was made of blades bat it away. It ignored the explosion, returning fire with a double barrelled heavy rifle that filled the air with loud cracks as it went off.

"Oh, no," Remmy said. "All squad members, retreat to crew cabin section and get ready to rally. That's the Beast, the Order's Prime Knight."

"They're opening a wormhole," Minh-Chu said. "Going to try to disrupt it with our generators."

"Are you sure it's him?" Jake asked as he watched Remmy start running.

"One hundred percent," Remmy replied. "Captain, stay here. It doesn't make sense for you to put yourself in its way. Seal yourself in, try to get us help."

"Disrupted their wormhole," Minh-Chu reported from the helm. "I can't leave this station unless we want them to drag us away from friendly space."

"Take all my marines," Jake said. "I'll stay here with Minh."

"Aye, Captain," Remmy said. "It's been an honour to serve with you."

Jake hated the finality of his statement, and a chill ran through him as the heavy bridge security doors closed. "Good hunting."

SIXTY

Extortion

THE CLEVER DREAM moved between much larger Order of
Eden warships like a stalking predator. Few of the enemy
vessels showed any sign that they were reactivating systems and
the ones that did still had cold reactors, minimal life support.
"Everything aboard those ships runs on their crappy software,"
Iruuk said. "The crews don't know what they're doing without
the automation."

"I can confirm that," Theodore said. "Some of them have
managed to get emergency communications working, and what
I'm hearing indicates that they may have one person qualified to
make their ships operational without software for every five
thousand thirty-three people. It's a training oversight typical of a
force that focuses on recruiting rather than properly training
their people."

Alice thought about commanders like Terran in their own

military for a moment, then renewed her focus and opened a channel to the Ion Runner. "Attention, Order of Eden members. I am going to begin destroying your ships, murdering your trapped crewmembers and I will continue until you leave your ship and release your prisoners to my ship." With a simple gesture, she set the message to repeat. "Can you make sure that goes across any band the Order are using for communications right now? I want them to know what's coming for once."

"Immediately," Theodore said.

She targeted the nearest Order of Eden Interdictor Cruiser. "All gun emplacements, fire on that ship. We're looking for soft spots with thin armour and their power systems. I don't want them to turn that ship on ever again."

"Are you sure this is the way to do this?" Iruuk asked quietly. "They're helpless."

The turrets aboard the Clever Dream began to fire as Ute directed the ship in a wide circle around the Interdictor Cruiser. "This is all they'll understand," Alice said. "Bring up the command codes for the Ion Runner and start sending power to its capacitor bank."

"I'm sorry, I can't do that," Theodore said. "After ten minutes and four seconds main capacitors will begin to explode resulting in the loss of life for several people aboard."

Alice took control from her station for a minute and started the chain reaction herself. "No problem," she said. "It's regulation: they don't get that ship." Out of the corner of her eye she could see Iruuk scanning it then nodding to himself. He could see what she did a while ago; there was no way the Ion Runner would be able to take off.

"This is Unit Commander Sabolea," came a response from the Ion Runner. "I see what you're doing, and don't consider your small ship a threat to our fleet. We are making recovery measures now and will be operational soon. We know you're not a murderer, that's why you're using your small guns to pester one of our cruisers. Just retreat, it's the only reasonable option. You'll escape with your lives at least."

Alice targeted both the unshielded bays of a large carrier with Javelin torpedoes. "Ute, keep us steady and keep both our D-Drives charging."

"Yes, Captain," Ute said, no doubt seeing what Alice was doing. "If it's not too bold, I think you should show them how serious you are. Two of your torpedoes would be able to penetrate the bridge of the carrier you're aiming at."

"You should have expected this," Alice replied to the Commander as she adjusted her targets. Two Javelin torpedoes would strike the main hangar, another would land deep inside the secondary, and two would impact the side of their bridge. Her fingers pressed the launch buttons without hesitation and she started loading a heavy seeker mine in the rear launcher. It would thrust towards her target and when it reached optimum range, fling hundreds of intelligent bomblets at critical systems.

The carrier's biggest hangars were torn apart from the inside, secondary fuel explosions adding to the damage as a violent impact on the bridge sent torn plating in all directions, the atmosphere within following out with them. Alice sent her mine towards a group of ships; three destroyers were huddled against another interdiction cruiser that had left its main hangar wide open. Her next Javelin torpedoes were set to destroy the hangar and bridge of a battlecruiser, and she launched them.

When another set of five javelin torpedoes were loaded, she sent them towards the only other interdiction cruiser in range, the one her gunners were picking pieces off of. A destroyer came up on her tactical screen, its power systems starting to come online and she made that her next target. "We're destroying that before its shields come up," she said coldly. Alice set her Saber seeker missiles to attack the destroyer and sent them behind a load of Javelin torpedoes.

The seeker mine she dropped earlier exploded in a cloud of destruction, ripping holes open in its targets and stirring the drifting ships. The destroyer that was powering up in front of her had forty two Sabre Missiles strike the hull protecting its main reactors, weakening it severely seconds before the Javelin Torpedoes struck one after another, decimating their engineering section.

"We're going to surrender your allies!" the Unit Commander said. "Hold your fire! We have seen your intention to destroy the Ion Runner, and I have no doubt that you will tear every ship in the sky to shreds given the chance. We are abandoning our attempts to control your ship, and your people will be waiting for you at the docking bay."

"You will not be in the hangar when we arrive. If you make any attempt to complicate our rescue, I'll make an example of you."

"That is clear, Captain," the Unit Commander replied.

"Ute, get us alongside the hangar and bring us in sideways. Gunners: if you can aim at the hangar our people are coming from, do it, and be ready to tear the inside of that thing up at a moment's notice. Not until I give the order though, we want our people back whole."

"Aye, aye, Captain," Woone said.

Alice looked at her tactical displays carefully. "I need your help, Iruuk," she said focusing on the scans of the carrier with her people aboard. "You have to watch the bigger picture. Start figuring out where we'll drop pulse mines on our way out. We need to do everything we can to slow this fleet down, but we won't have much time to do it."

"Working on it."

"Oh and watch for any other ships that are about to come online," Alice added.

"I am," he said.

Alice set the Javelin Torpedoes that were loaded to cruise along a long course between Order ships, bursting over and over again with electromagnetic pulses as they went until they ran out of power. She gave Iruuk the ability to change their course as he found better targets. The mines would do the same, only launching bomblets that would affix themselves to hull plating and pulse over and over again until it ran out of energy. The Sabre missiles she pointed at the open hangars of the carrier where her people would be delivered.

"They gave us a communicator," Gabe said. "Good to see you, Captain."

The Clever Dream slowed, moving into position next to the hangar. "Ready for a ride home?" she asked.

"Absolutely," Yawen shouted into the communicator. "The room service here sucks."

"There are soldiers coming into the hangar," Woone warned from her position in a turret.

"You didn't actually think we'd allow you to have our prisoners?" the Unit Commander said. "Victory is our right. Victory is our fate."

"Cover our teams!" Alice said to Woone and the other gunners. "Jump across to the Clever Dream, guys," she told Gabe.

"I'll get them inside," Theodore said, rushing out of the cockpit.

Alice watched her starboard side sensors as several of her people were gunned down despite the turret fire driving some of the Order soldiers back under cover. Of all the soldiers she'd come to rescue, seven were able to leap across the narrow distance between the edge of the hangar deck and the Clever Dream. Gabe was one of them, but she couldn't see Yawen, Regan or several others. There were several burned and torn bodies near the edge of the hangar bay, none of them showed any signs of life.

"We have everyone who could jump across," Theodore reported from the starboard hatch.

"Ute, take us out, then circle us around," Alice said, unloading one of her electromagnetic pulse mines and loading a high explosive one instead. It was set for the bridge of the carrier.

She entered the interface that let her control the critical systems aboard the Ion Runner and armed all its missiles. "Are you sure you want to do that?" Iruuk asked in a hushed whisper.

"We have to destroy it anyway," Alice said. The rear sensors showed her a clear picture of soldiers approaching the bodies of the Special Operations Team. Rage filled her as she watched them fire at the corpses, making sure there was no way to resuscitate them, to save so much as a scrap of grey matter. "Look."

"I understand," Iruuk said. "It's more than revenge. You're killing monsters."

The energy build up aboard the Ion Runner was almost at critical levels, and she pushed the generators aboard. There was more than a minute left before, but with her adjustments, the overload would happen in seconds. That overload would cause hundreds of Javelin and Decimator Torpedoes to explode along with thousands of bomblets. "I hope you're aboard that ship, bitch," Alice said to the communication line that was routed through the Ion Runner. She launched both her mines. One spun away, following a course that would take it towards two other carriers where it would hopefully cause enough electromagnetic damage to keep them out of the fight for weeks. The other strafed directly at the bridge of the carrier that became a tomb for many of her squad members. It burst, sending bomblets raining down on the bridge, bursting the transparent metal open and continuing to pummel the inner deck.

The Ion Runner was next, sending a blue then white explosion forth that nearly cut the large carrier in half. "Chart a direct course from here to the Haven System and use both D-Drives on full charge."

"That's only a theoretical use of those systems," Ute countered.

"Can you make it work?"

"It should work, yes," she replied.

"Then do it. I want to be back in the Haven system in twenty minutes," Alice launched the last Javelin Torpedoes Iruuk programmed and locked her station. She stood up and came face to face with Gabe, who had a mournful expression. "Yawen pushed me ahead of her," he said. "I'm sorry."

Alice steeled herself and nodded. "She always wanted to get cloned. Who else made it?"

"Knud, Jessen, Newell, Eckles, Nash and our objective; Wanda Teller," Gabe replied.

Clenching her teeth and clearing her throat, she turned back to the seat she left. It was as if her heart were in her head; she could feel its heat and its beat between her ears. Holding her grief and anger down was nearly impossible, but she did it.

There were other problems; that fleet wouldn't be down for long, there was another recovering fast near Iora, there were Citadel ships nearby that could return any moment, and she had a crew aboard who were depending on her. "Put some armour on if you're in shape to fight." Instead of facing Knud, she took her seat and unlocked her station. "We can't take anything for granted."

"We're ready to try this jump," Ute said quietly. "We'll know if it worked before we make the transit to extra dimensional space."

"Execute," Alice ordered.

A low, loud electrical hum filled the ship for a moment before a blue-white tunnel opening in space appeared. "That is a viable trans-dimensional corridor," Iruuk said.

"Take us in," Alice ordered quietly.

SIXTY-ONE

Knights

REMMY'S SENSOR suite was turned all the way up, causing so much visual noise that he suspected few people would be able to understand much of what they were being shown. It was the only way to manually watch for Clark Patterson's tricks. The Beast was trained by Freeground like Remmy, felt like Freeground Nation and the Puritan Party wronged them deeply. He'd lost every friend he had from that place.

Remmy's experiences were almost exactly the same with two exceptions. The first was the most obvious. Patterson was turned into a hybrid human, framework, Issyrian with a touch of Edxi mixed in for good measure. The second was something that Remmy hoped he could use.

Four Order Knights approached silently, invisibly. The only thing that ruined their cloaking profile was a stirring in the air. Remmy was the most visible person on the ship, hiding behind a thick bulkhead with the broad hatch beside him open. Dimitri and Sammi were at his side, ready with rifles. The output of his scanning system was turned all the way up. He was ahead of the Order's plans to break through the old-fashioned defences aboard the Nova Concord, but if they got one knight through that could flip in an instant.

The four Order Knights moved with the certainty of people who believed they were invisible. Remmy had split Captain Valent's entire squad into two groups. Each hid motionlessly in rooms adjacent to the main corridor running up the length of the command and control deck, their stealth systems on full. The Order Knights were almost in position when Remmy marked their position and sent a power system draining energy pulse in their direction with a small load of nanobots that would affix themselves to the Knights, defeating their cloaking systems.

He broadcast the Knights' locations and watched as Jake's squad broke cover, pointed fourteen heavy rifles that were becoming known as Knight Killers at the cloaked Order Elite soldiers and burned them down in a focused hail of explosive rounds. They were little more than a burnt pile of grease and metal melted to the deck.

"Damn, man, this is working," Dimitri said eagerly.

"No, it isn't," Remmy said. "It's forcing them to think of another way. They want to get to the bridge, this would be a direct route if we weren't prepared for them, but after three of their cloak teams have been greased, they're going to change to another strategy."

Remmy watched the main group of Order soldiers. The Beast was surrounded by Knights, twelve of them were visible to normal scanners. He was behind two bulkheads and the lift bank, too obstructed and far off for Remmy to get a read that would reveal cloaked soldiers. "We have to switch tactics first," he said, activating a program that started trying all of Clark Patterson's old identifier codes, starting with his Freeground civilian number. An Order of Eden emergency command code linked with him, and Remmy's heart jumped. He had a direct line open with someone who he hoped he'd never see again. It was like seeing a friend you thought was dead for years.

"Hey, man," he said casually. "It's Remmy, don't cut me off."

The image of the Beast flinched visibly, as though startled by someone appearing out of nowhere. He was already off balance. "If this is Remmy, then you're a conspirator with enemies of order, of humanity."

"I guess you could see it that way," Remmy said, looking at his tactical display and sending all but Sammi and Dimitri to the lifts behind him. He had a feeling Finn's hiding spot was about to get hit. That's where he'd send people if attacking the bridge didn't work; to engineering. Minh-Chu was too good at disrupting the wormholes the enemy was trying to drag them into. The Clark Patterson would have that shut down at the source and take Finn captive. "It's more like I joined the circus really. They'd leave your Order folks alone if they just let people live free and kick their hungry alien friends out of the galaxy. My circus friends back on Tamber just want to live free, have a day at the beach, a night at the club and get to the business of getting human numbers back up in the galaxy. You know they even have a guy with them named Carnie? He's actually the genuine article; travelled with a carnival and everything."

"This is a fight for our lives, the Order is maintaining a balance between the demands of the Edxi and humanity's survival. Without us, the Edxi would take every well populated world for themselves."

"Hey, I've got an idea..." Remmy said, programming three skitters he had in his backpack to go scouting on other decks.

They couldn't take more than a few direct hits, but they were fast, and could scan sections of the ship as well as any soldier. His were also loaded with high explosives, which he armed. "How about you and I declare peace between our factions so we can turn on those Edxi buggers." He snickered. "See what I did there? 'Buggers?' They're an insect race?"

"Surrender," Clark replied. Remmy had to remind himself that he was speaking to a person who took the name; 'Beast' willingly. It still sounded like his old friend, but there was a lot he didn't know.

"Man, you never had a good sense of humour. I'd make a joke and it would roll right off and you'd think I was just making conversation. Listen, this is getting tense. I've got a Captain behind me who can be... well... let's be honest... he's got a temper and your Order guys are a bit of a trigger."

"Goodbye, Remmy," the Beast said.

Remmy's hands gripped his rifle as he was surrounded by shrapnel, his shields brought down to forty two percent. With a gesture he reduced the scanning intensity of his suit so he could make something out in the visual noise. An armoured hand reached through the smoke, surging through his shields and grabbing him by the neck. His rifle was between him and his assailant as he was drawn off his feet, blasting the Order Knight at point blank range, cutting him in half. He made a serious mistake by closing in too close when he could have blasted Remmy and his squad mates while they were still recovering from the grenade strike they landed.

The hand let go of his neck and Remmy raked the torso with approximately twenty rounds in three seconds. Sammi was pinned to the wall to his left, an Order Knight was putting the muzzle of an oversized sidearm to her head and Remmy's first shots blasted that thing away.

"Help!" Dimitri said behind him.

If he turned, Sammi would definitely die and there was no guarantee that Dimitri would be saved, so Remmy riddled the Knight he was already aiming at with a barrage of rounds, bursting through his shielding then his armour, rending flesh and bone. In the next second he was facing Dimitri, blasting the Order Knight's dark green carapace like armour as it repeatedly fired its sidearm against the side of Dimitri's helmet.

Dimitri wasn't idle even though his rifle had been knocked out of his hands. As his helmet started to break down, he beat at the Order Knight with his fists, causing more clashing between their shields and a little impact damage on the Knight's arm and torso armour. Remmy and Sammi's rounds blasting the Knight were enough to finish the thing's shields off and Dimitri's next thunderous punch was an uppercut that broke his assailant's armour supports and the neck within. It collapsed in front of him and Dimitri stepped away, picking his rifle up. It took seconds for Remmy and his companions to blast what was left so it would never rise again. "Nice try, old buddy," Remmy said over the channel to the Beast. "You almost got me." He looked through his tactical scanners. Seven of Jake's squad were down, the rest were fighting for their lives. "Retreat to my location," he ordered. "We're outnumbered."

Three were able to extract themselves from the fray, running towards the heavy bulkhead Remmy rested behind. "Surrender Captain Valent and Commander Buu. It is the only way to get out of this situation without further loss of life," the Beast told him.

Remmy released his programmed skitters and they rushed into the service hatches that would take them to chutes leading to the other levels. He needed to know what else the Beast was doing. He had to keep him talking, splitting his attention as much as he could, but he was near the end of his patience. Casual talk was almost over, all he had was spite and hurt after that. "Last chance, Clark. You know you're related to one of your heroes? Yeah, Oz, or Terry Ozark McPatrick. His uncle let me in on it before I came here. You want a way to cross to the other side? That's it, a real chance. We won't even make you fight. You can work your way through all the hate you picked up when Freeground killed your sister..." Remmy started loading his hyper accelerator rounds in the front of his rifle and pointed at the narrow cone when Dimitri, his helmet half ruined, nodded at it. He and Sammi started doing the same, loading a type of weapon that had no business being fired aboard a starship. "... yeah, and then they exiled you. It's all different now. The Puritan Party has been disbanded, Freegrounders are refugees and freedom fighters. There's almost nothing left."

"You're missing a few of my dead," Clark replied.

"Oh, Isabel?" Remmy looked at his tactical scanner and saw that two of Jake's squad remained, they were five metres from joining him. He waited. "You got her killed after you broke her heart, buddy. I count her in my tally. You murdered that angel by dragging her into something she couldn't handle." Remmy was surprised at the hurt and anger that brought, just admitting that he blamed Clark for her death. "And who knows where that got Mary. You're a menace, but I'll forgive you if you switch sides now." He gave Clark two seconds to reply then sent a scan pulse down the long corridor. There was nothing in the way of the missiles they were about to fire. The pair of soldiers left from Jake's squad were secure behind the bulkhead with him. All their shields were recharged and the rest of the soldiers they had aboard were clear of the blast radius. They were ready.

"You can't imagine you have the upper hand here," the Beast replied. "Morally or tactically."

Remmy leaned into the hallway, Sammi and Dimitri doing the same, and they fired their missiles at almost exactly the same time. All three of them were blasted back by the pressure and heat as the missiles struck their target milliseconds later in the middle of the ship. The main lift column would be gone. Knights would be completely slagged, and if they were lucky the Beast would be dead.

A sharp pain in Remmy's side and an alert on his helmet display told him that he'd been stabbed, stabbed! He flailed towards the black suited attacker standing over him. It was armour he'd never seen before - sleek with form-fitted thin plating, a hood and mask without a face - and he managed to draw his sidearm and blast it on full auto, sending it reeling back. The sword was stuck on an edge of Remmy's armour, which pushed it out with the help of emergency nanobots. Dimitri was on his feet, rifle in hand, blasting at another darkly dressed figure.

A ripple in the air and a slim slice of visible armour where the cloaking field of the dark assailant was failing showed Remmy where another attacker was; behind Dimitri. "Sidestep, Dimitri!" Remmy said.

He did so, and Remmy took several shots at the dark assailant but it didn't deter it as it hacked Dimitri's head in half after three strikes against his damaged helmet. Sammi had her own nano blade out and blocked a strike from another assailant who was visible from the waist up. She was losing. Their shields had regenerated enough for them to survive a blast from a grenade, and as Remmy fired at the sword wielding bastard who was rushing back at him, he pulled a slim standard concussion grenade from his belt and tossed it into the middle of the room. "Grenade!" he shouted one second before it went off.

It sent their assailants flying, catching one hard enough to blast an arm off and break his side wide open. His shields gone, he leapt after Dimitri's rifle and came up firing at a dark figure only two metres away who had his blade raised. The weapon did what it was made to do: shatter armour and blast people to pieces. He turned towards Sammi in time to see her decapitate her attacker.

"I have Billy Finn," the Beast said. "His neck is in my hand. More Knights are coming. The outcome of this is certain."

Remmy cursed himself silently for believing that the Beast was where he thought he was; right in the middle of the ship waiting for someone to blow him sky high. Of course, he was elsewhere, skulking around the ship setting up an advantage.

The bridge doors behind them opened. Jacob Valent and Minh-Chu Buu emerged in full armour. "Let's make this our fight."

SIXTY-TWO

On The Verge

THE CLEVER DREAM emerged from the inter-dimensional corridor into normal space on the edge of the Haven System. "I have distress signals from an Aucharian ship called the Nova Concord," Theodore said. "There is an isolation field around the ship, that's the only way I can describe it. No transmissions are being allowed in."

"It's not coming from that old ship," Iruuk said. He was wearing his full armour, unable to fit in his seat properly, so it was minimized to a stool. "We're too far out for accurate scans inside but I can tell that there is a firefight going on. Temperatures inside are many times what we could normally survive, changing quickly, and there are five hull breeches that indicate explosions from the inside. There's only microgravity in there."

The tactical displays told Alice that there were nine ships on the way, one of them was at the head, it was the Noble Son, a refitted British Alliance Cruiser, still five minutes away. "Can you get a scan of what's docked with that old ship? The Nova Concord?"

"I'm trying, it looks like Citadel type cloaking, estimating its size..." Iruuk's voice faded away. The next instant she was on her feet, as though she disappeared from her seat and reappeared at the cockpit entrance, where Iruuk stood in her way, holding her shoulders. "Are you all right? You shut down our weapons and signalled surrender."

"I lost time," Alice said, feeling a powerful presence retreating from her mind. A glance over her shoulder was enough for her to see that Ute was guiding the Clever Dream away from the Nova Concord. "I've got you," she said, reaching out with her will, concentrating on that fading presence. In that moment she had a link with it, Alice made it impossible for its mind to retreat from hers.

It lashed back, it felt like an iron spike was driven from the front of her mind all the way to the back and she screamed, falling to her knees. "Oh, God, that one's powerful. That Geist is not normal."

"You already strained yourself," Theodore said. "Simple scans are showing signs of exhaustion."

"Wait, what am I doing?" Ute said, pulling her hands from the controls. "We're going the wrong way, but I don't remember turning the ship."

"Allow me," Lewis said. The Clever Dream flipped end over end and began thrusting towards the Nova Concord.

Alice didn't feel whatever it was in her head anymore, it was entirely gone, so she took her seat at the co-pilot's station. Their Prometheus beams were charging up again, so she targeted the dorsal side of the Nova Concord and set them to their lowest intensity, firing right away. "Let's see if we can find the enemy," Alice said.

"This is Gabe, down below," he said over the intercom. "We're all suited up, ready to go. Did you just signal our surrender?"

"Sorry, wrong button," Alice replied. "We're still moving in to help our people on the Nova Concord."

"Lewis?" Ute addressed. "I think I'm okay to take the controls, now."

"Then you have the controls," Lewis replied.

"I have control, thank you Lewis."

"There's a working airlock on the aft side," Iruuk said.

"Then that's where we're going," Alice said. The beams felt their way across a shape above the Nova Concord, affixed to it, and it matched a destroyer class Order of Eden ship. Alice could sense where the Geist was inside; near the front, outside of its most heavily armoured tank. She targeted that spot and burned it, turning her Prometheus beams all the way up. They would drain in seconds, require a recharge, but she wanted to frighten this Geist. With a few quick adjustments she fired five Javelin torpedoes at the hull plate covering the more armoured safe tank aboard the Citadel ship and followed it with a whole round of Sabre missiles. The Citadel ship's shields began to fail thanks to the Prometheus beams, and as they burned their last, starting a recharge cycle from zero, the Sabre missiles struck the armoured plate like the head of a big drum.

The Geist was almost there, retreating from the front of the ship, and she could sense it hesitate, slowing its swim. Javelin missiles hammered the same spot one at a time, almost blasting through that heavily armored plate. A presence tried to reach out to her mind again and she greeted it with a savage grin, remembering what it was like to feel a Geist die while it was connected to her consciousness. The Geist aboard the ship ahead of them may have been old, it may have been powerful, but the sensations she recalled with fresh clarity terrified it, and she learned something important. Geists could live forever, the thought of being killed or telepathically lobotomized was horrifying. Seeing evidence that someone had killed one of them, the Geist connecting to Alice attempted to recoil, but fear made it weak. "I am what your brother Geist made me," she told it, aware that she was speaking aloud. "A being who remembers a digital life, more than one biological life, and someone who can show you death. More than anything: I hate Geists," she told it, feeling her determination rise and her hate fade at a simple realization. If the war was to be won against the Order, against Citadel and all their allies, all the Geists had to die first. A little amusement surfaced in the Geist she was tied to, then she recalled that she had a teacher who was from Lorander and let him see her memory of Quan. All hints at levity faded. "He will train me to use my mind as a weapon that doesn't cut both ways," Alice said. A lance of pain struck her again but she refused to let go. Instead, she closed her eyes and focused. "Telepaths frighten you, don't they?" she taunted.

The pain forced tears to spill down her cheeks, but she fought to grip the Geist harder then pushed as though she was ripping through its skin. Something was working: it recoiled, but her head felt like it was being ripped in two from the inside. "Afraid I'll see something important?" she asked it.

"Alice! You can't take any more stress," Theodore said. "This will cause damage if you continue."

"We're docking with the Nova Concord," Iruuk announced.

Alice tried to let it go but found that it had a grip on her as well. Even through fear it saw reason and realized she was a serious threat. The Geist inflicted pain that was so severe that she opened her mouth to scream but couldn't make a sound. Her hands gripped her knee and the edge of the console as she rocked back and forth. "I have to sedate her!" Theodore said.

The pain eased then, and she heard Oz's voice in her mind. "It's all right," he soothed. "I'm blocking it now. Let go, Alice."

In that instant she saw Quan visiting Oz, spending precious time showing him how to put what he learned from Haus Geist to use, and how to use those skills for defence. It was only a beginning, but what once made Oz vulnerable to any Geist was already making him strong.

"The Citadel ship is detaching from the Nova Concord," Iruuk announced. "There is an explosive decompression on the dorsal side of the ship."

Alice swept the tears away from her face and looked at her tactical scanner, her head throbbing. She cancelled the sedation meds that her left command and control unit was about to administer. The Citadel ship was retreating quickly, too fast for anything to catch it. "Don't put me out, Theodore. That Geist is bugging out now that it realizes that it's outnumbered. Just gimmie something for this next level headache," Alice said.

"This is the last time I will do this before I must prescribe a period of rest and relaxation," Theodore said, sending medication into her arm through her command and control unit.

"We're ready to enter, the last firefight is about thirty metres in and five up," Gabe reported. "Your, uh, special troops want to take the lead."

"I'll be right behind you," Alice said, leaving her seat and patting Iruuk on the shoulder. "You have command, Fur-Face."

"I thought I'd go with you."

"Next time," Alice called over her shoulder.

SIXTY-THREE

Standoff

WARPED DECKS, a firefight that was pushing parts of the ship's temperature into hundreds of degrees, the arrival of more Order Knights than he knew existed, didn't make Jacob Valent doubt himself more than the fact that he could only see one plan that could save them from further losses. Minh-Chu and Remmy were directing the remainder of their forces to fallback positions near the front of the ship as the Beast and his Order Knights pushed forward primarily on the second lowest and the middle decks.

The Order Knights had a new trick, their shields could merge with Haven Fleet personal shields, so they were using their cloaking systems to get close to their enemies, then making contact, blasting their prey at point blank range. It was surprisingly effective, the kind of tactic that Jake shied away from when he considered using nano-blades years before.

Jake fought alongside Sammi Reynolds and Craig Kendrick, the first was from Remmy's squadron, the second was one of the last members of Jake's. They were both incredible fighters, and the three of them marched in a line, sensors turned up high, shields set to recharge using every scrap of energy their suits could provide. They were bait, made to draw as many Order Knights off from their retreat as they could.

The beauty of the Aucharian ship was lost. Superficial walls near the middle of the vessel were blasted through or blown out, leaving shreds of metal between supports and heavy bulkheads. They approached the middle, where the main elevator bank was, and it was a blasted pit that led to molten holes leading up and down. "We're going to get hit, this is their line," Jake said, watching his tactical scanner and a three-hundred-and-sixty-degree multi-spectrum view stretched out across the bottom of his in-helmet display. He didn't carry his rifle, but a basic sidearm in one hand with five fifteen-millimetre shell shots and he flexed his other hand, ready to spring his nano-blade and the energy weapon mounted beside it. The thing was set to close range, adjusted to break through shields.

A shape appeared for half a second on his three hundred sixty-degree view, it was less than three metres away, rushing Sammi, who saw it as well, opening up with her rifle on its highest setting, busting the Knight's energy shield down and blasting through its armour. Another came for Craig on his right, and he got the same reception, getting even closer. An alert appeared on Jake's display and he brought up the secondary shield on his arm, set wide enough to block him and the soldiers at his sides. Three micro-missiles exploded against it, the concussion blasting his shield so hard that he was forced back a step despite the extreme strength and fortification enhancements built into his suit. "Here they come," Jake said. "A rush."

"Now that our thermal sensors are completely blown out," Craig said, rifle at the ready. The heatsinks on the weapon were out, jagged fins extending from the top of the weapon to keep it from overheating.

Jake's sensors showed him vibrations against the floor in front of him and he blasted the spot with an acidic gel round. An explosion of green and blue liquid filled the space in front of him, taking the shape of three Order Knights as their personal shields reacted to the caustic solution. Jake stepped forward, touched his arm mounted energy weapon to the shield and let it blast the shield down with two high-energy, point blank range hits. The Knight tried to counter, bringing his sidearm up to Jake's head, but close range was where Jake shone brightest. He snatched the weapon away, flipped it around and fired it at the Knight's neck five times in quick succession as his companions blasted the Knights to his right and left with their rifles. There were more behind those three, he realized as his armour registered a pulse round hit. Headless, his quarry dropped, and Jake rose his rifle to blast in an arc in front of him.

His tactical system marked hits on four targets who were charging fast, drifting across the open hole in the middle of the broad deck through zero gravity. Jake and the pair with him opened fire on them, their explosive rounds going off against their enemy's shields. "Cover!" Jake said as the space between them was filled with white-hot pulse rounds, the Order Knights weren't hanging in space without guidance either. Small thrusters on their armour started firing, directing them down to the deck as they tried to fend Jake and his people off. The minor propulsion made them perfectly visible on scanners. "I count seven," Sammi announced as she dove behind a warped bulkhead, her suit anchoring her against it so she could immediately return fire.

"Confirmed," Craig said. "Six in a second." He and Sammi focused fire on the nearest Order Knight, a brat who was about to throw a grenade. He was torn to shreds before it could be activated.

"We have reinforcements coming in," Remmy said, using the hull as a conductor for communications. It was the only means of communication since the jamming started. "Four Nafalli bad asses and some serious Haven Fleet armour. Aft docking port."

Jake dropped a weaponized skitter and directed it to cloak and go after the group of Order Knights who just took cover behind the bulk head opposite them. It would take the long way, then blast them with an electromagnetic pulse before conventional explosives would follow up. It might not kill the Knights, but it would take a bite out of their shields and drive the less experienced of them out from behind cover. "Good timing, my groups' pinned down near the old elevator banks," Jake replied. "Do not send help, I'll try to break the stalemate and move on."

"We can push towards our reinforcements, we should press our advantage," Remmy said.

"No, stay on the bridge, fortify the position. More Haven ships are minutes away."

"Did you get a communication I didn't?" Remmy asked.

"No, but we're *in the Haven System*, reinforcements are definitely on the way, even though we're as far from Tamber as we could be. Fortify that position, I'll keep drawing them here, pushing them back if I can."

"If you're wrong, you're dead," Remmy said flatly.

"That's enough, Remmy," Minh-Chu said. "Fortifying our position, Captain."

SIXTY-FOUR

Breaking In

THE WEAPONRY ALICE'S Nafalli brought into her squad was stunning. When Woone and Faloo melted the inner airlock of the Nova Concord in less than three seconds with intense particle beam weapons that were mounted on hip rigs then charged forward, Alice was relieved. She knew the technical capabilities of the weapons, that all four of the Nafalli had hundreds of hours training on them with and without the harness mounts but seeing them burn a door through in a perfect square starting from the top and cutting right through to the bottom with expert ease was real reassurance that they were practiced with their gear.

They flooded the main aft causeway, catching fire right away. Knud, Jessen, Newell, and Nash represented the humans with Gabe and Alice in the middle. Woone and Faloo were running point, while the taller males Faloo and Krooke took up the rear. As soon as they were through, all the Nafalli fired several bursts from their personal energy cannons - that was the actual classification of their weapons - in all directions, revealing everything that was cloaked on their level and along the causeway above.

Alice's breath caught as she recognized the silhouette of the largest target amongst twenty figures that were attempting to remain cloaked. "Pick your targets and burn them down," Alice ordered, marking the large silhouette, the Beast of the Order of Eden as her primary target. "Missile burst!" she cried, unleashing a barrage of five micro-missiles in his direction and catching the pair of Order Knights at his side.

Their boots were holding them to the deck, their shield units were working together to form one protective bubble, and the Order Knights were throwing every kind of ammunition in their direction, but their shields were holding up, the charge bouncing between ninety-seven and ninety-nine percent as the focused beams of the Nafalli burst wide, revealing target locations, then focused in for seconds at a time, melting thin hull plating to get to some targets, striking directly at Order Knights who weren't wise enough to find cover.

"Where'd he go?" Alice asked. "Target zero, anyone have eyes on him?"

"I saw you nail him with two missiles and I can't find him now," Gabe said. "Auto scan isn't coming up with him either."

Alice got an idea then and pulled an automated pulse grenade from the slot under her arm. "Going to track this," she said, throwing it up towards the main concourse one level up. Two seconds later, their group was pummelled by concussive grenades, reducing their collective shield to twelve percent. "Move! Rush my waypoint," Alice ordered, marking a spot on her map part way down a hall that hugged the port side of the ship. There were bulkheads there, good cover.

Woone nudged into an Order Knight and broke rank, activating the savage vibrating bayonet on the end of her weapon and wielding it like a long staff. It clashed with the Knight's shield as she bashed him twice, knocking him to the deck. The third strike broke through his shields, and as the blurry, vibrating tip of her bayonet blade rattled and jigged against his armour, she activated her beam weapon, beginning a super-hot cut that burned through metal, flesh and bone from his stomach to the top of his head. Another struck her from the side, the round of his sidearm sending a splash of energy across the side of her armour, and Faloo was there, stabbing and firing at him.

The rest of the group caught up, finishing the Order Knights off. Alice dropped a timed electromagnetic grenade between their corpses to stop their regeneration. They went off as her group reached the hallway opposite the main aft airlock, rendering the Knights inert.

She found herself at the rear of the group, between Krooke and Noro, who were blasting at three Order Knights that fired at them from cover. The Beast came down from the causeway railing above, blasting through what remained of their shield, snatching Alice and hurling her down the broad hallway from port to starboard. She touched the wall of the corridor and affixed several metres out of sight from her squad. "Fabricate nanobot compound twenty-eight and load it into my sidearm." She said to her computer system as she scanned the hallway for the Beast with every system she had as well as her eyeballs. No one was attacking her, the Order Knights were focusing on keeping her people bottled up in the port side hallway. The Beast knew who she was, it was the only explanation.

Her shield was charged up to nine percent when a heavy

electromagnetic round struck her at high speed, depleting it and destroying half her emitter systems. She fired back in the direction the round came from then watched for any sign of a cloaked soldier. She was about to take a pulse grenade from her thigh pocket when she was struck so hard that the chest of her armour registered damage. Her boots held to the deck, the artificial muscle in the back and bottom half of her armour held her position, but the invisible figure had a grip on her rifle, and a blade strike was registered against her visor.

Alice grabbed at her assailant, her throbbing head clearing. Her left hand caught nothing but air, then her right got a firm grip on a metal edge, and she used every augmented physical system to punch with her empty hand as the other pulled. The crackling of his shield taking the hit and fighting to expel her as he activated it lit the space in front of her. The flaws she made in his cloak were revealing him only as a towering dark shape. Another strike from something solid, something made to pierce and cut hit her helmet, and she didn't need her computer to warn her about the impact, her head was jostled to the side.

With gnashed teeth, she struck at him several more times, trying to pry his armour open and his cloak failed, his shield failed before it could cut through her wrist. One more punch revealed that she was holding on to not only a piece of his armour, but the belly plate beneath, and he swung for her head frantically with his armoured, spiked fists as her last punch ripped it open, exposing him to the vacuum, making his stomach send blood into the weightless space between them.

All the while she ducked low, watching his swings, keeping her head out of the way. "Sidearm reload complete," her computer said.

"Time to end you," Alice growled through clenched teeth.

Pain lanced through her shoulder, then another wave of

excruciating agony as whatever cut into her from above, from her bleeding assailant was ripped free. The strength in her right arm was gone, and she let go of him. The Beast caught her by the helmet before she could get out of the way, stims and recovery medication flooding her system along with a small army of nanobots to take care of her growing injury list. Her suit was already beginning to seal.

Alice drew her sidearm and fired at the Beast's belly, which had already regenerated. If it penetrated, there was no indication. He grabbed her wrist, let her helmet go and ripped her boots free of their grip on the deck, damaging the synthetic muscle and plating in her armour. She flailed, her suit re-sealed from the void, the stimulants kicking in, and the wound in her shoulder burning, tingling as nanobot surgeons did their work. Getting her wrist free of him was useless, he was grabbing for one of her legs, and she caught his intention, kicking away and up, landing a boot against his jaw with more pressure than anyone outside of augmented armour could manage. It didn't faze him.

Light pulsed behind him, her squad was free, and charging. A dark figure came down from above, his boots affixing to the deck behind the Beast. She recognized the death's head helmet of her father's armour. The Beast let her wrist go, grabbed her helmet and drove a long spike against her chest armour, denting it severely. Alice kicked at him and struck his arm with a blow that snapped bone, but the Beast got his shot. A long spike drove into her beneath the breastbone, failing to press through the back of her armour, but running all the way through her body, and there was no pain greater. Then pulses of electrical current passed through the blade into her body, sending her into convulsions, the sound of her own screams filled her ears for long seconds before she passed out.

SIXTY-FIVE

Valents

THE BEAST FLICKED Alice off his long arm blade, sending her into a dark corner of the hall. Jake's systems told him that, despite two Nafalli beam weapons firing on him, his shields were recharging. The squad from the Clever Dream was representing themselves well, fighting at least two squads of Order Knights - driving them behind cover with expert cover fire - while advancing slowly on the Beast. It was how it should be done, it was the best way to keep your whole team alive while you tried to save your comrade.

The Beast's armour was self-repairing, he was about to take a step away, and Jake dropped his rifle, bumped into it on the way across the space between him and the Beast, sending it spinning through the gravity absent causeway. At the last instant, the Beast turned to him, and even through that horrific plating, Jake could see him smiling.

The Beast slashed at him with the same blade he'd used to impale his daughter, Jake raised his arm shield, deflecting it easily then bashing the Beast bodily at full charge, pushing him onto his back foot. Jake's intent was grim, not rage fuelled, but driven by more hate than he could stand. Jacob Valent's intent was simple. Murder him. Murder him quickly. His right-hand bracer unit vibrated as a nano-blade made to cut through hull material emerged. The Beast sidestepped Jake's swipe. He was about to regain his balance, retake the advantage.

Jake wouldn't have it and leapt at the Beast who narrowly dodged a body to body collision. He failed to deflect Jake's hand as it got a grip on the bulge of his shoulder plate. An electric surge burned Jake's energy shield out in one shot, a trick he'd adapt from the Beast's arsenal, and he felt an impact against his side. He risked shifting his grip, catching the Beast's neck and he hooked his leg around the bastard's waist, dragging his nano-blade across the thing's chest, watching his eyes grow wide. "I've got you now," Jake said. He felt the pierce of a blade shallowly penetrating his armour and clenched his teeth, hate bearing him through. The armour sealed the hole with a thin layer of emergency material. "I'm going to open you up and watch you start healing." There it was, another strike, but it missed the hole the Beast made the first time, he was panicking.

The first small crack started to form in the Beast's armour as the bastard bashed Jake's helmet with his unbladed hand frantically. His bladed fist found its mark, piercing Jake's side, digging in towards his stomach and Jake roared, holding to his enemy, cutting through plate, the breach in the Beast's armour growing, globules of dark blood shaking out of the crack into the air.

Another body collided with the Beast's shoulder, gripping him under the helmet, a sidearm in her hand. Alice pressed the muzzle against the opening Jake made in the Beast's armour and fired shot after shot until the Beast began to scream, it wasn't heard, but seen through the transparent section of his helmet. "Let him go, Dad," she said, their suits communicating through laser link.

As he did so, he watched as the Beast's armour sealed, but the transparent faceplate revealed an image that Jake couldn't believe at first. The crimson plates covering the misshapen head of the Beast were breaking down. The colour of the skin beneath changed from red and blue to fresh human pink. "Don't fire on the Beast. He's been neutralized," Alice said. "There won't be a framework cell left in his body in a minute."

"There are no Order Knights. Two other soldiers surrendered, we think they're Citadel. I'm sorry we couldn't go after you when he pulled you out of our formation, Alice," Gabe said. "Good job, damn good job."

"No worries," Alice said. "Rushing after me would have gotten more people killed. This was a victory. We have Clark Patterson."

"Well done," Jake said as he looked into the face of a young man who had an uncanny resemblance to Jonas Valent. "Someone get that thing in restraints."

He turned towards Alice, his stomach still burning and tingling, and pulsed his basic propulsion system in her direction. "Are you all right?"

"I was dead for a second there," Alice said, surprisingly cheery. "But I feel *much* better now." She allowed herself to be caught in his arms and chuckled as they gently bounced off the wall. "Welcome home."

SIXTY-SIX

Wrap Up

ALL IT TOOK for Alice to completely accept Jacob Valent as her father, biological and beyond, was his proximity. Her doubt and refusal, looking to Jonas as the person who initially made her so many years before as her true father, was purely intellectual. Watching how he spoke to people and sorted things out aboard the Nova Concord as quickly as he could while being effective at the same time made her feel like her father had returned. Her own squad sorted itself out quickly, by the time Alice directed them in restraining and securing the few prisoners they took, they were ready with a plan in mind.

It was clear to her that Gabe needed his own people. He stepped into a leadership role fluidly and was very good at it. Not quite as good as Jake, but experienced and confident. She wanted to work with him, maybe there was room for him aboard the Clever Dream. It was worth proposing.

Everyone gathered in the forward section of the ship on the lowest deck, where the Clever Dream was coming around to dock at one of the secondary airlocks and the first Haven Fleet destroyer to arrive was sending marines aboard to do another sweep of the ship and as they retrieved the survivors. Alice's attention was so split between watching her father and taking care of her own Squad, who seemed disappointed that there wasn't more work for them to do, that she almost didn't notice Minh-Chu, who approached her with a big smile. It was funny, she never realized how short he was until then. He was only a few centimetres taller, she could match or beat his height by standing on her tiptoes.

"Well, look at this. They grow so fast while we're away," he said.

Alice gave him a welcoming hug and smiled back at him. "I cheated." Being with Jake and Minh-Chu made her feel young again, almost as young as she did when they left. "What happened? Why did you come in on this ship instead of the Revenge?"

"We saw an opportunity to hit the Order where it hurts," Minh-Chu said. "I think it worked, but when the Order crashed our party, we were too far from the Revenge to catch a ride back."

"They're not back yet," Alice said. "But we're expecting them tomorrow."

Minh-Chu's lively expression darkened a little, worried. He was easier to read than Iruuk.

There was no reason to leave him in the dark, or to withhold reassurances. "Everything's fine, they said they were limping back but doing well," Alice reassured. "They'll probably be surprised when they find out you got here first."

"That'll be something," he said, his mood lifting a little.

Three shuttles docked along the wall, the doors opened to admit squads of soldiers. Each group knew where to go, passing around the survivors and into the bowels of the Nova Concord. It was time for them to do a sweep of the vessel, and Alice suspected that it was only the first wave. There would be hundreds of them in minutes.

"Captain Valent," a Commander said, his grin practically splitting his face it was so wide. "I'm Commander Sonnen, formerly of Freeground Fleet, now serving in your military. It's an honour to meet you."

Jake shook his hand. "Welcome to the Fleet," he said, half turning to Alice.

"Everyone knows you, Captain Valent," the Commander said with the same grin. "I wouldn't have been transferred if it weren't for you, a lot of people are grateful for the opportunities your actions brought us," he said, offering his hand.

Alice took it, and blushed, her heart skipping a beat when she saw Noah Lucas walking by behind him, joining Minh-Chu. "Um, thank you," Alice said, fighting to regain focus for a moment. "What opportunity did I give Freeground Fleet?"

"When you dressed down Terran, you made an important point to Haven leadership. There was a lot of outrage, but many experienced commanders started taking a closer look at the people who were brought in to manage your military efforts here, and hundreds of them were put out, a few thousand were demoted. Didn't you hear about it?"

"I was a little busy, I can't talk about it..." Alice said, eyeing a pair of marines standing nearby. There was no way they had clearance, and she really didn't feel like talking about her experiences over the last few days.

"I understand. To the point: If it weren't for you, the military merge between Freeground and Haven Fleet could have taken months, but now we expect to be finished by the end of the week. People who have been ready for promotions for years are finally being put in the right place, and the Freeground Nation are accepting the idea of relocation much faster. I just wanted to say thank you. Admiral Anderson has been a large part of the merge as well, possibly larger, if you could pass my thanks on, I'd appreciate it."

"I will, thank you," Jake said.

"For now, it's time for your people to board my shuttles," Commander Sonnen said. "We'll take you to the Hunter, from there you'll be going to the War Forge, Sir."

Alice thought the Commander was pleasant, but he definitely knew how to move things along. All but one squad of soldiers were already out of sight, moving into the Nova Concord on their sweep. "I'll be taking my people back to the Clever Dream," Alice said. "Good to meet you, Commander." She turned to her father. "See you aboard the War Forge."

"See you in a few minutes," Jake said.

Alice turned and looked to her squad, who seemed listless, leaning against the wall beside the airlock leading to the Clever Dream, with the exception of Woone and Faloo, who were leaning against each other, back to back. "We're finished here," she announced, holding her finger up and waving it in a small circle. "Pack up, we're standing down." It felt like the kind of gesture Yawen would make, the kind of thing she'd say, and Alice immediately missed her.

SIXTY-SEVEN

Reporting

ALICE RECEIVED an order to have the Clever Dream dock at a specific mooring point on the War Forge, to disembark with Gabe Vernor then send the Clever Dream on to a military hangar near the habitation section of the station. They followed instructions, but Alice was wary, feeling that there was something other than a pat on the back coming. It was only accentuated by the fact that Iruuk and Theodore wouldn't look at her while they made the trip.

They docked, and she felt the full weight of their silence as she slipped out of her co-pilot's seat. Ute broke it, her high voice confident. "I'm proud that I was on that mission with you, Captain. I couldn't have imagined how important it was, for me or you or even the fleet."

"For you?" Alice asked, genuinely curious. Ute was one of the most intelligent people she'd ever been in the presence of, not just scientifically, or where general problem solving was concerned, but socially as well.

"I am the first Mergillian to enter another dimension," she said. "I could go back to my people and my life would already be remarkable to them. I mapped a small piece of it, and that would have gone unknown for a long time if you didn't tell me it was something special. I'm a pioneer now, and I want to stay on your crew permanently."

"I'll make that request," Alice said, her eye drifting to Iruuk, who was busy working on his report while watching the scanner displays. "Thank you, Ute, I think even Lewis thinks you're a better pilot than he is."

"I do," Lewis said. "Your reflexes aren't better, but you think ahead further than any human I've ever had at the controls, and your style is... entertaining? I think that's the right word."

Alice left them behind, joining Gabe as they bantered on. They were through the airlock, walking down the hallway within the War Forge when he finally said; "I'm sorry I lost some of your people. There was nothing more I could do."

"I don't blame you," Alice said, keeping it short, afraid that if she thought about Yawen too much it would bring her grief to the surface. The room they were instructed to report to was within a dark hall with photo-resistive paint that interfered with all visual recordings. The double doors parted and they moved into the simple sitting room as a pair. Commodore Sawyer waited for them in the middle of a broad, semi-circular sofa. The wall past her showed the ongoing construction of a ship, small robots hovering around it, placing parts, arms reaching in, printing sections of the inner structure, and skitter bots delivering complex components within the frame.

"Congratulations to you both," she said, gesturing for them to take a seat on the semi-circular sofa across from her. "Welcome to the most secure conference room in the solar system, or one of them, at least."

"Should I be honoured or terrified?" Gabe asked.

They sat down, only centimetres apart. Alice couldn't believe how comfortable the seat was, it seemed inappropriate somehow. "This is going to be a long debrief," Commodore Sawyer said, leaning back. "Fleet is taking the Lorander philosophy: people are more forthcoming when they're off their feet and comfortable. We'll put a food order in shortly."

"So, we have your ear until?" Alice asked.

"Until you're finished," the Commodore said. "That's part of Haven Fleet's forming philosophy. The chain of command has to be knowledgeable and must demonstrate a true understanding of itself all the way up and down. When we have time, we have to communicate under the best conditions."

"So, this has nothing to do with the shakeup I started?" Alice asked. "Going forward, I'm going to disappoint you if you think I'll be that influential ever again. It's overrated."

Commodore Sawyer smiled, nodding. "The Admirals and Generals who don't know you or think they might be on shaky political ground are terrified of you. That's not why we're having this extended debrief. I ordered it as soon as I read your medic's report. If what he says is true, then I agree with his assessment."

"What did he say?" Alice asked.

"He was impressed by your capabilities, even though he was clear that they're beyond most people's understanding, including his, but he suggests that you take some time to adjust and to recover. There are recommendations that you consult with a Lorander telepath, be put on standby after the first few days so you can react to an emergency, but his assessment is that you should take your recovery in stages. Full rest for a week, put on standby part way through that, then training with your crew under your sole direction, and then ramping up to full duty at the end of a one-month period. There are serious vascular and stress concerns that he's highlighted here. The first were addressed and corrected, but the second will take time."

"There is an invasion coming," Alice said. "I have some thoughts on how to prevent it, and I'd like to be part of that effort."

"I agree," Gabe said. "Captain Valent showed good judgement during two crises that I've seen her involved in. I'd follow her into anything right now."

"I applaud your sentiment, but we need to go over the particulars. Especially now that Admiral McPatrick's actions today are under review." The Commodore paused for a moment, looking from Alice to Gabe then back to Alice. "You haven't heard. Well, minutes before the Nova Concord emerged on the edge of our solar system, Admiral McPatrick commandeered the Light Runner, a Haven Fleet corvette that was crewing up and testing its main systems. He ordered it to intercept Intelligence's classified Cache Site where the Exile Geist was being held under sedation. He issued a warning to the staff there and once they abandoned it, he launched nine Lance Torpedoes loaded with antimatter at the station and obliterated it. It wasn't a large station, two torpedoes would have wiped it out, but we're guessing he had to make sure. When the Clever Dream emerged, he was already on his way to the Nova Concord, but it was across the entire solar system. He states that he arrived in time to block your connection to the Geist aboard the Citadel ship docked with the Nova Concord, scaring it off and saving you from severe trauma."

"That last part is true, but I don't know anything about the Cache Site," Alice said. "I'm sure Oz saved me."

"All right. That's something that'll help him when he faces

the disciplinary board. Unofficially, I'm pulling for him. Officially, I can tell anyone who is cleared to listen that he was at least partially acting with the general good of the Haven System in mind. That is, if you think so."

"Definitely, Geists are..."

"Hold there, Captain," Commodore Sawyer said. "You're encouraged to share your opinions, but it's always best to preface them with facts."

Alice could only nod, she knew the regulations and the legal benefits of doing things exactly the way her commander was explaining.

"So, let's start at the beginning. I'll hear Lieutenant Vernor's report first, starting with your arrival in the Cefa system and any pertinent information leading up to that."

"While he begins, can I have a moment to send my father a message?"

"Go ahead," the Commodore said. "There's an anteroom through there."

Alice followed where she pointed, stepping through a door that was almost hidden in the side wall. The space was small, a waiting area with a sofa and two chairs, the table in the middle with a tissue dispenser implied that it was reserved for bad news. She called up her father's ident and called him. A few blip-blips later and a hologram of his head appeared. "I don't have long," he said. "I'm in debriefing with Admiral Karn and Riley."

"I'm in debriefing too. It looks like I'll be here for a few hours. I just wanted to warn you that Ayan has a big surprise for you, it's good, but you're going to be a little shocked." The concerned look on his face was enough for her to guess that she hadn't told him about Laura yet. "So, you haven't had a chance to talk to her? See her?"

"No, we're on separate ends of the station right now, it's huge. She's in classified meetings, I'm in a classified debrief."

"All right. Brace yourself, don't look up her personal profile before you see her, let her show you the surprise on her own, okay?"

"All right," Jake said.

Alice had a feeling that the moment her father disconnected the call, he'd look Ayan's personal profile up. "You promise me," Alice said as seriously as she could. "Don't go looking for information on what this is. Let Ayan tell you her own way."

"All right, all right," Jake said. "Good luck with your debrief."

"Thanks, see you soon."

SIXTY-EIGHT

Home

IN DAYDREAMS that were difficult to turn away from, Jake imagined that he would arrive at Ayan's door in the Everin Building and he'd find her eager to meet him but busy. That was the real impression he got from most of her messages, that she was always occupied by a Fleet that didn't have enough strong leaders.

The debrief was over, it was a strange meeting with a panel of Admirals, two Generals led by the ruling Triumvirate: The Minister of Public Welfare Pamela Grey, Science Minister Shawn Lourdes, and Defence Minister Carl Anderson who led the question period after Jake and Minh-Chu summarized their basic report. The question period went on for two hours with Carl Anderson squelching as many questions as were put to them, citing the report that Jake and Minh-Chu already had filed.

The question period about their new artificial intelligence weapon was led by the Science Minister, who seemed as curious as he was concerned, tugging on a short grey goatee as Liara and Remmy stepped forward to answer very specific questions. The Public Welfare Minister listened to everything closely, shifting in her seat whenever any combat in which someone was killed was brought up. Four of her questions were squelched, all of them indicating that she hadn't bothered to review any of the military reports from the Revenge. In fact, the worst question she asked was simply; "How did you come to the decision to bring Freeground Alpha to the Haven System?" which was squelched immediately by Anderson, who simply said; "You'll have to do your own reading on that. Moving on."

That was the largest flare up amongst the members of the Triumvirate, the ultimate ruling body for the solar system aside from Ayan, who left all decisions to them despite her official title of Queen. She could have been there, but Jake knew why she probably stayed away. At a guess, he thought she'd either feel like she was sitting on the wrong side of the table, or that she'd be a distraction, or that she ultimately didn't want to give any sign that she was interested in wearing a crown.

"That wasn't so bad," Jake said, hoping saying it would make it true. Most of the questions felt fairly mundane. While the whole ordeal was under way, he was getting status reports on members of his temporary squad. All but three were saved and he'd be able to visit them in the medical centre aboard the War Forge. The others were in line for consideration for the resurrection program.

They were effectively dead. Their existences were over thanks to a high level of brain damage. There was an excellent chance what was left of them would be used to put a body together so scans taken aboard the Revenge or by their armour could be written onto the new brains, and a copy of them would resume their lives. While it was good for the military, Jake still had reservations about it. None of that seemed like it would be as seamless or as easy as Haven Fleet seemed to think, and he wondered what complications would arise with relatives. Someone died, but everyone would be presented with a new copy that incorporated parts of the original body if possible, and a whole clone when impossible. Would some families want to honour the original with a funeral? Would most prefer to go on as though the replacement was the same as the original? He had a unique insight into the topic, but still didn't know where people would lean or how many complications there would be as the Resurrection Program was phased in. Time and testing would tell.

He and Minh-Chu made it through the scan check aboard the War Forge, marvelling at the sheer size of it. The rooms were tall, an extra half metre almost everywhere, and the halls were broad. The solidity and feeling of permanence he felt while he was there made him feel like they were entering a station that was affixed to an asteroid. There were no machine noises, even though it was mostly a manufacturing centre and shipyard, and the lights emulated the full healthy spectrum for humans.

"It's strange," Minh-Chu said. "I thought the Revenge would get here first." Jake felt immediate sympathy for him. It was clear that he imagined a happy reunion with Ashley when he arrived. He started at the arrival of messages on his command and control unit. "My sister. She's left five messages in the last two minutes," he said, activating his small holographic projector. "Oh, brother of mine!" she said, her face a little older, but not so much different from the bratty, energetic young woman Jake remembered. "They wouldn't let me greet

you properly. Something about you going for scans and classified checks at a super-secret site. I told them they'd better let
me be the first to welcome you, or they would hear about it
every time someone in Fleet uniform came to my restaurant.
You know what they did? Oh, wait, customer." The message
cut out.

Minh-Chu smiled a little and played the next one. Carnie
was already holding his mouth, keeping his chuckles in for the
most part. "I'm back! You know what they asked me when I said
they'd hear about this injustice? They asked if I would poison
the food! I could not believe the disrespect! I would never
tamper with food, and poison! The food doesn't deserve... Oh,
there's a group of them coming in now." The message ended.

"I'm back! Oh, customers." That message ended as well.

"Finally! It is no easy thing being the most successful restaurant owner in Haven Shore. Anyway, what was I saying? Oh,
yes. No tampering with food! The stomach rarely makes decisions, so why punish it with bad food or poison? That's what I
told him, and he laughed! I couldn't believe it, serious philosophy offered to him and he didn't have to buy so much as a
dumpling, and he laughs! I invited him to the restaurant. I think
he believes I will serve him excellent food, and I will. It's his ears
I'll poison! If I could pour hot dishwater soup on his mind, then
I would, but I'll have to let him hear all about it and embarrass
him in front of his friends. Ooh, I hope he comes in soon."
Minh-Chu burst out laughing at the conclusion of the message,
which gave everyone else permission to do the same.

When he started to calm down, he held his hand up. "Wait,
there's one more," he said, playing it. She appeared, smiling
sweetly with a framed picture of Minh-Chu from much
younger days beside her head. "I can't wait to see you, brother,
it's been too long. There are directions to my restaurant in the

message, but I know you can follow your nose. I am proud of you."

"She's a complicated woman," Minh-Chu said as the message faded. His words were critical, but their tone was filled with adoration.

"It was a long debrief," Jake said. "You should go straight there."

"You're right. She's probably climbing the walls." He looked to Noah. "You hungry?"

"Always," he replied. "Especially if you're paying."

They came through the last short hall before the waiting area and Jake's heart leapt as he spotted Ayan from behind. Her figure and her curly red hair were unmistakable to him. She was in a Fleet uniform, but there was something very different, even from behind, and it looked like she was holding something in her arms. She turned around with a big smile, but her blue eyes were asking a question. In a sling that hung high on her chest made from a fold in her uniform, she cradled a newborn.

He was across the room, at her side in seconds, and she greeted him with a brief, but warm kiss. "I know a little extra time passed while I was away, but," he said lightly and quietly as he put his arm around her gently.

"It's a big surprise, I know. An even bigger ask; you don't just get me, you have to take me and a baby and I never got a chance to ask you, but..." she trailed off. Before he could say anything Ayan looked up at him. "This is Laura. The daughter I thought I would never have. Alice's team rescued her from a refugee ship, and I adopted her."

"She's beautiful," he said, looking down at the black-haired newborn as her tiny lips worked into a shape that made it look like she was about to whistle. Her eyes half opened, closed then started looking around. "If you asked me, I would have made sure I was there for everything." Laura fussed a little, then her lips started turning upward. "Is she smiling?" A little 'poot' sound drifted up and he laughed.

"Passing gas," Ayan said. "So, taking our relationship out of order doesn't scare you?"

"We've started over enough," Jake said. "Maybe it's about time we skipped ahead a little."

Minh-Chu, his sister Kim-Ly and Noah were on their way to them, and Ayan looked up at Jake, her lips pursed. They stole a quick kiss. "I missed you so much, Jake," she whispered.

"I missed you too. Thank you for the messages." Was all he had time to say before they were joined by a trio who were mesmerized by Laura. "You made it up?" Jake asked Kim-Ly.

"They came down in front of my restaurant in a shuttle and brought me here. The windows were blacked out, and I had to wear audio blockers, as if hearing anything in space was even possible."

"Welcome," Ayan said. "I've been meaning to drop in at your place, but I've been busy. I've ordered a few times though."

"That's all right," Kim-Li said softly, looking at Laura. "You have a little dumpling of your own to take care of."

It wasn't the homecoming Jacob expected, no, it was complicated, and shocking, but he would rather be nowhere else. A check on his command and control unit told him that Alice was in a black section of the station, her exact whereabouts classified. "Congratulations, Admiral, Captain," Noah said respectfully before he turned to Minh-Chu. "There's an old friend on the station I have to connect with. I'll see you later."

Minh-Chu nodded knowingly then turned to Jake. "Welcome home, surprise!" he said with a chuckle, his voice low enough so he wouldn't startle Laura.

Jake laughed and nodded. "Best homecoming I can remember." In a moment's reflection, he realized that he'd never had two that were exactly alike. Every time there were changes. Whether his returns came with more good or bad news, it didn't matter, there was always catching up and adjusting to be done, but he was always happy to be back.

SIXTY-NINE

Of New Minds

THE MEETING WAS STATED in Alice's command and control unit. It wasn't marked as mandatory or optional, it was marked as fact. At oh-six-hundred she would be in Observation Room Six Three One Four. Theodore met her on the way. He knew his report would piss her off, it was written on his face.

Alice's stride didn't even stutter; he had to fall in step with her. "They have me on two weeks minimum leave. I won't be allowed to go on duty unless that invasion actually happens. That means the Clever Dream is down, my team goes into standby with Gabe taking over as leader, and if nothing comes up, they're in training starting at the end of week one. After two weeks, I'm on standby for a month with no assignments outside of the Haven System."

"I am looking out for your overall health. You've taken a lot in stride, there have been so many changes, but you've taken almost no time to adjust," Theodore replied apologetically.

"You barely know me; how can you tell what I can and can't handle?" Alice retorted, guilt nagging at her over the snap.

"I see the signs of too much stress for too long. You're quicker to anger, letting emotions factor into command decisions and combat acts, and then there's the suffering you endure at night, when you're trying to sleep. These are signs that you're trying to cope, and I can see that being under so much pressure is getting in the way. All this while your personality is still highly malleable. The worst thing about that are these telepathic encounters you've had. According to the Lorander psychological information I have, engaging in these violent contests of the mind could leave your core personality scarred and your potential for personal development severely limited."

The most annoying thing about Theodore's justifications for concern was that he was almost certainly right. Alice couldn't know for certain, but he could. "You should have talked to me first," was the only counter she could offer other than screaming and wailing and kicking her feet, which she wanted to do anyway, but there was no way she'd do it in the command section of the War Forge or in front of Theodore. Well, maybe in front of Theodore, just to freak him out.

"If you saw me pulling memory from my chest and damaging expansion ports, would you take me aside for a chat, or turn me off?" he asked with surprising conviction.

Alice stopped and turned towards him. They were a few steps away from her destination. "You're getting too good at arguing," she said, sighing. Alice deactivated her armour, parts of it fell off, too damaged to fold into a jacket.

Theodore picked the pieces up. "Thank you?"

"In a week or something I'll probably thank you for getting

me to take a breather if we aren't under attack. I'm not there yet though, okay?"

"Okay," he said. "Do you want me to take the rest of your armour to recycling, what's left isn't effective."

Alice gave him the jacket and boots section, glad that her vacsuit was able to make soles and draw an edge around her feet to make it look like she was wearing shoes. "Someday you'll get tired of taking care of people."

"Only if I'm not needed."

"I'll see you when all these meetings and briefings are done, okay?" Alice said. Her frustration at being put on leave was still fresh, but her irritation with Theodore had almost completely melted away. He was only doing his job. If anyone was to blame, it was her for putting him in that position.

"Oh, good, I thought I'd have to put in a request for quarters."

"Never going to happen, Theo," Alice said. "Unless you want a break from my drama."

"Your drama is amazing," he replied. "I'll see you later."

They parted ways, and Alice turned to watch him finish walking down the dark hallway before she sighed and pressed the button beside the double doors leading into the Observation room. They parted, allowed her through and closed the moment she was clear. Terry Ozark McPatrick stood in front of a completely transparent wall.

Sections of heavy hull plating were being held away from a thick frame as the War Forge's fabrication arms and worker droids worked on robust looking thruster and beam systems. They were actually looking at live construction, this wasn't a digitally created vista made to convince whoever was in the room that they were adjacent to a manufacturing line aboard the War Forge.

Oz turned and smiled at her, his uniform jacket marked him as a Commodore. "Thank you for coming, Alice," he said. Unlike the last time she saw him, he seemed approachable, well.

When she started towards him, her intention was to shake his hand, but it flowed naturally into an embrace, like an uncle greeting his niece. "How are you?" she asked.

"I was demoted two steps," he said. "My legal representative told me I should expect Rear-Admiral temporarily while I waited for the panel to convene, but they busted me down to Commodore because I told them to skip the panel."

"You plead no contest to the charges?" Alice asked as they parted.

"Aye," he replied, his manner still pleasant. "Considering one of the charges involved murder, I'm not surprised. If Anderson was part of the decision, I probably wouldn't have been dropped so far, but I'm still in a place where I can do some good. I've asked to take over SOCU. I'd like to rebuild the Special Operations Combat Unit. They'll let me have it, Sawyer will be reassigned to a carrier. It's a better assignment for her."

The thought of working under Oz never occurred to Alice. Imagining him as the new leader of the Special Operations Combat Unit was exciting. "You're going to have to do without me for a while, boss," she said. "But I can't wait."

"Good," Oz turned towards the view. "It's going to be an interesting crew, but you'll have a lot of time to get used to it while you take some time off. We're both on leave for two weeks. Your medic, Theodore, writes one hell of a report."

"I can't wait to read it," Alice growled. "I'm not allowed to do any heavy lifting for six weeks, mission-wise."

"Considering what you were trying to do out there with that Geist, I can't disagree with him. Neither of us are ready for the kind of telepathic work we were doing. Haus Geist did his best to train me while we were together on the Triton, but what you were doing takes years to learn to do properly. The kind of fight you were doing can scar both you and your opponent."

"Theo told me all about it," Alice said, turning towards the transparent wall. "It's all old science to Lorander."

"Lorander doesn't understand Geists," Oz said. "When you were fighting this one today, I was able to look right into your mind. There were no defences against me, you didn't know I was there at all. The Geist did. As soon as you let him go, he fled because he knew he could survive you since you were fighting out of fear, but it didn't know what to expect from both of us. When I told them there were three Lorander telepaths on the way, that was all it needed to know."

"I was not fighting out of fear," Alice said, at the same time trying to clearly recollect what that battle was like, whether or not it was true.

"All your willpower came from primal instincts, fear being the most powerful. I wasn't the only one listening in. Lorander telepaths who were on their way but too far from you to help could feel it. You were powerful, but you weren't controlled. You were fighting with a sharp knife, but it was all double-edged blade, no handle. Even when you were winning you were hurting yourself."

Alice's head still hurt, even though the medication made the pain seem distant. "I'll learn."

"You could," Oz said. "You should, actually. Find a Lorander trainer to help you defend yourself if a normal telepath tries to get into your head. Fighting Geists, that's a discipline that will either require a Geist like Haus, or a decade or two with Lorander trainers. That's if you don't want to burn your memories out, eventually turn into a vegetable."

Alice watched as a thick arm lowered one of the ship's main starboard hull plates into place. "What about you?"

"I'm not much different. Haus Geist found some telepathic potential in me, so I'm training, but where Geists are concerned we're the same. I'll be able to block one out like you could after some training, there's no way they'd get in, but fighting is dangerous. The wrong Geist or too many of them at once could burn me out in seconds. We'll always be a major problem for Citadel, though. I can tell you where a Geist is hiding within a million kilometres of here if one came into the system. They have a telepathic shadow that triggers our fight or flight instincts more than anything else. That is a huge problem for them, especially since they can't sense us unless we push back when we feel them nearby, when we feel them try to read us."

"So, if I sense a Geist and it's trying to get into my mind, it doesn't know I'm there unless I counter?"

"Exactly. We are invisible to it. The reason why we feel them at all is because they're reading the surface thoughts of everyone around us. It's their first strategic advantage. That's why the fleet is working hard to develop passive suppressors. The ones we have right now don't get along with cloaking devices."

"As in, they give everyone a way to find them when they're turned on," Alice said.

"Right. So, what do you think? Are you going to join a group of Lorander telepaths and work on your abilities full time, or are you going to stick with SOCU?"

"Is it really one or the other?" Alice asked.

"I won't let you stay in my unit if you plan on fighting Geists. Pointing them out, keeping them out, sure, but I couldn't live with myself if you had your mind wiped or destroyed. Not after everything you've gone through just to be here, just to be alive."

When Alice thought of her experiences with Geists, the first memories that came were of the pain they could cause. The thought of it made her cringe, what he said made sense. The knowledge that she'd never be an actual telepath was always there, and she'd already decided that being able to block people out was enough, how was making the decision where Geists concerned much different? "What if I counter-attacked a human? Am I facing the same risks?"

"Ask an expert," Oz said. "But according to what I know, no; humanoid telepaths who aren't engineered are different. Still, I can't tell you for sure. I don't know enough."

"Looks like I'll be hanging out with some creepy Lorander people," Alice said. "So I can learn more about blocking, and stay with SOCU."

"I actually thought you'd be joining the monks for a second there," Oz said.

"Gotcha," Alice chuckled. "Guess I'll have to enjoy teasing you while it lasts."

"Oh, the telepathy? I won't be able to master that for a long time, a decade, probably more. You'll have a lot of time to pull my leg. Just don't do it in front of anyone else in my command."

"Deal," Alice said. "So, which ship is this?"

"The Merciless," Oz replied. "Your father's ship. No one's seen anything like it. It took a lot of failures, and some research, but Ayan finally got everyone working together and now we'll have ships that use technology from every end of the galaxy. Everyone in command is holding their breath, praying that what we've seen in testing bears out." He shook his head. "But there's no need to watch them bolt it together when you have a family waiting for you."

"Meeting's over?" Alice asked.

"Adjourned," he agreed.

She turned towards the door and started walking. "Are you coming?" she asked as it opened.

"You go ahead," Oz said. "I have some thinking to do."

SEVENTY

Carnie's Tale: Reprise

IT WASN'T LIKE any place Noah Lucas had seen before. The directions on his command and control unit marked it as the Launch Room, a play on words he didn't expect in such a well-armed or generally serious military star base. It was new, open for one day, and as opposed to the rest of the halls and rooms he'd seen, every surface was softened with a special walking surface under foot, matte wall covering that had a velvet feel, and yellow lighting from above.

The wall across from the door and to the left were completely transparent so people on all three tiers of the place could watch as ships emerged from the front of the War Forge. The overall mood was high, everyone seemed pretty happy to be there. He wondered what it would look like when the news of the impending invasion got around.

There was a bar running through the middle of it with plenty of gaps for people to walk between the sides of the space, food dispensers along the walls and plenty of tables to sit at. It was where Theodore's message said to meet him, and he was looking for the only person in the place without a uniform, expecting it to be him.

He half expected his friend to still look like his mechanical self, and that was quashed the moment he saw a gentleman smiling at him, walking from the end of the bar. "Theo?" Carnie asked, excited, surprised. He was wearing a jacket marked with a red stripe going down the shoulders and arms, the letters S.O.C.U. on his chest under a red skull.

"Yes, how are you, Noah? Perhaps you'd rather be called Carnie?"

"No, man, that's all right," Noah said, hugging him enthusiastically. "I'm sorry I left you behind, I thought it would be a quick trip then I could use my pull to get you in with a fleet technician. You did all right, though, wow, I really didn't know it was you."

"They did an excellent job repairing me, and please don't worry about leaving me behind. I know you didn't have the means. I found us a table." He said, gesturing towards the side of the lounge.

"Man, I thought about you all the time while I was out there. I can't tell you how many times I thought; 'I wish Theo was here to see this,' and you've gotta meet Minh, he's, well, he's Minh."

"Meaning that he's unique, one of a kind," Theodore said with a smile. "I found myself thinking the same thing about you. I've seen a lot since I was reactivated and repaired. I'm a citizen now." A card emerged from his chest, the vacsuit parting just enough to let it come through.

Noah accepted it, realizing that he was holding a real Haven Nation Citizenship Identification Card. "You have seen a few things," he said, handing it back. "Congratulations, man. I don't know what to say."

They sat down, Theodore taking a moment to look at the ship having its plating bumped and checked. It was a severe looking warship unlike anything Noah had seen before. "I like watching the War Forge work. They say that her artificial intelligence is emotionless, but when I watch it put something together sometimes I see an artist's flair in how it goes about printing and building." He looked to Noah and smiled a little. "I'm sorry, I'm trying to share more of my random musings, it's something humans and other social races are encouraged to do when they're developing socially."

"No need to explain," Noah said. "I can't get over this place, or you, so if I go quiet it's because I'm stunned. So, what happened to you? Who picked you up and dusted you off?"

"Oh, that's a good story," Theodore said, a little excited. "I was activated by Alice Valent and Iruuk Murlen. They cured me of the virus that made me attack you. I'm sorry about that, by the way."

"No worries," he said, reeling from the name he just heard. "Alice Valent, Captain Valent's daughter?"

"Yes, and I have to wonder what he'll think when he finds out she's a captain as well, but we're getting ahead of ourselves."

"An admiral and two captains. That has got to be an interesting dinner table," Noah said.

"We'll probably find out."

"What?" Noah asked with a chuckle. "Okay, okay, start at the beginning. Alice got you switched on and cleaned up. What happened next?" Over three Salojin Ales and a full meal of broccoli, string beans and chicken, Theodore told him all the unclassified details of his time with Alice Valent so far. In the company of the best friend he ever had, the dark days he knew were coming seemed a little lighter.

THANK YOU AND CONTACT INFORMATION

Thank you for purchasing and reading Broadcast 11: Revenge. Watch for Spinward Fringe Broadcast 12: Invasion coming later in 2018. Here are a few ways you can reach me and other readers:

Facebook:
https://www.facebook.com/groups/spinwardfringe/
https://www.facebook.com/randolph.lalonde.3

Patreon:
https://www.patreon.com/randolphlalonde

Twitter:
@RandolphLalonde

My Blog:
www.randolphlalonde.com

www.ingramcontent.com/pod-product-compliance
Lightning Source LLC
Chambersburg PA
CBHW072010020726
47501CB00006B/1759